For June, the original Evie

Chapter One

For several days now, Evie Yeo hadn't been able to shake the queasy feeling that was nestling deep within the pit of her tummy.

She tried to convince herself it was because she was about to start her very first job, and therefore she must be suffering a bad attack of nerves at the thought of the earnest faces that would soon be looking directly up at her and listening (or, more worryingly, not listening) to what she had to say.

Or perhaps it was because the evening news reports of Hitler's advances and his successes in defeating the British forces delivered in a clipped BBC news announcer's voice seemed never to be anything other than awful. The few glorious weeks the previous autumn when the British fighter planes had held off the massive German air offensive seemed a very long time ago now.

Or perhaps it was because she, along with her younger sisters Pattie and Julia, only eighteen and nineteen, were being forced into an uncompromising adult world before they felt at all ready.

But Evie knew deep down she was kidding herself.

Timmy's latest letter to her, its envelope buried deep in the pocket of what had been her aunt Mary's once horribly unfashionable skirt (the best efforts of the three sisters during its recent make-over having only slightly improved it), gave little hint as to the emotional turmoil the letter's few short lines was fuelling.

This was following an embarrassing, and horribly fraught,

conversation the previous Friday with Timmy's pal Dave Symons, who'd then had the sheer affront to make a clumsy pass when he and Evie were squeezed into a nook in the cosy, dark-beamed snug of The Haywain. Evie now regretted agreeing to meet Dave Symons, but it was one of those things she thought she should do as he was probably missing his chum, now that Timmy had been called up, and she felt it was the sort of gesture that Timmy would expect her to make to a friend of his.

For, despite the cheerful message of the letter deep in her pocket, delivered in Timmy's previously welcome and carelessly florid script, full of descriptions of his new comrades and drills and other things new recruits had to get used to, every time Evie thought of her fiancé's buoyant words, she couldn't help but fume, her belly roiling.

Again and again she could only recognise anew the inexorable ring of truth to the revealing allegations that Dave Symons had crooned so intimately into her ear.

''E's given 'em all a snog, and then more – 'e tells me 'e loves you best, o' course, but what's a man to do when given the old come-on, 'e says? It's been going on since before you and he jumped the brush, or as good as, and I told 'im, it's no way to treat an 'andsome maid like you, but you know yorn Timmy – they queue up for 'im, they do!' he tipsily slurred. And then he tried to manoeuvre to a position whereby he could slide a comforting arm around Evie's shoulders. Dave Symons was well known as being happy to comfort many a young lady who had been upset by the louche behaviour of Timmy Bowes.

Feigning an urgent need for the lavatory, Evie had escaped abruptly, leaving Dave Symons with a look of surprised frustration fleeting across his pudgy, red-cheeked face.

In the cool of the public house's less than salubrious lavatories, she had then spent a grim, shaky-kneed minute or two splashing cold water on to her wrists and then her face, as she attempted to stem the tears that were precariously threatening.

Her delicate, diamond-encrusted engagement ring, which had been Timmy's grandmother's back when the Bowes family had been extremely well-to-do, and which Evie now wore on a delicate filigree gold chain around her neck, the ring nestling several inches above her bosom, felt as if it were made of nothing other than lead.

Now, inevitably, at each memory of Dave Symon's blunt but convincing descriptions of the shocking extent of Timmy's peccadilloes, Evie's stomach would flip once more, leaving her with the unfamiliar impression she was teetering close to the edge of a terrifying abyss.

Taking the letter at face value, in her calmer moments Evie could see that Timmy still seemed to be exactly the same happy-go-lucky young chap she'd fallen for.

As her friends Linda and Sukie had pointed out on several occasions, Timmy Bowes was quite obviously 'a catch', being funny and always ready with the glib comment, as well as very good-looking, with impish eyes twinkling out from under dark manly brows.

Indeed Evie knew that there was many a local lass who yearned for him to direct a little time and attention her way, and Evie could easily remember how she herself had felt immensely flattered when first he'd singled her out from all the others. In fact it was the feeling that she could show off a little, basking in Timmy's attention, which had initially been the most attractive thing about him.

Soon though, under his concerted attempts to woo her, Evie's feelings had escalated into something deeper.

Timmy had given her the impression that the same thing had happened to him too and that his head was likewise awash with thoughts of her.

Anyway, Timmy probably *was* still exactly the same happy-go-lucky lad he'd been all along, Evie had to admit, although now she knew there was something he'd gone to great pains to conceal from her.

To her distress (and shame at the imagined sympathetic looks that would doubtless come her way when family and friends learned of her predicament), what she had discovered during that oh so uncomfortable early-evening drink with Dave Symons in the bustling snug was that almost without a doubt her fiancé was a liar and a cheat.

And Evie realised that what rankled almost as much was that he was playing her for a silly fool. How dare he?

Also – indeed this was the biggest burr itching under her saddle – Evie could see that her blind and willing acceptance of everything that Timmy had told her, such as him needing time to swot up on pack-drill theory (as if), or that he wanted to spend the occasional evening with his mother before he left the village (pah!), had led to this disaster.

For, in reality, her inexperience of the ways of men with questionable morals had allowed Timmy the freedom to flirt, and then with all probability to go a whole lot further – although to do precisely what didn't bear thinking about, Evie decided as a lurid blush raced across her neck – with several willing young ladies he'd apparently made acquaintance with in various rowdy hostelries in the local market town.

As she leant forward in the early morning light to peer closely at her shadowy reflection in her carved, wood-framed mirror, her hip nudged the edge of the dressing-table top and caused the envelope to crackle as it buckled. Evie's stomach clenched tighter at the sound.

That April morning, the more intently she stared at her image glaring accusingly back at herself, the worse everything seemed somehow.

Her usually lustrous brunette hair appeared tangled and misbehaved no matter how much she brushed it, and she looked – and there was a very good reason for this, Evie could only acknowledge – as if she'd not been sleeping nearly enough, as her face was both puffy and uncommonly dry-skinned. There was even the suggestion of a deeply etched frown line between her brows that Evie was sure hadn't been there even the morning before.

All in all, she decided with a defeated sigh, who *could* love the rather unkempt and haggard face that was peering so disconcertingly back at her?

Even a glance at the photograph from just a fortnight ago, of her parents, Robert and Susan, their three daughters, and James, their only son, together with the two evacuee boys that they'd taken in, didn't really make her feel any better. Evie had wedged the photograph under the wooden frame around the mirror; it had been snapped just after their traditional Yeo family Easter-egg hunt in the garden on Easter Sunday.

Even though Timmy had left Lymbridge only days before Easter for training somewhere near the east coast of England, it had been such a happy afternoon, filled with jokes and laughter, much of which was caused by the sight of the paper eggs they'd all drawn blindfolded and then cut out and hidden from one another in the garden, before they made sure the evacuees Frank and Joseph found nearly all the 'eggs'.

Julia, almost always the most sensible one of the trio of sisters, had surprised everyone with the feathers she'd stuck on her egg, each one gaily painted using the remnants of what was left in the cracked and desiccated paint squares in their old tin watercolour box.

Evie smiled slightly at last as she thought of Easter Sundays from longer ago, back when she was that young child who was always so proud of being the oldest one of the girls, and when her parents had been more comfortably off than they were now, when Robert had owned his own garage before the Depression led to the business folding. Gone now were the larger house and the more assured position the Yeos had enjoyed in local society. But what hadn't changed one iota was the warmth and hospitality of the Yeo family, nor the high regard with which the family was held locally, aided no doubt by the willingness of both Robert and Susan to help out other villagers or to get involved in local events. In the run-up to those Easters of yesteryear, her mother and father would get Evie and Pattie and Julia to use the watercolour box to decorate real – so difficult to believe in these days of relentless food rationing! – white-shelled

5

hard-boiled eggs, while even little James would be encouraged to make a colourful daub or two. Her parents would then hide these trophies in their pretty but ramshackle country garden for the children to seek out.

Evie knew without a doubt that she was loved dearly by her family, and so she allowed herself a comforting moment to imagine what they'd all be doing at that very moment; she did miss the familiar sounds of ordinary mornings at the Yeo family cottage since she'd moved out.

But this day Evie's usually soothing memories of a happy childhood were roughly manhandled aside by rudely intrusive thoughts of damn Timmy and his damn letter.

And once more Evie's mind couldn't help but turn inexorably to the unavoidable concern that although Timmy had given her an engagement ring the night before he'd left to join the war effort, along with whispered promises of what a wonderful wife she would be to him as his fingers had tried unsuccessfully to find enough purchase to sneak behind the buttons of her best blouse, there was actually a very real possibility that Timmy didn't love her very much at all.

A month or so before Timmy had left, her mother had tried gently to quiz Evie as to whether she were quite certain that Timmy was 'the one', as it had been such a surprise to the family that a New Year's peck on the steps of The Haywain had led quite so speedily to the antique engagement ring.

Evie had been quick to reply to Susan that yes, she was quite, quite certain.

That conversation, which had taken place as she and her mother had prepared lightly buttered toast for tea after the Easter-egg hunt, seemed a long time ago, when an utterly different Evie had felt she could whole-heartedly reassure her obviously doubtful mother.

Now, standing in the early morning light seeping in through the bedroom window, at this moment the cold, nauseous feeling deep inside Evie burrowed deeper with one last cruel churn.

*

The occasionally erratic church clock was yet to reach the quarter-to when Evie turned into the gates of Lymbridge Primary School.

She was in an even gloomier mood – and indeed this was possible, even though she'd been convinced otherwise just a scant half-hour before – than when she had been considering her reflection in her pleasant bedroom at Pemberley, the rather grand house where she was lodging these days as a Paying Guest.

For although constantly drawn back to depressing thoughts of Timmy's fickle waywardness, as she had walked towards the school Evie had also started to suffer what were most definitely collywobbles at the thought of the day before her.

Why would anybody, even little mites of just five or six years, want to listen or, more incomprehensibly, actually believe anything she had to tell them?

What was the reason exactly that she had ever thought that teaching was in any way for her, or was something she just might be good at?

And, most perplexing of all, why exactly had she wanted to join the square-built, grey stone school in her home village that nestled close atop the dramatic heather-spiked West Country hills she'd known all her life?

Right at this very minute none of it made any sense to Evie in her unusually downhearted mood.

With a shake of her head, Evie gave herself a stern reprimand and tried to rally as she removed the key to the school's main outer door from the hidey-hole where headmistress Mrs Bowes had told her it would be wedged, and then unlocked the door and slipped inside the schoolhouse.

To one side of her was the vestibule for hanging coats, with the toilet block beside it; there was a small kitchenette on the other side of the school's entrance area. Immediately ahead of Evie were sturdy doors to a pair of adjoining classrooms, the larger one for the juniors, and the smaller one for the infants.

Through the window panes of the door to the juniors' classroom, Evie caught sight of the huge canvas world map peppered with the familiar pink of the British empire, hanging half rolled down from its wooden case high on the wall above the blackboard, and she was transported back in time.

She could remember all too clearly the seemingly endless and now merged-together sea of dull lessons she herself had endured under Mrs Bowes, lessons that sometimes she had only just managed to keep awake for, and then she recalled how alarmingly quickly she would forget what Mrs Bowes had been teaching. The lessons she had enjoyed remained as vivid in her memory as if they had taken place yesterday. But Evie knew she'd still be in a pickle if asked to name by rote all the Pacific Islands.

Anyway, the plan was that from now on Mrs Bowes would continue teaching the juniors, who were all seven years or older, while Evie would be in charge of the infants.

Evie could remember what a hard task-mistress Mrs Bowes had been as a teacher, and so she was in no doubt that she would prove to be an equally challenging employer, and that she would expect Evie to push her pupils hard to reach the standard expected of them.

The problems didn't end there.

For Mrs Bowes was Timmy's mother, and she worshipped to distraction the very ground her darling son walked on. This meant that she wouldn't tolerate a word against Timmy from anybody, and least of all from Evie.

Evie tried to cheer herself by privately promising that during any difficult moments she might experience in the schoolhouse, she must always remind herself that she was very lucky to have this opportunity.

For although she had completed her teacher's training at a specialist teachers' training college in Cheltenham, and had been all set to seek a permanent job in Plymouth or Exeter, when the Phoney War proved to be anything but, it soon became clear that it might not be a good idea for her to leave the sparsely populated Devon countryside in which Lymbridge nestled, and Evie had put her ideas of teaching aside.

Robert and Susan had made it clear that they wanted her

at home with them, or if not actually with them now that the evacuees had arrived, then safe in another Lymbridge dwelling such as Pemberley. And Evie realised that in the face of Jerry's vigorous night-time attacks, she didn't feel particularly brave either and not did she relish the thought of living many miles from her family in these troubled times. So she had decided to make the best of things, and she would help out in the busy Yeo household as much as possible and then do some summer harvesting work to bring in some money.

However, a fortnight ago Mrs Bowes had asked to speak to her.

There was a totally unexpected opportunity for Evie that had arisen right here in Lymbridge itself!

The vacancy of infant teacher had come up as the class's last teacher, Miss Coombes, had been abruptly sent away in disgrace at the end of the spring term once she could no longer disguise the fact she was in the family way and, scandalously, was without a wedding ring on her finger.

Evie couldn't help remembering the tricky teatime on the last day of term at Mrs Bowes' prim and fussily over-neat cottage at the far end of the village (a rarely used parlour bursting with small china figurines aside).

After reminding Evie how lucky she was that Timmy had deigned to give her a second look, or words to that effect, as naturally someone with the many advantages of Timmy could have the pick of any local girl at all, the headmistress had smoothed her thick and sensible tweed skirt across her ample hips with slightly chalky fingers.

Mrs Bowes mentioned, in her rather plummy voice, the current vacancy at the school. Then she added, much to Evie's delighted surprise, that she was prepared to offer the post temporarily to Evie as, although inexperienced, at least she was a qualified infant teacher. And Mrs Bowes didn't think Evie could get up to too much mischief in just the one term until the summer holidays, after which a 'proper' infant teacher would be appointed.

Although sitting close to his mother and Evie, Timmy had

paid no attention to their conversation as he wolfed down his supper, and then without so much as a glance toward them turned his attention to perusing what in these straightened times passed for the sports page in the *Western Morning News*.

The upshot of the conversation was that despite having the windfall of an unexpected job, Evie had been left under no illusion that Mrs Bowes had anything other than the lowliest opinion generally of teachers (and all infant teachers in particular) other than Mrs Bowes herself (naturally). Or that she, Evie, was anything other than merely a convenient choice, being *very* lowly in the pecking order as lowly infant teachers went – and that was even though she was engaged (and obviously very lucky to be so) to Timmy.

Evie did, however, enjoy one big advantage in her favour in Mrs Bowes' view, namely that she lodged extremely close to Lymbridge Primary School, as Pemberley was situated on the adjoining piece of land, and so Evie would be on-hand if anything untoward happened out of hours that a teacher needed to attend to.

Pemberley was a spacious and once rather splendid house that was located in extensive grounds, and Evie delighted in being grandly described as a paying guest, or PG. When she had told Timmy that she was moving to Pemberley, his first comments were to ask whether visitors to the PGs were allowed as overnight guests? These were thoughts Evie had to immediately disabuse him of.

Anyway, as Mrs Bowes spoke to her that teatime about the vacancy at her school, Evie felt unable to say anything to the older woman's rather steamrollering, ungracious offer of the temporary post of stand-in infant teacher, other than she'd love to take on the class for the forthcoming summer term.

No promises of a full-time post, mind, Mrs Bowes had been quick to reiterate. But Evie had already got the point.

Later that same evening Evie had had to shrug off the jokes made by her sisters Pattie and Julia to do with favouritism and her being given the job of the new teacher at the village school purely because she was making whoopee with the headmistress's son.

Evie responded by saying that if this were favouritism, then she didn't care to think what the alternatives might be, as she was feeling very firmly put in her place.

Evie had then had to contend with Pattie, who never hid her opinions, pointing out that there wasn't really another option for a teacher at such short notice, and so hiring Evie had been shooting fish in a barrel as far as Mrs Bowes was concerned.

'And of course everyone knows that the old trout herself will most definitely be pure murder in a teacup to work for. I love you, Evie, but you need your head examining for agreeing to step in to help her out without, it seems to me, a second's thought to the merry hell you'll be in for. Or without the promise that the job may become a full-time post. You're quite the soft touch,' Pattie had finished.

For a moment Evie felt thwarted at Pattie's words, although Julia's reassuring squeeze to her arm persuaded her that, just possibly, there was a small and remote chance she wasn't after all the worst person in the world for the job. She'd been at the top of her class at the teachers' training college in Cheltenham, Julia was quick to remind her.

And, Evie could remember from her subsequent teaching practice at a school near Barnstaple in North Devon, it was certain that the children would be sweet and lively and endlessly entertaining at least.

Chapter Two

As Evie expected, the infants' classroom had the distinct smell of floor varnish and boiled cabbage about it, long shared by all schools across the land. In fact, as Evie stood and had a quiet minute to gather her thoughts, she turned around slowly to take in the four corners of room and realised it was the first time she had actually ever been in any classroom completely on her own.

Despite the shafts of hazy sun coming in from the high windows, with dust motes dancing, her infants' classroom was bleak, as nothing could disguise the fact that it looked like a forbidding space that was unlikely to yield any sense of wonder or enthusiasm in her young charges, tiny as they were.

Evie had intended a name game as a short ice-breaker so that she could make sure that she knew who everybody was and the infants could learn her name. Now, the more Evie considered the blank walls that seemed to be sucking all energy away, the more uncertain she felt that there wasn't a better way for them all to begin their first morning together.

She'd spent the last few nights making bunting pennants so that later in the morning the class could string those on to long lengths of plaited twine, and Evie could then quickly tack the pennants at regular intervals. She had thought her class could then hang the bunting in the new Nissen hut that had been erected just after Christmas at the bottom of the school field. And once they'd done that, the plan had been for Evie to read the class a jolly story as the children sat cross-legged in front of her on the floor.

This idea had arisen following a visit Evie had made to Miss Coombes. Although she and Miss Coombes had only chatted now and again when they'd bumped into each other in the village, Evie had taken her predecessor a pair of tiny bootees, wrapped in tissue paper, that she'd hastily knitted the night before from wool unravelled from an old baby jacket Susan had saved. Miss Coombes had been packing her belongings ready to return to her parents' home in Exeter, but she seemed pleased to see Evie, wishing her luck. And she was clearly touched by the gift of the bootees.

When their conversation turned to the Nissen hut, which was to be used if there was any sort of emergency at the school itself, it was with a small chuckle that Miss Coombes told Evie of the pandemonium when close to the end of the spring term the infants had been sent to the hut together with the juniors when there was a rumour of an unexploded bomb on the school roof. Before a false alarm could be declared soon afterwards, the box of baggy spare pants and knickers had had to be raided several times by Miss Coombes as the little ones decided, with predictable results, that the Nissen hut was the home of a host of creepy crawlies all determined to eat INFANTS!

Although Evie had laughed as Miss Coombes described the kerfuffle, as she walked back to Pemberley she'd decided she should accustom the infants to the hut. Then, if it ever did need to be used again, all her young pupils would already be familiar and comfortable with it, creepy crawlies or no.

But now she was standing in her austere classroom, Evie thought it was more important for her to make it feel bright and welcoming, and a place of security and happiness, or at least as much as it could be in these testing times.

And so, she decided on the spur of the moment, that the morning's lesson plan would now have to change. It would be the name game, then some painting, followed by a story in the classroom that would by then have the paintings displayed proudly on the walls to brighten things up. Later, once everyone had eaten their packed lunches, Evie's pupils could turn to finishing the bunting.

Luckily Evie had had the foresight the previous week to seek help from Mr Cawes, the school caretaker, in making her up something her pupils could use as paint. He'd been very helpful and had managed to concoct three or four pots of colour using goodness knows what, and he'd even been to the local weekly newspaper in Oldwell Abbott, their local market town. There Mr Cawes had begged some paper offcuts that couldn't be used on the huge metal printing press, returning to Lymbridge with a tremendous cache. Evie had been impressed by how resourceful he'd been. The paper was quite fragile but Evie thought if it were folded it would probably be perfectly serviceable for what she wanted it for.

Evie decided that she and her pupils could end the day by playing some sort of game that would decide whether the bunting be put up in the classroom, or else hung in the Nissen hut.

These poor children had so little choice over anything to do with their lives these days, and especially so in the case of the two evacuees in her class, Jonathan and Michael, who'd come to Devon from London and were missing their families dreadfully, which wasn't surprising as they were still only five. They made, along with Frank and Joseph (who were in Mrs Bowes' class), a total of four evacuees who lived in the village and attended the primary school.

In fact there were a further fifteen evacuees still resident in the surrounding area, boys and girls, most of whom had been sent to outlying farms, but they had been allocated to other village schools. There had been more evacuees sent to the area, but they had already returned home.

None of this was ideal, of course, and so Evie was keen that the children she was going to teach could discover that they could sometimes influence what was going to happen, even if it was something as seemingly meaningless as where some home-made but nonetheless cheery-looking bunting might be hung.

As the church clock struck eight o'clock, Evie heard the unmistakeable sound of Mrs Bowes' rapid but heavy-footed gait, heralded by the clang of the school gate behind her.

Putting her basket containing several storybooks and the half-made bunting on the teacher's table behind her, Evie turned to face the classroom door with what she hoped was a positive and cheerful expression on her face as she waited to greet her headmistress.

'MISS, MISS. ARE YOU OUR NEW TEACHER? MISS, MISS!' roared scabby-kneed Bobby Ayres as he ran towards her. His mother, Betty, gave a small wave and a sympathetic grimace in Evie's direction as she turned to go.

Evie smiled brightly at Bobby. 'Yes, I'm Miss Yeo, and I'm very much looking forward to teaching you and your friends.'

'MEOW?' he hollered back, clearly puzzled.

'Miss. Yeo,' Evie enunciated slowly in what she hoped was a quietish but crystal-clear voice, remembering Miss Coombes saying to her that little Bobby was a sweetheart and really will-ing, but that he tended to get the wrong end of the stick as he often needed his ears syringing. Now, Bobby nodded back at Evie with a serious expression as his tongue wobbled a loose front tooth, leaving her uncertain as to whether he'd understood what she had said to him or not.

But Evie couldn't dwell on Bobby and the problems to do with his hearing, as the next ten minutes yielded in quick suc-cession another eight members of her class, whose mothers each came into the playground to speak to her. Evie actually knew who they all were already – this was an advantage of having grown up in the village as it was a tightly knit community – but it was the first time she had spoken to some of them.

She had been at school with a couple of the mothers herself. These fellow old pupils were girls who had married as soon as they could. Evie exchanged friendly and slightly bashful grins, rather than what she hoped were the calm and in-charge smiles she directed towards the other mothers.

The reality was that much of this was a big bluff. Although she would be twenty-one before the end of 1941, Evie felt barely more than a child herself, and so the thought of having given birth to and then being responsible for her own five- or six-year-old offspring, as these former school pals were, took her aback slightly.

As Evie waited for her final three stragglers – there were twelve children in her class – she tried to keep an eye on the ones who were already milling around.

The little girls looked to be mostly quiet and content to stand near to one another, some still clutching a reassuring parental finger while their mothers chatted to one another.

The boys seemed more rowdy, with some already darting about, and Evie couldn't help but suppress a small sigh when she noticed that one youngster had already drawn a moustache on another's face. It looked very like Hitler's moustache, and although it was rather well done, Evie cringed inwardly as she imagined what might have been used to mark the other lad's face, given that pencils and ink pens were so precious that they were always accounted for and kept purely for lessons.

The final three pupils arrived together, and it wasn't long before Evie felt it was time to send the remaining mothers away.

Once she was alone with her class in the playground, she made sure she had twelve small faces looking up at her (she'd double-counted them to make sure all were where they should be).

And then she said in a tone she hoped combined kindness with gentle authority, 'I am your new teacher, Miss Yeo, and I'm very much looking forward to teaching you all until the summer holidays begin.

'We're going to line up, and then we'll go inside. I want you each to stand beside somebody else, and then each pair can stand behind another pair – this means we can practise counting to two, and then all the way up to six.

'When we get inside, we'll do some lovely paintings of your very favourite thing, and then you can all have a go at drawing a picture of me, and then we can hang your paintings on the walls right away, with your names and ages at the bottom...' At which point Mrs Bowes walked by, parading ahead of her own class of older and slightly more ordered pupils, her characteristic tweed skirt and sturdy sensible shoes reinforcing the impression that she would brook no mischief.

Evie saw that unfortunately Mrs Bowes' eyes were opened wide, and her eyebrows were raised pointedly in Evie's direction while her head slightly kinked in the direction of the moustache on the young boy's face.

'But first, let's go and wash our hands and faces,' Evie heard herself finish rather lamely.

She felt worn out, and it still wasn't even nine o'clock.

Chapter Three

It was quarter to five before Evie was able to walk in the lengthening shadows down the mossy stone path to the battered front door of Bluebells, the old cob cottage in which the Yeo family had lived for nearly ten years.

She had survived her first day as a bona fide infant teacher.

'Hey sis, how'd it go? Knocked 'em sideways?' said her brother, James, as he rushed out of the door just as Evie arrived, causing her to step aside abruptly. He loped up the path without waiting for a reply while seamlessly stuffing a slice of bread and jam into his mouth and then, grabbing his bicycle from the hedge into which he'd carelessly thrown it, he jumped on and cycled off without a backward look.

Evie smiled to herself as she thought about how James, the baby of the Yeo children, always looked to be in a tremendous hurry (even when he was sitting still, somehow), and how he would make a point of never listening to the answers of the many questions he'd ask. Fifteen was a very difficult age, Evie thought, and although these days he looked very much a man, and had been shaving for over a year now, she hoped the war would be over before there'd be any danger of James being called up.

The next second Joseph and Frank, the ten- and eleven-year-old evacuee brothers billeted with the Yeo family, burst through the front door to the cottage in their normal harum-scarum manner, grabbing on to each other's jackets in order to try and be first into the front garden. With a boisterous *Hello!* yelled more or less in Evie's direction, they sped off to meet their school pals to play a game of knockabout football on the village's tiny hardstanding beside the draughty village hall with an old and hard leather ball James had managed to scavenge for them, almost definitely using as goalposts the woollies that Evie and Susan had knitted for them after painstakingly unpicking the wool from a variety of old garments.

If one of those woollies got kicked again into the murky village pond that abutted the gravel beside the village hall, as had happened once during the Easter holidays, Susan would have sharp words to say, Evie knew.

There would have been a time that the game of football would have been played on the village green, but now the green had been devoted to livestock belonging to various villagers, and there were several pigs of varying ages and sizes who spent their days rooting around, as well as a couple of henhouses.

Evie paused for a moment longer at the cottage's front door to check if the coast was now clear for her to enter, only to find Shady, the family's mongrel, slipping every which way as his massive paws failed to gain proper purchase on the linoleum as he attempted to rocket down the hall towards the door, intent on finding exactly where the football had gone to. He shot past her without a sideways glance, although Evie could hear his baggy soft mouth slapping against his teeth as he charged by; he must have just eaten not to spare her a glance just in case there was a snack being proferred.

The Yeo family had had a lot of fun over the years trying to guess Shady's parentage – his giant feet, stumpy legs (shorter at his front end than at his rear), coarsely haired body, extravagantly fanned tail that was invariably wagging, and lugubriously bulldoggish face with his saggy lips and tiny tombstone teeth suggested a very mixed parentage. James was always keen to add that his unnaturally high-pitched bark denoted in his lineage something very small and yappy, a Pekinese or a daschund maybe, while Pattie insisted that his copious bad wind must indicate that whatever breeds of dog had been involved in his lineage, they had been without either a nose or an adequate digestive system. Evie felt this to be a wee bit unfair, and that Shady's affectionate nature and his acute guard-dog hearing more than made up for any ability to clear a room in seconds, a feat that always led to him looking behind himself in puzzlement, which was why Pattie was convinced he didn't have a sense of smell.

'Cooeee, anybody home? I'm starved,' called Evie down the hall as she went in, expecting the traditional family welcome.

Instead there was silence. Total, and rather flat silence.

She walked through to the kitchen, as homely as ever and clearly the scene of a meal already eaten. Drat – she'd hoped to be in time as Susan was much better at making something appetising out of nothing than her landlady Mrs Worth (or, more precisely, whichever woman from the village Mrs Worth had persuaded to help with the evening meal, there being a rather alarming turnover of helpers, suggesting Mrs Worth might share a characteristic or two with Mrs Bowes). Evie hoped Susan had saved something nice for her, as she had told Mrs Worth that she would be eating with her family; all meals were carefully planned to avoid wastage, and Evie suspected she'd have slim pickings if she had to fend for herself back at Pemberley.

Peeking out of the back door across the rows of carefully tended vegetable plots that now took the place of what had been the rear lawn and a larger grassy area between the apple and pear trees that made up the orchard, there was still no sign of the rest of the Yeo family.

Then a clang and a swearword erupted from the garage, and so it was there Evie found the rest of her family looking at the family's elderly but reliable car, as her father demonstrated to her mother and her bored-looking sisters how a car should be immobilised.

'It's not just if the Germans invade, you know. I was talking today with old Bert from yonder farm, and he said there was a story in Monday's *Western Morning News* that there's been another escaped convict from Dartmoor Prison, and he'd found a car that hadn't been immobilised, and so the clever bugger just drove off in it. Talk about making it easy for those felons. And for the B-word Jerrys!' exclaimed her father.

'And so the long and short of it is that we've all got to know how to do it. Will you pay attention, Pattie? This is important, and I'm going to make you show us what I was just telling you if I catch you looking up to the rafters again. Those lads'll just have to hold their horses for you to go a-flirting.'

Robert's bark was always worse than his bite, and so Pattie wasn't the least bit chastened.

As Evie watched her father, dressed in his favourite corduroy trousers held up by braces over his oft-washed checked flannel shirt, point out the car's distributor and the water tank and the place the oil went in, she was able to catch her mother's eye and her warm smile.

'Right, that's all really good to know, Robert, and we're all grateful to have such a good mechanic on our hands. We are, really. Obviously' – cue smirks and raised eyebrows from Pattie and Julia – 'but Evie's just arrived, and she must be dying to have a spot of something, and to tell us about her first day as a fully fledged teacher.' Susan firm words brooked no dissent as deftly she herded the family back towards the kitchen. She was very good at that sort of thing.

Susan refreshed the large earthenware teapot, liberating it from its crocheted tea cosy that had been worked into elaborate swirls and waves in order to create air pockets that would help keep the heat.

'Sorry, lovey. I got carried away back there for a moment,' said her father to Evie. 'I do like a car engine.'

'And to tell us about miles to the gallon. And horsepower. And the new traffic lights in Exeter, and the diversions in Plymouth around the rubble,' said Evie, as she gave her father a kiss on the cheek.

Robert was a large man, gentle as a kitten and hard to anger, and he took his new role with the Ministry of Agriculture very seriously. He was responsible for making sure the yields of the local farmers were as high as possible, cycling on his huge old bone-shaker from farm to farm come rain or shine. Although important, his job didn't mean an extra petrol ration.

Susan was the parent who'd disciplined the children when they were little, but she too had a heart of gold, although hers was a bit more deeply hidden than her husband's. These days she more or less ran the village shop for owner Mrs Coyne, despite only being paid a shop assistant's wage. Evie felt Mrs Coyne took shameless advantage of Susan's good nature but, wisely, she had never shared these thoughts with her mother, who could be a tad touchy about such things.

'So, was it as hideous as it promised to be? Or, more exactly, was Mrs Bowes as hideous as she promised to be?' asked Pattie with raised eyebrow, as Evie accepted a cup of tea from her mother, and Julia made a start on clearing the teatime debris from the table.

'No, it was all quite peaceable and pleasant actually. Well, after I'd washed the Hitler moustache off the chops of little Danny Blewitt, and until going-home time, that is.'

Evie went on to describe her day at school. The painting had gone down well, indeed much better than she'd expected. She'd asked her class of little ones to paint pictures of their favourite things, so after dissuading some of the older infant boys that guns weren't really what she was meaning, she'd been given eventually pictures of a few hard-to-distinguish cats and dogs, a rather scary-looking hamster, a Christmas tree, an ice cream, and several mummies and daddies.

When everyone had finished their first painting, she helped each child write their name and age on their picture. And then she asked them to make a quick portrait of her, with predictable results, with even the irascible Mr Cawes barely being able to suppress a chuckle or ten as, while the class was at morning playtime, he tacked the pictures to the wall with drawing pins, the favourite things on one side of the room, and the gallery of green creatures – sorry, er, Miss – on the opposite wall.

After playtime, Evie had yet another last-minute change of plan as to what her first day should be (she really was going to have to get more organised as to her teaching, she reprimanded herself sternly, otherwise Mrs Bowes would have her guts for garters), and soon she was helping the children to write their own names.

Then they did counting, and a few basic sums using the children themselves as the counters to show what one plus one, and two plus one meant. This took them up to dinnertime, the children eating their packed lunches at their diminutive desks before Evie took them outside for a welcome runabout.

Miss Bowes had told her while the children snacked that Evie could send her charges home half an hour early that afternoon. This was normal for the infants for the first week of term apparently, as the littlest children got so tired that they could end up petulant and tearful, and this could set the others off even though they were that little bit older.

Evie was pleased as she thought a couple of her pupils already looked pretty close to their limits. And now that she had nearly a whole day of being in charge of a classroom under her belt, and as she had now met the children, she wanted to put a proper lesson plan together. A lesson plan that she would stick to, come what may.

If Evie were honest with herself, she had meant to have started work being much more organised. But her swirling and unsettling thoughts to do with Timmy had put paid to those lofty ideals. Try as she might, she couldn't stop thinking about what he had been up to, or how hurt and humiliated she felt.

Luckily her pupils were too young to notice that she kept changing her mind. But Mrs Bowes would be much keener-eyed, and so Evie knew that although she would probably get a day or two's grace while she settled her knees under the teacher's desk, she most definitely needed to organise her thoughts as to how she was going to help her charges achieve the correct level for when Mrs Bowes would take them over at age seven.

Anyway, for the lesson after lunch she'd decided that as the weather was pleasant a nature table would be a good idea, as that would let the children relax a little.

A few days earlier Evie had remembered a gold crown in the Yeos' dressing-up box. When she and her sisters had grown out of wanting to wear it themselves, they had delighted in insisting that James wear it when he was small enough for them to boss him around without fear of reprisal. In fact, they would still jokingly threaten him with enforced wearing of 'The Crown' as a punishment if he was annoying them, which was quite often.

Earlier that afternoon, removing this slightly battered childhood relic from her basket with a flourish before the rounded eyes of her infants, Evie explained that it was a crown and that whoever was the first to find leaves from *five* different shrubs or trees or grasses in a small area to the side of the playground (Evie held up her hand and indicated counting to five, using each of her fingers and her thumb) would have the honour of wearing the crown for five minutes (another counting hand gesture) as king or queen of the class that day.

Whoops of laughter ensued as the children darted around hunting down their quarry, quickly drawing Mrs Bowes to the window with a stern face. But when she saw how earnestly even the tiniest children were counting their leaves she retreated back inside to concentrate on her own (much duller, Evie suspected) lesson.

Finally, after a short break, a lively game of hopscotch was initiated on the grid that had been painted on a far corner of the playground before even Evie had been a pupil at Lymbridge Primary School, with everyone calling out together the numbers and even the youngest children being able to do at least the first jump. The game was still going on when the parents came up to collect their children.

Several pupils made as if to walk home on their own, which rather took Evie aback as they seemed too small to be trusted to find their way home unaided.

But Mrs Bowes had come out to check that everything was running smoothly, and she assured Evie that it was quite normal for even five-year-olds to make their way home on their own if their parents allowed it and they didn't live outside the confines of Lymbridge village.

To her surprise Evie had really enjoyed her first ever day of properly paid work. The time had flown, and the children seemed happy to do what she asked.

Her good mood wasn't to last, however, as just as the last junior pupil crossed the playground to go home, Mrs Bowes had said to Evie that she needed to speak to her.

'I've been informed by the Ministry that there's a very good chance that Lymbridge Primary School is going to be doubled in size at least,' said Mrs Bowes in a somewhat uncharacteristically flat tone of voice when they were at last able to sit down in the empty juniors' classroom.

Mrs Bowes continued, 'The nightly air raids on Plymouth have been very bad, with the loss of several schools as well as many homes. Added to which, there's a new wave of evacuees likely from northern towns where the nightly bombardment has likewise been kept up for weeks.

'The details are still being worked out, but if the rumours I hear from on high are correct we may have to go up to teaching as many as forty children in each class, although goodness knows what we'll be seating them on in that case. And it could be that we are made to segregate the girls from the boys, which will be what most of those children will be used to, and I don't quite know how we'll manage that either. If a lot of children come from one school, their teachers might accompany them, but we can't take anything for certain.

'The long and short of it is that you need to be ready to have a much larger class, Evie, perhaps across all the ages in the whole school if we have to separate the girls from the boys, and you need to be able to do this at the drop of a hat. Naturally, if that is to happen, I myself will take the boys, as they will need an experienced hand. Of course,' Mrs Bowes was able to finish in her usual authoritative tenor.

Then, as she so liked having the last word, and in case Evie has missed the point, Mrs Bowes added, 'This means your class could be from five years up to eleven. That is a challenge for even the most proficient of teachers. You will be expected to keep all the children in line.'

Evie couldn't think of anything to say in response that didn't sound like an outright criticism of the war effort, and she would have rather cut her own hand off than murmur anything that sounded unpatriotic in the slightest.

But the reality was that she felt the class she had already was the perfect size for someone of her scant experience, and that some of the younger pupils seemed shy and very uncertain of themselves, and they would feel threatened by an influx of children they didn't know. And she wasn't at all sure she would be able to teach a wide age-group of pupils at the same time.

Unfortunately Mrs Bowes wasn't yet finished with her gloomy news. 'Also, Evie, I've volunteered you to help with the billeting of these new children, and so on Wednesday afternoon you are to report to the village hall at four o'clock, where you will be allocated with duties of finding accommodation for these displaced children, and possibly several pregnant or nursing mothers.

'And if I were you, I'd make sure you have a bicycle along with you as, being young, I daresay they'll send you off to the furthest farms. Some of those roads are very hilly and so I'd make sure you get a good night's sleep beforehand. Still, Timmy likes a trim girl' – an inward snort was only barely snuffed out by Evie, knowing that Timmy wasn't particular as to trimness or plumpness, just as long as the young lady was willing – 'and so that will help keep your rear as it should be, as I'm not sure if you're aware of it or not, Evie, but you're getting quite broad in the beam, and that really isn't going to do.'

As Evie finished describing her day to her family while enjoying a welcome second cup of tea and a slice of bread topped with, as a treat, a smear of last year's honey from their hives at the end of the orchard, Mrs Bowes' allusions to the size of

Evie's bottom were greeted with gales of laughter by her family. It was Pattie who pointed out that Mrs Bowes was a fine one to talk as her own tweed skirts were very well rounded in this respect. And Robert chipped in with, 'What rubbish, a real man likes a bit of meat on his sandwich,' which provoked a thump on the arm from his wife, who then looked at Evie and told her not to worry in the slightest as she'd got a lovely figure, being slim but womanly.

After the sisters had gone to compare the size of their posteriors in the long mirror in the large upstairs bedroom, with howls of laughter ringing out when it was obvious that Julia, who worked as a postmistress and therefore actually spent a significant amount of every day cycling up and down those self-same laborious hills on her way to the far-flung outlying farms to deliver letters and packages, proved to have the largest derriere of the sisters by quite some way.

After Frank and Joseph had returned from football pink of cheek and with eyes shining, cheekily asking if there was anything else they could eat as they were so peckish that their bellies thought their throats had been cut, Evie announced that she had to go.

'Mrs Worth promised she'd heat water for me and all the others to have a bath tonight, so if I don't go now, I might have to wait until the weekend for my bath,' said Evie as she left.

She felt a pang of homesickness as she walked down the garden path, leaving everyone in the kitchen.

Her spirits were raised though when Julia pounded down the road after her to say that if Evie came around the next night she'd practise doing pin tucks on her hair with some setting lotion.

'How lovely. I might even bring my Coty and my Ponds, and we can make it a beautifying session. You can try my Tangee lipstick – I still can't get over how it looks orange but turns to cherry,' Evie promised.

Feeling much happier than she had that morning, Evie headed back to Pemberley with a renewed spring in her step.

Chapter Four

In fact the hair and beauty session had to be delayed until later in the week, because on the Tuesday evening Evie helped Mrs Worth prepare rooms ready for a new tranche of PGs set to arrive the following day. Mrs Worth was keen to fill the house with PGs, as otherwise there was a danger the house would be requisitioned, she explained to Evie, who had indeed previously been a bit curious as to why Mrs Worth, who didn't seem particularly short of money, would want to have a motley crew of PGs rampaging around her large and comfortable home.

And on the Wednesday, Evie was kept out until past nine o'clock having a disappointing evening pedalling Julia's unwieldy bicycle from one outlandish farm to another as she tried to find beds for the evacuees who would soon be arriving.

Then on the Thursday morning Evie had to get up early as before school she was to meet with the village Evacuee Committee to report on her success, or not, at finding billets.

Although the previous evening Evie had been disheartened by the paltry response she'd elicited, it turned out that in actual fact she had done better than anybody else had from the village, as she had found four families willing to take a total of five children, with the result that she went to school feeling she'd actually done rather a good job.

So it wasn't until the Thursday evening that Evie returned to her parents' cottage. Although officially unnamed, the girls had dubbed it for years as Bluebells purely as a means of annoying their brother, who hated anything obviously feminine, and the name had stuck to the extent that now all the family knew it under that moniker, even James.

Julia and Evie spent an enjoyable couple of hours playing about with each other's hair and making up an oatmeal face pack as part of a general beautifying session, which included a painful eyebrow pluck. They wrapped up the evening with careful applications of the famous Tangee lipstick, just to check it would change colour as if by magic. It was a couple of hours that were punctuated by lots of gossip and many cups of tea from a constantly refreshed pot.

Julia had sent away to London for a magazine detailing various pin-curling techniques, and as she was getting to be quite the dab hand with hair styling, she was hoping that she would be able to make a little extra pin money from doing sets for local women who would already have had their hair permed by a proper hairdresser in Oldwell Abbott or Plymouth, but who needed regular sets to keep their hairstyles in order. These sets would help Julia eke out her rather paltry wages from the Post Office.

Evie had found out long ago she didn't really have either the patience or the nimble fingers that pin curls required, and at night the most she could usually be bothered to do was to squash her own hair inside an old scarf she'd then knot at the top of her head to sleep in, and keep her fingers crossed for what she hoped would in the morning magically be revealed as a sea of lustrous curls and glossy waves. This hope wasn't granted very often, she'd discovered.

It was therefore lucky that Julia had only let Evie pin curl the back of Julia's own head, and that Julia, no matter how she angled her hand mirror the next morning, couldn't really see the rather erratic results.

Both Pattie, who was out that night, and Julia, were very disciplined about pinning their hair every bedtime, although it always left Evie bemused that they could sleep on a head with so many sharp hair pins threatening to dig into their scalps. Even when tightly wrapped in a scarf, in Evie's experience there was always, without fail, a pin that made itself a nuisance.

Evie and Julia's companionable beautifying was frequently broken by the sound drifting in through a window of loud exclamations and sarcastic comments from the rest of the Yeo family. This was because everyone, including the evacuees, were outside in the rear garden in the gathering gloom, as Robert was organising them to dig some more of the grassy areas up to get ready for yet more vegetable production, despite the fact it was already too late in the year to plant up all the varieties he claimed they could produce.

Even the normally stoic (well, aside from when woollies were kicked into the village pond, that is) Susan gave vent to a rare moment of unabashed ill-mood, and it was at this point that Julia called from the kitchen window that she would make fresh tea for everyone, but it had to be in ten minutes as she just needed to finish what she was doing to Evie's hair or the setting lotion would dry out before she had time to get all her sister's hair in place.

Still, potatoes in their jackets with some cream cheese that Julia had been given by a farmer on her rounds, and yet another pot of tea soothed any feathers that remained ruffled. And soon Frank and Joseph were showing off with varying degrees of impressiveness the card tricks they'd learnt somewhere disreputable in Peckham.

With a jolt Evie realised that somehow it had got to nine twenty, and so she had to hurry back to Pemberley as Mrs Worth closed the outer front door at nine-thirty sharp. An arrival after that would mean that Evie would earn a black mark by having to knock to be admitted as although she had a key for the inner door, she hadn't been given one to the large front door on the outside of the glass-sided porch.

*

30

Later, in the small hours of the night, it was the first time that Evie was actually to see bombs dropping in the distance over Plymouth or, to be more exact, the distant luminosity of fires and explosions that these faraway bombs had led to.

On the horizon of this moonlit night as she gazed from her small window in the eaves of the roof on Pemberley's second floor, Evie having lifted the blackout curtains after checking there was no light emanating from anywhere in her bedroom (a lighted match outside on a clear night being apparently visible to pilots at 5,000 feet), Evie could see the glow of other people's unhappiness, and the rising smoke drifting in lace and ribbons across the twinkling stars.

It was terrible but it was also eerily beautiful. And suddenly Evie could hardly tell whether the sound in her ears was what she was imagining as crashes, splintering glass and booms from the exploding bombs dropped during the determined assault by the Germans, or the beat of her own heart pulsing blood around her body.

Soon she could hear the thrum from the engines of the retaliating British planes flying southwards from airfields in the north of Cornwall and elsewhere in Devon, and this drowned out these other sounds. Again, it was both ominous and invigorating, and Evie felt a surge of excitement course through her.

For the first time in over a week, Evie wished Timmy were there and not many miles away. She didn't quite know why suddenly she felt like this, especially considering Timmy had been such a rotter, but she didn't think she had ever felt so awake, so full of life itself. She yearned to have Timmy's arms wrapped around her and to be able to feel his muscular, strong body close to her much softer one, their hearts beating next to one another.

Indeed she could hardly believe how much she wanted his reassuring and familiar Timmy smell to be enveloping her.

Previously she had scoffed when she had heard raucous comments from her sisters about how frisky wartime was making everyone, but now she sensed there might be some truth in the claims.

Evie's reverie was disturbed when Mrs Worth knocked at her bedroom door to say that everyone else in the house was removing to the recently constructed Anderson shelter that had been built in a gully to the side of the house's substantial garden, and made of corrugated iron and covered with earth, just in case a stray bomb were to land on Pemberley.

After a few moments Evie got up unwillingly. She had battled good sense against the warmth of the comfy bed with her panoramic view of what was happening across the moors, and of course the reluctance to let the rest of the household see her in her tatty sleeping scarf, which she'd worn home over Julia's artfully arranged army of hair pins (try as she might though, she had had to take various of these hairgrips out when trying to get comfortable on her pillow). She had just put on a sweater over her nightie, with her dressing gown on top, and her winter slippers, and was busy removing her pillow and eiderdown from the bed when she could hear everyone else traipse back into the house, with Mrs Worth asserting that they had decided it looked as if Jerry had given up for the night once the British planes were heading towards the coast

Evie crawled back into bed still wearing her dressing gown and sweater, only to find she was still wide awake, a state that continued until the first bird-calls heralded the new and cruelly bright morning.

Feeling very bleary and not at all ready for the day, Evie was taken aback at breakfast time when she entered the dining room to find there were four new PGs seated around the large table laid for breakfast.

She'd forgotten they were coming, and she realised that they must have been unpacking in their rooms when she had returned to Pemberley from Bluebells the night before.

Two of the PGs introduced themselves as a husband and wife called Mr and Mrs Wallis, who had moved to the West Country from Canterbury following a concerted series of air raids there. Mr Wallis looked much more mature than his rather fashionable wife, and so Evie assumed that he was too old to have been called up.

Then there was another older and some would say rather dashingly handsome man called Mr Smith, as well as a chronically shy younger man with slightly poor skin and a bad stammer, and rather unruly hair, who managed to say, after an agonising pause while he tried to force the words out, that he was called Peter Pipe.

Evie surmised that to judge by their suits and smart shirts and tie, the two unaccompanied men looked as if they worked in Whitehall or some other official capacity. Mr Smith was probably the most dapper man she had ever seen, as he was very elegantly attired, and especially so for a country village, while Peter Pipe looked as though he wished he was somewhere else and in less formal clothes, Evie thought. And what an unfortunate name for someone with such a pronounced speech impediment.

Evie explained across the breakfast table that she had just started as an infant teacher at the village school next door, and that although the wartime news was so often bad, she did find that being around the children cheered her up no end.

Mr Worth, who was normally a totally silent presence at the head of the dining table in the face of his wife's ebullient, not to say sometimes domineering presence, drifted across the dining room holding a cup and saucer to interrupt what Evie was saying. Looking at Mr Wallis he launched into a rather tedious description of his important work as a solicitor (it was too important, apparently, to be diluted by being thought rewarding), and then Mr Wallis replied he was a solicitor too, or at least he had been before the war.

Five minutes later Evie felt she had heard quite enough about torts, deeds, wills, addendums and the difficulties nowadays in finding reliable legal secretaries for that particular morning, and with a final mouthful of toast she stood up to leave. She caught Peter's eye, and was horrified to see him flush instantly a deep crimson as he began to inspect his plate with an earnest attention.

As she was walking into school just a few minutes later, Mr Cawes sidled up to Evie and muttered, 'Yorn fancy man won't like the fact there's a young 'un as a PG at yorn big 'ouse, 'specially if 'e's a proper 'andsome lad intent on cozying up an' making merry wit' a young maid like yerself.'

'I doubt Timmy would give a moment's thought to any such thing, as he's always much too busy thinking of more interesting things. And the new PGs all look very proper and well-behaved,' Evie said in her snootiest tone as she walked or rather, she hoped, flounced by. By 'more interesting things' Evie meant Timmy himself, but Mr Cawes wasn't to know that. And there was nothing special about Peter Pipe. Nothing special at all.

Mr Cawes' responding 'Harrumph' was surprisingly eloquent in its brevity.

The morning was fresh and sunny, and the perfect temperature for an outing.

Mrs Bowes told Evie that together they could walk the children around the village and some of the closer fields, encouraging the children to name different parts of buildings and plants, and the types or breeds of animals they saw, while she and Evie could talk to them about historical things they knew about the village, such as the age of the church and the whereabouts of ancient burial mounds, or cloud formations or indeed anything else they came across that they thought the children might be interested in. And when they got back to school the children could be given some work to do that would be connected to what they had seen.

Mrs Bowes explained that in the summer terms she was always keen for the children to get out into the fresh air as much as possible. The winter weather could be treacherous this close to the moorland tors, and so there would be long months ahead come the autumn with very little opportunity for outside time for the pupils.

It was a very pleasant hour or two out in the sunshine with the children, although Evie was slightly surprised at how often some of her small charges needed to go to the lavatory, although less surprised than Mrs Bowes appeared to be at Evie's encyclopaedic knowledge of cars and tractors, and a better than rudimentary understanding of how engines work, demonstrated by her answers to questions from some of the elder junior boys (Evie didn't have an engine-mad younger brother and father for nothing).

A little girl called April Smith, with messy blonde pigtails and a slightly holey cardigan over her summer frock, asked in a breathy voice if please may she hold Miss's hand as they walked, and Evie thought her to be very sweet as soon afterwards the small girl pulled her to a gate to make sure that Miss had a good view into a field of what looked like twin lambs.

While they were out, Julia cycled by on her mail round, cheerily waving and then, after Evie had flagged her down, pausing briefly to open her bag to show the school children the letters she had to deliver and to explain her route in broad outline.

And then, just as they'd turned to make their way back to Lymbridge Primary School, the farmer's wife at Switherns, the nearest farm to the school, called to them that if Mrs Bowes and Evie thought it a good idea they could all stop by and have a glass of milk. Mrs Bowes and Evie did indeed think it a good idea.

At a nod from the farmer's wife, Mrs Ward, Evie asked if anyone knew how to milk a cow, and it turned out that five of the junior pupils said they could.

And so while the rest of the school jostled around to find the best position to watch, these five children were each allowed a brief go on the soft teats of a massive black and white Friesian who was next in line in the milking parlour. The Friesian was called Winston, and Mrs Bowes tutted audibly, to Evie's amusement, at what the headmistress obviously considered to be sacrilege and disrespect to the prime minister at having a cow as his namesake, although privately Evie thought it most likely that Mr Churchill would be rather flattered that such an obviously productive creature with massive udders had been named after him.

Winston clearly had udders practically bursting with milk ready to be collected, and each of the children with milking knowhow managed to get at least a couple of squirts of milk into the grey metal milking pail.

After that, all the pupils watched the tremendous speed at which the deft and practised hands of the farmer's wife could draw the milk, the children clapping with delight when she stopped with a half-full pail. Then each pupil was allowed to have a drink of the fresh, still-warm creamy milk that was scooped for them from the milking pail, Mrs Ward using for the purpose an old wooden dipper that had clearly seen a lot of service over the years, before the children trouped back into their classrooms in good humour.

Unfortunately Evie was down in her teaching plan to teach arithmetic as her next lesson – it was absolutely not her favourite subject – and to make a start on the two-times and three-times tables, and so the jolly mood of earlier dissipated rather rapidly.

The three Rs – reading, writing and arithmetic; or reading, righting and rithmatic – were the mainstay of the school curriculum. And so Evie knew she mustn't stint on tackling sums with her infants.

Then she remembered that she was supposed to be making the infants think about their walk around the village, and so everyone perked up no end when Evie ditched the times-tables for *one* church, *two* wheels on Julia's bike, *three* pigs on the village green, *four* teats on Winston's generous udder, *five* sets of twin lambs, and so on.

However, once the arithmetic lesson was over and the children had had their lunch, even Evie sitting them on the floor in a semi-circle around her and reading them a story from their favourite Enid Blyton book couldn't quite restore the relaxed and happy mood of their walk, no matter how many funny voices Evie tried to employ in telling her story. The children were obviously tired and Evie was concerned that she and Mrs Bowes might have walked the littlest ones just a bit too far.

By the time Evie was waving her pupils home, she was relieved that it was Friday and she now had a couple of days to herself. She had survived her first week as an infant teacher.

She was going to hurry home and get ready. Tonight was a night out in Bramstone, the large village a mile or two away, which Evie would borrow Julia's bicycle to get to. She had arranged to meet up with her old school pals Linda and Sukie.

Evie could hardly wait – she hadn't yet told them, or indeed anyone else, what a blighter Timmy had proved to be.

The ladies bar of The Wheatsheaf was busy. It wasn't quite six o'clock yet, but there had been a rumour all day that, following the flurry of recent air raids in Plymouth which had led to all night-time entertainments and public houses in the city now closing at eight-thirty, public houses in the outlying areas such as Bramstone or Lymbridge might start to follow suit.

The landlord of The Wheatsheaf said, when Evie asked, that he'd had no official direction on closing time, but if he heard that other hostelries local to him were closing early, then he would do too. The rumour had spread and so clearly his patrons were getting their drinking in early.

Sukie, who had been by a long way the prettiest girl at school as well as the most outspoken, said to Evie and Linda that in that case they'd better get a move on with having fun, and she was going to have a large lemonade rather than a small one! And she might even have a beer to finish the evening.

Linda smiled, saying, 'Steady on, old girl; drink too much of that and you'll spend too much time in the W.C. rather than eyeing up who you can flutter your eyelashes at.'

'You jest! I have both the bladder of a camel, and an uncanny ability to bat my eyelashes despite immense physical discomfort,' Sukie replied in a trice.

Evie wasn't quite sure that camels did have large or strong bladders, and so she said, 'I'll buy the drinks. And then I've got some news or, more exactly, a moral dilemma to tell you about.'

Armed with their lemonades, her friends sat rapt as Evie described the awkward evening of just a week ago when Dave Symons had revealed the extent of Timmy's amorous escapades.

'And I've not yet told my sisters or my mother, as I wanted to have time to think about it first – and I'll never tell father or James, as they'd kill him if they could get their hands on him. Of course Timmy's away right now, but I think they'd have long memories,' lamented Evie.

'The truth of it is that I don't know what to do. Timmy's letters are the same as ever, but I believe Dave Symons was telling the truth to me, in large part as I fear he's too dim and dull to be able to make up anything that could sound so convincing.'

Linda and Sukie gave the appropriate responses of shock and despair at Timmy's poor behaviour, and Dave Symons' likely lack of imagination, just as Evie had known they would.

'I do wonder now that if perhaps Timmy and I rushed into getting engaged,' she went on. 'But it very much seemed the right thing to do at the time, and Timmy made me feel so special and as if we could be happy together.

'And it was exciting, as we did it despite Mrs Bowes very much putting her oar in on the side of dissent, and this made me think that we were meant to be together, come what may. And I thought that we would be able to get through anything and that Timmy would love me whatever happened. But now I see that can't be true.' Evie's voice was now tremulous. 'I've felt sick and out of sorts all week, and as if I'm on the edge of quicksand and am just about to sink. I feel jealous, and angry, and I go to sleep thinking about it and it's the first thing I remember on waking.'

Sukie squeezed her knee, and Linda told her to keep her chin up and that at least she'd found out he was a cad before she'd married him, rather than after, as was usually the case.

Sukie, who was also imposingly tall and had something of the Valkyrie about her, looked very regal as she stood up to get their next round of drinks, and said, 'Evie-Rose, sweet, if that devil Timmy were here right now, I'd give him a piece of my mind and a punch on the nose. He's lucky a girl like you has even given him five minutes, let alone agreed to marry him, and I wish I could remind him of that.'

Evie gave her friend a rueful smile, before continuing with a once-again serious expression on her face to Linda. 'I really don't know what to do. Timmy hasn't had a chance to defend himself, and I had a letter on the Saturday and then a postcard yesterday in which he seems exactly the same as usual – and, useless creature that I am, I've written back in just the same cheery tone as I always use, pretending everything is just as it should be. I think if I weren't actually working for his mother and seeing her every day, I might have said something to him. Or maybe I wouldn't. I don't know.

'In any case, I've only just started at the school and I do like being an infant teacher very much, or at least I think I will once I know what I'm doing, and so I don't want to risk rocking the boat by upsetting Mrs Bowes, which would be the likely outcome. Oh, hell and damnation. Men . . . I'm just not sure they're worth it.'

As Linda disappeared to the lavatory, the lemonade clearly having more effect on her bladder than Sukie's, Sukie returned with their drinks and pronounced, 'Evie-Rose, don't be sad. You listen to me. Men are nearly *never* worth the trouble, let me go on the record as saying. And you know that I know what I'm talking about when it comes to men. Anyway, right now it's probably wise for you to lull Timmy into complacency while you plot your revenge, as that way you have a chance to get him on the back foot. And in fact you could think about trying a touch of his own medicine, as I see that the rather handsome chap over there can barely take his eyes off you.'

Evie couldn't resist peeking at the old brown-splodged mirror on the wall in front of her in order to catch a sneaky glimpse of her would-be admirer staring at her from behind. But she couldn't see anyone who was looking her way or who was remotely handsome.

'Give over, you daft old maid!' Evie giggled as she gave Sukie a playful swipe.

'Got you going, you have to admit! See, there's life in the old dog yet, and so I'm thinking that if Timmy's got any sense he's going to make very sure that you feel he's the most faithful fiancé ever before too long,' laughed Sukie.

'Thanks. You play a trick on me and then call me a dog. That's not what I call being a good friend!' chided Evie.

'Get on with you – it made you laugh, and that's more than that worthless waste of space of yorn is doing, isn't it?' Sukie retorted with a rebellious toss of her head.

As usual, the evening ended with Sukie disappearing off somewhere with some young man she'd managed to ensnare, leaving Linda and Evie to declare that they were done with talking about Timmy Bowes for the night, and then to get down to the serious business of putting the rest of the world to rights.

Linda had nearly finished her apprenticeship to be a farrier. Being a farrier was a really important job in a rural area as it was crucial that the local farm horses were kept properly shod with metal shoes protecting their hooves from splitting so that no day of work would be lost on the land. Linda was rightly proud to be the first woman farrier in the county.

Now, she confessed to Evie, she was rather taken with a young farmer called Sam Torrence, who owned two gigantic pure-bred Suffolk punches broken to harness, as well as a couple of youngsters of more mixed parentage that he had yet to bring on.

Linda described Sam in glowing terms, but privately Evie thought Sam seemed to be very dense about Linda's increasingly obvious signals towards him. Dense, or perhaps a little frightened by Linda's extremely apparent enthusiasm for him.

'Men. Too stupid and too much trouble, and yet we can't live without them. Before the war I'd have consoled myself with a large slice of my mother's cake, and now that option's not even open. It's too painful!' Evie wailed, only half in fun, as she rang the changes by this time asking for a glass of weak bitter shandy.

'And, Linda, now it looks as if you might have found Mr He's A Bit Slow On The Uptake, I've got Mr Faithless, and our own dear Sukie's run off with Mr I'll Have Forgotten Him By The Time I'm Putting My Sleeping Scarf On Tonight. It's enough to make a girl weep.'

Chapter Five

Darling E

*All fine and dandy with me, and so I know you'll be
cheered up by that as I daresay you are missing me
furiously. And if not, why not!! Anyway, I'm pretty busy as
these military types I find myself with now certainly know
how to have fun, I can tell you! We all complain about the
food but it's all right really, and although I can't let you
know where I am, we haven't yet set sail or seen action.*

*So we have lots of time to paint the town red, and boy,
we are doing just that at every moment we can! I don't
think the local hostelries have seen anything like us, and
so we are certainly showing the local lads what real men
are. And I've been able to teach some of the others in my
in-take our famous West Country drinking games – they
think I'm a proper good chap, I can tell you! Although they
still think I'm lying about the ferret-legging competitions – I
don't understand what's so funny about ferrets!*

*In short, I am making you proud of Your Timmy, I can
tell you!*

Hope you and ma are well.

X from your very own T

Evie couldn't help but sigh deeply early on the Monday morning as she re-read Timmy's latest letter.

All that was clear was that he was in his element, and intent on being the ringleader in what sounded like plenty of extra-curricular activities, most of which appeared to be to do with energetically joyful carousing.

It was just as she expected, Evie supposed, but somehow it was disappointing nonetheless.

While Timmy had never been *that* different, she had been hoping against the odds for a little more from him, such as perhaps even a throwaway query as to how she was spending her time, in order that she could then perhaps plant the tiniest seed of doubt in his own mind as to precisely what she might be up to herself.

But clearly Timmy thought she was too dependable and boring to be doing anything out of the ordinary in any respect. It was very irksome, I can tell you! Evie told herself glumly.

And he uses too many exclamation marks, was her next rejoinder, although then she chided herself for turning into too much of a schoolmarm where punctuation was concerned. It was wartime, after all, and so the pros and cons of a full stop versus an exclamation mark were pretty trivial by comparison.

As she headed down to breakfast after dressing for school, through the gracious, large window that was pitched halfway down on the turn of the stairway Evie caught a glimpse of glowering grey clouds that looked for all the world as if they were sitting right on top of the imposing moorland tors she could spy on the horizon. Grey clouds to match my current grey mood, she sighed.

She had hoped she'd be up too early for the other PGs, as she didn't really feel like making pleasant conversation right now. But, tiresomely, the ever-smart Mr Smith was already sitting at the breakfast table (didn't any of his clothes ever crease?), and of course he looked in anticipation in her direction as she came into the room. Evie found him the most difficult to talk to of all Mrs Worth's paying guests, as they didn't seem to have much in common and of course he was so very much older, and therefore immediately Evie regretted not bringing a book with her to breakfast that she could immerse herself in.

Sure enough, after their good mornings to one another, there was an uneasy pause. But then Mr Smith began to ask her in an interested and gentle voice about the village of Lymbridge, before he enquired as to how she was getting on in her new job.

Evie began by giving quite short answers to this query. But then she opened up, and began talking about what it was like being such an inexperienced teacher, and especially so when the only other teacher was so very knowledgeable and had seen it all before.

Mr Smith, who said he had noticed Mrs Bowes walking home from school only the Friday before, when he nipped out to the village shop to see if they had any pipe tobacco, wondered if the headmistress might not be a velvet fist in an iron glove, rather than the more usual way around?

Evie shot him a wry look.

Mr Smith then asked Evie how long her family had been living in Lymbridge.

Soon she found herself telling him about the various members of her family, even explaining to Mr Smith that their evacuees Frank and Joseph were really two Jewish brothers who had been rescued and brought to Britain from Poland by train in 1939, sadly leaving their parents and older brothers and sister to an uncertain fate.

When the boys had had to be evacuated from Peckham along with the rest of their school, Evie explained, it had been thought best that their names would no longer be Franz and Josef, but should instead be changed to Frank and Joseph. She wasn't herself sure this had been a good decision, but the boys hadn't seemed to mind too much.

And although now virtually all their old school mates had now returned to their families in south-east London, Frank and Joseph's foster home had been destroyed and their foster parents sadly killed, and so Evie told Mr Smith that without parents in London, and as her own parents were happy that they should stay on in Lymbridge, it very much looked as if young Frank and Joseph would see the war out billeted with the Yeo family.

Evie was surprised then to hear herself confessing that initially she had had very mixed feelings about her parents taking in the boys. The Yeos had once been a little more prosperous than they were currently, but Robert's small garage in Bramstone had failed in the difficult years in the early 1930s, and money had been very tight since then, and Evie admitted to being worried about how her parents managed financially. Susan had once been herself a qualified teacher, but she had stopped working when she had her own family, now adding to the family's meagre income with a few hours each day helping out in the village shop. Evie said that two extra mouths, ration books or no, must be placing a strain on her family.

Mr Smith nodded sympathetically. The years of the Depression had made life difficult for many people, he knew, and rural living meant that there were fewer opportunities and it was especially difficult to get back on one's feet.

Evie stopped short of confessing all. She wasn't proud about this, but try as she might to feel otherwise, the truth of it was that she had felt seethingly jealous when Robert and Susan had first announced to the family that they would take in the boys.

If Evie were honest, her taking lodgings at Pemberley had been done initially in a moment of pique, as a means of her wanting to let Robert and Susan know that she felt that the Yeo family, and their finances, were being stretched too thin. Evie hadn't been working at that time, but she had had a small inheritance left to her by her grandmother, and so she decided to use this 'rainy day' money to make her point.

Robert and Susan had urged her to remain at home with them, saying that the boys could have their beds made up in the rarely used parlour and that it was everyone's duty to look out for people less fortunate than themselves, but Evie had insisted she would move out, and so Frank and Joseph now topped and tailed in her old bed.

When Robert and Susan said they felt disappointed by her uncharitable attitude concerning the two displaced and frightened boys, it had cut Evie to the quick, largely because by then she agreed that with her silly and snappish behaviour she had let herself down.

It had taken her a while to look at the Peckham lads with anything approaching charity, and she had buckled in this respect only after Julia and Pattie described a little of what they'd said the bombing in London had been like, after which she was able to soften towards them.

Now Evie was terribly ashamed of her shabby behaviour and didn't care to think about it too often.

'What about if their parents cannot be traced back in Poland when, thank God, it's all over?' Mr Smith's question brought Evie back to the breakfast table with a wump.

'We can't bear to think about that, for their sakes. But I do know that Mother and Father wouldn't let Frank and Joe leave Bluebells unless it was to return to their proper family or to a really good foster family in London. They're mischievous and very lively, and are always up to this and that, which is just as young boys should be. There's not an ounce of bad in either of them, and these past months they've very much come to feel part of our own family, and we've all grown to care for them now very, very much. For them this is important, as well as for us,' Evie explained in what she hoped was a hearty voice, although she could see there was a danger she was over-egging her enthusiasm. 'Every time we look at Frank and Joseph it really does feel like we are doing our bit, and that we must all band together to beat the Jerrys.'

To change the subject Evie described to Mr Smith her younger sisters, Pattie and Julia, and her brother, James, adding that the various guests at Pemberley might well get to know Pattie and Julia over the next few weeks, as in view of the size of Mrs Worth's dining table, which was about twice the size (at least) of anything else in the village, the local sewing circle were now going to move their cutting-out and pattern-pinning nights to Pemberley. It would really help them to use such a large table as then larger pieces of cloth could be spread out across the whole table, and fortunately Mrs Worth had willingly agreed to this idea of Evie's as she was also keen to do something more to help the war effort.

The ladies of the sewing circle, to which Mrs Worth and Mrs Wallis were going to be the newest recruits, were busily turning old clothes and whatever else they could find into usable garments to send either to London or Plymouth to be given to the desperate people who had lost their homes and all their possessions in the aerial bombings that had destroyed so many streets and homes. Evie explained to Mr Smith that she enjoyed sewing and knitting, and she enjoyed having 'new' clothes to wear, and so she was one of the keenest members of the Lymbridge sewing circle.

'Goodness, I had no idea the Pemberley was going to be such a hive of commendable activity,' said Mr Smith. 'Now, tell me a little more about what made you want to be a school teacher.'

It was at that point that Evie realised with a start that time had waited for no one – and certainly not her – and if she didn't make a dash for it right NOW, she would have to face the indignity of arriving at her classroom in the wake of her pupils. And Mrs Bowes would be livid if she were late, especially as she had the shortest distance of anyone to go!

Still, thought Evie, as she scampered towards her classroom, whoever would have thought that such a dull old chap as Mr Smith would actually turn out to be very pleasant and so easy to have a conversation with?

In fact, Mr Smith had made such an impression on Evie that she even mentioned him and their breakfast conversation to Mrs Bowes as they were helping each other to tidy their classrooms at the end of the school day.

The headmistress's immediate response quite took Evie's breath away.

'Well, I really don't know what Timmy would make of that: you and an older, unaccompanied gentleman having breakfast on your own together, and if that's not bad enough, then you talking to him just as if he were your equal. What on earth is Mrs Worth thinking about, letting you have breakfast together unchaperoned? I know that we are in difficult times these days, in which the old standards might not always hold true, but there is absolutely no need for you to be personally and morally lax, now is there, Evie? You must agree, surely? You simply must know better than that.

'Furthermore, and I want you to take note of this with all due seriousness, I'm sure my Timmy would expect you to be decorous at all times, and to know your proper place in the scheme of things – and this place is certainly most unlikely to be chatting away too freely to someone called Mr Smith, who after all might or might not be here in Lymbridge masquerading under an alias for all we know, or up to all sorts of no good. And there you are letting the side down by speaking to him as if you've known each other all your life,' the pompous notes in Mrs Bowes' voice rung out. She wasn't finished either.

'Timmy has been brought up to behave properly in all respects, and he is always very mindful of what is correct and proper, and the need never to speak or to act out of turn. He is the very model of proper and stalwart behaviour, as we all well know; in short, he is the very best example of what is expected of decent folk. And he will expect you to be likewise, naturally.

'I know it's not easy for someone like you, Evie. That is, a girl coming from a modest background. But I had expected more from you, really I had, and especially seeing as you've recently spent several years improving yourself in Cheltenham where the world renowned Ladies' College is. I was hoping some of that more refined culture would have rubbed off on you. A vain hope, I understand now.'

Struck by the various levels of unfairness inherent in Mrs Bowes' numerous and ungracious comments, Evie found herself utterly speechless, very possibly for the first time in her life. She simply couldn't think of a single thing to say in her own defence.

It was not a good feeling, and one made worse by Mr Cawes touching a finger to his cap in her direction as she hurried away from the school building a few moments later. Evie was sure he'd heard every admonishing word from the harsh lips of Mrs Bowes through the still-open sash window of the juniors' classroom.

And although Evie felt strongly that she had done nothing wrong nor that she'd acted improperly in any way, she could sense that her cheeks carried a sharp slash of crimson shame as she headed homewards, vowing to miss her breakfast completely if ever again there was a lone male guest in the dining room. Oh, heavens to Betsy, the screaming injustice of it all.

After tea at Mrs Worth's, during which she found herself utterly unable to finish her single tinned sardine on a slice of unbuttered toast, which meant she then had to go through a ridiculous and thoroughly undignified charade of finding a way to sneak it out of the dining room, as to leave wasted food on a plate was unconscionable in these straightened months, Evie headed to Bluebells to pick up Julia's bicycle. She had to go on another dreaded round of seeking out billets. Still, Evie couldn't quite hold back a smile when she saw the unbridled joy in which Shady gulped down the offending sardine and toast.

Something more positive that had happened meanwhile was that Mrs Bowes had told Evie the day before that the large numbers of recently displaced children they had been warned they should expect, had failed to materialise, and so this meant that, for the time being at least, they were only going to have to make room for an extra seven children at the school.

This was a huge relief to Evie, especially as most of them were older and so she was going to have to make welcome just an extra two in her own infants class.

And she and Mrs Bowes were going to be able to keep the school's pupils split up as present, into juniors and infants,

49

which meant that Mrs Bowes and Evie could continue to teach each class as mixed-sex, and again this was extremely welcome news as far as Evie was concerned. She thought the little girls softened the behaviour of the more boisterous boys, while the shyest girls could learn much to their benefit from the British Bulldog attitude of the young lads.

Nonetheless there were still another two billets yet to find, and the situation was pressing as the evacuated children would arrive late afternoon the following day. It was imperative that a solution to the billeting be found that very evening.

Evie was in for a challenging and ultimately disheartening few hours.

It was with relief that each of Evie's previous prospective billets confirmed they were still willing to take a child (and in one case, two), as they had promised her on her last visit (all the families offering the five billets wanted the oldest children possible: these last-tier billets were on outlying farms and so now that so many local men had joined the forces, understandably the farmers were already thinking ahead to harvest time and how useful it would be to have an extra pair of hands to call on to help with the harvesting, and especially extra hands that wouldn't have to be paid and, furthermore, would help eke out the family's rations with their food stamps).

But no matter how much she begged and pleaded, Evie was absolutely unable to find anyone prepared to billet the two smallest children.

When she returned to Mrs Ayres, who was in charge of organising all the local billets, it was to the news that nobody had come forward elsewhere locally when the other people sent on billeting duty had done their rounds that same evening.

'Goodness knows what will happen tomorrow,' Evie said despondently, chin resting heavily on her upturned palm, later that evening when she was sitting disconsolately at the kitchen table at Bluebells – she had come to return Julia's bicycle – as she watched her sister attempt to tame Susan's unruly mass of hair by giving her a home permanent.

'Those poor little mites – they're two girls aged five and six, I believe – and they have lost their homes in Plymouth already; their fathers are fighting, and one mother is in hospital badly hurt, while the other poppet's mother has been killed, ironically, by an ambulance that didn't see her in the blackout.' Evie sighed.

'It's all so tragic for both of them, and now they'll probably have to be put up in the vicarage with crusty old Reverend Painter, who knows not a jot about families or small children, and who probably can't even tell the difference between a small girl and a cassock, or what young children like to eat, and I'm sure that within a day of arriving these poor children will surely wish they'd never been born, if they don't already, which they probably do.'

Susan and Julia tutted in agreement, and nodded along with Evie that the blasted war was making everyone's life extremely troubled, and that it was giving some poor people almost unbearable burdens to carry. While everyone knew that God only gave to people the burdens that they could bear, these seemed very large burdens for little ones of such tender years; and so on.

Evie traipsed home, thinking that all in all she'd had a perfectly horrid day.

But there was a surprise to come.

For at ten o'clock there was a sudden unexpected and loud rapping of the front-door knocker at Pemberley, even though the large outer door had already been locked.

Evie was heating milk and water in a pan for a cup of weak cocoa in the kitchen as she rinsed through her undies and precious stockings in the scullery sink (it was her last pair of fully fashioned stockings, and so she was determined to look after them as well as she could, as stockings of this quality had become like gold dust in the shops – well, actually, gold dust would be easier to find, she was convinced, if her last visit to Plymouth at Easter was anything to judge by). Lost in bleak thoughts, she looked up and was shocked to see a rather stern-faced Mrs Worth shepherd her father Robert and a bright-eyed Julia into the kitchen.

Wearing a put-upon expression on her still-lipsticked but distinctly pursed mouth, as late-night visitors were considered in A Very Dim View, as had been mentioned several times previously to each of the PGs, Mrs Worth made to leave, but Robert forestalled this by indicating that the landlady should stay to hear what he had to say.

'Don't worry, lovey,' Robert then said reassuringly to Evie, 'no one's hurt or anything. But Susan and I have got to talking about yorn little evacuee girls; it's a right proper shame what's happened to them. So, we've decided that we'll take the little maids in ourselves if there's no one else that'll have 'em, and they can top and tail in Julia's bed. But that's only if, and I do mean if, Julia can find somewhere else to lodge and –' at this point Robert turned his gentle but unwavering gaze towards Mrs Worth – 'and so me and Susan wondered if Julia could move in here and share Evie's room, Mrs Worth, as we just haven't the room otherwise, and our Julia's a good lass who's no trouble, and of course she'll be happy to pay you what Evie is paying, or perhaps a little less as they'd be sharing the same room? And in that case we're very happy to have the little evacuee maids at Bluebells.'

Evie thought it to be the most excellent idea. She had made sure weeks ago that her initially callous attitude to Frank and Joseph had been well and truly trampled upon, and of course she now knew what lovely lads they had turned out to be. She also wondered whether the experience of Timmy's apparent affection for her, and her definite affection for him over the few months when she had felt head over heels in love, had opened the gates to a more readily available wellspring of care and consideration towards others on her part. So Robert's idea looked to be the perfect solution for those desperate little mites, as long as Julia was happy about it too. And to judge by the warm look in her limpid dark eyes, her sister certainly was. Evie held her breath anxiously as she waited to see what her landlady would say.

But Mrs Worth could only smile in the face of Robert's appeal to her better nature. And the net result was that she agreed with alacrity to the plan of Julia becoming yet another PG, not least (Evie thought) as besides some extra weekly rent from her sister (in spite of Mrs Worth even agreeing to reduce Evie's own payment slightly 'because of the inconvenience'), which must be welcome as it had to be expensive trying to maintain a grand house of the size of Pemberley, it would mean too that Julia's ration book would be added to the house's catering cache of rations.

And as Julia would be doubling up in Evie's room, where luckily there was already an old day bed that one of the sisters could sleep on, Mrs Worth wouldn't even have to find an extra berth for Julia and nor would she have to give up one of the two remaining empty bedrooms that she was hoping still to find PGs for.

And so, before Evie's cocoa had had time to chill, hands had been shaken on the arrangement, and it was agreed that Robert would help Julia move her possessions over to Pemberley the following afternoon.

The sisters tossed a penny for who'd get the day bed, although this was more for form's sake than anything else, as when Evie won the right to have the proper bed to herself, she decreed that she and Julia should swap beds on the first of every month as she wouldn't be happy if she knew Julia was always sleeping on the much less comfortable mattress.

As Evie escorted her father and sister to the front door, Julia whispered that in actual fact Pattie had wanted to be the one to move across to Pemberley, and she had kicked up a bit of a stink at not being put forward. But Robert and Susan had felt that she'd want to be out late at night too often to keep Mrs Worth happy, and that it would all end in tears, and so the rest of the family had united in the decision that it would be Julia who would move out to join her sister, everyone seemingly having forgotten that the front parlour could have been made into a bedroom as previously suggested.

Evie thought her parents were probably right to suggest Julia rather than Pattie, much as she always found her youngest sister to be tremendous fun. Mrs Worth liked things done a certain way, and all the current PGs seemed happy enough to fit in with her rules despite the occasional grumble, whereas the more naturally rebellious Pattie, lovely as she undoubtedly was, would nevertheless have delighted in flouting the rules at every opportunity and in causing general mayhem. Robert and Susan were very good at ignoring her and not giving her anything to kick against, and so they could live with Pattie reasonably harmoniously, whereas it would have been only a matter of days before Mrs Worth would have been thoroughly riled.

That night as Evie snuggled under her ancient feather eiderdown and gaily coloured crocheted blanket she'd put together several years earlier from wool oddments unravelled from various jumble sale, moth-eaten old and felted woollies that had failed to sell, she felt only the tiniest jealous pang at the thought of the two girls taking up residence at Bluebells.

In response Evie told herself firmly she was very lucky she was to have two such caring parents, who had such a lot of love spare to give to those less fortunate than themselves.

The Yeo family certainly wasn't rich in terms of money, but in terms of warmth, happiness and security, they were nothing short of millionaires.

Chapter Six

The two little girls from the recently bombed-out streets in Plymouth, Marie and Catherine, duly arrived as expected the next afternoon. They were completely traumatised: wide-eyed and almost unblinking, obviously very grubby, slow to move and unwilling to speak. Evie was determined to think about them in a more charitable manner than she had when Frank and Joseph had arrived, but when she saw their timid, fearful faces she found that quite naturally her heart went out to them, and she dreaded to think what they had been through to end up in that condition.

At the appointed time Susan came to collect them, and she simply knelt down, gathered them into her arms, filthy and knotty-haired as they both were, and enveloped them together in a long hug, telling them each how very, very happy she was that they were going to stay with her and her family, and how much Shady was looking forward to having them as his new playmates and best friends.

As Evie watched her mother stand up, take hold of each of their hands and then lead Marie and Catherine slowly away to their new home, she was sure that it wouldn't be too long before they were chatting away like any ordinary little girls. If anyone could help them forget the trauma of what they had survived, it was going to be Susan Yeo.

For quite some minutes afterwards, Evie squared her shoulders and puffed out her chest; she knew she still had a way to go herself, but her parents always tried hard to do the right thing, and she felt very proud of being a Yeo.

The other children to be billeted were all collected as promised too – this was a first, as previously there'd always been some sort of drama over where at least one child would sleep, no matter how rigorous the pre-arrival organisation.

In all the milling around Evie was kept very busy, as she wanted to be certain that she had said hello personally to each and every one of this latest batch of evacuees before they left with their new guardians, and she made sure that they all knew she'd be at their new school every day and that they could find her there at any time to ask her a question or to say hello, even if she wouldn't actually be teaching them.

Evie thought that it might help these displaced children settle in more quickly at the school if there was at least one face they knew before they arrived for lessons. And she wasn't sure that Mrs Bowes would provide quite the sort of reassuring welcome that in all probability these anxious children needed.

Meanwhile Julia's rather hurried arrival at Pemberley livened things up no end. She had an agreeable and calm way about her that people were instantly drawn to, and so the atmosphere across the whole house seemed to lighten a couple of notches immediately.

Indeed it was only a couple of nights after Julia had got settled and unpacked all her belongings that Mrs Wallis, who had brought some records with her when she and Mr Wallis had relocated to Devon from Canterbury, asked Mrs Worth if she'd mind very much if the old gramophone was dusted off. The dining table could be moved to one side to make space in the dining room, which was one of the biggest rooms on the ground floor of Pemberley, for a little dancing after tea one evening.

'We'll finish by nine o'clock, and then we'll make sure that we move everything back to just as it was, I promise, so that everything is fine and dandy for breakfast,' said Mrs Wallis in her posh, tinkling voice.

Rather taken aback by this unexpected request that put her somewhat on the spot, Mrs Worth hadn't been able to think quickly enough of a good reason to say no, and so a night of home dancing was planned for later that week.

In fact the evening turned out to be a tremendous success, with Mr and Mrs Wallis proving to be impressively expert dancers who looked almost as if they were gliding around the room rather than dancing and, surprisingly, Mr and Mrs Worth showing all and sundry present that they were also pretty nimble in this respect and not nearly as old-fashioned in the way they danced as the more sceptical of the PGs might have expected.

Julia and Evie partnered together, with Evie trying (with varying degrees of success) to lead, and then Julia danced with Mr Smith, who also revealed he had rather an energetic set of heels.

As Evie thought would be the case, Peter Pipe refused to dance but he watched the goings-on amiably enough. And in fact Evie was just thinking that Peter seemed a little less shy and withdrawn these days, and that although she had wondered several times quite what job he cycled off to each morning, there was a rather appealing air of mystery about him as he was very adept in sidestepping any hint of interest in what he was doing or why he was in Devon. She was just thinking that Peter had one of those smiles that totally transformed his face, not that he could be provoked to smile very often, when she realised that for the first time since the breakfast that had led to her unfortunate dressing-down by Mrs Bowes, that Mr Smith was directly addressing her.

Trying to keep a polite distance between themselves in terms of both space and emotional jolliness, she felt herself colour up when Mr Smith laughed openly. This was because she hadn't been able to prevent herself gasping out loud and then quailing obviously, being quite unable to stop her previously polite expression slipping when she realised that he had suggested that next time a little evening dancing was planned at Pemberley, then perhaps Evie should see if Mrs Bowes were interested in joining them for a few turns around the floor.

Later it turned out that Peter was exceptionally accomplished on the piano and this meant that he could bash out most of the current popular tunes. He could sing too, and rather well, Evie had to confess to herself as she noticed that the stammer that could be so prevalent when he talked seemed to disappear as he sang.

Soon everyone was standing around the piano and the evening turned into a general sing-along, with favourites of the time being crooned out loudly by everyone who lived at Pemberley.

Despite Mr Worth's completely tuneless 'singing' being so awfully bad that Evie and Julia didn't dare catch each other's eye for fear of a fit of the giggles, it was the most fun anyone could remember having for quite some while.

Suddenly Pemberley seemed the place in the village where everyone wanted to be.

The final two bedrooms were let, this time to WRVS (Royal Voluntary Service) girls called Sarah and Tina, who'd had to move away from Exeter when their flat (two friends sharing a flat together – the very idea was so daring, in Evie's opinion, yet how thrilling!) had to be condemned following the loss of the bombed-out house next door. They seemed nice young women, very wholesome and pleasant, and Evie and Julia warmed to them at once.

Then Rev. Painter was heard crunching up Pemberley's long semi-circular drive early one evening. He had a special request, which was to see if the young ladies of the house would take over putting on the annual village summer Revels. He felt new blood was needed in these dark days to breathe life into a long-standing summer event for the village that sadly had come to feel like little more than an unwelcome chore in recent years for those who usually put it on, with a corresponding drop-off in stalls and attendance.

This year Mrs Bowes had agreed that the Revels could be held on the school grounds as the village green was indisposed; and then it turned out to be she who had also volunteered Evie – of course, for when wasn't it Evie who Mrs Bowes volunteered whenever something needed doing? – as the logical choice for the person who would organise the other organisers, and indeed, it seemed to Evie, everything else to do with the Revels. Mrs Bowes seemed to think that with Timmy away, Evie didn't have enough to fill her time.

Evie thought Mrs Bowes was very adept at manoeuvring her into a range of tasks that were strictly outside her school remit, but actually in this case she didn't mind too much as she thought that putting on the Revels might well be fun. And as the date of the Revels wasn't until early July and it was only just May, there was plenty to time for her to persuade her family and friends to get involved, and for her to chivvy the village's inhabitants to put on a good show in order to prove to Jerry that times might well be tough, but that those who were lucky enough to live in Lymbridge were not the types to be easily put off from enjoying a little frivolity in the summer sun, with the added bonus that they could raise some money for local good causes.

Julia, and Sarah and Tina too, seemed happy enough to be involved, and so they determined among themselves that they would move heaven and earth to make the day of the Revels a fun afternoon for everyone who came out to support them, as well as a suitably patriotic day where absent loved ones could be remembered with pride.

The village sewing circle now met at Pemberley several times a week, and so there could be up to fifteen women seated around the dining-room table working with their heads bent forward over their sewing.

Evie had to admit to herself that while she'd always been rather a good knitter, she was now quickly becoming a dab hand at picking various clothes of all types apart, and then after washing and careful pressing, turning the material the other way around, and remaking various garments with the fresh and less-worn side of the material showing.

Sometimes the unpicked clothes would be completely restyled and made into something very different from their original incarnation. In this respect Evie was particularly proud of a smart pin-striped skirt she had made for herself from an old pair of her father's trousers that he had ripped badly below one knee on a stray nail standing proud of the wall, when poking around at the back of the garage in the blackout one night while, ironically, looking for a nail to bang in something in the kitchen. The weather was currently too sunny for such a warm skirt but Evie was certain that it would really come into its own during the autumn and winter months, and she liked the rather mannish look of the pin-stripes.

During these companionable, wholesomely domestic Make Do and Mend evenings, Mr Smith would quite often sit in the corner of the dining room reading or doing a crossword (he was good, although nothing like as quick as Peter who could do a whole *Daily Telegraph* crossword in under ten minutes), while Julia and Pattie would joke and entertain the other members of the sewing circle, larking about as Mrs Sew-and-Sew, a character they had made up.

Mrs Sew-and-Sew was an outspoken, er, so-and-so. But, despite her hilarious snootiness and ridiculously posh ways, she also offered really good tips and many cunning tricks on how to breathe new life into old clothes. Who, for instance, would have thought that the inside of pockets would have made such a good place to find spare material if a patch were needed? Only Mrs Sew-and-Sew of course! The best method of darning a worn heel in a sock? You couldn't say One, Two, Three before Mrs Sew-and-Sew would be charging to the rescue with the very best method, a way so simple that even the most novice of seamstresses could manage.

Quite often Evie felt that Mrs Sew-and-Sew bore just a little bit too much of a bossy resemblance to Mrs Bowes to be either comfortable or particularly amusing to her ears. Everyone else, however, thought her screamingly funny.

Peter would also put in an occasional appearance in the dining room on these sewing-circle evenings, although he'd always leave it an hour or two before daring to peer around the dining-room door.

Gradually he gained in confidence, soon turning out to be a very welcome visitor as he would regularly be the one who would come in hefting Mrs Worth's largest tray, the one with the cane edging and bead-threaded handles twining out of a casein base, that would be groaning under the weight of much needed cups of tea for everyone. Once, as a rare treat, he'd included two bars of Fry's Five Boys chocolate, broken into pieces on a saucer decorated with painted flowers so that everybody could enjoy a taste of something sweet. Later Evie laughed off Julia and Pattie's quips that Peter had made sure she had got the largest piece of chocolate, and that she had responded by glancing up coquettishly at him through the untamed curls of her fringe.

Of course, despite these many distractions, Evie still felt overwhelmingly concerned about Timmy and his inconstant heart, although she was no closer to having made any sort of decision as to what she should do about him or his behaviour. Her heart told her she was being less than truthful with Mrs Bowes every day the poor woman was kept in ignorance of her beloved son's wrongdoings – Evie liked to pride herself on her honesty – although she couldn't imagine actually ever finding the courage to broach the subject directly with Timmy's mother. Evie also still felt conflicted about her own feelings towards Timmy – love seemed a much trickier territory to negotiate than she had anticipated just a couple of short months ago. And the war hanging over them both made it even worse, as Evie felt young men who might be called upon to make the ultimate sacrifice should perhaps be allowed more leeway than normal in accepted 'good behaviour', but that she found it most painful having to experience this more lax attitude directly.

Also, although it wasn't in any way a nice feeling she was experiencing, Evie realised that unfortunately she was getting used to the uneasy feelings Dave Symons' comments had provoked, as well as the idea that she might have fallen in love with a feckless man who, she could now see, if they were to go on to marry, would deeply hurt her feelings as often as not. She still wanted to love Timmy in the uncomplicated manner she had before he had left Lymbridge, but it was difficult knowing now that her hopes of loving an honourable man had been dashed.

Part of the problem was that she knew that to end her liaison with Timmy would be to severely hamper her chances of a 'good' marriage. There just weren't very many suitable prospective partners living locally, and although Timmy was flawed, he was attractive, and fun too, and as his wife, he offered her a position in local society that most people would be envious of. It all needed thinking about very seriously.

She had now confessed to Julia and Pattie all her suspicions as to Timmy's uncouth and wanton behaviour, and, as she had expected, her loyal sisters were hot under the collar and unashamedly furious on her behalf.

Occasionally Evie and Julia would lie in bed at night as they planned ever more ludicrous plots of revenge, all designed to Teach Timmy A Much-Needed Lesson, such as Evie only feeding him turnips after they were married, or that when she would do his washing, she would put itching powder (Julia claiming that James knew a good recipe) inside Timmy's clean underpants. And then, briefly, the sisters would have to put their pillows over their faces to muffle their hoots of laughter.

After moments like this Evie would be plunged into moroseness, experiencing Timmy's casual cruelty wash over her once again; it was as if she needed these lighter moments as a measure to calibrate in some way the grave extent of her heartbreak, although she would immediately feel guilty over her ability to laugh whilst also feeling sad. In some ways thoughts of Timmy felt like a scab she knew she shouldn't fiddle with, but felt compelled to pick at all the same.

Once she tried to explain to Julia how strange love was, and how very odd it felt to know that although she was upset and hurt by what Timmy had likely done, sometimes there was an almost uncontrollable impulse to give way to wild laughter, and that at these moments she felt as if her heart were inconstant and would be the undoing of her. Julia, who had never had a young man of her own, stared back at Evie in incomprehension, and Evie decided not to mention these complex feelings again.

Generally, she felt various degrees of down-heartedness and felt sorry for herself; maybe it was easier if she allowed everybody to think this was all she was feeling all the time. Well, everybody other than her fellow PGs, her parents and Mrs Bowes, that was.

Then, out of the blue, Pattie arrived with devastating news.

She took Evie out to the lichen-covered stone bench that was artfully set in the shade of the large elm toward the bottom of the large garden at Pemberley, so that they could have some secluded privacy.

There, Pattie told Evie that she had been out one evening with a friend in Oldwell Abbott, where she had caught a swift glance of Tricia Dolby, one of the girls Timmy had supposedly been over-attentive with, who had been walking down the street.

Pattie held Evie's hands and stared into her eyes as she said, 'Evie, dearest, this is difficult for me to say, and I'm only telling you because I love you so very much, and therefore I want you to hear this from me rather than one of the many tittle-tattles around here, like that ugly beast Dave Symons—'

'For crying out loud, spit it out, Pattie – you're scaring me,' interrupted Evie in a tone that she herself could hear was close to yelpish. She didn't like her sister's serious expression.

'All right, all right my darling. The truth of it is that I can't be sure, but Tricia looked, um, bulgy. In other words, she was a bit too round in, um, the stomach area, if you know what I mean,' Pattie said, and followed her statement with a dip of her head in Evie's direction and a meaningful raising of her eyebrows.

For a second Evie stared back at her younger sister with a look of complete incomprehension.

Then she cried 'Oh!' in a small anguished voice as she raised a fluttering and shaky hand toward her throat and the engagement ring hanging on its delicate golden chain just under the neatly embroidered collar of her cotton blouse.

'Look, let's not jump to conclusions, Evie, sweetie. Tricia might just be plumper than I remember her. But, and do remember that this is a big but, *if*, and note that I do say "if", she is indeed in the family way, there could be rumours about her and Timmy that won't be to the good as far as you are concerned. Rumours that someone somewhere will make sure you hear sometime, as you know how gossip is the lifeblood of these moors,' Pattie said in a soft voice rich with care and gentleness.

'Of course, even if Tricia is expecting, that is not necessarily a guarantee that Timmy is involved. But I thought you should know what I saw, Evie, and so I wanted you to be prepared for any news that may come your way, and to have a chance to get used to these possible developments in private beforehand. I think it's better that way, unpleasant as it is, rather than you having to run the risk that at some point you might, out of the blue, have to take any potential bad news of this sort on the chin. News that would perhaps be given to you in front of a crowd of people who'd all then be gawping at you to see how you'd react.'

Pattie was right, Evie could see. What her sister was saying wasn't pleasant to hear – but it would be a whole lot worse if she were hearing it from the mouth of a malicious stranger in front of Tricia or Tricia's cronies.

But the result was that however low Evie had felt in the weeks since she had heard about Timmy's infidelities, it was as nothing to the deep depths she felt herself sliding towards at this very moment. She realised she had been harbouring a vain hope that Dave Symons had been lying, and it was all some horrible mistake. Evie looked at Pattie and saw that in spite her stressing '*if*', Pattie believed Tricia to be pregnant; with a shudder Evie felt it incontrovertible that Timmy was the father.

Now she understood for the first time in her life the true meaning of the word heartbreak; at this very moment her heart felt as if it was literally cleaving in two.

As salty, hot tears of despair started to well and Evie's chin and lower lip quivered uncontrollably, Pattie could only take her beloved sister in her arms and hold her tight until the wave of sorrow started to subside, Pattie giving silent thanks that she had had the foresight to tuck not one but two clean and starched hankies into the waistband of her skirt before leaving Bluebells to break the bad news to Evie.

Damn that Timmy Bowes. Damn him.

Chapter Seven

Evie wasn't quite sure how she managed to get through the next few days; everything and everyone around her felt strange, and a long way away. It was almost as if she were looking at the world through a kaleidoscope; it seemed familiar, yet constantly, subtly and subversively different.

In fact, she couldn't decide what was worse: the knowledge that her private humiliation in choosing a feckless fiancé might at any moment explode into public knowledge; or that there was something of the sense of a Sword of Damocles hanging over her slightly tricky relationship with Mrs Bowes.

For if Timmy had made another woman pregnant – and let's hope in that case, it was just the *one* woman, Evie said to herself – she had no expectation other than, unfair as this might be, Mrs Bowes clearly laying the blame at Evie's doorstep for Timmy's inability to keep the flies on his trousers firmly buttoned.

Or were the anxious looks that Julia and Pattie cast in her direction if they thought nobody else was looking worse? Or perhaps even more horrid was the relentlessly nagging worry about what her father might do to Timmy when he came home on leave if Pattie's suspicions turned out to be true.

Hour upon hour each night would be spent writhing in torture in the blacked-out garret bedroom, with Evie doing her level best not to toss and turn, as she knew that Julia needed every moment of sleep that she could get as she'd have miles to cycle the next day on her delivery rounds for the Post Office. And so by each morning a worn-out Evie would find her body aching furiously from toe to tip with the tension of trying to lie still.

She was flat and uninspired in her teaching too, Evie knew, and she could feel Mrs Bowes casting an occasional piercingly scrutinising look in her direction.

And once – unforgivably – Evie snapped at sweet little Bobby Ayres when he'd misheard something she'd said. When she saw the hurt and puzzled look fleet across his normally happily open face in response to her barbed comment, Evie could have laid her head on her arms and wept. He didn't deserve such shabby treatment, and her heart went out to him.

Evie came to dread the sound of the letter-box, as to make matters worse Timmy's typically cheerful letters were becoming even more ebullient.

Her replies were as terse as possible, but he seemed to interpret this as nothing more than tiredness from being kept on the run-around at the school by his mother and so he assumed that she might be overdoing her efforts at Lymbridge Primary School.

With each new letter written to Timmy, Evie tried to gather her courage to confront him with her suspicions about what might have gone on between him and Tricia Dolby, but she would chicken out with a disheartening and humiliating failure of resolve, and then she would as usual resort to the same old topics that weren't dangerous or contentious. His letters were also a constant reminder that he was away from Lymbridge to fight a war, and it was possible that he might not come back. Emotive feelings swirled about, and slowly Evie came to dread the sight of yet another envelope with her name on the front.

Oddly, it was when Sukie had cycled over to Lymbridge for coffee one Saturday morning that Evie turned the corner, and started to feel better or, if not better exactly, slightly stronger.

By way of simple gossip, Sukie mentioned innocently Tricia Dolby's expanding waistline and inflated bosoms, and the rumours that were starting to circulate to the effect that it very much looked as if Tricia might be having a 'happy event' in time for Christmas.

Previously Evie hadn't confided to Sukie or Linda the names of any of the girls who Timmy was claimed to have philandered with – when she had told her friends about Dave Symon's assertions, she assumed that if she'd said who the girls supposedly were, it would make it feel all the more real somehow – and so Evie had declared at the time of her confession to her pals that she wouldn't pass on that portion of the gossip, on the basis of 'what goes around comes around'. Sukie and Linda had joked about her moral high-mindedness; Evie knew better – it was nothing aside from her wanting to avoid further humiliation.

But at Sukie's unexpected words this particular Saturday morning, Evie was suddenly swamped by the feeling that life was going to play out in this respect precisely as it would do, and the reality was that there was nothing she could do about it any which way, other than for her to take the view that she really shouldn't feel so personally defeated. After all, Timmy's behaviour wasn't her fault, although the pity of it was that it didn't feel like that.

Sukie, a close friend since they had met on the first day at school when they were just five years old, and the friend that over the years had always seemed most attuned to the slightest change of Evie's mood, saw her friend's face blanch at her mention of Tricia Dolby. Sukie understood at once that she had unknowingly blundered into choppy waters.

When Evie explained why this was, Sukie's next response, after apologising for putting her size seven foot firmly in her mouth by mistake, was to ask what precisely did Evie intend to do about this pretty parlous state of affairs?

This was, Evie realised, the first time anyone had immediately assumed she should take some sort of offensive into her own hands, rather than merely offering Evie some not very reassuring words of comfort and consolation.

'I've said it before, Evie-Rose, and I daresay I'll be saying it again. But men are nothing but trouble,' Sukie was saying with conviction. 'You give them an inch, and they take a mile. All men are like yorn Timmy. Full of dastardly thoughts and actions. Or at least they would be if they thought they could get away with it. And in his case I blame Timmy Bowes' damn mother – she's spent decades telling him how wonderful he is and that he's God's gift to everybody, and now, the deluded fool, he believes it. The cheek of that woman – and she'd already got a lot of ground to make up with me for boring my pantaloons off with the sheer dullness of her lessons all those years ago.

'As long as you remember, Evie, that Timmy Darling is nothing more than a pain in the behind. And that you are too good for him. No, that's not right! You are quite simply MOST ASSUREDLY too good for him.'

Sukie continued in this vein, and although Evie felt she was letting the words her friend was saying wash over her, she had to admit that hearing Sukie so vexed on her behalf was quite a pleasant feeling, all the same.

'I know he made you love him, Evie sweet, but men like Timmy Bowes are masters at that sort of thing. They know what to say to make nice, trusting girls like you think they care for them. And then, once they have you right where they want you, that sort of wastrel immediately stops trying. So their game then becomes one of making sure that they can hang on to someone like you while also playing footsie with whoever else they can dupe.'

And in that emotionally barbed comment Evie could feel the ring of what felt like an obvious truth.

Her loyal friend had always been a stunner in the looks department, and she had been immensely popular with boys since infants class and so Sukie knew what was what when it came down to men.

It was also undeniable, Evie had to admit, that Sukie had had a rapid turnover of dates over the years as the Devon lads tended to be naturally conservative, with the result that they found Sukie's outspoken views perhaps less attractive than her golden hair and depthless dark-blue eyes. Indeed some of the more easily jealous Devon lasses had occasionally accused Sukie, sometimes even directly to her face, of being 'fast', a term that Sukie always took great exception to. And she was often taller than her beaux, which perhaps hadn't helped her chances either. At any rate, Sukie didn't think much of how the majority of men behaved, and was quite happy to point the finger at their various weaknesses.

However, prior to her recent experiences with Timmy, Evie had always felt that Sukie held a somewhat jaundiced view of the opposite sex.

But now, for the first time, she wondered if Sukie might not be right after all.

Evie knew that she herself was woefully inexperienced when it came to love.

Sure, she had walked out with Steven Hodges for a couple of weeks when she was sixteen, but when Steven had finally plucked up the courage to kiss her, Evie had been horrified when he'd tried to slip something warm and slimily sneaky between her lips – she'd recoiled instantly when she realised it was his tongue!

And now poor Steven was dead, having the sad honour of being the first Lymbridge man to die in action in this war, although the war memorial had a metal plaque with a depressingly long list of the village's losses from the Great War.

Evie had felt unbearably sad when she had heard the tragic news about Steven at Christmas, when she had hoped very much that before he had died he had found a young lass or two who liked his inching, slug-like tongue rooting around their mouth a whole lot more than Evie herself had done.

It wasn't until a whole two years after Steven that Evie had met a pleasant enough trainee solicitor called Edward while she was at teachers' training college in Cheltenham. But after a couple of chaste visits to matinee cinema performances, Edward's mother had put the kibosh on the relationship, making it clear she had designs on a better-connected wife for Edward than Evie looked to be. Rather disappointingly, Edward had put up little struggle in opposing his mother's plans, seemingly content to listen to and then follow her filibustering opinions as to the matters of his heart.

Then, racily, there had been a single incident of some passionate kissing in a Cheltenham alleyway after an evening at a dancehall. A young man called John (Evie never found out his last name) had whisked Evie around the dance floor in his expert arms for several turns, before treating her to her first port and lemon. Then, after offering to walk her home, he had persuaded her to step with him into an empty doorway at the entrance to the alley.

Evie surprised herself by being very happy to be so enticed. For a couple of minutes she had lost herself in the unexpected thrill of being held in strong arms and kissed by a man who very noticeably, even to a green Evie, knew what he was doing. Heat flooded across every fibre of her body, and she had responded to John's enthusiastic kisses with an eagerness that took her breath away.

But when he tried to press her against the wall and she could feel his growing excitement, she'd realised she wasn't after all ready for what it was now glaringly obvious that he wanted. And so she slipped from under his arms with an apology; and, after two or three deep breaths to marshal his feelings as he stared at the wall, John gave her a look that managed to combine longing, regret and acquiescence to her wish that matters should stop, before politely offering an arm for her to take as he walked her home in a suitably gentlemanly fashion.

For weeks afterwards Evie had tortured herself with, at times, intensely pleasurable thoughts of what might have happened if she had stayed in the doorway.

In the times she had seen Timmy, she had been careful to use her knowledge of those heady minutes in the alley to make sure that she was never really in a position whereby she had to say a firm no to Timmy, who she soon found could be surprisingly persuasive.

It had become a dance of manners between them, as Timmy would try every trick in the book to get Evie on her own in an isolated spot, while Evie employed all of her feminine wiles to make sure she was never close to being compromised. If Timmy had thought matters would change once they were engaged, he'd been in for a rude disappointment.

She didn't think she was a prude, and she didn't judge *too* harshly Sukie and Pattie's seemingly more relaxed attitude to men and whatever it might be that these men were wanting (and what – or not – Sukie and Pattie might go on to deliver to them, Evie would wonder about, knowing though that she would never be so coarse as to ask for any lurid details). However, the truth of it was that Evie was determined to be a virgin on her wedding day.

Already Evie could tell that some people would feel her quaintly old-fashioned in this ambition, but it was important to her, and so she didn't feel able to compromise. Or, more exactly, she felt she hadn't yet met the man who made her feel that perhaps she should think otherwise.

Now Evie thought that while Sukie might hold an unjustifiably harsh opinion of men in general, in the case of Timmy Bowes in particular, Sukie was very probably correct in her assumptions about his behaviour, and that it was high time that Evie called him out on what he had been up to.

'You're right, Sukie, lovey. I've waited too long, and Timmy must feel he's got away with everything. I am going to write to him and tell him what's what. No, I've a better idea – you and me are going to sit down together right this very minute and a draft a letter that will leave him in no doubt that I Am Most Definitely Not Pleased,' Evie announced with an uncharacteristic authority.

Dear Timmy

It has come to my attention that there are things you have not told me and which you should have; in fact you should not have done these things in the first place. For I believe you have not been true to me.

I have been informed that you have had, for want of a better word, 'interludes' with Susie Pine, Anne Oakley, and also that dark-haired girl with the sizeable rear you like speaking to and who works in Woollies in Plymouth (I don't know her name, but I have seen her giving you the glad eye), as well as Connie Farmalow and Beverley Tavey. I have heard tell also that Tricia Dolby is expecting a baby, due in November, the rumour is, and that YOU are the father.

I am upset and very cross with you. In fact – and you know I am not one given to hyperbole – you have broken my heart.

I thought you were a better man than that.

As far as I am aware, your mother has no idea of the rumours circulating about your behaviour, although Lymbridge is such a small place that she must be bound to find out soon.

Evie

Evie and Sukie had spent nearly an hour on the few lines of this letter, and had had several trial runs. It needed to be simple, in order that Timmy, who wasn't particularly bright, could not argue he was confused as to what Evie was driving at; and of course it also needed to be firm in showing Evie's disapproval of his behaviour, and her subsequent devastation at the loss of her belief in their perfect love story.

Sukie was also rather for Evie giving Timmy some sort of 'shape up or ship out' ultimatum, but Evie felt she should leave the letter relatively open-ended as she wanted to see what Timmy's response was to her allegation. Phase two could be an ultimatum.

At any rate, Evie forbore putting any sort of kiss after her name, which even though her feelings had been freshly churned through writing the letter, was hard for her not to do. All the women left at home once the men had gone to fight were very aware of the real peril their loved ones were or were about to be in.

As she stuck the stamp on the envelope containing the letter, Evie felt that some of the legal chit-chat and solicitors' reminiscing she had heard at meal times between Mr Worth and Mr Wallis had rubbed off on her, and added clarity and a sense of conviction and determination to her sentences. That was what she hoped, anyway.

It wasn't an eloquent or a great letter in any sense, Evie knew, but she felt it should do the job.

The reply though, when it came three days later, was vintage Timmy.

Dearest E

I am well; or normally I am well, although right now I have rather a heavy head following a hotly contested game of pinochle last night.

Yes, that is a list in your letter!

Here in camp, I think only of you, I promise! You are the one for me.

Don't breathe a word to Ma – it will only lead to trouble. And remember, Evie, I am going to make you proud!

Your Timmy x

Sukie's response was to roll her eyes and to sigh dramatically.

'I don't know, I really don't,' agreed Evie, although without the sigh; she was too dejected. 'I can't tell if he's acknowledging that he did dally with those women, or if he's saying instead that whatever went on it's all been blown out of proportion, or that nothing really happened. Goodness me, he's annoying – indeed I think Shady, who's not been averse to visiting every single one of the bitches in Lymbridge, has better morals than Timmy Bowes.

'And besides being evasive, Timmy seems to think I was threatening to tell his mother about these women. That's just

74

as annoying, as obviously he doesn't know me at all if he thinks I'm going to stir up *that* particular hornets' nest. I do have to work with the dratted woman after all.'

Sukie and Evie decided that perhaps the response that Timmy hadn't bargained for would be silence, and so Evie vowed that she wouldn't contact him for a fortnight.

But this vow was to no avail as the very next day she received a postcard with a hastily scribbled message that said simply: 'E, by the time you read this I will have been shipped out, and so I think our correspondence will face delays. Wish me luck! Loving thoughts, Txx'.

It seemed to Evie as if the fates were conspiring against her in her desire to deal effectively with the bothering issue of, to quote Pattie, The Tricia Trouble.

Chapter Eight

Evie found she didn't have too much time on her hands to sit around feeling sorry for herself.

That very evening troubling news came concerning her and Sukie's friend and former classmate, Linda. She had been visiting a hilltop farm only eight or ten miles from the South Devon coast to shoe a couple of workhorses, and had been helping the farmer lead them from their pasture to the farmyard for their shoeing when a lone German aeroplane had flown across low overhead, even though it was the middle of the afternoon and it could be quite clearly seen. There was nowhere for them to hide and guns from the light aircraft had strafed both Linda and the farmer.

It was extraordinary – nothing like this had occurred before in the region.

The farmer, Bill Stewer, was hit in the hand and leg, and one of the horses had dropped stone dead, crashing to the ground with a grunt and loud thud, from a bullet taken to the head between the ears. The normally gentle giant of a horse that Linda was leading had panicked in the furore and had quite literally run over her, inadvertently kicking her in the chest, cracking a couple of ribs and causing her lung to collapse. A bullet had also sliced the skin on her arm, although this was merely a glancing injury.

Both Mr Stewer and Linda had been taken to hospital in

Plymouth, and of course Sukie and Evie made haste to go to the hospital to see their friend.

When they arrived on the ward Linda was in, Sam Torrence, the young farmer Linda had told Evie she liked so much was standing at the end of her bed looking extremely uncomfortable as he shuffled his weight from foot to foot and constantly turned his hat around in his hands. Linda looked equally uncomfortable too, although Evie thought that might be because of her injuries.

When he spied Sukie and Evie, the young chap introduced himself and, quickly giving their right hands each a rather painful single tug floorwards, he made his excuses with a 'well, I'll be off then as them cows need milking dreckly', and then fairly galloped away down the ward towards the exit doors.

Linda looked at her friends with slightly raised eyebrows and, as well as she was able (which wasn't very well), tried to shrug in a nonchalant manner. 'Sam is such a nice chap, and I can't believe he came in to see me when I know how extremely busy he is at the farm as there's always so much for him to do there now that he has practically no help.

'But once he got to the end of my bed, then he got all tongue-tied; and I had to keep the conversation going with no help from him, and frankly I just didn't feel up to it. After what seemed like the longest age, he was just starting to get going himself again by asking questions that I'd just told him the answers to, when you two arrived, and then we couldn't see him for dust. Honestly, I don't think I'm ever going to be able to get this relationship off the ground. Snails are faster than him, and I'm running out of excuses to just turn up at his farm on the off-chance of running into him.'

'Well, given the amount of effort you've put into making Sam Torrence as comfortable as possible, you don't seem to be as badly hurt as I expected,' said Evie, a mite primly. 'And I agree with your comments of a week or two back when you told me quite often that he is rather manly and strong-looking, and so perhaps Sam is the tonic you need to aid your recovery. Therefore, speaking as the world-renowned Doctor Evie, once you are up and about again, I prescribe visits for you to Sam Torrence's farm as often as required. Dreckly so...'

Linda tried to grin, and then she went on to say that she and Mr Stewer, the poor farmer who had been strafed, had both been interviewed by the military, the Devon police and also by a reporter from the *Western Morning News* who was going to write about them for the paper, Linda stressing that the horse who injured her was in no way to blame. Luckily the farmer's injuries weren't life-threatening. Linda had allowed the reporter to send a photographer to her bedside, and he had taken a hasty photograph of her as the ward sister had tried to shoo him out once she realised what he was about.

This was, apparently, the first incidence of something like this, and so nobody quite knew what to make of it.

Adding that she should make a full recovery within a few weeks and that she would be back farriering again not long after that, Linda added, 'They're going to get me up and walking about tomorrow as I'm less likely to get fluid building up in my lung that way.

'It hurts like buggery though, but I think that's more where Hector's hoof caught me – he was terrified, the poor chap, and of course his hoof must be close to the size of a dinner plate, although a plate with a bloomin' great metal horseshoe nailed to it. The real tragedy though is the loss of Mabel, of course, as this pair were inseparable and had worked together for years. I hear they had the very devil moving Mabel's carcass off the path, which is no wonder as she was massive. And of course poor Hector must wonder where she's gone, especially as she won't now be stealing wisps from his hay net as she was wont to do from right under Hector's nose, not that he minded, the sweet old boy. They were such a hardworking pair and were so easy to handle that one of your infants could have ploughed with them, Evie. They were loaned out to farms all over the place to help with ploughing and hauling and whatnot, and so I don't know how the local farmers will manage to get over a loss like this.

'And Mabel was the dearest old girl possible, absolutely one of my favourite horses, and whenever she saw me coming she'd always raise one of her feet up and just hold it in the air, waving it about for all the world as if she was saying that she was ready and that just like me she was a girl who does like to have new shoes. This blimmin' war...'

Evie and Sukie did their best to cheer up Linda whose soliloquy had ended tearfully. Linda seemed upset only about the hurt of the horses concerned and not at all worried about herself, and not very worried about poor Mr Stewer either, and so Evie and Sukie stayed by her bedside until Linda began to look drowsy.

They knew their friend was playing down the horror of the whole event, and that she was very lucky to be alive.

Chapter Nine

On the night after the visit to Plymouth Hospital, Evie slept poorly. She had unsettling dreams of her and Timmy being strafed by a lone German plane as they strolled around the school playing field; then they were taken to hospital in a trailer driven by Sam Torrence who somehow turned into Mr Smith on the journey. And then at the hospital Timmy was somehow the doctor who had to give her a very grim prognosis, namely that her heart would need to be removed and that Peter would be the surgeon leading the operating team. Evie had woken with a gasp and a start, and then had spent at least an hour in the pitch black replaying all the whys and wherefores in her and Timmy's relationship.

So it was a weary Evie who went down to breakfast the next morning to discover that Lymbridge was alive with two further pieces of news. The military had requisitioned a once-grand manor house called The Grange that was about three miles away from the village, on the edge of a frill of moor, and apparently it was going to be turned into a hospital for recuperating, gravely wounded servicemen returning from various offensives.

And Switherns, the farm where the farmer's wife, Mrs Ward, had allowed the children into the milking parlour on the morning when Mrs Bowes and Evie had taken them for a walk around the village, was to have a troop of about one hundred conscripted men from the Rhondda Valley in Wales billeted in a couple of their hay barns as these were quite large and were currently empty as the hay was yet to come in.

These men would be arriving the next week, and apparently they had been offered the option of either going down the coal mines to work for the war effort in a reserved occupation, or else signing up to fight. These Welshmen due to arrive in Lymbridge were those who had opted to fight, and they were going to do their preliminary training in Devon, before being shipped off from HM Dockyard Devonport to end up wherever those doing the strategic planning would decide they could be most useful in fighting Jerry.

And so within a day or two Evie found that her lessons were punctuated by the sound of military lorries rumbling past with supplies such as stacking beds and other necessities.

Pattie, whom Evie felt had seemed to be languishing in the doldrums since Julia had moved out from Bluebells, got something of her old twinkle back at the thought of this many young men actually being stationed in sleepy old Lymbridge, in short, right on her doorstep, even if they were only to be there for a little while. And Sarah and Tina were clearly excited by the prospect too.

In fact Evie and Julia joked that they could fairly hear the crackle of hormones whizzing around!

Life at Pemberley and at the village school had settled into a pleasant routine for Evie. Now that she'd survived a month at work, she'd received her first brown envelope with her pay inside. She paid her rent to Mrs Worth, and then presented her mother with two crisp £1 notes to help out with the housekeeping at Bluebells.

Then on the next Saturday morning, Evie went to Plymouth with Sukie to spend a little of her hard-earned gains, and to visit Linda once more.

However, when push came to shove, after an hour of wandering around the shops Evie could only bring herself to part with two of her clothing coupons, which she used to buy some pretty flower-sprigged cotton to make herself a blouse (and actually she thought that if she was clever in laying out the new pattern she'd just bought, and provided she kept to the short-sleeved option, she might even be able to squeeze a second blouse out of the remnant of material, in which case she would make it up for Julia). But, try as she might, the looked-forward-to shopping trip to Plymouth wasn't as much of a splash-out as Evie had anticipated.

Plymouth was still very clearly bearing the signs of its pro-longed night-time bombing, with plenty of shops having boarded windows even though somehow they were managing to keep open for trading, and Evie and Sukie had decided on the bus in that it would be sensible for them to do their shopping first, after which they would go to see Linda in hospital.

Before they headed to the hospital they decided to drop into the saddler's to see if they could find something appropriate as a welcome home gift for Linda as she was being released from hospital the following Tuesday, provided she continue to improve at the current rate.

At the saddler's they discovered he was selling some foul-smelling homemade fly repellent. It was the perfect present for Linda, they decided, because as noxious as it was, it would mean that when their pal was back at work in the coming hot summer weather she could dab it on whatever horse she was shoeing in order to ward off the flies, and then Linda would be a bit less likely to be bitten to death by the many flying creatures that always gather in the hot weather around horses. This was Linda's only gripe about her occupation.

As Evie paid the saddler for the fly repellent, she spotted some smart brown and cream dog-tooth-checked fabric folded haphazardly on a shelf on the back wall of the shop but tucked low down and almost obscured from view beside several boxes of grooming brushes, and so she asked the saddler what this material was. It turned out to be a strong duck cotton ordinarily used for the underside of the padded bits of saddles or harness collars.

When Evie discovered that, for now at least, this material didn't require a clothing coupon to buy as it was deemed to be of essential use, and that it was very reasonably priced, she nabbed herself a couple of yards. This was only after Sukie had batted her eyes at the middle-aged saddler, who had first said no, although he then went a coy shade of rose under the scrutiny of Sukie's pleading look. Luckily he understood that he had met his match, and so he made Evie, and Sukie, who couldn't sew to save her life and who had been saying she was stony broke anyway following a little too much in the way of going out in the early evenings, promise on their mothers' lives to keep quiet about precisely where the fabric came from as he absolutely wouldn't be able to cope with an influx of young women wanting to buy some as well, if either Evie or Sukie let the cat out of the bag.

As they left the shop, Evie turned to see the saddler tucking the remains of the checked cloth under the counter well out of sight.

Outside, Evie had to bully Sukie into accompanying her back to the newsagents to buy another pattern, or more precisely a magazine Evie had spied that was giving away a pattern, this time for a suit, before they could head to the hospital for their visit to Linda.

She had done much better now, in terms of splashing-out, Evie decided.

That evening Evie set to work cutting and pinning, and by the end of the week she was the proud owner of a very smart and flattering two-piece suit, comprising a neatly fitted jacket and a slim skirt that ended just below the knee.

Evie had never worked with checked material but, rather to her surprise, there were no problems (she had to acknowledge that it was clear that her sewing skills were definitely coming on in leaps and bounds under the tutelage of Mrs Sew-and-Sew).

And when Julia declared that Evie had never looked finer than when wearing the suit, which couldn't have fitted her better if

Hardy Amies himself had made it for her, Evie thought it very likely that she and her new suit would become very good allies over the course of the war. It was so useful to have an outfit that could be worn on just about any occasion, as the beauty of the suit was that it could be dressed either up or down, although as the densely woven material was also rather thin despite its obvious strength, she would need to add a coat or jacket over the top when venturing outside on chilly winter days.

On the next Saturday morning there was the thunder of heavy goods engines, and a convoy of khaki lorries deposited the Rhondda men at Switherns.

For the rest of the day the village of Lymbridge was to echo with the shouts and laughs of these raw recruits, who made plenty of loud exclamations when they realised that the bathroom facilities consisted of a cold tap in the farm yard, and a wooden-sided latrine dug quite some way down the nearest field.

The cows grazing in the field where the toilet block had been constructed were fascinated by the young men who were soon gingerly picking their way towards the latrine.

The cattle had, apparently, never seen anything as exciting in their lives before, with the result that it wasn't long before every single black and white creature in the field had come to see what was going on. They drifted across the pasture to stand together in a raggedy line, forming what for all the world looked like a guard of honour indicating the way to the lavatories.

Evie couldn't help but wish that she had a camera with her as she didn't know what was funnier: the placid, enquiring faces of the phalanx of large-eyed and tail-flicking cows, who clearly thought this all a very entertaining way of spending a Saturday as they looked on with immense concentration at the lads at the same time as they chewed their cuds; or the anxious faces of the Rhondda boys, who clearly weren't used to cows and had no idea how large or interested these bovine beasts could be as they passed by the guard of honour to answer their calls of nature.

Inexorably slowly the cows inched forward until the stronger-bladdered recruits, who were the last of the troop to risk the run to the lavatories, had only a narrow pathway down the field in which to walk, and any one of them could easily have reached out to touch the moist noses of their patient audience.

After church on Sunday, Evie and Julia returned with the rest of the Yeo family to Bluebells, as Robert had been able to nab a couple of rabbits for the pot, and Susan had promised them all a lunch of hearty rabbit stew.

'It breaks my heart,' announced Susan as she carefully stirred the stew, making sure that the dried crusts of the gravy from the side of the casserole dish had been scraped and then stirred back into the stew for added flavour, and then she added some dumplings for the final half hour. 'Have you seen how very young those Rhondda lads are? They're supposed to be men, but half of them look as if they've not started shaving yet. James is close to their age, and I can hardly bear to think of him perhaps one day having to go to a strange place away from us all for training, and then be sent off to who knows where.

'I hate to think that some of them are likely to get killed when they are sent off to fight. Those who were in church this morning looked homesick, scared to death and very much in need of a mother's hug. And I know that if our James were away, I'd be wishing a local family would be thinking kindly of him, and trying to come up with a way of making him feel welcome.'

Evie could only nod in agreement. She too had been surprised and then rather shocked to see how young, open-faced and naïve these Welsh lads had looked when she was standing only feet away from them in a nearby pew. She had also thought that if the resolution of the war didn't hurry up – and it showed no signs of doing so in the twenty or so months since the start of war had been declared – then her brother, James, would most certainly be called upon to serve his country. James was already saying he was keen to go to fight, but Evie thought that this really didn't bear thinking about.

And so by the time the rabbit stew had been served, consumed and plates wiped clean with an extra slice of Susan's delicious homemade bread, a plan had been hatched.

Robert would bag another brace of rabbits for Evie to give to Mrs Worth, and then Evie would ask her landlady whether it would be possible for her and Julia, and Susan too, to organise a tea party for the Rhondda lads at Pemberley.

It was the obvious place for such a tea party, as Pemberley was the only house in the village with the benefit of graciously large reception rooms and a substantial garden (if, fingers crossed, the fine weather held). Pemberley also had French windows from the dining room opening directly out to a sun-trap stone-flagged terrace, complete with small green plants and various lichens and mosses peeping out from between the flags, and wide stone steps down to a small patch of lawn below that nestled in front of numerous, recently dug vegetable plots.

There looked to be too many soldiers billeted at Switherns to have them all over to Pemberley at one time, Susan and Evie agreed, and so perhaps the tea party could be spread over adjoining afternoons, with the lads being split into two groups, meaning approximately fifty soldiers would be expected to visit each night.

Then, provided Mrs Worth had been agreeable to the general idea, Susan would ask the CO (Commanding Officer) if he would allow the village to welcome the soldiers over the two nights.

It was certainly a plan, Evie thought as she got ready for bed that evening, and a very good one too.

The gift of the softly furred, light-tummied rabbits to Mrs Worth did the trick, and once Evie had assured Mrs Worth that she didn't need to provide any food or drink, if she didn't feel she could, an agreement was quickly reached as to the viability of the tea parties for the Rhondda boys.

Susan then went to see the battalion's CO, who was only too happy to agree to the plan, and so it was decided that the tea parties would take place on the next Thursday and Friday.

Tina and Sarah were co-opted to help Evie do some cooking, while Julia, Pattie and Susan would visit every house in the village, asking each household for a small gift of food for the parties.

Nearly everybody agreed to give at least a little something, even if it was only a splash or two of some homemade fruit cordial or a few potatoes for some potato salad.

Julia and Evie got to baking, using a recipe they'd carefully cut out of the *Western Morning News*. It was for a sponge cake comprising two thin rounds held together by a filling made of mashed parsnips flavoured with banana essence, a concoction that fortunately was much more pleasant tasting than it sounded. And they decided to give vol-au-vents a go, using mushrooms that James picked for the purpose to make a savoury filling – sadly the vol-au-vents were not as successful as the sponge cakes as the medicinal liquid paraffin with which Evie and Julia had eked out the fat for the pastry turned the pastry a rather un-appetising shade of pale grey, and there wasn't the slightest flake to the pastry either. Evie had hoped that cooking would improve the look of the pastry, but to no avail. No matter: these small delicacies would be served anyway.

The village shop donated a few tins of fruit salad and numerous small waxed-paper party dessert bowls (goodness knows how these had come to be stocked, and at such quantity, in the tiny shop in the first place, Evie thought).

Susan combined the fruit salad with several packets of cubed jelly she'd managed to rustle up from various village wives, and then she helped Marie and Catherine pour the jelly mixture into the bowls. Never had two small girls looked so pleased at such a simple achievement, especially as Shady stood by, slowly wagging his tail like a banner of encouragement. Next the process was repeated with some Little Miss Muffet raspberry junket Susan had been saving for a special occasion.

Meanwhile Mr Smith and Peter put extra leaves in the dining table, and then practically wore themselves out charging around the village on missions to collect chairs, plates, napkins and the much-used giant metal teapot from the church hall, which had now become a depository for all sorts of things that were collected together to help in various ways during the war effort.

At three-thirty on the Thursday, plates of food started to materialise, as did of course the trays bearing the first batch of Susan's and the evacuee girls' many fruit jellies and junkets.

Soon the grand dining-room table was groaning under an assortment of food and large jugs of homemade fruit cordial. Evie thought it looked as if the spread was a bit 'kiddies' tea party', but she would have bitten her very tongue out rather than give voice to any criticism when everyone in the village had been so kind and had clearly tried very hard to provide something that would remind these young Welsh soldiers how very appreciated their war efforts were.

Just as the fifty soldiers marched up the drive in pairs, their uniforms neatly brushed and their shoes shining, Mr Smith and Peter manoeuvred the piano out to the terrace, with Peter and Evie sharing a grin of complicity as she followed with the piano stool.

Various villagers, Rev. Painter, and everyone from both Pemberley and Bluebells, jumped to attention to welcome all the guests, and before long the young soldiers' plates were piled high with food while Susan and Mrs Worth went around offering either cups of tea or glasses of fruit cordial.

Peter stayed at the piano, playing some popular tunes. It turned out that both Sarah and Tina had lovely singing voices that harmonised well with Peter's deeper bass, and that they all knew a lot of the words to a variety of songs, and even when they didn't know precisely the right words, they were very good at either ad-libbing, or tra-la-laaing.

As Evie stood near the piano and watched the tea party – Mrs Bowes and Mr Smith spending rather a long time chatting together, she noted with a slight quavery shiver – she realised that the small pieces of party food were precisely what these young men had needed to remind them of home and warmth and security, and very probably also of parties they had been to during their childhoods. Evie chided herself severely for having been so low as to think mean thoughts about the childishness of the spread.

Evie was pleased to note though that the small evacuee girls, Marie and Catherine, looked much better, and certainly a whole lot cleaner. Shady was at the party in obvious attendance too, and was clearly in his element, revelling in the huge amount of pats and belly-tickles he was getting from those of the young lads who were clearly fond of dogs.

And when the request was granted that these young men could provide their own thank yous by singing some Welsh hymns, it turned out that Peter knew the tunes to these too (was there indeed anything he couldn't accompany on the piano? Evie wondered).

As Evie smiled in Peter's direction once more, to be rewarded with a brief and all too rare dazzle of Peter's splendid smile, she turned around to look over the tea party as the Welsh voices united in a soaring burst of song.

She could see she wasn't the only one brought almost to tears by the haunting melodies and strong lilting voices that were rising around her – for an instant she felt utterly transported by the beauty of the moment.

The next day everyone united once again to put on just as good a show for the second group of men as they had for the first tea-party, and it all went down equally as well, although this time around the singing voices of the young lads were arguably even more impressive.

On both evenings Pattie, Sarah and Tina stayed out late afterwards. And for quite some days they each seemed to have an extra spring in their steps and a distinct twinkle in their eyes.

Sukie turned up for the second tea party, and whispered to Evie that she had been to see about an opening in the administration department at the new recuperation hospital, and so now it was a case of 'fingers crossed'.

Evie decided that there wasn't a man present who wasn't casting a longing glance in the direction of Sukie's trim figure and bouncing blonde curls as she added her own tuneful voice to the rich outpouring of song.

Well, there might be one man, Evie realised later.

While Peter seemed to spend an inordinate amount of time staring at the piano's keys with a serious face (the country air and simple country fare evidently having cleared up his skin no end), the few times he looked up, it seemed only to be to check where she herself was standing. This realisation gave Evie a slightly fizzy feeling all over. Later, when getting ready for bed, Evie thought for the first time that she had never directly mentioned to Peter that she was engaged. She supposed she should, but then she told herself that it was most presumptuous of her even to think for a moment that he might be the slightest bit interested in her availability, or not, and determinedly she put such thoughts from her mind.

A fortnight afterwards, the Rhondda boys had all left Lymbridge, leaving behind a clutch of home-made peg dolls for Marie and Catherine as a final thank-you gift in return for the village's warm and heartfelt welcome.

Shady spent a morning searching for where they might be. Evie thought that the softer-hearted of the men had probably snuck him an occasional treat, and that Shady would sadly miss both the treats and having his tummy tickled with such abandon.

Evie was never to find out how many of these brave but understandably terrified and apprehensive Welsh lads were to survive the war, but she thought of them often over the coming years.

Chapter Ten

Dear E

Well, I have now had my first taste of combat. And it was awful. Truly awful – Bill Tinder (I daresay you remember how he always used to try and grab you when we used to play kiss-chase in the school playground as little 'uns?) was shot yesterday afternoon and killed before my very eyes, his body falling right at my feet. I had never imagined anything so terrible. He was a good lad, and it's a proper shame.

The sight of Bill's lifeless eyes staring straight up towards Heaven is something I will never forget.

It has made us all realise properly, and in my case for the first time I think, the enormity of the fact that any one of us here could within a few short seconds be badly maimed, or worse, dead. It was a bad shock, especially being brought home to us all in a manner so forceful. I never expected to see anything like it, and I dreamed about it last night again and again.

It's also made me think about something I'd never thought about before, which is that by the next time you see me, I might very well have killed someone. I really don't know what to think about that. Once I would never have thought I would have it in me, but now after seeing the body of poor Bill, I don't know – I think perhaps it could be something I might have to do.

All I've ever wanted from life is a good time; and you too, of course. I have imagined in my mind's eye you and me living in some pretty cottage in Lymbridge with you dandling one of our many children on your knee, and me teaching our sons to play football, and you teaching the girls to do your clever knitting.

Until today, I couldn't wait to wake up each day and have more of it.

And now, far away from everything I've known and loved, I don't like at all the fact that my life may well end up differently to how I've planned it.

So the long and short of it is that seeing what happened to Bill, and the shock of how much smaller his body looked in death than it had in life, has made us all serious and fearful, and there's a grim quietness in our mess tent.

The weather is warm though (our uniforms are a bit too hot, is what I mean), and the food not too bad as long as I don't think about it too much.

Of course the loss of Bill has brought the rest of us closer together, proving, as Ma would say to me, that every cloud does have some sort of silver lining, although in respect of Bill passing I have had to look hard to find it.

And we are extremely glad we had such a month or two of the high life, and fun and rightly good jinx, before we left Blighty, as now it is all solemnity and determination about us.

I spend a lot of time thinking of your beautiful face and your lovely hair (and all your other beautiful bits too) – and thoughts of you make me feel much better.

Of course it gives me pleasure too to think of you and Ma keeping each other company. I worry about the both of you, and so I hope you are taking good care of each other, and are speaking nicely of me.

Your loving fiancé

Timmy x

Well, there was a lot in the letter that had been crossed through by some official, and so this was how Evie laboriously pieced together what Timmy was trying to say (and there was a lot of leeway where she might have got some parts misconstrued). There were blacked-out lines that were to do with, Evie guessed, where Timmy and his friends were stationed, and also to do with the combat he was writing of.

All in all, Evie thought it to be an extraordinary letter, and that Timmy seemed very, very far from his normal devil-may-care self. Whatever had happened – and there were rather a lot of sentences that had been taken out by some far away official so as not to show poor morale – he looked to have experienced a brutal and very salutary lesson, wherever it was in the world he had been sent to.

Evie decided that the fact that Timmy had not used a single exclamation mark in his whole letter probably denoted what a dreadful experience he had just had. She didn't think she had ever read anything that Timmy had written that didn't contain at least one exclamation mark.

Cross as Timmy had made her these past few weeks, Evie's heart still went out to him, and she hoped fervently he was feeling a little happier right at this moment. While she could cheerfully have slapped his chops, she realised that she still cared for him enough to wish him well wherever he was.

Timmy's sombre mood was matched by relentlessly gloomy news of the war's progress in the newspapers and on the wireless. Britain's forces were fighting hard, but were clearly sustaining heavy losses, no matter how positively the clipped-voiced newsreaders would read their bulletins, and Evie was rather inclined to think that Britain was very much on the back foot and that it might not be too long before Hitler mounted an invasion. And if that happened, goodness knows where they would all end up.

At night there was usually the monotonous drone of fighter planes flying across the moors, and while Julia's sleep was rarely disturbed (cycling for so many miles each day over such unforgiving inclines was clearly wearing her out), Evie would lie awake hoping that what she was listening to were British aircraft going to defend their precious land and cause, rather than German planes mounting an offensive that was going to prove to have a much more sinister outcome.

Although sometimes the horizon towards Plymouth would show fires burning, causing the other PGs to get up to go to the safety of the Anderson shelter, Evie increasingly opted to stay in her room with Julia, despite Mrs Worth's dim view of this. And while Julia peacefully slept, Evie would pull the blackout curtains open and lie on her side in the pitch-black bedroom with her head propped on her hand as she stared out across the moorland trying to work out whose planes were making the most noise.

Even the children at school seemed to have picked up on the nation's general worrisome mood, as they were being quieter than usual, and not running around nearly so much at playtime. Rowdy games of chase, it and football, seemed to have given way to the quieter and less boisterous pursuits of making dens and epic contests of marbles. Evie's infants were too young to join in properly with either of these pursuits, but they seemed to enjoy tagging along as a willing audience, content to stand and watch with interest what the older children were up to.

Despite Evie's best efforts, the evacuee girls from Plymouth, Marie and Catherine, were still worryingly withdrawn in her infants class, although Susan reported that they were opening up a little at home. Evie felt at something of a loss as she didn't know what else she could do to help them settle in and relax a little.

Then one rainy afternoon a young tabby and white cat that Evie had seen getting its nose pummelled by another cat in the farmyard at Switherns wandered into the schoolyard, and sat mewling outside the door to Evie's classroom.

When Evie opened the door to check the cat wasn't trying to bring in a mouse or – horror! – a rat, she was surprised by the tabby darting into the classroom between her legs and jumping straight on to Marie's bony lap.

After's a moment's surprise, the little girl looked delighted and enveloped the puss in a clumsy cuddle. This only seemed to encourage the cat further, and it spent the rest of the lesson padding between Marie and Catherine's tiny laps, purring furiously and causing the rest of the class to laugh when the purrs reached such a crescendo of high-pitched tones that they could be easily heard right across the classroom. It was incredible that such a small cat could house such an extraordinarily loud purr.

The girls had obviously both enjoyed the cat's attention, and so at the end of the lesson Evie asked if they'd like to give the puss a name.

'Keith!' squealed Catherine instantly in a raspy voice.

The elegant feline face turned to Catherine and seemed to dip its nose in agreement, causing the whole class to laugh uproariously once again.

And so Keith, despite very obviously being a female, became as often as not a fixture in Lymbridge Primary School's infant class. Keith would answer to her name and she seemed to have an unerring instinct for the child who was feeling most wobbly at any particular time, sitting as close to them as possible, if not actually on their lap, while making the racket of a purr that Evie always found so at odds with her slim and lithe body.

Mrs Bowes was distinctly unimpressed at first that Evie had allowed Keith to be made welcome in her classroom, although when she saw how soothing Keith could be to a tense and unhappy small child, Mrs Bowes said, with a sigh, that she supposed the tabby could stay until she blotted her copybook. And if that were to happen, Evie wasn't to let her in again.

Evie crossed her fingers and hoped Keith realised that she must be well behaved at all times, and that she must never scratch anybody. Luckily Keith seemed house-trained, and she never showed any desire to unsheathe her claws, even if one of the littlest pupils was occasionally a little over enthusiastic with the strength of the pats and strokes doled out to her.

And when Keith purred at full voice, as she was want to do at any opportunity, often she would stare straight at Evie with happily narrowed eyes, which Evie also found strangely comforting, feeling that if Keith was so unashamedly happy then life couldn't be as bad as all that.

Soon, at the start of every lesson, Evie would open the classroom door to look to see if Keith was going to join them for arithmetic or writing or painting, and if she wasn't there Evie would find herself calling her in especially.

In fact the odd gift of a miniscule rodent corpse aside (several shrews, and a tiny mouse), which Evie would swiftly flush down a lavatory before Mrs Bowes could get wind, the arrival of Keith was so successful in boosting her class's morale generally that Evie thought the children ought to have more school pets. For, if Keith's presence was anything to judge by, the presence of animals encouraged gentleness and consideration in her young charges, and the uncomplicated affection given back by Keith was a small but nevertheless bright joy in an uncertain world.

Evie wondered, if by any chance Mrs Bowes wanted her to return to her class of infants after the summer holidays – and nothing had been said in this respect to indicate that indeed might be the situation, of course – then it might be an idea if she suggested that Mr Cawes build a school chicken run down by the Nissen hut, so that the children could keep a few chickens and ducks. And perhaps if that were to happen, they could even get a goat too. The eggs and milk would all be put to good use, Evie was sure. She decided not to say anything just yet, but she did feel that extending the school menagerie was a good idea.

One evening, when everyone else at Pemberley seemed to be otherwise engaged after tea, Evie found herself alone in the sitting room in the gathering dusk writing a list of things that needed to be done for the day of Lymbridge's Revels, a date she had realised only that morning was sneaking up with alarming alacrity.

Unfortunately she felt plagued by a sense of ennui, and was

therefore rather bereft of ideas, as aside from a table of jumble, a coconut shy and a lucky dip, her piece of paper was blank, and so she was tapping the end of a pencil against her teeth as she stared at the back of an old used envelope on which she was making her list, hoping for some sort of divine inspiration, when Peter came into the room with a welcome cup of tea for her.

They passed the time of day, and then Peter asked what she was doing.

'Well, I'm trying to come up with ideas for the Revels. It's only just over a fortnight away, everyone seems very busy, and I need to get things going that will actually happen, and that will cost next to nothing as nobody has a penny spare these days. Ugh! And meanwhile, the minute I remember that Mrs Bowes will have my guts for garters if I don't put on a good show, my mind goes a complete blank,' Evie sighed with a touch of dramatic despair.

'Let's put our thinking caps on,' said Peter in a positive voice. 'What about a raffle for a jug of some of Mr Chugg's scrumpy – that would prove popular, I'm sure, although possibly a bit lethal – a tug of war between Lymbridge and one of the other villages nearby – probably Bramstone as they've still got a few lads there, and I think Lymbridge could give them a run for their money? Then you could have a guess-the-weight of a piglet stall, rides for the children on Mr Sutcliffe's ancient old donkey – the beast, although small and friendly-looking, will need to have a muzzle on, don't forget, as it tried to nip me the other day when I refused to give it a carrot from the bunch I'd just pulled from the garden when I caught it loose in our vegetable patch. And then there could be a "most inventive" jam competition, a tombola, a fancy dress competition, a skittles contest—'

'Whoa! Steady the buffs – I can't keep up with you, Peter,' Evie cut in as she scribbled furiously. 'You should be organising these blessed Revels; you've got ideas coming out of your ears. And I can't believe you've only been in Lymbridge for a month or two, as you already seem to know who everybody is and how it all works around here.'

Peter blushed a deep scarlet at Evie's admiring words, and muttered that he supposed he must have good powers of observation.

Evie tried to ignore the vibrant shade he had gone. She realised that she had no idea what Peter was like as a person. Indeed she knew next to nothing about him, other than that he was a dab hand at making tea, was a whiz on the piano and quick at difficult crosswords, and that he coloured up easily. She had no idea where he came from or whether he had a family or a sweetheart, or what he did for work or where he would cycle off each morning to.

Of course, in these days of careless talk costing lives, it wasn't unusual for people not really to ask each other questions about what they might be up to, but nevertheless she had a vague feeling that she had been left wanting in some indefinable manner.

The Yeo sisters prided themselves on knowing all the gossip, and now Evie realised she and Julia had been missing a trick as far as Peter Pipe was concerned. He seemed a nice enough chap, and she felt she'd been verging on rude to show so little interest in him, and especially so when he had always been so thoughtful in keeping her supplied with cups of tea. She decided that at some point she would ask him about himself, and she would then casually slip into the conversation the fact that she was engaged to Timmy. It would be a friendly chat between two fellow PGs, but it wasn't a conversation she felt ready for just at the moment when there was suddenly a hard-to-read feeling in the ether between her and Peter; it felt a little stirring but also awkward.

The silence between her and Peter stretched heavily for what seemed like ages, and then Evie decided it had gone on too long for her to be able to act in a casually throwaway manner.

Evie sipped her tea politely, and tried not to feel uncomfortable as she pretended to look at her envelope. She failed. Then she thought that if she could have a good idea of another event they could add to the roster of events for the Revels, then the difficult pause in the conversation might be averted without Peter noticing.

So, now that Peter's colour had returned to something approaching normal and he looked to be distracted by retying both the laces of his black leather brogues, she said with an overly encouraging smile, the smile she reserved for her youngest pupils, 'Okay, Mr Clever Clogs –' cue another burst of scarlet '– let's see what you can suggest that the littlest children might be able to do.'

As a tactic for smoothing out an embarrassing moment, this was hopeless – Peter was as crimson as earlier, and now it felt as if there were a heavily charged atmosphere swirling between them.

Still, Peter found somehow the wherewithal to step back into the fray. 'What about a conker competition for the slightly older boys? I know it's still too early for this year's conkers, but you're not telling me that some of the lads won't have got a few conkers from the end of last season set aside for this year – we used to do that, anyway, and get our mothers to boil them in vinegar, and then we'd leave them on the mantelpiece above the kitchen range for the whole winter to dry out and go rock hard, and very successfully too, I might say.'

As she listened slightly dreamily, Evie noticed that Peter's stammer wasn't nearly so noticeable when he was confident in what he was talking about. Or possibly she was just a bit more used to it these days and so it didn't seem so obvious.

'And,' he added, 'perhaps the girls could take part in something like a daisy-chain competition? Or an egg-cosy knitting competition?'

'This is good for starters,' said Evie in her 'rallying school-teacher' voice. Oh dear. Where had that come from?

'Right, I'd like you to meet me here again tomorrow with at least as many ideas as you've given me this evening. And then I think the Lymbridge Revels will be in business,' Evie finished in a breathy rush, as she stood up abruptly to take her empty teacup back to the kitchen and swiftly strode from the room, leaving Peter looking distinctly pink around the gills and a trifle side-swiped.

The next evening his idea was that a mixture of a tea dance and a barn dance could close the Revels. A ramshackle band would be put together, and the villagers could take part in both traditional country dances and a mixture of contemporary dances to modern tunes. The children would be able to join in too, of course. Peter would lead the musicians on the school's piano, and he was sure that Mr Smith could compere the dancing.

Yes, thought Evie after a moment or two of deliberation, I think I've now got the Revels all in hand.

Linda was recovering well from her collapsed lung and she felt ready to return to work, and so to celebrate this, the three Yeo sisters arranged to meet Linda and Sukie early one evening in the ladies bar of The Wheatsheaf in Bramstone, an enjoyable thirty-minute walk along a heathery path that wended occasionally across patches of moorland and between fields abutting the edges of the moor.

As the sisters strolled along, laughing and chatting, they couldn't help but remark how wonderful the moors smelt, as the faintest but nonetheless alluring whiff of sea air from the coast to the south of them was combining winsomely with the rising scent of the bracken and gorse, not yet fully at its summer height, and the thickening heather that had been warmed by the day's sunny weather. A small herd of wild Dartmoor ponies followed them for a while, a pretty caramel-coloured foal with a sticky-up mane keeping close to the haunches of one of the bay mares.

At The Wheatsheaf they were delighted to find that Linda looked more or less returned to full fitness, and she was happy to report that earlier in the day she had been to see Hector, the horse who had injured her so badly. And although apparently he still looked for Mabel and would neigh for her before he'd begin pulling his own hay from his evening hay net, otherwise he appeared to be more or less back to his old calm and gentle self.

Then Sukie was keen to tell them all that she had landed the job at the recuperation hospital, working in the hospital's office helping with patient administrations, and that she would be starting very soon. She added she was rather hopeful of meeting a nice young doctor.

'I'd have expected no less from our own snazzy Sukie,' laughed Evie.

Pattie had some news too. She had also managed to fix herself up with her first job since leaving school over a year before. Although she wouldn't be living with the other local land girls, who were mainly down in the West Country from the southeast of England, billeted on various farms, she was going to join them over the summer and autumn period, mainly to help with making sure the animals were all mated to ensure that next year's young would arrive as early as possible in the year so that they could be as mature as possible before the harsh weather of winter would set in. And Pattie would help with bringing in all the different harvests, as well as a little hedge and dry-stone-wall husbandry.

Robert had suggested Pattie when he'd heard about the job when he was out and about on his old boneshaker, and it certainly sounded as if Pattie was set for a very busy summer.

Evie was really pleased about this as Pattie, the youngest of the Yeo girls, was now eighteen, and Evie knew that Robert and Susan had felt it was high time that she got herself fixed up with something proper to do rather than just earning some pin money as and when, as she had been by doing an occasional evening collecting pots at The Wheatsheaf (Robert being particularly keen that this occasional work would come to an end, as inevitably it would be he who would have to collect Pattie on the evenings when she was on the late shift to escort her home. He felt it was too dangerous to expect Pattie to walk or cycle home on her own across the stretch of moorland; and if not kept a close eye on, she was apt to spend too much time late at night with one lad or another if they were walking her home).

Evie had also thought privately that if Pattie didn't get fixed up with something of note to do, she might find she'd be sent to work in a munitions factory or something similar that would be very probably outside the county. From what Evie had been able to glean, such work was difficult, dangerous and dirty, and she felt Pattie would have hated it, but then she would have had little choice in the matter.

As the heat slowly faded from the day, the group of young women decided to get the last of the sun by moving to the large table in a courtyard just to the side of The Wheatsheaf.

It was a jolly party and it was clear that Julia and Evie were on good form too, as after everyone had said their news, they kept them entertained with impressions of the various people living at Pemberley. Evie even dared to do a short impersonation of Mrs Bowes and the imperious way she would marshal the juniors after playtime, which then encouraged her to attempt the faces the juniors would then make behind Mrs Bowes' back if they thought they could get away with it and if they thought the eagle-eyed Evie was looking elsewhere.

Then the gales of laughter emanating from their happy table in the outside forecourt of the public house ended abruptly.

Without warning, Tricia Dolby had stepped through the door from the ladies bar and into the courtyard.

Evie froze, her glass still in mid-air, as she and Tricia stared at each other.

Everyone on Evie's table immediately glanced towards her. It was clear that they were all too aware of the rumour concerning Timmy and Tricia.

Evie's face was immobile, and her expression difficult to interpret. As the blood pounded close to her ears, Evie didn't dare glance downwards to Tricia's belly.

Then Tricia turned sideways and swiftly stepped back inside the public house. It was evident to anyone who cared to look that she most assuredly was pregnant.

'Well, I do declare!'

'Such brazenness!'

'What behaviour . . .'

'Oh my goodness.'

Evie cut across the comments of her loyal friends and sisters, to say, 'You must stop it, all of you. If Timmy is the father of Tricia's baby, then Tricia must feel alone and frightened. And to judge by the letter I had from Timmy earlier in the week, he is feeling just as alone and frightened right now, although for very different reasons. These are difficult times for everybody. And so we must all behave well. And this means that we can't be mean about either of them.

'And in Tricia's case, it must have been a terrible shock to see me, and the rest of you sitting there. Let's not forget how charming Timmy is – I'm not sure I can blame her if she did give in to his demands. I am cross with her, make no mistake about it, but the truth of it is that I feel differently about it all after reading Timmy's last letter. I'm not sure why, but I do.'

As the rest of the table stared at Evie open-mouthed in surprise at her magnanimous words, Evie stood up and quickly followed Tricia's retreat without so much as a glance behind her.

There was no sign of Tricia in the bar, or in the ladies' lavatories, and so Evie went outside through the public house's main entrance. She looked to the right, but the road was empty. She looked to her left and at last she could see Tricia heading rapidly down the road. Tricia was on her own, and so Evie thought she had probably planned to meet a friend in The Wheatsheaf's walled forecourt, and had had the misfortune to be the first to arrive.

It would have been unexpected and devastating for Tricia to see Evie sitting there surrounded by a group that was so obviously all on Evie's side, Evie thought.

'Wait, Tricia, please. Wait!' she called.

Reluctantly, Tricia stopped, and turned slowly around to allow Evie to catch up with her.

Evie wasn't sure what she wanted to say to Tricia, and so she halted about three feet away from her and they stood in silence for several moments. To judge by Tricia's querulous expression she thought she was in for a verbal larruping from Evie, and so Tricia decided to be the first to speak, perhaps as a means of averting any harsh words.

'Evie, I'm so sorry. Every day I 'ate myself for what's 'appened. What's done is done, I know, but there's not a moment passes I wish it weren't another way,' Tricia said contritely, a tear threatening to roll down a plump cheek.

So, this was the confirmation of Timmy's shoddy behaviour she had been seeking, Evie supposed as she felt a lurch inside.

Even though in her heart of hearts she had known the truth for a while now, she experienced a heart-piercing pang.

But Tricia's desperate expression and genuinely remorseful demeanour (as far as Evie could tell, anyway) were worming their way into Evie's heart too, and almost before she knew it she reached out and touched Tricia's arm in a gesture of comfort.

'And 'e were my first and only, and we did it standin' up behind the church 'all, with my skirt lifted and his braces still up. And yorn Timmy 'ad given me some scrumpy and swore on 'is mother's life that if we kept stood up, I wouldn't get caught and so he didn't need to wear a rubber – 'e said 'e needed one as much as a toad needs a pocketwatch. And it were over before I knew it almost, and I'd not really 'ad time to know quite how far we'd gone. And now I'm 'eaded for disaster, and it were never worth it, because if that quick fumble is all there is to it, it wouldn't matter to me if I never did it again...'

Tricia's voice was wobbly and tearful, rich with the soft Devonian burr of the country farming lasses, and the combination of this with what Tricia was telling her made Evie feel most peculiar too.

She didn't want to know the gory details of precisely what had gone on between Timmy and Tricia, but all the same there was undeniably a little bit of her that was fascinated with the intricacies of the actual act of procreation – and this rather sturdy young woman had had, after all, an experience with Evie's fiancé that she herself had taken care to avoid.

And although a hurried grope behind the church hall didn't sound particularly tempting, nonetheless Evie was curious about what sexual intercourse might be like, and especially curious as to what it might be like with Timmy.

Perhaps none of this would have happened if I had allowed him to go all the way with me, Evie thought. But then she gave herself a stern reprimand. It was very unlikely he'd have kept his trousers buttoned with those other women, whatever she had done, and it could well be Evie herself who'd be standing with a growing belly, just like Tricia, and then she would have her father and James on the warpath and baying for Timmy's blood. What a dreadful thought! she told herself.

'I can't say I'm happy about this, Tricia, or that I know what should be done,' Evie said then to a snuffling Tricia who was battling with teary eyes and a running nose, promting Evie to pass Tricia her own clean hankie as it seemed as if Tricia didn't have one with her. 'But I know now the sort of man that Timmy Bowes is, and that he could charm the very birds from the sky, and so I don't blame you as much as him. I suppose our engagement will now definitely be broken, and that Timmy will marry you—'

Evie was interrupted by the anguished squeak of Tricia's strident *No!*

'No. Oh no! That's not goin' to 'appen, Evie. I've known *that* all along.' Tricia then continued in a gloomy but mercifully calmer voice, 'That batty witch of a mother of 'is would never allow 'im to stoop so low as to be puttin' a ring on the finger of the likes of me, a lass who'll never amount to more than scrapping along workin' in a dairy parlour.'

Evie privately agreed, now she thought about it properly, that indeed Tricia's assessment was pretty likely to be true.

Tricia definitely wasn't the sort of daughter-in-law that Mrs Bowes would want. Mrs Bowes prided herself on her and Timmy's social position in the village, and Tricia's dumpy figure, workaday clothes and attitude, and her broad working-class country accent would leave no doubt about her lower social status. It left Tricia in a precarious position, with a loss of reputation that would in all likelihood continue to dog her for years; and without reputation, she'd now be virtually unmarriageable too. And to think of the poor baby, who was going to be the blameless victim in all of this. How would they both cope?

But what Evie said was, 'Well, Timmy is going to have to take responsibility for his actions, isn't he? It's not fair that you should be left alone to bear this burden, while he gets off scot free.'

They talked some more, and then Tricia headed homewards, her farmgirl's walk threatening to become something of a waddle, while Evie turned around to plod back towards The Wheatsheaf, her shoulders feeling burdened down by Timmy's infidelity.

Once back at the courtyard to the public house, it was to find an unexpected furore going on.

Tricia's two friends had turned up ready to meet her, and now there was a bit of a set-to going on out in the enclosed forecourt with Words Being Said from supporters of both sides.

Evie arrived just as one of Tricia's friends hissed 'fast madam' in Sukie's direction, and Evie was only just able to step in between the overheated young women as the situation looked about to descend into undignified fisticuffs.

Feeling slightly dazed by the jolting the last few minutes had given to her, somehow Evie managed to soothe ruffled feathers all around while her sisters and pals continued to look daggers across at Tricia's pals. Evie suggested that as Tricia had gone home, perhaps Tricia's friends should follow her to see how she was doing as she had had an unexpected shock.

Even when these two young women had been gone for ten minutes or so, Sukie was still furious, although she had to chuckle when she admitted that she didn't know what she was most cross about, being called a 'fast madam' or that Evie had

had to come face to face with the dratted Tricia. It was a close-run thing either way, they all agreed.

Later that night, Evie lay in bed and thought about how cruel and ironic life could be. She had been wronged by both Timmy and Tricia, and yet it had turned out to be she who had been the one to spring to Tricia's defence and who had tried to comfort the scared young woman. It was also Evie who had realised that the grim things Timmy was experiencing, perhaps even at this very moment, could possibly in some way quell her anger toward him.

It was all very complicated, Evie decided.

On the following Monday morning it was left to Peter to notice that Evie looked paler than usual and a bit tense as she pensively bit her lip and distractedly poured her morning cup of tea.

Somehow Evie found herself spilling out a selective and sanitised version of the sorry tale of her awful Friday evening to Peter as they walked down Pemberley's drive together a few minutes later, Peter pushing his bicycle beside her. Evie neglected to clarify her and Timmy's own relationship or the precise reasons as to why Tricia's unexpected appearance had been deemed so incendiary, but she thought that Peter's sympathetic utterances denoted that it was very understandable that she still felt so raw.

Then Evie and Peter spent a few minutes deep in conversation standing close together at the gates to the entrance to Pemberley, Peter slowly wheeling his bicycle backwards and forwards over three or four inches of path gravel until he had worn quite a groove among the small stones.

He didn't say much in response to Evie's slightly shaky voice, but Evie was left feeling the best she had done since accosting Tricia, despite being, when she thought about it later, slightly embarrassed at being so forthright to a man she hardly knew. There was something reassuring about Peter Pipe, there was no doubt about it.

Chapter Eleven

No sooner had Evie got inside the school gates after her con-
fiding a proportion of her woes to Peter, than she heard the
imperious, tummy-sink summons of Mrs Bowes.

'Evie? Evie! I need a word,' trilled the headmistress.

With a sigh, and a quick check to see if her blouse was properly tucked in and the side seams of her skirt were straight and
as they should be, Evie went into the juniors' classroom. It was
still early and so the pupils hadn't started to arrive yet.

'Have you heard from Timmy?' said Mrs Bowes.

Evie knew how very much Mrs Bowes doted on her son.
And she was painfully aware that this might well be a heavily
weighted question that could catch her out, bearing in mind
what Timmy had been up to right before he'd left Lymbridge.

Mrs Bowes and Timmy had lived on their own together for
more than fifteen years, since Mr Bowes had run off with the
manageress of ladies clothing at Spooners, the large department
store in Plymouth. This had been a tremendous scandal at the
time, Susan had intimated to Evie, causing Mrs Bowes to walk
around the village for quite some time with a determinedly
lowered head and a refusal to catch anybody's eye.

Although apparently he still lived less than ten miles away, it
was claimed that Mr Bowes had never dared show his nose in
Lymbridge since. Timmy had told Evie that although his father
sent generous presents on his birthday and at Christmas, the last

time he had actually seen him was when Timmy was only six years old, and his father had seemingly left for work as usual one day.

After her initial reticence about the match, Evie felt that Mrs Bowes had actually been reasonably accepting of Evie as a future daughter-in-law, all things considered, although Evie knew that in some ways Timmy's mother would always expect preferential treatment of herself over any wife of Timmy's.

It wasn't necessarily ideal, and it was easy to imagine that there would be times when there would have to be a battening down of temper and expectation as far as any wife of Timmy's would be concerned, although Evie supposed that this was an understandable situation given Mr Bowes' desertion of the family home, as it was certain that an experience like this would bond a mother and her son very closely together.

'I had a letter from Timmy,' replied Evie cautiously. 'He said that poor Bill Tinder had been killed.'

'Ah, so that's what happened. That must explain it. My letter on Saturday was very odd – I had the impression that dear Timmy was holding something back from me that he didn't want me to know. I hadn't realised he and Bill had become so close, and so that must be it, as he didn't mention Bill's death,' said Mrs Bowes in a relieved voice.

Phew, thought Evie, hopefully this meant it would be a little while longer before it was all out in the open for public consumption about Tricia, although with the size of her spreading waistline the clock simply had to be ticking on this news.

But with a bit of luck it wouldn't be until the summer holidays, Evie could only hope, as it would be incredibly awkward between Mrs Bowes and herself if the news about Tricia's pregnancy and Timmy's further peccadilloes were to come to light before the end of term. The news was bound to cause a few fireworks, and of course it would also signal the official end of Evie's engagement, and if it were already the summer holidays then at least Mrs Bowes and Evie wouldn't have to see each other every day.

'Anyway, what I actually wanted to talk to you about is that I think we have a thief, or even a team of thieves, in our midst,' Mrs Bowes was saying, and Evie hoped she hadn't missed anything important while she had drifted off in her pervasive thoughts over The Tricia Trouble, although the words that the headmistress was saying about a possible thief seemed hardly creditable. That sort of thing didn't go on in Lymbridge.

Mrs Bowes continued as relentlessly as usual, but perhaps in a more excitable manner than normally she would deem as acceptable.

'Evie, this is very serious. I had seventeen shillings and six-pence in my purse yesterday morning first thing; I remember most clearly as I had broken into a pound note the day before in the village shop. But this morning I went to leave some money for Miss Pluckett, who comes in once a week for an hour to run a duster around the house; it's always so clean, as you know, and she doesn't really need to do more than that, but I haven't the heart to stop her coming. Anyway, imagine my horror, Evie, when I discovered that I only had twelve shillings and sixpence left in my purse!'

Evie thought Mrs Bowes' distracted and wandering sentences must be an indication of how upset she was; normally she was such a stickler for ordered speech.

The tirade continued. 'And I know that's not right as there was definitely a whole five shillings more there yesterday. I double-checked, and then looked in my pockets and elsewhere in my handbag.

'My handbag has only been with me at school, and at home. I've had no visitors at home, and I hardly think you –' Evie couldn't help but gulp guiltily at mention of her name, despite her innocence '– or that old buffoon Mr Cawes would have the nerve to go rooting through my purse to steal five shillings.'

'Indeed not,' said Evie firmly, although she felt just the slight-est bit miffed at Mrs Bowes' ungracious assumption that she was necessarily lacking in the gumption department. Although probably not as miffed as Mr Cawes would be if he heard Mrs Bowes declaring him a buffoon.

'This means we must have a thief somewhere at this school.

I think the pupils in your class are probably too small to be the perpetrators, and so it must be one or more in my juniors.

'Until we have identified the culprit I want you to be especially vigilant, and naturally not to leave anything of value lying around. This problem needs to be solved before the end of term, or else everyone will get tarred with the brush of suspicion.' Mrs Bowes' strident tones rang out dramatically across the classroom just at the clang of the school gate heralded the first pupil's arrival for the day's lessons.

Evie went out into the playground deep in thought. While five shillings wasn't a massive amount of money, and Mrs Bowes was comfortably off and so the loss of it wouldn't in any way be the sort of disaster for her that losing such an amount would be for one of the village families much closer to the breadline, nevertheless it was still a sizeable amount, and especially so if it were indeed a child who had dared to take it. Their pocket money, if they got any, was most likely to be less than sixpence a week. And in any case an apparent theft and a likely circle of suspects whereby the thief could only be part of the local tightly knit community, was an unpleasant slur on everyone.

Evie watched distractedly as the pupils arrived in ones and twos, with some of the infants still being walked to school by their parents, while others were now trusted to make their own way.

The children, whether juniors or infants, all looked so wholesome and so honest, and Evie found it hard to believe that any one of them had been brave enough to open the drawer to Mrs Bowes' school desk, where everyone knew she kept her huge and ancient brown-leather handbag, delve inside its capricious interior to extract the well-used matching brown-leather clasp purse, and then choose to take out the five precious shillings.

Such dishonest actions beggared belief.

That teatime Evie went to Bluebells and enjoyed a family tea with the rest of the Yeos, excepting Julia, who had got a rare date that night with a man from the divisional Post Office's HQ, and so was hopefully having a good time right this very minute in Oldwell Abbott (although not *too* good, as Susan had been quick to say, followed by 'and as long as she gets the lift home to Pemberley she assured me she's been promised').

After tea, and once Frank and Joseph had run out to play with the other village children, James had disappeared to who knows where (with Susan's calls of 'and DON'T be back too late' reverberating in his ears), and with Marie and Catherine having been taken outside by Robert to help with a spot of weeding in the vegetable patch, Evie told an increasingly dumbfounded Susan and Pattie about Mrs Bowes' allegations of theft.

'By lunchtime her anger had swelled alarmingly, and she was all for calling the police in immediately. I did my best to dissuade her as I'm worried that this wouldn't do anything other than cause more problems,' said Evie.

'The more I think about it, the more I can't believe that this is just a desire for money. It seems so out of character for people who've grown up in Lymbridge, as here honesty seems something that unites us all, and so I suspect something else must be at play. And in that case, if the police come and start poking around and asking all sorts of difficult questions, who knows where it all might end.'

'Yes, we've always been a trustworthy lot here in Lymbridge,' agreed Susan. 'As far as I know it's only your Mrs Worth who locks her doors, and even then she only does it late at night. The rest of us have never felt the need to bother as there's never been any need.

'I do remember once that Reverend Painter thought his bicycle had been stolen, but the silly old buffer had taken it when he went up to old Mrs Bean's, and he walked home after he had forgotten he'd cycled there, with the result that the next morning when he went to get his bicycle it wasn't where he expected it to be. It was Robert who noticed it leaning against Mrs Bean's back wall a couple of days later and he wheeled it back to the vicarage. But I think that's the closest we've got to any allegations of theft.'

'Yes,' Pattie agreed with her mother and Evie. 'I find it hard to think of any of those kiddies opening that old dragon's purse and taking her money. Whoever it was is very daring, and I'm almost impressed!'

'That's silly. And not at all the point, Pattie,' admonished Evie. 'I just hope the mystery of whoever it is doesn't drag on. The longer it does, the more the suspicion will move from person to person, and that simply can't be a good thing in such a small village as Lymbridge.'

The conversation was brought swiftly to a close by Robert and the two evacuee girls coming back into the kitchen to wash muddy hands at the scullery sink.

Evie jumped up to pour some more hot water into the teapot. And Marie and Catherine climbed on to the laps of Pattie and Susan for a cuddle, and Evie encouraged the little girls to talk about Keith and the funny things Keith would do while Evie was trying to teach the children.

The jovial mood continued as Robert went on to describe in tremendous detail his latest training meet-ups with the local Home Guard, about which he was most circumspect. Apparently there'd been a fair amount of drilling, although the inevitable conclusion drawn by everyone in the local Home Guard unit was that most of Lymbridge's older men who'd been keen to volunteer were unaccountably afflicted by two left feet.

Apparently there'd also been a lot of discussion about what would happen if there were an invasion. The local signposts and location signs on train stations had been long removed as it was thought this tactic might confuse Jerry.

'I can't see it myself, but there you go,' said Robert. 'I think the old boys just want to do something. It all went a bit comical when on Sunday we went to that old bridge down the river from Bramstone, to practise what we should do when we see the Germans coming. It was chaos, with the right hand not knowing what the left hand was doing, or if indeed the right hand even knew if it was the right hand at all.

'And so I can say with certainty that if Jerry does invade, the locals are going to be at much greater risk of being hurt by the Home Guard than anything Jerry can throw at us.'

Robert had the timing of the best comedians, and as they laughed, Evie was glad that Marie and Catherine had found billets at Bluebells. As she looked at the now drowsy girls, she was sure her steady parents were giving them a good home.

Chapter Twelve

For the next few days Pemberley was awash with make do and mend activity, and the sounds of chatting and laughing, and the softer noises of the fragile tissue of paper patterns being cut to size and then pinned on material, and then the regular clunks of metal on the wooden table under the tablecloth as the large fabric scissors were used to cut out fabric around the pinned patterns on the huge dining table. Indeed it was all so busy that Evie hardly knew if she was on her head or her heels.

Almost without her realising it, the question of who the thief at large might be slowly drifted to the back of Evie's thoughts, as did equally unwelcome thoughts of Timmy and Tricia. Evie still felt an underlying queasiness to do with Timmy, but she was determinedly not thinking about him.

Firstly, as at last there was a plan of what they would do to celebrate Lymbridge's day of summer Revels, there now was an awful lot of organising and running around that was needed in order to make sure that everything went as smoothly as possible on the day and, more importantly, that everyone had a good time and raised as much money as possible to be spent on local needy causes.

Luckily Peter proved to be a tower of strength in putting these outline plans of Evie's, or, more accurately, his own, into action.

Indeed, as Peter tore around the village at Evie's every whim and wish, rustling up various things from all and sundry that were required, and making sure that the villagers who would be running stalls or games knew exactly what they needed to do, he seemed taller and broader, and not at all the painfully thin and shy, round-shouldered young man Evie had first met who'd appeared so nervous of his very shadow.

Julia teased Evie about her bossiness. 'It's clear that the influence of the dear Mrs Bowes is rubbing off on you. And then some. The result of this is that you're keeping Pemberley's Peter running hither and thither purely at your say-so, the poor chap, although it's not escaped my notice that he quite seems to be enjoying being so useful, most of the time, at least.'

Needless to say Evie didn't care a jot that she was being bossy, and she told herself that it was quite immaterial to her whether Peter Pipe was smiling or not, as she just wanted to make sure that everything – and there was quite a lot of 'everything' – was going to plan as far as the Revels were concerned.

Also, she would remind herself quite often, if Peter told her he was going to do something, then at least she knew it was going to happen.

So she started to think of extra things for him to do, and to look forward to hearing how he had got on in completing the tasks she had set him.

To Evie's surprise and gratitude, Mr Smith proved invaluable too as a helpmate, as with his habitual calm manner and wryly amused expression on his face, he seemed likewise content to trot around the village at Evie's word, even persuading a rather surprised-looking Mrs Bowes to be more actively involved in helping him make sure that the planned arrangements were all in hand.

And once Mrs Bowes had been coerced into joining Mr Smith on his rota of errands, any lingering recalcitrance on the part of a reluctant villager they might encounter was, naturally, quickly steamrollered into oblivion.

That's the ticket, thought Evie.

*

However, organising the Revels was only part of the reason why Evie felt so busy; the sewing circle was meeting at Pemberley most evenings after tea. There was a problem they needed to attend to.

For the last couple of years Sukie had done a little book-keeping and some letter-writing duties for a number of local dairies and farms, as well as the village shop.

Now she'd managed to land her first job in a proper office – as her new post at the recuperation hospital entailed – she would be expected to wear smart outfits in her impressive-sounding role. It was only after a farmer's wife had mentioned this to Sukie (she'd known it in theory but she'd not really thought about it) that poor Sukie realised she had been somewhat caught on the hop.

She had rushed home and heaped her clothes on her bed, only to discover to her horror that her meagre collection of outfits, while they might be fine for an afternoon's work at the kitchen table of some outlying farm or other, or the odd night out at The Haywain or The Wheatsheaf, when given close scrutiny it was painfully apparent that they really weren't up to snuff for what this more grown-up, more important-feeling Sukie would require for her new role at the hospital.

Evie had chuckled good-humouredly when Sukie had bemoaned the situation. 'Honestly, Sukes. It's only because you're so stunning, that up until now you've never had to think about what you're wearing – you could make a burlap sack look like the latest fashion from Paris, and so you've never really had to bother.

'But now that you're about to embark on Project Snag Sukie a Doctor, you're having to join the world of the rest of us! Just be thankful that you've managed to escape the woes of the wardrobe for such a long time.'

The result was that now it was all hands to the pump as far as the younger members of the sewing circle were concerned. Evie had put out a call to arms that there was a wardrobe-needing-emergency-resuscitation crisis, and almost before they knew it,

Sukie's friends had agreed to pool their time to rustle up outfits that could give their pal a fresh look every day over a whole week at work.

The sewing circle decided that if this went to plan smoothly, then they could at some time in the future do this for any one or other of them in the circle, should there be an important event looming such as a new job (wise nod of head and purse of lips), or a wedding (sigh, downward look and shy smile), or a baby coming (gulp, straight-ahead look with wide eyes and stiffened shoulders).

Sukie's own skills with a needle and thread were negligible, to say the least – in fact, Mrs Sew-and-Sew was much less polite about Sukie's needlework skills – but Sukie was extremely good at pinning a pattern and cutting out (she really could squeeze the most from a too-small piece of material better than anyone else), as well as making cups of tea for the sewing circle now that Peter, their regular tea-boy, was being kept so busy running the errands on Evie's ever-expanding list of To-Dos for the forthcoming Revels.

The members of the sewing circle decided therefore that the most sensible plan would be to divide Sukie's new wardrobe into days.

Sukie had scrounged an old cream-coloured linen driving coat of her mother's that dated from just after the end of the Great War, and which had been worn when Sukie's father was busy a-wooing, and so this garment's seams had been carefully unpicked and was now in the process of being remodelled into a smart shift dress. Worn with one of Sukie's old blouses underneath, this was Monday's outfit.

Evie, still flushed with the success of making her dog-tooth check suit, had thought that some blackout curtain lining could perhaps provide Sukie with a very serviceable version of the same suit, this time with an elbow-length sleeve.

Linda popped over to Lymbridge one teatime to help Evie and Sukie trawl from one household in the village to another to ask those who'd made blackout curtains whether they had any scraps of material left that they could take to try to do something with. Linda couldn't help remarking, after about an hour, that she felt lucky she could wear breeches every day to work and her beloved stout boots. 'I'm not ladylike to look at, but I sure am comfy. And as everything I wear gets covered in horse slobber, I have to make sure it's slobber-proof. And if I'm trimming the hooves of sheep then I end up covered in even worse!'

After this concerted effort of the three of them, Evie and Sukie were left with a reasonable collection of pieces of leftover blackout-curtain lining, albeit each in slightly differing shades of the peculiarly dull and lacklustre greyish-white fabric.

As a gamble, they decided to try dying the largest pieces in cold tea, which rather to their surprise gave the material a lovely and surprisingly uniform fawn colour. The next day the pieces were carefully washed to see what effect that would have – and to everyone's delight the tannin in the tea had firmly dyed the fabric, and it didn't seem to want to go patchy when washed.

Then, after a tremendous amount of head-scratching and moving the pattern around this way and that, eventually Evie and Sukie were able to work out a way that the material pieces they had could indeed yield Sukie a suit, although Evie commented that Sukie had better not eat much from now on, as it had been a terrible squeeze to eke out the fabric and even then the skirt was going to be very snug-fitting indeed over the hips and waist.

When the suit was finished it would be Tuesday's outfit, Evie making sure that the jacket's high top button would preserve Sukie's modesty if she decided to wear it buttoned up and with no blouse underneath. Sukie said it was perfect as once a month she would be expected to attend a meeting of all the management staff, and so she didn't want to look like some hayseed secretary when she was taking the minutes of the meeting; this suit was deemed Definitely Not Hayseed.

Wednesday would be the skirt of the suit, and to accompany it Evie donated to Sukie a knitted round-necked short-sleeved jumper that Evie had made for herself the previous autumn but hadn't actually worn as she couldn't persuade herself that the wool's muddy-brown colour did anything other than make her look completely washed out (it had previously been an old woolly of James's that he'd worn through on the arms, and had then grown out of; Susan only ever got him clothes in earthy colours as he was so prone to getting mucky and Susan liked to think that the dirt wouldn't show on her preferred muddy and mossy palette of 'James' colours).

Now, however, it was undeniable that Sukie's blonde hair lifted a sweater that had most definitely looked drab and dowdy on Evie into something that appeared to be incredibly chic and fashionable, and particularly so when the muted brown of the wool was set off by the contrast of the suit's fawn skirt. Evie could only sigh at how unfair life could be at times.

Thursday could be the suit's jacket worn over the cream shift dress, while Friday could be Sukie's best blouse together with the suit's skirt.

James, who could be surprisingly handy when he wanted to be, although he'd found it was a good policy if he tried his best to appear otherwise, had been asked by Evie if he could think imaginatively as to jewellery, and so his contribution to Sukie's wardrobe was a carefully carved wooden brooch of a Dartmoor pony that he stuck on to an ancient brooch clasp – Susan had long ago knocked the original resin front-piece off the clasp – as well as a simple hair comb that James made for Sukie from the same golden wood.

Sukie's warm hug and surprising kiss of thanks on his right cheek made James blush just as much as Peter was prone too, much to the amusement of the three Yeo sisters.

Showing initiative, Sarah and Tina had cut out of the newspaper a week or two before a pattern for a knitted brassiere. Sarah was the more competent knitter but even she was surprised at how well the brassiere she had made turned out, and a pleased Sukie pronounced it a perfect fit.

Linda took one look at the Sukie-sized dimensions of the

intricately constructed woollen under-garment (James had caught a glimpse of it before he had hurriedly left the room, although he'd not been able to get to the door before he'd turned pink a second time), and instantly Linda gave a bark of laughter as she then glanced downwards at her much more ample bosom. 'I think I'd need something a bit more substantial than a few rows of baby's two-ply wool,' she joked, although there was a slightly wistful undercurrent to her words.

And then everyone else chimed in very quickly to say that *both* Sukie's and Linda's figures were lovely, and wasn't it wonderful that just as many chaps liked a more cuddly-figured girl than a slender one, and vice versa?

Back to the Snag a Doctor wardrobe, and luckily Sukie had a pair of brown shoes she'd hardly worn, and an elegant brown handbag that was a near perfect match, even though it was almost twenty years old, having once been her mother's. The bag wasn't too badly worn or scuffed, and Mrs Wallis was able to buff it up with a dab of her precious nourishing shoe cream until the leather of the bag gleamed as good as new.

Evie was quick to say that with her cleverly worked new outfits all in various co-ordinating hues of brown and cream, and her unusual wooden accessories, Sukie was going to look almost as if she had stepped right off one of the pages of the glitzy film magazines that Pattie so loved to browse.

On the eve before Sukie's first day at work, the final button-hole was stitched and the last thread trimmed.

Before the new clothes were all carefully wrapped into a large brown paper parcel to keep them pressed and clean while Sukie carried them home, Sukie had her hair done by Julia, with Sukie paying close attention to the hairstyling so that she could replicate the look in the days to come. She said she wasn't going to waste her precious lipstick until it was confirmed there was a handsome doctor around for her to set her cap at.

Julia explained that she was inspired for Sukie's new look by Katharine Hepburn in the previous year's smash, *The*

Philadelphia Story. Comments of 'Ah, I love that film' drifted skywards from the lips of several members of the circle.

Sukie was then persuaded to perform a fashion parade that Mrs Sew-and-Sew dubbed in her snobby voice 'Pemberley a la Mode'. Sukie perambulated up and down on the terrace outside the dining room in her smart fawn suit, with the fading sunlight giving it almost an apricot hue, swinging an umbrella as a prop for a parasol. To a continued commentary from Mrs Sew-and-Sew, she then posed as if she were about to use one of Mrs Worth's delicate bone china teacups and saucers, just as she would do if meeting Cary Grant in a scene from *The Philadelphia Story*. (Mrs Worth had gone to a whist drive in the church hall that evening, as they wouldn't have dared to touch her best china if she had been in the house.) Finally Sukie drew the show to a close by looking as if she were about to smoke one of Mr Worth's Senior Service cigarettes as she peeped alluringly out from beneath a heavy wing of lustrous blonde hair now obscuring one eye, looking for all the world as if there might be a fashion photographer or a Hollywood talent scout wandering close by. Unfortunately there wasn't.

But Mrs Wallis, who was easily the most fashionable lady in Lymbridge, as before decamping from Canterbury she had built a fine wardrobe of good quality clothes purchased from prestigious London stores, had watched the fashion show, and then declared that she was going to move heaven and earth to find some material for Evie to make her a suit, for which she promised to pay Evie handsomely.

Sukie was quite overcome at how wonderful her new clothes looked.

'I feel as if I've been walking around in rags these past months. I simply couldn't have done better if I'd had all the money in all the world, and the cloth rations to match, to spend on anything I wanted in Spooners,' she said. 'I'm so grateful to you all for putting yourselves out for me, I can hardly say; only when it comes to returning the debt I owe you, just remember, please, that I am not allowed to sew but that I can cut out patterns pretty niftily.'

At school both Evie and Mrs Bowes had decided that their classes should each put on a short performance at the Revels.

Mrs Bowes decided that the juniors would take part in a display of country dancing. There was an ancient piano at the school positioned against a wall in the juniors' room that even the slightly tone-deaf Evie could tell was extremely out of tune. She quickly came to dread the scrape of table and chairs being moved to the edges of the classroom that would always manage to muffle its way through the classroom wall to her class of infants. Then she pictured the tension-filled moment as, presumably, the juniors reluctantly lined up, and finally there would be the squeak of gym shoes on the wooden floor and the thump of children jumping about on the herringboned parquet wooden floor as Mrs Bowes attempted to bash out tunelessly and with an erratic tempo a traditional country-dance melody on the piano's yellowing keys.

After a couple of days of this torture (for the juniors, and Evie, at least), Evie started to see the funny side. As she reported to Peter that evening, 'Goodness knows what has caused Mrs Bowes to become so ambitious. She's decided the juniors WILL perform a traditional country dance come hell or high water, and that she'll accompany them on the piano.

'The children have never done anything like that before and, it sounds like, neither has Mrs Bowes. I don't think that before this Monday Mrs Bowes knew a thing about country dancing, and despite dancing every day this week, it's not going well. Neither is Mrs Bowes' piano playing going well – every time she plays the piece of music she wants them to dance to, it comes out differently, and so the poor loves are constantly at sixes and sevens, and I can hear Mrs Bowes getting crosser each day that passes. And the boys hate dancing with the girls. The girls don't think much of it either, and I can hear them saying when they pass me on the way to the playground afterwards that the boys' hands are grubby and sticky, and that they don't like holding them.'

'Ever it thus!' Peter laughed, and then added that he had an acquaintance who knew a little bit about pianos and tuning, and so he would see if he could pull in a wee favour in order to try and sort something out before the big day. And then he added that if Mrs Bowes' playing didn't pick up, and provided she would allow him to, he could play the piano for the children's country dance.

'What a wonderful idea. I'll suggest to Mrs Bowes that if you play the piano, then that will leave her free to clap in time to give a clearer beat for those poor children,' replied Evie minx-ishly; she had been angling for Peter to make this suggestion. 'Maybe that will prevent humiliation all around. Mind you, Mrs Bowes has a fearsomely loud clap – it must be all those years of calling her pupils to attention at the end of playtime – and so you might want to suggest it would be more beneficial to the polish of the performance if she stand on the opposite side of the dancers to where you are to make sure wherever the children are at any particular moment the beat of what they are dancing to will be very clear.'

Evie decided meanwhile that what she would do with her infants would be to divide the class into teams of boys and girls, and then each group could recite a short nursery rhyme to the audience. The audience would be asked to vote for which nursery rhyme was delivered with the greatest style. Of course, the votes would be wrangled, and the competition would be declared a tie, but Evie thought it might make the children enthusiastic and keen to out-do the other group.

She decided to choose nursery rhymes with a country theme, and ones that the children might know already. The boys could recite 'Cock a Doddle Doo', as she knew they would throw themselves into the line of 'cock a doodle do' that began each of the three verses. And the girls could recite three verses from 'Mary Had a Little Lamb', and Evie would see if there was a late lamb on any of the nearby farms she could borrow for one of the girls to hold (maybe April Smith, as she'd shown such an interest in the lambs when they had had their school walk). The boys could have a cockerel to go with their rhyme, although this had better be in a cage, otherwise Evie could only imagine chaos ensuing.

Evie's next thought was that a photograph of the infants with the lamb and the cockerel could well make a picture that the *Western Morning News* might be interested in running, and so she decided to ask Mrs Worth when she got back to Pemberley after school if she could use the telephone in the hall to phone the newspaper and see if they would like to send a photographer to the Revels.

As Julia would quite often finish her day's work at about two-thirty in the afternoon, seeing that she would start her postal delivery rounds so early in the morning, Evie quickly co-opted her sister to give a hand in helping the infants learn their nursery rhymes, Julia trying to tame the exuberance of the little boys while Evie attempted to encourage the girls to say their nursery rhyme in just as loud and as bold a collective gusto-filled voice as the boys. To Evie's delight Marie and Catherine proved to be thoroughly thrilled with both the nursery rhyme and their roles in the performance, and to have the loudest voices of the small girls.

Pattie didn't escape Evie's bossiness either, even though she was now working long hours on various farms. Evie charged her with finding a lamb and a cockerel (and some sort of contraption to keep the cockerel in), and in getting them all to the school one afternoon for a dress rehearsal, just in case any of the little ones proved terrified of either of the creatures when they were up close. The rehearsal with these live props went well.

And then Evie reminded Pattie that it was now her job to bring, look after and then deliver back to their homes the lamb and the cockerel on the day of the Revels. Pattie looked less than wholly pleased.

Lying in bed on the nights after they had been drilling the

children to make sure they were word perfect with their nursery rhymes, Evie and Julia would tease each other by reciting the other's rhyme out loud, just as the other sister was on the point of dropping off.

'The things you do to be annoying,' wailed Julia.

'Rubbish. I'm just trying to keep you jolly,' said Evie.

'Jolly?! Ye gods...'

'Needs must in a time of war.'

It was only as she woke up the morning following this particular exchange that Evie realised she hadn't once thought of Timmy Bowes the previous day.

On a Friday afternoon, the day before the Revels, Susan and Robert came to the school to have a word with Evie, who had just waved her final pupil off home, and who was now trying to get as much organised at the school for the morrow as she could.

She had just neatly stacked the chairs close to the door out to the playground, the plan being that the next morning they would be moved close to the tea table that would be set up in the playground as near the school's small kitchenette as possible. She was glancing up at the sky above as she deliberated whether the current fine weather was to hold through the Saturday. It would make life so much easier, Evie thought, if the weather remained clear. If it rained they could do quite a lot of the events inside, of course (excepting the tug of war and the various races or the donkey rides), although it would be a terrible squeeze and it would be much nicer if as much as possible could be outside.

Evie felt a stab of concern when she noticed her parents heading across the playground toward her classroom. This was very unusual, and all the more so as the expression on each of their faces was very serious.

'Evie, lovey, have you got a moment?' said Robert.

'We wondered if we could have a quick word,' added Susan.

'Whatever's the matter? You both look a bit green,' said Evie.

Susan explained that it seemed as if her purse had been stolen from where she had left it lying on the kitchen dresser at Blue-bells the previous evening; inside it had been almost £5 (four £1 notes, a ten-shillings note, and some pennies, threepenny bits and a few florins), money that had already been earmarked for a whole host of things.

Evie told her parents there had to have been some sort of mistake, as purses didn't go missing from Lymbridge kitchens.

What must have happened, Evie surmised, was that James had probably moved the purse to the mantelpiece above the range when he was using the kitchen table to strip his bicycle back, or to do something equally messy that also needed a lot of space.

'I'd love to think so,' said Susan glumly. 'But he denies all knowledge and he's not been in much lately anyway, with these long summer evenings, and so your father and myself have hunted everywhere for the blasted purse, and it's quite disap-peared. We've searched the house and the garden from top to bottom, even in all the bedclothes and under the beds, and in the parlour where we hardly ever go, and we've also asked at all the places I went to yesterday in case I dropped it somewhere when I was out.'

Robert looked intensely uncomfortable. 'The thing is, everyone was out after tea on the day it went missing, except for me and Frank and Joseph, that is. Pattie was working, James had gone to Bramstone, and Susan had taken Marie and Catherine to play with the McCarthy twins. The boys were helping me with the runner beans, but then they both went inside to have a drink of water and so they were, for a little while, alone in the kitchen.

'And while I don't want it to be either or both of them who are implicated in any way in the disappearance of Susan's bloomin' purse, or Mrs Bowes' five bob, I can't help but wonder if some of Peckham's less than savoury ways haven't rubbed off on the lads, with the result that they helped themselves to the purse when they saw it lying there.

'Do you think we should mention it to Mrs Bowes, as they are in her class?' Robert ground to a halt in voicing his suspicions, and looked across at his daughter with his kindly brown eyes full of concern.

Evie shook her head furiously – she couldn't think of a worse idea. She could hardly believe what she was hearing. It didn't seem possible to her.

'What rubbish – I won't believe it of either of them as they are such good boys, so don't say anything. Oh dear, I fear this isn't good news at all,' was all she could think of saying in response to the suspicions about evacuees Frank and Joseph.

The very thought of the two thefts, one of them so close to home, put Evie in a grumpy mood for the rest of the evening. She was monosyllabic and distracted when Peter tried to speak to her, and she made her excuses and stumped up the stairs to bed as soon as she decently could.

Chapter Thirteen

The next morning it was Saturday, and the Revels were going to happen come what may.

Evie awoke to the chirps and tweets of a very carefree sounding dawn chorus, and although this was a sound that usually was immensely cheering to her (not that she was often awake at this godforsaken hour), on this particular day Evie lay in bed crankily, still feeling extremely out of sorts.

When it was properly light although still very early, she crept from bed and tried to dress in clothes that she'd already worn and that were waiting for her in order to wash as quietly as she could so as not to disturb Julia; she might get dusty as she worked on getting things ready, and she planned on washing and changing at breakfast time. Her sister didn't stir, her deep and rhythmic breathing continuing at the same tempo. It was only when, by mistake, Evie lightly tapped the handle of the water ewer with her wooden-backed hairbrush that Julia moved. Evie paused with the brush still aloft in mid-air, then Julia gave a deep sigh that bordered on a groan, turned over and burrowed deeper under her bedcovers.

Relieved, Evie went down to the kitchen, where she gazed at the contents of the pantry, such as they were, before deciding she didn't feel hungry or even in need of a cup of tea. She had a drink of water, and decided to head over to the school, even though it was really too early for her to do a whole lot that was useful.

There were threatening grey clouds in the sky, and Evie felt them appropriate to her melancholy mood. She was, she realised, quite nervous about the day ahead, and she was also extremely weary as she hadn't slept at all well.

In fact she wished it were the evening already, and that the Revels were galloping away into the mists of time. Why had she ever allowed herself to be put forward as the main organiser? She would learn from this, and make sure she was otherwise engaged next year, that was for certain.

At the school, she set to giving both classrooms a good tidy and putting the remaining tables and chairs into position for displaying the competition prize-winners, Mr Cawes having already moved the furniture needed for outside into the playground where he had then shrouded it all in a huge tarpaulin.

Evie and Mrs Bowes had decided that as many examples of the children's work should be on display in the classrooms as possible (fingers crossed for no rain) although the bulk of the day's activities would take place outside in the playground; the classrooms would be open to anyone who wanted to see the day's earlier competition winners on show, and there might be a fair amount of people moving through the classrooms who would be interested in what the children had been up to that term. After three o'clock there would also be a short whist drive starting in the juniors' classroom.

It would all look a bit more inviting if the bunting from the Nissen hut could be strung around the doors into the school, Evie decided. She had already scavenged several union jack flags from various sources in Lymbridge, and Mr Cawes was going to pin those up when he arrived later in the morning.

After an hour or two of doing a bit of this and that, and retrieving the bunting from the Nissen hut, Evie felt in a more equable mood, and she decided she now felt a little peckish and so it was probably time that she headed back to Pemberley.

But this was not before she had collected a handful of drawing pins and a gigantic poster she had prepared over the lunchtimes during the previous week when Mrs Bowes had volunteered to take over playground duty in order that the poster could be got ready.

With pins in each corner and four midway down each side, with an extra one stuck on the top and bottom sides, she attached the poster on to the slightly rickety old wooden sign where ordinarily black letters stood out against a white background proclaiming Lymbridge Primary School. The sign was positioned beside the gates to the playground, staring over the dry-stone playground wall and down the single road through the village. The poster was so big that it hung above and below, and to the sides of the sign, and Evie had had to use some of the drawing pins as low down as the legs of the sign.

Evie had needed several goes before she had been able to complete the poster to her satisfaction, and she had had to attach several pieces of paper one to another in order to arrive at a big enough space where the Revels' schedule and all the other bits and pieces could be written in full.

She hoped Mrs Bowes' ears hadn't been burning on the fourth lunchtime running that Evie had spent on this, as Evie had been muttering less than kind thoughts about her as she struggled to squeeze everything in.

And later that evening she had had to persuade Tina and Sarah to give her a hand making rosettes for the first prizes; again there was a fighting chance that Mrs Bowes might once again have had rather hot ears.

♣ ♠ ♥ TODAY ♣ ♠ ♥

Lymbridge Revels
Lymbridge Primary School
1 p.m. to 5 p.m.
All money raised to go to local good causes
Adults 6d. entry
Children 14 yrs and under free

FUN, FRIVOLITY AND FROLICS FOR ALL THE FAMILY

9.00 a.m. gates open for competition and some racing event entries

12.30 P.M. GATES OPEN TO REVELS PROPER – PLEASE ARRIVE PROMPTLY

1 p.m. Revels declared open by Rev. Painter

1.05 p.m. Prayers for loved ones fighting, and for those Lymbridge residents who have made the ultimate sacrifice

1.15 p.m. Performance by Lymbridge Church Choir

1.45 p.m. Punch and Judy Show

2.05 p.m. Magic tricks performed by the Amazing Adamstrel

2.30 p.m. Country dancing display by Lymbridge Primary School juniors

2.45 p.m. Nursery rhyme competition recited by Lymbridge Primary School infants

3 p.m. The various stalls to open

3 p.m. Fortunes told by Queen Sheba of Bramstone (tent at side of playing field, to left of vegetable plots)

3.00 p.m. Miniature whist drive (juniors' classroom)

3.30 p.m. Tug of War: Lymbridge vs. Bramstone (road outside school gates)

4.00 p.m. Country and modern dancing for all on hardstanding to left of school; moves for country dancing called by Mr Smith

5.00 p.m. Thanks and close: Rev. Painter

Beer tent (open 12.30 p.m. courtesy of The Haywain,
15 yrs and over only, please), Tea tent (open 2 p.m., 'cream'
teas and fancies, rock cakes)

Jumble; donkey rides on 'Susie' (3d. – no feeding, please); guess the weight of the piglet'; lucky dip; raffle; tombola; fishing for sixpence; baking competition; coconut shy; 'most inventive' jam competition; best biscuit baked by a child of 11 yrs or

under; daisy-chain competition; fancy-dress competition (judge Mrs Bowes, 12.30 p.m.); skittles; conker competition; egg-cosy competition; best vegetable competition (three classes: carrots, leeks, and greens); ferret-legging competition (ferrets to be kept in the marked corner of the playground – please keep dogs away from this area); test your strength; test your stamina; fastest knitter of ten rows with each row 100 stitches as one plain one purl; recorder competition (performance of one minute); dog with the soppiest eyes; most obedient dog (two classes: household pet and working dog); three-legged race; fastest boy under 11 yrs; fastest boy under 15 yrs; fastest girl under 11 yrs; fastest girl under 15 yrs; fastest father; fastest mother; egg-and-spoon race – egg shortage meaning tennis-ball-and-spoon race (all racing events to be judged by Mrs Bowes – the judge's decision is final); poultry with shiniest or most unusual feathers; best talking budgie; best watercolour painted of Lymbridge; best card trick (to be judged in the beer tent at 3 p.m. by Mr Smith); best limerick (to be judged in the beer tent at 3.20 p.m. by Mr Smith – nothing too saucy, please!); auction of the morning's competition winners (3.40 p.m., auctioneer Mr Smith) (Note to those interested in 'Best Card Trick', 'Best Limerick' and 'Auction of Competition Winners' – as Mr Smith is calling from the dancing at 4 p.m., it is imperitive that the timings of these events be kept to, otherwise Mrs Bowes will have something to say ...)

Rosettes, bunting and prizes. Deckchairs
and sunshine (with a bit of luck!)
Music provided by Mr Peter Pipe
And much more
All competitions 2d. to enter.

All welcome to enjoy the excellent classwork of pupils at Lymbridge Primary School, displayed in the infants' classroom

All competition entries to be at the school by 9 a.m.
to be registered by Mr and Mrs Robert Yeo (Revels'
stewards for the day)

Judging of some competitions to take place in the morning;
most of these competition entries will be placed on display
in the infants' classroom (though not animals, sporting
or competitions taking place later in beer tent)

A photographer from the *Western Morning News* will be
present; private photographs can be arranged with him for
2 shillings a picture (or two photographs for 3s.), to be
posted on to recipients next week

Around the edges of the poster Evie had plonked small and
simple one-colour potato prints of things like balls, crowns,
balloons (these were from the 'ball' potato, but with a string
drawn on afterwards), a piglet, card-suite symbols, a cracker,
and a teacup.

After she had pinned the poster up, she glanced skywards
just to make sure it didn't look like it was about to pelt with
rain, as she wasn't convinced that the writing and illustrations
on the poster would prove to be watertight. The clouds looks a
little less grey; more dove now than battleship. Fingers crossed
for no rain.

It was, Evie decided as she took a couple of steps back to
assess her work from a distance, not *too* bad an attempt for her
first-ever public outing as a poster-maker.

As Evie considered heading back to Pemberley to have some
breakfast, and to bathe and change, she chuckled as she thought
of the threat of Mrs Bowes' ire hanging over the goings-on in
the beer tent between 3 p.m. and 4 p.m. – it was, she admitted
to herself, probably the only time that she would ever be grateful

that her headmistress was acknowledged throughout the village as a harridan. Well, other than when Mr Smith and Mrs Bowes were chivvying up people in the run-up to the Revels.

Evie also smiled at her cheeky line 'And much more'. To be honest there wasn't anything planned she'd not got on to the poster already (and what a squeeze to get everything in that had been!). But she'd thought it seemed an appropriate way of ending the description of the various attractions planned, and that she would take the risk that nobody else would notice.

The best-talking-budgie class was also a bit of a con, but dear little April Smith – she was a sweetie – had stopped Evie in the playground the week before and had asked in her lispy little-girl's voice if there was going to be something that her blue budgie Tomasina could be entered for. As far as Evie knew, Tomasina was the only budgie in the village (and goodness knows what Tomasina was fed on these days), but in a soft-hearted moment Evie had heard herself promising April there would indeed be an appropriate class for her beloved feathered friend.

The staunch efforts of Peter, Mr Smith and Mrs Bowes in their chasing up and confirming various stalls and events and so forth had made sure that everyone knew the Revels were happening this Saturday, Mrs Bowes having also ordered Rev. Painter to mention them at both the morning service and evensong the previous Sunday.

And Tina and Sarah had made much smaller and simpler posters highlighting the date and the main attractions that had been pinned up in the village shop, The Haywain and on the village noticeboard, and also in The Wheatsheaf in Bramstone and on Bramstone's village noticeboard. Mr Smith had arranged for the Revels to be in the Forthcoming Events sections of the *Western Morning News* and the *Oldwell Abbott News*. Every one of these posters had directed villagers to the porch of Lymbridge church, where Evie had hung a complete list of the competitions and, where appropriate, rules of entry.

Evie couldn't think of anything else they could have done to publicise the event.

Pattie and Linda's contribution had been to make The Official Scoreboard. This sounded grander than it was, as Mr Cawes had painted white an old piece of hardboard, on to which Linda had painstakingly marked out a grid, and then Pattie had listed all the competitions, leaving space for the winners' names, and any times or other useful bits of information. At the top, Pattie, who definitely had an artistic side to her, had written out 'Lymbridge Revels 1941', and in red letters at the bottom she had written, beside another box, 'Grand total raised for local good causes'; the total raised would be entered into the empty box at the end of the day, and either Susan or Robert would list the various competition winners as part of their stewarding duties.

Rev. Painter had promised that long-term The Official Scoreboard could take pride of place hanging on a wall in the church hall, and that beside it would also be hung a large picture frame with a montage of photos of the day that the *Western Morning News* photographer would take, provided they could strike a deal on the fee for these photographs. Evie told Rev. Painter not to worry about the cost of the pictures, as she was pretty certain that Sukie would be able to work her magic on the photographer, with the result that a wonderful bargain would be struck.

Rev. Painter had then said to Evie that he hoped the Revels would be a rejuvenated annual event everyone would start eagerly to look forward to, and that in time the walls of the church hall would be covered with Official Scoreboards from various years.

'It's so good in a time of war to have a day when we can all do something together – it reminds us of what we are fighting for, and that we can tell Jerry we will never be defeated,' said the Reverend.

Evie thought that this was overselling the power of the Revels a bit – she couldn't imagine Hitler quaking in his boots at the thought of the Lymbridge daisy-chain competition or anybody guessing the weight of the piglet. Possibly the ferret-legging competition might be a bit more of a caution...

But anyway, while she agreed generally that the Revels would be a nice day whereby those in Lymbridge could have a pleasant few hours together, Evie's one thought was that next year, the Rev. Painter's begging aside or no, she'd definitely allow the privilege of being chief organiser to go to someone else.

As Evie left for Pemberley, the men who were erecting the beer and tea tents had arrived and were hard at work, and Mr Cawes was busy with tacking up the Union Jacks and the bunting, and suddenly the school seemed to be full of bustle and whistled tunes (and the odd swear word when anyone banged their thumb).

Fortuitously Evie timed her walk back at Pemberley perfectly. As she headed in the opposite direction to a straggle of villagers who, even though it was too early, were now arriving with competition entries for classes such as 'most inventive jam' or 'best leek', Evie found she'd neatly avoided having to talk to Mrs Bowes. Just as she turned into Pemberley's drive Evie could see the headmistress, wearing her familiar tweed skirt, marching towards the school. There were so many classes planned that Mrs Bowes' judging skills would be put to the test within the hour, with the judging of the egg-cosy competition kicking off the proceedings.

Evie smiled when Mrs Bowes answered Evie's cheery wave with a slightly off-putting salute of her hand to her brow with her hand held there for a beat or two longer than it needed to be. Then she felt her heart give a small slither downward. Whenever she unexpectedly saw Mrs Bowes she would instantly think 'Timmy', and as the days passed with Evie still frozen in inaction, and with Mrs Bowes still in the dark, she felt evermore uncomfortable about the whole situation. It was a mess, but with a small shake Evie told herself to concentrate on the Revels for now, and to worry about Timmy and Tricia afterwards.

And as Evie went in the front door and headed to the

downstairs cloakroom to wash her hands, she spied Mrs Worth just bringing the generously-sized teapot into the dining room, and Evie suddenly felt ravenous and, as always, gasping for a cup of tea.

Her nervousness about the Revels had dissipated during her few hours at the school that morning to almost nothing, she realised.

She had done her best, and if it all went wrong now, then so be it.

Although it still wasn't yet eight o'clock, the rest of the PGs were all in the dining room, and everybody seemed to be looking forward to the day ahead, and they asked quite a lot of questions of Evie as to the running order of various events and competitions.

Mrs Wallis was going to enter a watercolour she'd made of the church into the painting competition, and, amid much gentlemanly chortling a couple of evenings previously, Mr Worth and Mr Wallis had both written limericks they'd be reciting in the beer tent later, although they deemed it wiser not to read them out at the breakfast table. Mrs Worth was keen that everybody knew she was going to do a stint in the tea tent.

Peter said that when Evie was ready to go back to the school he would accompany her as he wanted to try out the piano, as his piano-tuning chum was turning up soon in order to try and get it slightly more tuneful. And then at ten-thirty he and Mr Smith would become the marshals for the racing events to be judged in the morning, after which they would help Evie's parents make sure as many competition entries as possible were displayed in the infants' classroom.

Once she had eaten, Evie felt much more fortified and she nipped upstairs to get ready.

She gave herself a hasty sponge-bath and then put on her dog-tooth-check suit, but with no blouse underneath the jacket (and she had pushed the sleeves up practically to elbow length) after she had looked out of the window to see the dove grey clouds had given way to clouds that looked fluffier and edging towards oyster. She wanted to be smart, but not too hot, and so hopefully she was striking the right balance.

Although ordinarily they wouldn't be her preferred choice as she thought they made her look squat and frumpy, she decided to wear her old tan-leather sandals that she'd had since she was fifteen; they'd been trusty and faithful friends through the years, and what they lacked in glamour they made up for in comfort. Evie had a feeling she was going to be on her feet and dashing about for the rest of the day, and so comfort seemed a vital consideration.

As she and Peter headed over to the school ten minutes later, there was the tiniest chink of blue sky showing among the clouds.

'If that gets big enough to patch a pair of sailor's trousers, then we're in for a nice sunny afternoon, I'm sure. Or at least that's what my mother would say,' said Evie.

'Let's hope so.' Peter smiled across at Evie as side by side they entered through the gates of the playground, and Evie grinned back at him.

Her happy look was slightly knocked askew, however, when Peter looked at the poster and pointed out to Evie that 'imperitive' was really spelt 'imperative'.

'Bother!' said Evie. 'I'll have to alter it, and keep my fingers crossed that Mrs Bowes hasn't noticed. If she has, I'll never hear the end of it.'

'Or,' said Peter, 'you could add another competition to the list: spot the deliberate spelling mistake in the poster competition. Also, you are fibbing with that line "And much more". And as you've completely obscured the sign to Lymbridge Primary School, let's hope that everyone knows where it is.'

Evie tried to give Peter the most disdainful and withering look she could.

But the twinkle in Peter's eye meant she had a difficult time frowning quite to the desired level.

*

The morning passed in a flurry of activity. The piano tuner turned out to be a really nice chap. He only had an hour to do what he could, and so he wasn't able to get the piano to concert-hall level, but once he'd had a tinker, the old piano sounded distinctly less grating on the ears than it had done.

Peter had time for a quick run-through of the various tunes that Evie had told him were going to be needed for the juniors' country dancing, and for the choir.

As Peter wrapped up what had to be the shortest rehearsal of all time, Evie explained to Mr Smith how the judging of the various morning competitions would work – this would be the baking, jams, vegetables, paintings etc. and, regardless of the actual class, Evie's advice was that whatever Mr Smith thought best was fine, as long as the same person didn't keep winning all the classes. Her father, Robert, would tell him if there were several people entered for a slew of classes; 'in fact, anything you want to know about anything or anyone, ask my father; this has worked very well for me over the years,' Evie explained.

Before Evie could move on to how she wanted the entries to those morning competitions arranged in the infants' classroom, while ignoring the slightly put-upon expression that was already fleeting across Mr Smith's face – he didn't mind doing what he could, but this was verging on slave labour, the tremor in his neatly trimmed moustache seemed almost to be suggesting – Evie was forced to pause when she looked up towards the gates to the playground.

It seemed that about every villager was arriving with an entry for at least one of the morning competitions, and they were all now converging on the school gates.

Seeing Evie distracted, Mr Smith sidled out of her orbit with obvious relief and headed off to organise the villagers as they came into the school playground.

With a rapidly beating heart Evie called slightly squeakily for Peter and Mrs Bowes, and they came to do their bit with the incomers.

In fact Mr Smith, Peter and Mrs Bowes, and Robert and

Susan, were so efficient that for the next hour or so Evie found herself at rather a loose end, as she had delegated so brilliantly that she hadn't actually left herself with anything to do, other than to oversee the stacking of the wooden boxes with small air-holes drilled into the wood that contained the six ferrets they had begged and borrowed from various farmers.

To look busy when everyone else was working so hard, she spent a long time correcting the spelling mistake she had made when writing her poster for the Revels.

Several hours later, Rev. Painter hovered in front of the bunting-decorated school doors at least ten minutes before he was due to open the revels officially.

Exactly as the church clock struck one, Evie clapped her hands together to get people to stop what they were doing in order to listen to the grand opening, and when that didn't work she tapped a wooden paintbrush handle on an empty but clean milk bottle.

But it was Mrs Bowes' bellow of 'Order!' that made sure Evie's more polite call to arms was obeyed.

'Welcome, everybody, to the annual Lymbridge Revels,' Rev. Painter began.

So far so good, thought Evie.

Chapter Fourteen

The next couple of hours passed in a blur of activity, with the result that by teatime early that evening Evie found it quite difficult to remember exactly what happened and when in relation to all the events she'd organised. But it was clear the Revels were a tremendous success.

The beer tent did a roaring trade, the various stalls were well supported, and the sizeable crowd, swelled by visitors from neighbouring villages and outlying farms – quite a lot of people whom none of the locals recognised or knew where they came from – laughed when they were expected to during the Punch and Judy show (the puppeteers coming from Plymouth for the performance) and the magic show of the Amazing Adamstrel (who was a local young farmer called Adam, about whom Pattie whispered to Julia, 'Yep, pretty amazing all right!').

The country-dancing display by the Lymbridge Primary School juniors looked surprisingly polished, although Evie noticed that Frank and Joseph bumped conspiratory shoulders and could barely contain their smirks when Mrs Bowes had to gallop heavy-footedly across the playground to get to the group of dancers so that she could clap out the beat, as she had been deep in discussion with Mr Smith and had failed to notice Evie's frantic signalling, or Frank's clarion call of 'Miss!' when the children and Peter had been poised and waiting to start the display for a minute or two.

Peter was smiling too at the flustered headmistress, and he and Evie caught each other's eyes as Mrs Bowes was reduced to blustering, 'Right, children, look sharp and stop dawdling – heads up and shoulders back, and on my count of three.'

Then it was the turn of Evie's infants. There were so many people jostling to get a look at them as they stood so sweetly in their two teams on either side of the top step of the school entrance that Evie was worried they'd be stage-struck.

But to a child, they behaved like complete professionals who had been doing this sort of thing for years, although the cockerel and the lamb looked a bit less keen about the whole endeavour. The children were all word perfect as they stared gravely at Evie who smiled her encouragement.

When it came to the vote of whether the boys had beaten the girls, or vice versa, there were loud cheers and applause for both teams, and the cockerel cockadoodledooed for each team too, and so Evie was in all good conscience able to declare the nursery rhymes had been equally well performed by both teams, and that the result was an honourable draw.

Then there was a moment of high drama.

The energetic clapping and the cheering from proud parents of the infants upset the piglet that people were supposed to be guessing the weight of, and with a super-piglet wriggle and a hop and a leap, he was up and out of his tiny, high-walled pen with a high-pitched squeal (who'd have thought such a pint-sized creature, who'd been blissfully asleep since he'd arrived, looking as if butter wouldn't melt in his mouth, would have such a spring in him?). And then his little pink trotters were going nineteen to the dozen as he hared down the field to seek refuge behind the Nissen hut.

'Go on enjoying yourselves, everyone, please, but perhaps move a little further away from the piglet pen,' commanded Evie, as she tried to hold her laughter in. 'I think he's scared of all the noise, and so if everyone stays in the school playground, I'll go and get him.'

She trotted after her porcine fugitive, while Peter went to collect a box that might be helpful in the catching and holding process – a precious porker was valuable and definitely couldn't be allowed to disappear into the yonder in these times of scrimping.

There was no sign of the piglet in the secluded area behind the hut when Evie and Peter first peeped around the hut's corner. But then Peter put his finger in front of his mouth to indicate they shouldn't speak, before pointing to a slight hollow underneath the hut. Evie nodded that she understood.

Peter lay down on the grass and put his hands gingerly into the hollow. Evie crept close with the box as Peter inched forward until almost the full length of both arms was under the hut.

A piglet squeal, and a windmill of thrashing stubby legs, and Peter had caught hold of the little chap and carefully pulled him out from under the Nissen hut. He writhed furiously (the piglet, not Peter), and Evie had to help Peter hold the piglet before he attempted to make another dash for liberty. It was the closest that she and Peter had ever been to each other.

It was a bit of a tussle, but with lots of sssshs and other soothing words, she and Peter took a lot of care making sure they were gentle and calm, and soon the piglet's frantic actions were pacified by their constant stroking of his little pink body, their fingers sometimes inadvertently touching for an instant.

Once he was lying placidly in Peter's arms they were able gently to place him into the box and fold the lid down, and Evie quickly sat on the box to make sure he couldn't lift the lid up from inside in a final show of defiance. There was one last muted piggyish snuffle, more of indignation at being put somewhere dull and dark rather than anything else, it seemed. And then the piglet, who had a rather fetching ginger fringe on top of his head, agreed he was beaten, and quickly settled down.

As she sat in victory on the box, Evie was breathless, and she couldn't help laughing – it was all so funny and ridiculous, and she laughed harder when she noticed that Peter had managed to get his white shirt quite mucky in his wrestle with the piglet.

Peter was now kneeling on the grass close to Evie's knees, still panting a bit with his own exertions of having to chase the piglet and then catch hold of him, and he leant down to get a closer look at the little porker who was watching him with a baleful eye through the space in the side of the wooden box that had been cut for a handle-hold.

Peter looked up at Evie and slowly the smile faded. His expression intensified as he stared at her, deep into her eyes. And in that moment Evie felt caught on a tide of significant silence, with the happy sounds of the Revels a mere murmur in the background.

Her heart flipped and started to hammer, and she couldn't quite get enough breath.

It was a dizzying feeling, and all she could see were Peter's gold-flecked eyes and long eyelashes glinting in the sunlight.

Without quite meaning to, somehow she couldn't help leaning towards Peter just at the moment he leant towards her.

Before Evie was properly aware of what was happening, his lips were brushing hers with exquisite softness. It was a split second of heaven.

'Miss, Miss! Where's the piggy?' bellowed little Bobby Ayres as he blundered around the corner.

Evie and Peter sprung apart. The spell was broken, and they could only glance at each other in shock. What had just happened? Had they dreamed it?

'The PIGGY?' queried Bobby.

With a swallow and a valiant but failed attempt to speak in a normal voice, Evie said, 'We've just caught him, and put him in the box for safety, Bobby, and I am sitting on top of the box while we work out what to do with him. I think you and the others recited your nursery rhymes so very well that everybody was really impressed, and this meant that they clapped so loudly they frightened the poor piglet. Why don't you go back to the Revels, and Mr Pipe and I will put the piggy in his box in the Nissen hut so that he can have a little time on his own to calm down, and then he can come back to the Revels and be put back in his pen, and you can look at him then.'

'Yes, Miss,' said Bobby obediently, and turned around to go.

Without looking at each other or saying a word – Evie and Peter seemed now struck with crippling shyness and awkwardness towards each other – together they were able to manhandle the box back around to the front of the Nissen hut, and then hoist it inside. They found a couple of heavy hessian sacks containing Mr Cawes' groundsman odd-job tools to put on top of the box to make sure that the lid stayed closed.

And then they looked at each other in the dim light. The atmosphere felt charged with electricity. They stepped closer together, their eyes locked.

Gently Peter stroked the side of her face and Evie found it such an intimate gesture that she closed her eyes and held her breath. The sensation, piercingly intense, lasted only a few moments, and Evie found that without her being aware of the intention to do so, her hand had crept up to touch Peter on his forearm where she could feel his skin and his firm musculature underneath. The feeling flooding through Evie was almost more than she could bear.

Once again Peter's lips skimmed hers. It was like being kissed by lips soft as a rainbow.

And then without saying anything or looking at her again, Peter turned and slipped out of the door.

As she breathed out with a shudder and continued to stare at the door he had gone through, Evie almost swooned at the thought of what had just happened.

She felt terrible at her inexcusable behaviour – she was still engaged, officially, to Timmy, after all, and she knew that allowing Peter's advances was something that no nice girl should do – but she felt knocked sideways by a totally unexpected and overwhelming feeling of desire that felt almost animal in its nature.

It was all she could do not to run after Peter and beg him to return to the subdued light and bone-deep quiet of the Nissen hut with her.

As the piglet gave a piglet-sized snuffle and lay down in his box, Evie longed for Peter to kiss her again. With Peter's arms wrapped tight around her, and his lips on hers, she would be happy at that moment to die, she felt.

Evie had never felt like this about Timmy, she realised. And what did that mean about her love for her fiancé? Suddenly she knew that the feelings she had believed to be love those months earlier, were now revealed as being much shallower, as if she had been playing at being in love or had been talking herself into it, perhaps swept away in part by the general excitable mood of the times. And although Peter's lips has been on hers only for a second or two, now she felt as if she was on a helter-skelter, as if she couldn't return to being the old Evie and instead was plummeting towards a heady world of sexual knowledge and desire. To realise she was capable of such feelings being so quickly aroused was scary, but undeniably wonderful too.

Chapter Fifteen

A while later Evie had collected herself sufficiently to try to wander unobtrusively back to the hubbub of the Revels. She peered through the small window and then listened carefully at the door before making a swift exit – it would be disastrous if Mrs Bowes caught any whiff of a suspicion of what had gone on.

Still, she was buoyed by the unexpected kisses, and felt almost reckless. It was as if she were a quite different Evie to the Evie of only an hour ago.

The scales had fallen from her eyes – she was infused with a yearning she had never dreamed she was capable of. And those two velvet kisses might not be enough to slake the headiness of this feeling of desire.

Evie wasn't sure whether she should be thrilled or terrified.

Sukie, well versed in matters romantic, noticed immediately that something was up. She'd seen Peter exit the Nissen hut with a strange expression, and now she tried to catch Evie's eye as she raised a suggestive eyebrow.

Damn and blast! Evie felt herself blushing furiously as she gave a cursory wave to her friend and pretended she was walking to do something very urgent that needed to be sorted out Right Now that was somewhere towards the infants' classroom and that was most assuredly so important that she couldn't spare a second to stop and speak with Sukie.

Luckily, before Sukie could come over to find out what had

happened (she wasn't the sort of woman who could be fobbed off by a simple wave and someone else looking as if they were busy, Evie knew), Susan called a word in Evie's direction that ordinarily would have given her a moment of discomfort.

'Ferrets!'

And so although she felt a bit woozy and confused as to what was happening around her this sunny afternoon – how could everything look so ordinary and mundane, when her world had just been knocked off its axis? – Evie was able to sidestep neatly Sukie's inquisition as she went to stand at her mother's side.

There, as she felt the small hands of both Marie and Catherine slip into hers, one on either side, Evie looked on with glittery but unseeing eyes as her father and her brother took part in the ferret-legging. They were the final two competitors, the scores of the previous entrants already written up on an old blackboard propped on an easel.

It was very likely the Yeo family reputation was about to be badly besmirched, as the ferrets had proved to be a cantankerous bunch so far, with the school's first-aid kit being plundered several times.

Robert had opted for loose trousers – they were his corduroy winter gardening trews that Evie could always remember him wearing, and so they must have been donkey's years old. It wasn't a particularly successful strategy as it turned out. Instead of snuggling down as if for a nap, Robert's ferrets proved tetchy.

James was wearing a pair of more snugly fitting trousers he'd borrowed from a friend. His ferrets settled down immediately with the result that James was able to stand there calmly.

And so it wasn't long before James was declared the overall winner of the competition. He knew he was lucky as the ferrets had probably been made drowsy by the warm afternoon and had lost the excitement of going down the trousers of the early contestants, and so had decided they'd have a quick snooze in the dark of the trousers. Nonetheless, James was thrilled as it was the only time he had ever been first at anything, a feeling made all the better by beating the best of the local young men who were still in the area in reserved occupations.

Evie noted James holding himself with a hint of swagger as Sukie came near. She pecked him on the cheek in a kiss of congratulation as his fellow competitors cheered and catcalled him. Then, playing up to the audience, with a provocative look on her face, Sukie slung her arm around James's shoulders and pressed the length of the side of her body against his. James looked as pleased as punch, while several of the other competitors looked as if they were regretting calling themselves out so early – if a cuddle with Sukie had been billed as a prize, they might have endured another nip or two from the ferrets, their expressions suggested.

As the camera clicked for the *Western Morning News*, the raucous mood of those standing around suggested The Haywain had been doing a roaring trade in the beer tent, and Evie had already noted just before the piglet ran off that the landlord's son had been sent back to the public house to collect another keg.

Evie could also see that in part Sukie had used her effusive congratulation of James as a means of closing in on Evie, and that she was itching to sidle even nearer in order to discover what had been going on in the Nissen hut. Yoicks!

The prize for winning the ferret competition was a large tankard of 'Knock 'Em Dead', which was the strongest variety of scrumpy The Haywain offered. It was made by the public house from locally grown apples. Rumoured to have an occasional joint of meat thrown into the brew as it was fermenting to give it a bit of extra kick, Knock 'Em Dead was so lethal that The Haywain proudly proclaimed nobody could drink three pints and stay standing up.

As James downed his tankard in almost one long draught, with Sukie smiling on encouragingly as she managed also to look pointedly in Evie's direction, Susan stood among the crowd, her stance a study in censure. Susan rolled her eyes dramatically when James banged down the empty tankard as she didn't really approve of alcohol, and certainly not of fifteen-year-old lads, and her only son in particular, downing strong cider in the middle of the afternoon.

But Robert laid a reassuring hand on his wife's arm, saying, 'Let him be, Sue. He'll feel like a man just now, and so let him enjoy his afternoon, and his photograph with Sukie. I'll stay close to him to make sure it doesn't get out of hand.'

It was only when Pattie and Linda came by a little later and asked Evie about the ferret competition which they'd missed as – they admitted – they'd been flirting in the beer tent, Linda having to make do with whoever was around as Sam Torrence had had to work, and Pattie not being too particular either, that Evie realised she'd hardly even known it was happening, and she only had the vaguest sense now that her brother had won the competition.

'Don't think you're getting away with it, Evie-Rose. I'm on to you,' whispered Sukie as she passed close by on her way to speak to Pattie and Linda, who were now distracting Susan from staring too obviously at her son.

Evie hardly cared. All she'd been able to think about for the past few minutes were Peter's lips gently – indeed as softly as if he'd brushed a feather tenderly across her lips, or slid a pure silk scarf over her waiting mouth – kissing her. It felt like a memory she'd treasure for ever.

The only fly in the ointment during the rest of day – well, actually there were two flies – was Evie seeing Tricia's parents, Mr and Mrs Dolby, staring at her rather pointedly. There was no sign of Tricia, thank goodness, but Evie, still cocooned in warming thoughts of her and Peter and the piglet, tried to keep a reasonably bland expression on her face under their scrutiny. Mr and Mrs Dolby must know of her own association with Timmy, she thought.

Then she noticed they were standing only a short distance from Mrs Bowes, who fortunately was still clearly ignorant as to their significance as she wasn't paying them a scrap of attention as she bossily instructed a put-upon Mr Cawes to do something or other.

Peter then neatly distracted everyone by walking by carrying aloft the box containing the piglet, and he now popped the once again snoozy little tyke back into his pen – someone had taken the precaution of heightening the sides substantially.

After some urging, Peter was persuaded to hold the piglet again, and pose for a photograph with the errant escapee taken by the chap from the *Western Morning News*, who seemed to have been doing a lively trade in snapping pictures, carefully noting down in his reporter's notebook who the various people he was photographing were, and the addresses to which he should send the photographs once he had developed and printed them up.

The photographer joked with Evie that as far as he could tell, Shady was in every single shot he'd taken; Shady clearly was having a field day of the highest order. And, apparently, the photos that Shady wasn't in, all looked as if they were very likely to have a small tabby and white cat strutting around with her tail as upright as a flagpole, just as if she owned the place, seemingly oblivious to any visiting dogs, donkeys or ferrets. Evie laughed as she knew that school cat Keith was very good indeed at making her presence known.

Later, Evie felt peculiar when she caught an unexpected glimpse of Peter, and particularly so when she noticed Mrs Bowes looking at her.

But when Mrs Bowes came over to mention that she'd just been alerted by Mrs Wallis that Rev. Painter had already had one pint of Knock 'Em Dead, and had just asked for another, and that he probably shouldn't have any more after that if there wasn't to be a debacle in his speech to close the festivities, Evie was able to relax as the spectre of the Dolbys having some sort of fracas with her and Mrs Bowes faded away. Evie reassured Mrs Bowes that she would have a word with The Haywain's staff manning the beer tent, and that she would ask Robert to make sure the Reverend didn't get too tipsy.

As she walked promptly towards the beer tent Evie thought she'd probably had enough sticky moments for this afternoon.

That particular wish wasn't to be granted just yet, however.

Vince Short, one of the older juniors who would be leaving Lymbridge Primary School when term ended in a couple of weeks, and who would be starting at the secondary school in Oldwell Abbott in the autumn, came up to Evie.

He told her that he had seen Frank and Joseph looking significantly at handbags on the arms of visitors to the Revels, almost as if they were hoping somebody hadn't done the clasp of their bag up securely, because if the owner of the handbag hadn't, perhaps there would be a purse that would make, in Vince's words, 'easy pickin's'.

The Smith family weren't particularly popular in Lymbridge as one or other of them always seemed to be at the bottom of any rare discord in the village. Vince was a sometimes surly, rather unpleasantly demanding child the other children didn't appear to take to much either, and at least twice that term Evie had heard Mrs Bowes reprimanding him for being too boisterous in playground games with younger children, and apparently she had had to have further words when he had been daring some of the younger juniors to play tricks on Mr Cawes, such as hiding his paintbrush or screwdriver.

Evie wasn't quite sure what to say to Vince's allegations. She'd never particularly warmed to the boy herself, but of course there was a possibility that as much as Evie would like to think otherwise, he was telling the truth and that Frank and Joseph were up to no good, and so she thought that for now at least she probably should give Vince the benefit of the doubt. At any rate, Evie didn't want him to feel that she wasn't paying attention to his allegations as that would smack of favouritism as everyone knew that Frank and Joseph were billeted with her parents.

'Thank you, Vince – I'll deal with it now,' said Evie, with a manful effort at keeping any edge of irritation from her voice. 'I think I see your father looking around for you.'

'Doubt it. Ma sent 'im home in disgrace as 'e'd been making sheep's eyes at yorn maid Pattie in the beer tent.'

'Right. I see. In that case I'm sure your mother will be wondering where you are. She might have things she needs you to carry for her if your father has had to go,' Evie replied in a brisk tone that she hope would allow no argument.

Once Vince had gone, Evie looked for Frank and Joseph, and saw them peering at the donkey Susie, marvelling at how she had a metal bit actually in her mouth, lying across her tongue, her teeth having a convenient gap so as not to get in the way of the bit. They had obviously never seen a donkey at close quarters before, or a bridle, nor given any thought as to how any sort of riding animal could be controlled.

Susie, who was enjoying having a rest in the shade of a tree and a welcome bucket of water after spending a couple of hours giving rides to eager small children, looked bored at their attention, and was standing with half-closed eyes and an occasionally twitching tail.

'Frank! Joe! Can you pop over here, please?' called Evie in what she hoped was a suitably rousing voice, her hastily conceived plan being to keep the boys busy until all the visitors had departed. 'It's almost the end of the afternoon, and so I wonder if you can help us organisers with some of the clearing up. I'm not asking any other juniors – I only want people who are up to the job.

'Perhaps you can ask Mrs Bowes if there's anything you can help her with. And if she hasn't anything, then you could help Mr Cawes clear away all the markers for the running events that are still pegged into the ground the other side of the vegetable plots. And as the ferrets have all been taken home, that area of the playground will need sweeping to clear away the loose pieces of straw from their boxes, and then all the sweepings very carefully picked up.

'By the time we leave here this evening, everything needs to be shipshape and Bristol fashion. And while we sort things out you two can tell me all about what you've most enjoyed doing or watching today.'

Evie tried hard to listen to Frank telling her about his prowess at the tombola and Joe saying he'd managed to eat three whole toffee apples, but it proved to be almost impossible when pleasurable thoughts of Peter were so distracting.

A squiffy but fortuitously not embarrassing Rev. Painter was able to draw the afternoon to its official close thirty minutes after the planned end of the afternoon, the demand for dancing making it impossible to close up shop promptly at five, and then quite a lot of the villagers stayed on for a while to help put things back to rights.

Mrs Bowes and Mr Smith seemed to have disappeared off somewhere together, the rumour being that Mrs Bowes had some unusually coloured lupins in her garden she thought the Mr Smith might like to see.

Still, Mr Cawes was around to make sure that the school and the grounds survived the grand clear-up.

Indeed he seemed invigorated as he bossed people around with lots of 'look lively mind you' and 'that's gwain over there', as chairs were stacked and tables and desks moved to just outside the school doors ready to be lifted inside once Evie, Julia, Linda and Sukie had sorted out the classrooms, Evie being kept on her toes as she had to make sure that Sukie didn't get an opportunity to grill her. Meanwhile Pattie was off somewhere with the Amazing Adamstrel, and so the odd comment was made about shirkers and shirking. Tina and Sarah were helping The Haywain crew move everything in the beer tent back to the public house; apparently this fell under the banner 'shirking' too.

Peter was in charge of collecting all the money the various stalls and events had made, and he joked now that the Knock 'Em Dead had definitely helped boost the takings at the auction. Before he'd gone to see the lupins, and once the dancing had been drawn to a close, Mr Smith had announced proudly that he had been able to sell virtually everything in the auction, and what he'd not been able to sell, he'd put in the piglet's former box to take back to Pemberley, and then he had slipped Peter three crisp £1 notes to add to the overall funds raised and to cover generously his haul of leftovers.

Evie grinned, and her heart gave a small flip when she saw Peter perched on one of the diminutive chairs that her infants sat on in class, writing on an equally diminutive desk as he worked out on a scrap of paper the grand total of money raised.

It was an extraordinary sum, a tremendous £102 8s. 10½d., more than double the amount raised at the annual Revels of any previous year.

Peter carefully painted the grand total in its box on The Official Scoreboard, and then he put in the final winners and timings of the competitions. He then carried the scoreboard across to the church, accompanied by Frank and Joseph who were manhandling the easel the board would be placed on. Once atop the easel, The Official Scoreboard would take pride of place to the side of the altar for the next couple of weeks before it would be hung for perpetuity in the church hall.

As Evie watched the cheerful way in which Frank and Joseph struggled with the heavy wooden easel she still couldn't really believe that they could be the thieves that were blighting the honest ways of Lymbridge.

After an hour of hard and sweaty work – 'Ladies don't sweat, they only perspire, we must remember!' Julia claiming at the same time as she looked distinctly shiny of face – the school looked back to normal and almost as if the Revels had never happened. Julia was feeling very pleased with herself as several village women had approached her to see if they might come to an arrangement over Julia's fledgling hairdressing skills, of which people were starting to speak highly, and so Evie felt pleased her sister had had a rewarding day too.

At last the helpers all trudged off and Evie was left on her own to have a final check around the premises, collect the handtowels from the lavatory that she would wash at Pemberley, and to lock up. As she replaced the key in its hidey-hole, she turned to see that Peter had remained behind also, and was busy unpinning the poster from the school sign.

He came up to her with the poster carefully rolled, and handed over the drawing pins, which Evie put in the hidey-hole too as she couldn't quite bear the thought of unlocking the door again just for something so small, although she reminded herself that she must say to both Mrs Bowes and Mr Cawes at church tomorrow that the drawing pins were there and therefore if they were first to the school on Monday they needed to be careful when removing the school key not to jab their fingers on the sharp points.

'I thought that you might like this as a memento of the day,' said Peter, as he nodded towards the poster she had so carefully made, and then he handed it to her, saying, 'You did a wonderful job, and the Revels were a magnificent success. And it's all down to you.'

'Yes, they were, weren't they?' said Evie with a smile. 'And you worked really hard to make them a success too, and I do very much appreciate it. Indeed I don't know what I would have done without you.'

They realised they were looking intently into each other's eyes, and they both began to blush. They each noticed, and then blushed more furiously. It was very awkward, until Peter broke the tension with a laugh, and Evie joined in.

They walked back to Pemberley, not really saying anything to each other or daring to look at each other. Evie's heart was beating unnaturally fast, but it seemed enough to stroll home side by side in the cooling sunlight, close enough to each other that their shoulders occasionally bumped. There didn't seem the need for either of them to mention what had happened between them earlier.

Just as they turned into Pemberley's drive Evie noticed the dreaded sight of the telegram boy riding his motorbike through the village.

'I do hope he's not bringing someone terrible news,' she said. 'It's been an almost perfect day, and so it would be tragic if it were spoilt now.'

Chapter Sixteen

The news that came in the telegram was bad. Very bad indeed. It was just about the worst thing that could happen.

Evie had no sooner got back to Pemberley and was sitting in the kitchen enjoying the sensation of the cold stone-flagged floor under her slightly throbbing bare feet (she didn't think she had sat down once since leaving Pemberley in the morning, other than that minute or two on the box behind the Nissen hut). Having kicked off her shoes and removed her stockings the moment she got home, she was now sipping gratefully at the best cup of tea in the world that Mrs Worth had just poured for her, when Mr Smith came in with an extremely worried look on his face.

He had hurried over from Mrs Bowes' cottage. As Mr and Mrs Worth looked on anxiously (he'd whispered to them in the hall what he was going to say to Evie), Mr Smith crouched down by Evie's chair, and held her hand softly as he gently broke the awful news.

The telegram had been for Mrs Bowes. It was to say that Timmy had been gravely wounded in action and was being treated somewhere abroad in a military hospital unit. There had been no description of his injuries, or exactly where he was.

Evie sat still and as if frozen. She was quite numb and it was as if she'd been submerged very suddenly into the icy water of one of the glistening Dartmoor streams. She didn't know what to say, or what she felt.

She doubted she had heard correctly and so turned large eyes to Mr Smith in a look of puzzlement and incomprehension. Even more gently, Mr Smith had to repeat his words.

Seeing Evie's lost-at-sea expression, Mrs Worth sent Mr Worth to call for Julia, who was having a well-earned bath upstairs, the household water having been heated especially so that those involved in the Revels could have the treat of a bath on Saturday evening, if they so wanted. In a few minutes Julia hurried down the stairs and into the kitchen, damp still, and with a look of extreme concern on her face. She had clearly been planning on an early night as she was already wearing her dressing gown and slippers, and had her hair pin-tucked and tied up in her sleeping scarf.

'Evie? Evie, darling?'

There was no response. Evie continued to stare unseeing at the imposing Welsh dresser before her. Her eyes weren't quite focused and the muscles in her normally animated face had gone slack.

Julia leant down and gently caught hold of her sister on either side of her upper arms, deftly manoeuvring Evie on to her feet and into the small library adjacent to the kitchen, where she carefully guided Evie until she was sitting on a small sofa that was placed with its back to the window. Julia lifted Evie's feet on to the sofa too.

'Another cup of tea, with sugar please, if we have any, I think, Mrs Worth,' said Julia with efficiency, as she placed a handy crochet blanket throw around Evie's shoulders and another over her legs. 'To me it looks like she's gone into shock. Is there a nip of brandy or other spirit anywhere, Mr Worth?'

From what felt like a very long distance away, Evie heard Mr Worth in the hall, explaining to Peter what had happened, and then asking if he could go to The Haywain to see if they had any brandy.

Julia popped her nose out of the door, and saw Tina hovering in the hall too. 'Tina, dear, I think Evie needs her mother – it would be wonderful if you could go to Bluebells and see if she can come over.'

Then Julia perched on the edge of the sofa beside her sister, and put a comforting arm around her. Evie was shivering, and seemed still only able to gaze unseeingly into the middle distance.

Feeling as if she were fathoms underwater, Evie couldn't quite work out what was happening around her or why she felt so terrible.

It was as if someone had told her that Timmy had been injured. But maybe she had got that wrong? Or was this some sort of dangerously subversive dream?

Then a reassuring squeeze of her shoulders from Julia snapped her back at last to the here and now.

How dreadful. Poor Timmy!

Evie turned watery eyes towards her sister.

And then – and at this Evie could have groaned out loud at her woeful lack of moral staunchness or any common-sense compassion – the very next feeling that pushed all other thoughts aside was one of nothing less than mystification about the depth of her reaction. In short, she was dumbfounded she felt so side-swiped at the news of Timmy being injured, dreadful as it certainly was.

Of course it was always a tragedy when any young man in his prime was cut down. But the reality was that she didn't care for Timmy in the way that she was supposed to. To her now, he felt as if he was more a stranger than a cared-for fiancé.

Evie caught a glimpse of the concerned faces of Mr and Mrs Worth peeping around the library door to see how she was, and she felt unworthy of their anxious expressions. They all assumed she was heart-broken, and paralysed with worry. But she wasn't really; indeed, far from it.

She had known for a while now that it was almost definite that her engagement to Timmy was about to end, and that he hadn't turned out to be the man she had once hoped he was. Her love for him had withered, of that there was no doubt. And the only reason she had not already brought the relationship to a close was that, aside from the difficulty of doing so while actually working for Mrs Bowes, in an ideal world she would have like to have done it to Timmy's face. While a period of leave for Timmy hadn't looked likely, she had been supposing over the past couple of weeks that she would write to end their formal attachment at some point in the looming summer holidays, once she didn't have to see Mrs Bowes every day.

But everything to do with Timmy that Evie had been feeling now all seemed to have melded into one confusing and repugnant juggle of conflicting emotions.

And her transporting moment with Peter and the piglet, feeling so long ago now when Evie fleetingly thought about it, felt likewise depressingly tainted and uncomfortable.

It wouldn't be going too far, Evie felt, to say that the stolen kisses seemed somehow perhaps to have evoked this tragedy. While those moments had been wonderful at the time, those feelings of exhilaration that Evie had experienced were now firmly being trampled into the ground by thoughts of how badly she had behaved in the wider scheme of things. It had been behaviour that was certainly unworthy of a woman engaged to another man.

Evie was ashamed, and she felt that she would rather die than have anyone know what had happened behind the Nissen hut.

And should she feel that poor Timmy's injuries were the dire result?

In some ways the worse thing about it all was that Timmy had always been such a lively, vital person. The sort of man with boundless energy and a tremendous vitality for life, the sort of person that everyone, both men and women, wanted to be around, the sort of chap with an ever-ready laugh and an enviably easy way about him. Quite simply, Timmy Bowes made everything more exciting, a quality that Evie could see had been the very thing about Timmy that had first drawn her to him.

Would she have fallen for Timmy in peacetime? Evie couldn't

say; all she knew was that he had seemed like a beacon of something positive and light that she could hang on to in this horrid war. He offered the lure of excitement and laughter, and although the Evie of three or four years ago would have assumed that she was a more serious person, she had found herself bowled over by little more than the way Timmy had made her smile and, on occasion, laugh uproariously.

And even though Evie still felt very bruised and fragile following his cavalier treatment of her – and she was sure he wouldn't have thought he was really stepping out of line in how he had behaved, or not *too* much at any rate, and he would have expected Evie to rap his knuckles but probably not much more – she could acknowledge that Timmy was a very manly man, and that many would feel that someone like him epitomised all that was good about the British Tommy. Somehow Timmy's inherent vitality and manliness made the telegram's news that much worse.

And if his injuries perhaps meant the loss of a limb or his sight, he would hate it, Evie knew.

Perhaps the situation was even more tragic, and he'd be bedridden for ever, or he might even die. In fact, it was very possible that he might already have succumbed and died of his injures.

If that were the case, then Evie realised with a further sinking heart (yes, tragically this *was* possible) that in some way she would always feel as if she herself and her shoddy behaviour were culpable.

She had behaved badly and dishonourably. No matter that Timmy hadn't been perfectly behaved himself; two wrongs could never make a right was the sad truth of it. And while he would have been injured before she kissed Peter, she knew, that hardly mattered, as she still felt as if she were in some way to blame for the pain he was suffering.

Poor, silly, stupid Timmy.

His poor yet-to-be-born child. Not forgetting poor naive Tricia.

Timmy's poor mother.

And her own poor self.

It was all so dreadful.

Susan arrived, her usually placid and calm face etched with deep lines, and she asked if she could be alone with Evie, aside from Julia that was. Calm, as ever, and wise, it wasn't so much anything that her mother said in her quiet and reassuring manner that Evie found so comforting, but more that her mother seemed such a pillar of support and the symbol of all things as they should be. Susan was the type of person that Evie had hoped to emulate, and part of what made her feel so badly now was that Evie knew that she had been tested, and she had been found wanting. It was bad enough she had let her mother down with her snipey feelings to do with having to share her parents with Frank and Joseph when they first arrived; now she had transgressed further, beyond what even that morning she would have thought possible.

Evie was persuaded to drink the sweetened tea, and also some whiskey that Peter had brought back from The Haywain in a glass, covered by a saucer to prevent splashing, as they hadn't any brandy.

Evie couldn't bear to look up to see if Peter had actually come into the room. But her impression was that he seemed equally wary of her, merely standing in the hall and passing the glass of whiskey to Julia through the opened door, before he made himself scarce, swiftly leaving Pemberley, presumably to trek disconsolately back to The Haywain to spend an hour or two drowning his own sorrows.

Julia persuaded Evie to put on her thick winter cardigan, and slowly the shivering abated. The tea and the alcohol worked further magic, and soon the result was that at last Evie was able to look around with eyes that could now focus and to speak much more coherently to Susan and Julia.

It wasn't long before Evie announced that she must go and see Mrs Bowes.

Mr Smith had returned immediately to Mrs Bowes after

breaking the news to Evie, but Evie said it would be inexcusable if she didn't also go now to see Timmy's mother. Mrs Bowes would be simply devastated, Evie was sure, and so she must go there to help the older woman put on the show of strength that Lymbridge village would expect of her.

Evie kissed her mother, and thanked her. 'I'll be fine now,' she said. 'I think it had been such a busy day and I'd had nothing to eat or drink since breakfast – well, other than one of Mrs Tully's rock cakes, which took the word rock a bit too seriously. I've spent all the time since then running around; and I just hadn't been expecting anything like the telegram, and so it was a total shock that knocked me for six. I feel so much better now, although still a bit queasy at the same time.'

Ten minutes later Julia and Susan walked Evie across the village to Mrs Bowes' cottage (Julia still with her hair pinned and wearing her sleeping scarf, such was her concern about her sister, although she had wriggled back into a dress), and together mother and middle daughter stood in the road and watched Evie make her way up the path of the pretty, well-maintained garden, and tap quietly at the front door.

Mrs Bowes answered very quickly, and Susan and Julia could see Mr Smith standing further back down the hallway. In a gesture of true warmth the older woman clasped Evie to her bosom, and Evie clasped her back with a genuine affection that would have surprised Evie if her store of surprise for the day hadn't already been used up.

The two women stood there, one sturdy and one slender, their heads touching tenderly and with pent-up emotions quaking their shoulders.

There was to be no sleep for Evie or Mrs Bowes that Saturday night. They sat, along with Mr Smith, in the small parlour that was cluttered with myriad cherished china ornaments, and talked through the telegram and all the various permutations of what its scant words might mean.

Mr Smith was wonderful about keeping them supplied with

hot drinks, and at about two o'clock in the morning he was able to persuade them each to eat a slice of dry toast. Evie had to force her toast down, but she knew she had to eat and keep her strength up, for who knew what they all might have to deal with in the coming days? Besides the bad news about Timmy rendering her hungerless, who would have thought guilt about allowing Peter to kiss her would also have proved to be such an appetite queller?

Mr Smith also tried to make sure that they dwelt on the one positive factor of the news – when the telegram was written, although Timmy had sustained serious injuries, he was still alive.

Evie, however, didn't find this thought to be nearly as soothing as Mrs Bowes appeared to do.

While Evie was still thinking through the possible ramifications of the news in the telegram, she noticed in the small hours of the night that Mr Smith and Mrs Bowes were sitting very close to each other on the chintz-covered sofa and that they seemed to pay a huge amount of attention to anything the other said.

With a start Evie saw suddenly that there might just be some sort of romantic attachment blossoming between Mr Smith and Mrs Bowes. Certainly Mrs Bowes seemed to be paying a lot more attention to what the dapper PG was saying, and she was clearly drawing much more comfort from his words than Evie would have expected the ordinarily stand-offish headmistress to do from anything said by a man who had only recently moved into the village, and who Mrs Bowes had once questioned as to whether his intentions were honourable or not.

Evie didn't feel like dwelling longer on what might or might not be going on between the older pair.

Privately she felt much more cautious about Timmy's prospects, although she wasn't about to voice these opinions. Timmy had been alive when the telegram had been sent, yes, but she was all too aware that a lot could change in an instant when anyone is badly hurt, and so Evie thought it might not be wise to read too much into the two short lines of the telegram.

For the second day running Evie witnessed the dawn chorus. What a lot has happened in these last twenty-four hours, she said to herself, with so much of it a total shock.

An hour or so later there was a timid tap at the front door, and Mr Smith went to usher in Julia, who was worried about Evie.

'Evie, sweet, I think you need to come back to Pemberley now, and get some rest,' said Julia in a low voice. 'You'll have all those kiddies tomorrow keen to tell you about their performance at the Revels, while I'm sure you'll want to go to church later this morning, and it's not going to help Timmy one iota if you make yourself ill.'

Mr Smith nodded in agreement, and Mrs Bowes told Evie that Julia was right, and it was time for Evie to go home in order that she might catch up on an hour or two of sleep.

'Thank you for coming, Evie, and for staying with me for such a long time,' said Mrs Bowes. 'Timmy has made an excellent choice in you as his wife, I see now, and *when* he is back with us all in Lymbridge, I'm sure that thoughts of his forthcoming marriage to you will really help him make a speedy recovery.'

Oh dear. These weren't words to gladden Evie's heart. But she knew that they were said with good intentions, and so she replied, 'I'm going to go home and try to nap for a little, and then at church later I'm going to pray with all my might for Timmy. I'm sure that wherever he is, the knowledge of your love for him is going to add to his strength.'

Mrs Bowes and Mr Smith accompanied the Yeo sisters to the door, and with a final hug for Timmy's mother from Evie, she and Julia set off arm in arm towards Pemberley.

There was a silence, and then Julia said, 'I know this won't be what you're thinking about just now, but I couldn't help noticing that your Mrs Bowes and our Mr Smith seem to be very, er, united... Do you think there's something going on between them? I noticed there was never any suggestion that he was going to come back to Pemberley with us.'

'Yes, I think you're spot on. I'd never noticed anything

previously between them either, not that I'd been looking, of course, but they definitely do seem rather fond of one another. I'm sure it's all very proper and decorous, but I suspect that cupid might have shot an arrow or two in their direction,' agreed Evie.

'Ho hum,' said Julia. 'I'd love to fall in love by the time I'm twenty, but all I can see is that I'm heading to be a dried-up prune of a spinster. And yet Mrs Bowes, who's not Hollywood glamorous in any way, nor the epitome of charm or the type of woman who courts male admiration, looks like she might be lining up husband number *two*, and a husband who's most debonair and distinguished-looking to boot. Honestly, life can be so unfair sometimes.'

'Don't worry, dear, there will be a man for you at some time, I'm sure. Probably the sort who'll be impressed at the speed you can now cycle up those dratted hills on your postal rounds.'

'Hrrumph. The real danger is that all those hills will do is show up my prospective Romeo as someone who can't cycle up them himself. And that my thighs will by then be too muscly and huge to fit into my trousers.'

'It's almost as bad for me, Julia – I'm now going to have to find a way to stop my prospective mother-in-law, and my headmistress too let's not forget, hugging the breath out of me. Twice tonight is quite enough, and now those embraces must end,' said Evie. 'And whatever the state of Timmy's health is, as far as I am concerned I can only foresee a potential minefield of social etiquette faux pas, and especially so when Mrs Bowes gets wind of Tricia Dolby and Timmy's indiscretion, and finds out that I am party to this knowledge.'

Chapter Seventeen

At school on the Monday, Evie found to her relief that the children were all very well behaved, indeed almost spookily so. Lymbridge was such a small village that the news of Timmy's injuries must have spread like wildfire, and so Evie assumed that parents had urged their offspring to make sure they weren't naughty and that they must do everything that Evie asked, the very moment she did so.

Evie didn't have any heart for teaching that day but, she told herself, it was nearly the end of term now, and so it probably wouldn't matter much for this final week and a half if the children ran riot just a little. In some ways the time since Dave Symons had broken to her the news of Timmy's infidelities had flown and in other ways it had sluggishly plodded by. But it would be ten weeks ago now, as school had started on the Monday after his revelation. The news about Timmy's injuries seemed to have virtually halted time, and Evie could never remember feeling so out of sorts or so exhausted.

And so she decided the infants could help Mr Cawes with a bit of vegetable plot weeding. Mr Cawes was much less enthusiastic at this prospect than Evie, but he acquiesced with a glum shake of his head and a toothless chomp on his ancient, unlit pipe that more often than not was poking out of his mouth, and just two grimaces and 'it's a bad lot, a bad lot.'

And once the infants had done an hour or two of that, then they could do yet another nature table, Evie thought.

Bobby Ayres particularly enjoyed the nature table as he was able to find some of the piglet's droppings close to the Nissen hut that had presumably been deposited as the piglet had scurried by on his bid for freedom. Bobby carried the droppings carefully to the school steps where Evie was encouraging each child to bring back and arrange their finds, and with his familiar 'Miss, Miss', he delighted in showing her his precious discovery.

The sight of the nuggets of piglet dung then made Bobby's pal Simon Bridge want to see what similar 'gifts' donkey Susie and the ferrets might have left.

Evie knew that luckily Mr Cawes had assiduously scattered Susie's dung on to the vegetable plots and dug it in, as horse or donkey dung was an excellent fertiliser. And as she herself had made sure that Frank and Joseph had done a thorough job of sweeping up after the ferrets, there wasn't much dropping danger from that quarter either, and so she said that Simon could look for donkey and ferret dung if he wanted. Meanwhile Bobby could now go and wash his hands – 'use some soap, Bobby, not too much, but definitely use some!' – before he did anything else.

Through the open window of the juniors' classroom, Evie could hear pupils reading painstakingly and in slightly bored voices out loud from various books, and then saying their tables out loud. She supposed that Mrs Bowes felt as washed out as she did, and so for once was allowing the children to do most of the work.

At Pemberley that evening, Pattie, Linda and Sukie came by to see Evie. To be honest, Evie could have done without it, as she felt bone-weary and exhausted (much more tired actually than she had felt the day before). But she knew her friends were just trying to be kind and to do the right thing by her, and so she tried to put a brave face on her lack of enthusiasm.

Sukie, whom Evie have been slightly nervous about seeing in

case she made mention of the time right before the ferret-legging that she had been so keen on Saturday afternoon to buttonhole Evie about, behaved impeccably, which was a tremendous relief.

It actually turned out to be a very pleasant hour, and Evie, who knew this anyway, was reminded all over again how lucky she was to have sisters like Julia and Pattie, and friends such as Linda and Sukie.

Sukie was now in her second week of her new post at the rehabilitation hospital, explaining, 'We won't have patients for a couple of weeks, and the doctors and nurses haven't arrived yet. We're setting up the administration systems and making sure we know what we are doing, and we're overseeing the supplies coming in. And there's quite a lot of workmen around, putting in things like extra plumbing, and doing a bit of painting so that everything can be as hygienic as possible. And they are making an airstrip with a short runway nearby so that smallish planes can bring some of the patients to us.'

'And while you wait for the entrants to the Sukie-Snags-a-Doctor competition, are there any handsome workmen there for you to keep your hand in with?' asked Pattie.

'As if! Not only are we rationed for food and clothes, but also for good-looking men, I fear.'

The arrival of Rev. Painter drew the visit to an early close, which was a good thing as both Pattie (who was finding that her hard physical work on the land, which she wasn't used to yet, was using nearly all her energy) and Julia (who'd had to do a double round today as they were managing on less staff as people were signing up or moving to other sorts of valuable war work, and so there was now a rota of double-shifts) were clearly worn out.

Rev. Painter's visit was a courtesy call to Evie. After requesting that she not get up from her chair as he was only going to stop by for a minute, he told Evie he had said special prayers for Timmy at both church services the day before, and he hoped those prayers had been of comfort to Mrs Bowes and Evie.

Evie had had a few words with him right after the service the previous morning, although now she couldn't really remember what they had said to one another; and so now she thanked him for the prayers, in case she'd not done so properly the day before.

He also wanted to thank Evie for the tremendous success she had made of the Revels, and to add that he was going to go on praying daily for Timmy.

Evie felt comforted, but all the same she wished they had some concrete news about Timmy.

Mr Smith was doing what he could – he seemed to have some influence in the corridors of power at Whitehall – but there was no further information forthcoming yet.

Although everybody was being so kind, Evie felt frustrated and anxious.

Just before bed, as she was making herself a final warm drink in the kitchen which she thought might help her drop off (Sunday night had been a time of tossing and turning too, and Evie now felt extremely sleep deprived and in a strange state that felt almost beyond sleep), she couldn't help but flinch when Peter walked into the room unexpectedly.

She looked at him, and felt her skin go goosepimply. Obviously not expecting to see her standing there either, Peter looked equally wrong-footed. Indeed he looked quite aghast.

With a deep breath, audible to Evie from the far side of the large kitchen, Peter then mustered his reserves, and crossed the room to stand a polite distance of three or four feet in front of her.

'I am so sorry to hear about your fiancé,' he said in a clipped voice. 'It is terrible news, but we must all hope for a positive outcome. You must feel very worried.'

Peter's stutter had returned. Evie realised she'd not heard it for a while.

Their easy way with each other of just a couple of days previously had quite disappeared. This was difficult and uncomfortable.

Evie felt awash with guilt that she had never talked with Peter about her engagement to Timmy. She should have made her association with Timmy clear weeks ago.

She presumed that her thoughts to do with her errant fiancé had been so conflicting since she had been at Pemberley that while she hadn't intended initially to be evasive, she hadn't really wanted to talk about Timmy much either, as in all conscience she hadn't been able to feel relaxed enough to chat away about a fiancé who, rather than putting her first, had almost definitely made another woman pregnant.

And then as she had got to know Peter, increasingly it had never seemed quite the right time to bring up her association with Timmy. Evie wasn't proud about any of this.

Had Peter known all along about Timmy? It was reasonably possible that he had, as Pemberley residents Mrs Worth, Tina and Sarah, and of course Julia too, were all aware that she was engaged to be married. And, Evie assumed, Mr Smith would know too, bearing in mind how much time he and Mrs Bowes had spent together.

But it was just as possible Peter hadn't known of Timmy's existence. He didn't come from the area, and by the time he moved into Pemberley Timmy had already left Lymbridge. And the engagement ring, still on its chain around Evie's neck, was rarely, if ever, in public view.

If Peter had been ignorant of the engagement, then Mr Worth's hastily whispered command that he needed to dash to The Haywain to get some spirits for Evie to drink on the Saturday evening as she was in shock following the news of the grave condition of her fiancé must have come as a terrible surprise.

Peter was such a proper sort of chap that Evie decided that he almost certainly hadn't known about Timmy; she couldn't imagine him making so bold as to kiss her if he had, she was sure. She wasn't about to kid herself that she was so devastatingly pretty that he would have kissed her regardless.

Either way, Evie felt incredibly bad about the situation. And Peter's downcast expression suggested he didn't feel too thrilled either.

Briefly Evie consoled herself with the thought that there hadn't really been an indication of any frisson between her and Peter until the day of the Revels, to Evie or anyone else around her.

Well, that was what she hoped. But she remembered Julia joking with her about her bossiness and Peter's willingness to pander to her every whim, and she wasn't so sure that Julia hadn't been aware of something going on between them that Evie herself at that time insisted on remaining oblivious to.

What a muddle.

As Peter stood before her now, looking stiff and hurt and gawky, but nevertheless determined to behave properly, Evie was thoroughly miserable.

She felt she needed to be strong and true to Timmy, so that she would have no worry from now on that any bad behaviour on her part would contribute further to his illness or, a thought too horrible to contemplate, his demise. In the intellectual sense, Evie knew these feelings were mistaken and downright silly, not to say self-indulgent, as nothing she did or didn't do in this respect would have any impact on whether Timmy lived or died.

But, mistaken or not in her peculiar logic at this point in time, she felt that even from afar her behaviour might somehow have an influence on the eventual outcome of Timmy's wellbeing, and so she absolutely must behave correctly from now on.

This was all very well, but what really was causing pain to Evie at this minute was how strongly she longed to go to Peter and have him take her in his arms, and to feel his lips once more on hers.

Peter's face was doleful and his demeanour taut, Evie saw, and for an instant she comforted herself with the possibility that he might be thinking similar thoughts to her.

Perhaps if he moved towards her, she could allow herself a moment of pleasure.

But Peter was a complete gentleman. Evie saw that he would never breech the invisible fence that the now openly acknowledged existence of Evie's engagement had constructed around her with such impenetrable strength.

She wanted to weep hot tears of temper and exasperation in frustration.

Unable to trust herself to speak, instead she had to settle for watching Peter turn and disconsolately leave the kitchen, with her silence and guilty half-smile the best she could summon up.

They felt like strangers to one another. What a desperate feeling.

Chapter Eighteen

The next couple of days passed in something like a hazy blur as far as Evie was concerned.

She'd get up, toy with her breakfast, go to school where she would just about manage to keep an eye on the infants to make sure that they weren't hurting themselves or others, but not really do any teaching as such, as she found it easier to read them stories or allow them to run around and let off steam outside. Then she'd go back to Pemberley, push a little supper around her plate (sometimes on a tray in her room so she didn't have to see anyone), and retire early to bed. She was now sleeping very heavily each night, in a deep and dreamless sleep, but would wake each morning groggy and with a headache.

Mrs Bowes and Evie were gentle with each other – mercifully the hugging had stopped – but they hardly talked, as they'd said everything about Timmy and his plight that there was to say, and they couldn't really face talking about anything else. When they greeted each other in the mornings, they would each give the other an enquiring glance to see if there was any further news, and then they would each give an almost imperceptible shake of their heads before going about their business.

No new is good news, was what they might have said, but somehow it didn't really feel like that.

If Evie were honest, and she was trying to be honest with herself these days, she spent just as much time thinking about herself and Peter as she did about poor Timmy lying somewhere in a hospital bed. There was no thinking about herself and Timmy, Evie realised after a day or two.

Meanwhile Peter appeared hardly ever to be at home at Pemberley, and Evie was determined to keep a low profile, as the sympathetic looks from her other companions in the house were hard to bear, and so she'd not seen Peter since that night in the kitchen. She imagined all sorts of scenarios where she could go and find him to speak to, but the reality was that she knew she wasn't going to relent and give in to this impulse.

Mrs Worth was treating Evie with a generous amount of unasked for kindness, even checking with Evie if it was still all right if the sewing circle went ahead at Pemberley as usual. Evie said yes, of course, although she wasn't sure if she could face it herself, at least for the next few days. Mrs Worth agreed that this was perfectly understandable, and that she personally would make sure that the sewing circle kept their voices down and that Evie would hardly know they were there.

Later Evie mentioned to Julia about how considerate Mrs Worth was being. 'Honestly, I've always found her to be a nice woman in general, but these past few days she's been absolutely wonderful, and I feel she's gone quite out of her way and far beyond what she's needed to do in trying to make me feel better.'

Julia replied that while Mr Worth had been sorting out something in the garden and Evie had tried to nap on the Sunday morning before church, Julia and Mrs Worth had together cleared away the PGs' breakfast things, and Mrs Worth had confided that a similar thing had happened to her in the Great War. Her fiancé at the time had been wounded at Passchendaele, but had sadly later died of his injuries. Mrs Worth had been heartbroken, and it wasn't until ten years later that she had married Mr Worth, who'd been her next-door neighbour in Southampton and who had devoted many years in waiting for her to feel less grief-stricken. They'd stayed in Southampton for quite a few years, but had moved to Devon and bought

Pemberley five or so years ago when Mr Worth had been offered a partnership in a larger firm of solicitors based in Plymouth.

'I think you and Timmy, and the news of his injury, has brought a lot of those old feelings flooding back to Mrs Worth,' said Julia. 'This time we are going through right now seems so awful to you and me, but of course we forget that people of our parents' and Mrs Worth's generation have already been through it once before and it really wasn't that long ago. The Great War might seem like history to us, but talking to Mrs Worth last Sunday, it was as if it was just yesterday for her.'

'I guess the same must be true for Mrs Bowes. Timmy told me his father had a good war generally, but that he was invalided home just before the end, as he'd been hurt, although not in any life-threatening way,' said Evie in a sympathetic voice. 'He was expecting to return to France once he'd recovered, but it never came to that. Perhaps Mrs Bowes feels her luck was used up first time around, and that it might not be such a good outcome for their son when we finally get proper news.'

'Don't say that, dear. Until you know otherwise, you must think positively, for everyone's sake,' said Julia.

I am trying, thought Evie, I am trying. I just wish that Timmy and I had never got engaged. He didn't really want to, I daresay. And now, while I hope he manages to get better and be the old Timmy once again, I can't help wishing I was free of any emotional responsibilities, other than that of being a good friend to him. Why, oh why, did I rush things so much and go as far as getting engaged to him? Mother could see it, I know, and I'm cross I didn't listen to her as she would only ever have my best interests at heart. But it didn't feel like that to me. It's almost a case of 'marry in haste and repent at leisure'. And now, besides hurting myself, I've hurt Peter too when he absolutely didn't deserve it. What am I going to do?

Life went on though, and Evie was persuaded to meet up with friends and family on the Wednesday evening at Bluebells, although only on the proviso that herself and Timmy weren't talked about, and that everyone tried to behave as they would have done before the blasted telegram arrived.

So both Linda and Pattie reported encouraging signs in their own love lives, and Evie tried to be happy for them.

Apparently Sam Torrence had called for Linda's help over a bad case of cracked heels on the hind legs of a young colt he was hoping to break for harness in a year or two, and Linda had been happy to take him some sore-udder cream that she swore was a miracle worker in all sorts of animal skin conditions despite being manufactured with cows in mind. 'And it works on humans too; now I've found how brilliant it is, I use it as hand cream every evening and my hands are much softer and less battered than they were,' Linda said to a couple of raised eyebrows belonging to her friends seated around the kitchen table.

Anyway, while they were peering at each other around the nether regions of the colt, apparently Sam had asked Linda if she wanted to come in for a cup of tea afterwards.

'Blimey,' said Linda, 'I couldn't help but think that this was Sam virtually asking me to marry him. You can guess that he was very awkward once I'd stepped inside, and meanwhile his mother had taken herself off upstairs so that we could have the kitchen to ourselves – I expect she had to take a lie-down at the shock of Sam actually plucking up the nerve to ask a young woman into the farmhouse – but once I got Sam talking about foot ailments the various animals had had on the farm, he was fine.

'It was a bit sticky when I had to go as he kept standing in front of me and I didn't know what he wanted me to do. Eventually he turned around and just pushed my bicycle to the gate. And then he said he hoped I'd be back the next day to check on the sore heels, which I did today; and yep, the udder cream is working. This morning it only took him about five minutes of dithering about and doing his odd foot-to-foot shuffle before he could ask me if I wanted to go to the market at Oldwell Abbott with him on Friday to help him choose a couple of piglets. Now

I know he doesn't need any piglets as that black old sow of his had fourteen not so long ago, so if that doesn't amount to a proper date, I don't know what does!'

'Well, ladies, now it's progressed a-speed to the piglet stage, I think it's quite clear that we ought to be brushing our wedding hats off,' said Sukie wryly.

At the unexpected mention of the word 'piglet' Evie felt as if the air had been sucked from her lungs. It was still less than a week since the lively piglet with the sweet little coil of hair between his ears at the Revels had led to the opportunity for Peter to kiss her.

For just the merest instant she allowed the heady memory of the intoxication of Peter's gossamer-light kisses to wash over her body, before she brought herself back to the here and now, and the slightly quizzical expression on Sukie's face as she peered at Evie.

Luckily Pattie came to Evie's rescue as she reported a dalliance with a young barman at The Haywain, whom she had met at the Revels in the various moments she'd not been larking about with the Amazing Adamstrel. 'He's called John and is apparently a distant cousin of Barkeep Joss, and he got a head injury in the blitz and so he can't sign up now as he was having fits right after the injury. Still, the war effort's loss is my gain – and I can certainly vouch that he's pretty—'

'Pattie!' rebuked Susan sharply, who then went on with raised eyebrows and a significant expression on her face that left no doubt as to her meaning, 'We do not need any lurid details, thank you, and especially so in front of Marie and Catherine to whom you must always be a good example. And your father and I are trusting you to be a good girl, always remember.'

Unchastened in the slightest, Pattie smiled gaily at her mother. 'I'm only teasing; John has been a perfect gentleman so far. Unfortunately!'

Susan couldn't help but smile at Pattie's cheekiness, although she managed to combine this with an admonishing shake of her head.

Evie wasn't particularly worried about Pattie's honour, at least with Barkeep Joss's relative. Pattie loved men but, up until now at least, she had been content to settle for kisses and little more; she was very aware of how easy it was to get a bad reputation in a small country area, and so she took great care not to step too far out of line as she didn't want to take herself out of the pool of marriageable girls.

And Barkeep Joss – everybody always added Barkeep before his Christian name, so that now across all of Lymbridge, Barkeep Joss *was* his Christian name – would keep a close eye on any shenanigans too. He wouldn't want anyone he was responsible for bringing into the area to cause problems or, just as worryingly as far as Barkeep Joss would be concerned, any potential loss of custom to his beloved public house. If a lass's family and friends decided to boycott his establishment because a relation of his caused ripples of discontent by acting in an improper manner with any local young lady, then Barkeep Joss would have words to say on the matter. Money was always hard to come by in a rural area, and so business concerns would override any chance of impropriety from that quarter, Evie was certain.

Later, Susan was putting Marie and Catherine to bed, and Robert was still working on the vegetable plots with Frank and Joseph, while Pattie was in her bedroom with Julia and Linda, showing them her new shoes with green suede uppers and a wooden sole. And it was now that Sukie finally cornered Evie.

'Right,' said Sukie in a tone that made Evie quail, 'I want to know what went on down at the Nissen hut on Saturday that made Peter look as if he'd won a million pounds and you look very shame-faced indeed. I've been very patient and understanding that everyone has been distracted by the news about Timmy, but it's now time for you to fess up, Evie-Rose.'

Evie sighed inwardly and her shoulders dropped. Then she decided to come clean with her old friend. What was the point of not being honest? She needed someone to lean on and she trusted Sukie. She bent forward in her chair towards her friend, and Sukie pulled her own chair forward so that her ear was only a couple of inches from Evie's mouth.

'Sukes, you absolutely cannot tell a soul, and especially not Julia as that would put her in an awkward situation, seeing as we all live together. And you cannot say anything to Pattie, as she'll tell Julia. And you can't say anything to Linda either, as she'll tell Pattie, who will tell—'

'Julia!' hissed Sukie quietly but with tremendous meaning. 'For goodness' sake, get on with it, Evie-Rose, before someone comes in.'

'Right. So, not a word?' whispered Evie, eliciting a dramatic roll of the eyes from her friend, who made an impatient chivvying movement with her hand.

Evie shuffled her chair closer to Sukie, and then whispered right into her ear, 'We kissed!'

'You kissed!' squeaked Sukie, although much more loudly.

'Ssssh, or I'll stop,' breathed Evie with a threatening look, allowing a pause to grow between them. 'Peter and I had to hare down the field to get the guess-the-weight piglet after he'd escaped from his pen when all the parents were clapping at my infants – weren't they wonderful, by the way? – and the noise scared him. The naughty little fellow went to ground in a hollow under the back of the Nissen hut, and Peter had to lie down on the ground to pull him out. Then I helped calm him down, which meant our hands were accidentally touching each other's, after which I had to sit on the box to stop the little chap getting out again. And Peter was kneeling at my feet and we were laughing at each other, and it was then that he kissed me—'

'I assume the little chap is the piglet and not Peter. What is it with my pals and farm animals and romance? First Linda, and now you,' Sukie wondered innocently enough although she couldn't disguise the twinkle in her eye.

'Okay, okay, you laugh at our country ways and all that,' replied Evie. 'You'll be smiling on the other side of your face when your doctor proposes to you down at the hospital's chicken run over a plump Buff Orpington and a clutch of eggs; you wait and see if I'm not right!'

'Just go on...'

'Well, the moment Peter kissed me, my whole world changed. It sounds so daft and sentimental and like some of the trash reading that Pattie is so fond of. But it was true – his lips were so soft but so *right*, if you know what I mean... It was simply the best thing that I've ever experienced,' said Evie with a dreamy look.

'Then we carried the piglet in his box into the Nissen hut so he'd have a chance to settle down again. And it was a bit smelly and dim in there, but after we'd weighted down the lid of the box, Peter stood beside me and stroked my face, and he kissed me again. It doesn't sound like anything much now, I know, and it only took a matter of seconds, but honestly it was the most romantic experience, even though there was a slight piglety smell on his fingers as he touched my cheek. I practically fell to the ground at his feet in a big ungainly heap. He left before I could stroke his face back. And then I stood there for ages, completely beside myself. I felt as if I'd fall over if I tried to walk too soon. And Timmy never made me feel like that in the slightest.'

'You sly fox, Evie-Rose. I knew it!'

'And I saw you, and then it was the damn ferrets, and then I had to keep Frank and Joseph busy as that pest Vince Smith told me, or as good as, that they were eyeing up handbags to steal from. And Peter and I walked back to Pemberley – and do you know, as we headed home it was better us not saying anything about what had happened when we were with the piglet, as us knowing what had happened but choosing not to mention it made everything the more secret and special somehow. And then I can't have been home ten minutes when Mr Smith told me about the telegram and Timmy,' said Evie.

'You poor love. From top of the world to down in the dumps in a few seconds. What a shame,' said Sukie.

'And aside from the fact I feel guilty about quite forgetting my engagement and allowing Peter to kiss me, and I feel sick with dread that poor Timmy may be lying somewhere quite dead right now, I also feel guilty that everybody, and Mrs Worth and Mrs Bowes especially, are being so nice to me, which I really don't deserve,' Evie went on. 'On top of all of this, I know I've hurt Peter dreadfully. It's all changed between us now, and at this minute he can hardly even bear to be in the same house as me. Perhaps he knew about Timmy and me before, and perhaps he didn't, but at any rate my heart feels broken in two.

'When Tricia Dolby came to light I felt humiliated and made to look stupid because of Timmy's treatment of me. I took that feeling at the time for one of heartbreak, but really I see now that that feeling was just a silly, young girl's humiliation at being shown up, and not really a whole lot more. Now I have a worry about Timmy that doesn't relent, plus my heart really *is* broken in two – Peter is the man I want and the man I think I could love; and although I think he liked me for a while, now I'm the person he hates.'

Evie had no sooner got the last word out, than Susan bustled back into the kitchen, and Evie and Sukie could hear the sounds of Julia, Pattie and Linda pounding down the stairs. The moment Susan was distracted by filling the kettle for another pot of tea, Sukie gave Evie a commiserating look and a squeeze of support to her knee.

Evie felt very low and insignificant in the big scheme of things, and the happy voices of her sisters and friends, who were now obviously forgetting their attempts of a few days ago of treating her with kid gloves, was a relief but somehow also reminded Evie of how very far she had fallen.

Chapter Nineteen

All continued in much the same way until Friday. There was no news of Timmy, and no sign of Peter. Evie thought it was almost as if she were caught in limbo, destined to live the same sort of 'nothing' day again and again.

And then three things happened almost all at once.

The first began on the last Friday of the summer term. During the afternoon there were no lessons as Evie and Mrs Bowes had decided that they should give the children an end-of-year tea party, with lots of running-about games, to celebrate the looming end of term.

The pupils' last day at school would be the following Tuesday, although Mrs Bowes and Evie would finish their term on the Wednesday evening as they would spend their final day making sure their record-keeping was up to date, ordering supplies for the next school year and so forth. Mrs Bowes explained to Evie that it didn't really work having an end-of-year party on the last day of term, and on the Monday of the final week it wouldn't work either as that was the best time for the teachers to try and prepare the children for the hard work they'd be expected to put in during the autumn term, and so she didn't want the pupils to be distracted from these more sombre, responsible thoughts. On the last day of term itself the pupils wouldn't be interested in a party as they would want to get home to enjoy the start of the long summer holidays.

Evie wasn't sure she quite agreed with all that Mrs Bowes was claiming, but she didn't have the energy to put up any resistance.

Mrs Bowes and Evie tried hard on the Friday to give the children a nice time. And although the children didn't seem to notice as they charged noisily about the playground in some hastily arranged games and competitions, and then wolfed down slices of bread and jam and some homemade fruit cordial, in reality both of their teachers were subdued.

Luckily, the previous week, Evie had planned and written out clues for a treasure hunt – well, two sets of clues actually, simple clues for her infants of pictures on cards for what they needed to look for, and a more challenging set for the older children – and so the treasure hunts took up a welcome chunk of time during which neither she nor Mrs Bowes had to expend too much effort, once Evie had explained clearly to the pupils how a treasure hunt worked.

The children seemed to be in good spirits, and they were very well behaved generally, but it was with a distinct sigh of relief that Evie closed the school gates on the last one as they all left for home and their longed-for weekends.

Evie headed back inside the school, where she and Mrs Bowes did a stock-take of supplies, and then checked the condition of the buildings and the grounds, and each table and chair, in order to draw up a To-Do list of odd jobs for Mr Cawes over the holidays.

As they worked companionably side by side, Mrs Bowes said Mr Smith, who had been in London since the beginning of the week, had been applying pressure on the authorities in order to get some news of Timmy and his condition, and so she was hopeful they would hear something more soon.

Evie said she hoped so too, and that she thought Mrs Bowes was doing a wonderful job of putting a brave face on things and going about her business almost as usual. Mrs Bowes thanked Evie for her thoughtful words, and then she said that she felt Evie was showing an enviably stiff upper-lip too.

As an overwrought and worn-out Evie meandered home to

Pemberley, she thought: if only you knew the truth of the whole situation, Mrs Bowes, you wouldn't feel so charitable either to me or to your dear Timmy.

Before Evie had made it all the way up the drive to Pemberley, the second thing happened. She was taken aback to see Julia running out of the front door and towards her, waving something papery furiously in her hand, while screeching, 'Evie, Evie, look at this!' Julia must have been watching out of the window for her return.

Evie's heart plummeted as she didn't think she could bear any more bad news just at the moment.

But then she realised that Julia was charging towards her with a delighted expression on her face, and that Pattie, who had Friday afternoons off as the rest of her workweek covered such lengthy hours, was now also dashing towards her, looking equally as pleased as punch.

Apparently too excited to speak, Julia grabbed Evie's hand, and propelled her back to the house and straight into the kitchen, where Mrs Worth was also beaming broadly. Pattie seemed not to be able to stop laughing.

Evie felt too depressed and weary to be excited by any of this – it seemed almost to be playing out in front of her as if she wasn't quite there. Her dream-like state only intensified when she saw that what Julia had been waving around so flamboyantly were two official-looking pamphlets.

On closer inspection Evie saw they had been issued by the British Board of Trade and featured a rather scary-looking puppet-like housewife called – what?! Yes. Yes, truly! – Mrs SEW-and-SEW. And this pamphlet puppet Mrs SEW-and-SEW was bossily sharing tips and instructions on how to mend clothes, just as their own irascible Mrs Sew-and-Sew had done to the ladies of the Lymbridge sewing circle.

There was a red and cream leaflet, complete with illustrations and diagrams, called 'How to Patch a Shirt', and a purple and cream one called 'Deft Darns', and this one covered a host of darning dilemmas, from darning holes in linen to lock-nit seams or a slit in fabric.

Puzzled, Evie could only stare at the leaflets with incomprehension, and then she looked across at her still beaming sisters and Mrs Worth.

'My goodness, I don't know what to say. Where on earth have these come from?' she murmured after a while. 'How odd that someone else also would have the idea for a Mrs Sew-and-Sew. And how strange she is so like our Mrs Sew-and-Sew.' Her voice trailed off rather as she gazed once more at the leaflets.

Julia was looking at her sister intently to gauge her reaction.

'Oh. It's nothing to do with Evie then, obviously,' Julia declared rather abruptly.

'We don't know what has happened!' Pattie cried. 'Isn't it a mystery, Evie? We were all convinced it was something to do with you. We can't think who it can be otherwise. And we can't imagine how this Mrs SEW-and-SEW speaks just like our Mrs Sew-and-Sew. But these leaflets are real indeed – Mrs Worth checked!'

Mrs Worth explained that in the morning's post there had been an envelope addressed to her, and inside it were the two pamphlets, but that there was no accompanying letter, note or card. At first she thought it was some sort of peculiar hoax, or a jape that she hadn't been able to see the point of. But the more Mrs Worth looked at the leaflets, the more she could see they'd been professionally produced. And, she noticed, the envelope had a London postmark, which was all the more perplexing as how could someone so far away have caught wind of Mrs Sew-and-Sew?

Mrs Worth had had to wait for Julia to get home to see if she could shed any light on the matter, and then Julia had run down to get Pattie when she thought her sister would have finished work. But neither of them had been any wiser as to what had gone on than Mrs Worth had been.

The long and short of it was that Mrs Worth then plucked up the courage to telephone the Board of Trade, with herself and Julia and Pattie squeezed around the small semi-circular table in the black-and-white tiled hall on which Pemberley's old-fashioned phone grandly sat, the sisters hoping to listen in to the discussion their landlady was poised to have.

Eventually Mrs Worth had got put through to what she thought was probably some sort of government public information department, and the nasal upper-class voice at the end of the phone soon established beyond any doubt that the leaflets were real.

In fact they were going to be part of a London-wide push to encourage all women across the capital to make do and mend, and there was even talk of having Mrs SEW-and-SEW as a regular cartoon strip in the national press, sharing her tips on how to breathe new life into old clothes. Mrs SEW-and-SEW looked like she was about to become very famous indeed.

And when Mrs Worth, quite overcome to discover the veracity of what she was holding in her hand, gave a garbled account to the upper-class voice of how their own Pemberley Mrs Sew-and-Sew came to be invented by Julia and Pattie *at her very dining table* to make the other members of the sewing circle laugh, and that she said exactly the same things in just the same touchy manner, the British Board of Trade official at the other end of the line asked for Mrs Worth's telephone number.

He said that he needed to make some enquiries to find out how the Board of Trade had come to produce the Mrs SEW-and-SEW leaflets. And if there was any link to be found, it could well be that he would send down to Pemberley a government press officer to collect more information, and to speak to Julia and Pattie, in order that a story on what had happened could be fed through to the national newspapers. The national press were apparently very keen to find some 'home-grown good-news stories', in order to offer a little welcome light relief when there was so much depressing news from elsewhere to read about.

Even Evie, in her dejected state, couldn't help but perk up at this peculiar turn of events, although not nearly to the extent of Julia and Pattie, who were by now jigging about, once again almost speechless with excitement. After all, Mrs Sew-and-Sew had been their creation.

It wasn't clear what had gone on, or why precisely, but it did seem that Lymbridge sewing circle might just have gone out of its way to help the war effort.

It had all been quite unintentional but, all the same, what a lark if there was indeed a link between the two domineering know-it-alls with a yen for sewing.

No sooner had the furore about the pamphlets subsided a little – although Evie knew this was only likely to be a short period of grace as once Tina and Sarah returned to Pemberley, which would be in an hour or so, Mrs Worth, along with Pattie and Julia, would become excited all over again as they recounted the story – than there was less welcome news for Evie. This third thing came just as she got the kitchen to herself for a welcome quiet minute or two.

Robert arrived with a gloomy face with the news that there had been another theft, and he wanted to ask Evie's advice as to whether it was now that he should go and have a word with Mrs Bowes.

This time the theft had taken place at the village shop, where Susan worked. She was only at the shop until two o'clock each afternoon though, and so she'd not been there that afternoon after school.

But within the last hour the shop's owner, Mrs Coyne, had been to Bluebells in order to speak with Susan. The shopkeeper said in her broad Dartmoor brogue that a group of boys from Lymbridge juniors had been to the shop after school, and when they had gone Mrs Coyne discovered that all the liquorice bootlaces had disappeared too.

Frank and Joseph had been among those juniors who were in the shop.

Food thefts were taken very seriously by everyone these days, and so the police were being called in, Mrs Coyne had added.

Evie and her father agreed it was a terrible state of affairs.

It was still hard to believe that Frank and Joe, who were such lovely boys at home and who had become so very much part of the Yeo family, could be so light-fingered.

But the evidence against them seemed, most definitely, to be steadily mounting up. They had had the opportunity to do all the thefts, and Evie couldn't help but be reminded of young Vince Short's snide allegations as to Frank and Joseph eying up handbags at the Revels.

Susan was beside herself, Robert went on, as she felt somehow implicated in what was going on as she was directly connected now to two of the thefts. And she believed that she and Robert must be letting the boys down in some way if they were stealing, as perhaps they weren't being clear enough in explaining right from wrong. Neither she nor Robert could work out the best way of handling such a transgression as they'd never had any trouble like that with their own children.

Evie felt desperately sorry for all concerned, and she said she would mention the theft, and the possibility of Frank and Joseph's culpability, to Mrs Bowes as she would almost definitely be seeing her the following morning as a courtesy call to find out if there was any news on Timmy's condition.

'Beggars belief,' concluded Robert in a melancholy manner, 'especially as Frank doesn't like liquorice, and Joe's not knocked out by it either.'

Robert had been gone about five minutes, and Evie was quickly filing a hangnail before going up to change (she didn't want to risk snagging her stockings on a rough nail as she rolled them down her legs) as she planned on doing her week's washing while the clothes line was free. There would be stiff competition for space on the clothes line by the Saturday morning, and on such a pleasantly warm evening with the promise of a night of fine weather ahead, Evie hoped she could steal a march on her fellow PGs and get her clothes nearly bone-dry by the morning.

Mr Smith arrived at Pemberley in his motor car. He clearly had an essential occupation to be given the petrol allowance with which to run a car, and he was hotfooting it back from London, where he had been since the start of the week. Evie was sure that Mrs Bowes must have missed his comforting presence.

Recently Evie had begun to wonder whether Peter might have an important profession too, bearing in mind how unobtrusively efficient and watchful he was, and the way he took care not to draw attention to himself when he wasn't playing the piano, and how he didn't seem to have an obvious reason for not being signed up.

But thoughts of how Peter might spend his days were pushed aside when Mr Smith said to Evie in an urgent voice that he'd just seen the telegram chap on his motorbike, and so he'd asked if it were a telegram for Mrs Bowes. When there had been an answering nod of agreement, Mr Smith had driven straight to Pemberley to collect Evie as he was sure that both she and Mrs Bowes would want to share whatever news the telegram contained.

In Mr Smith's car on the way to Mrs Bowes' house, Evie felt dizzy and nauseous; she'd not had anything to eat since her frugal breakfast many hours earlier and now she was paying the price. But she wanted desperately to find out what the telegram had to say. It had to be about Timmy.

Mrs Bowes opened the door to Evie and Mr Smith before they'd even got through the garden gate. She was crying, the sight of which caused Evie almost to turn tail and flee; she wasn't sure she was strong enough for what might be about to happen.

Mr Smith might have sensed Evie's sudden reluctance, as immediately she felt his comforting hand slip under her elbow. Her spirits felt a little fortified, and together she and the older man entered the house.

Actually the news wasn't as bad as might have at first been feared, although it was undeniably serious. Mrs Bowes was crying as much from relief as she was from grief.

Timmy wasn't dead, although he remained critically ill. He had been wounded in the head and in the back, and he had been in a coma for several days. He had now come out of the coma without medical intervention; this was a good thing, although the medical people hadn't been able to establish (at the time of writing the telegram, at least) if he had sustained lasting brain damage.

His spinal cord was so swollen that it was also impossible for anyone to know with certainty quite the extent of his injuries in that respect. He was mildly sedated, and the medics treating him were trying to stabilise his condition so that, hopefully, his own body could heal itself enough in order that he could be soon repatriated to a hospital in England to recuperate further.

Mr Smith and Evie both read the telegram several times, and then Evie said, 'This isn't the worst news we can hear. There is a glimmer of hope in this telegram. And let's remember that Timmy is young and is in the peak of his physical fitness, and so if any body can heal itself, my money is on Timmy Bowes' body being the one to do this.'

Mr Smith had encouraged Mrs Bowes to take a seat on her chintz sofa, where she'd plonked herself down in an oddly askew manner, and Mr Smith poured her a drink of a lethal-looking colourless spirit from her drinks cabinet – he obviously knew his way around the headmistress's cottage quite well, Evie couldn't help noticing – and then Mr Smith raised an eyebrow in query in Evie's direction to see if she wanted a snifter too. She shook her head as she simply couldn't bear the thought of drinking alcohol in front of Mrs Bowes, and so Mr Smith poured only himself a short measure of the spirit.

Mr Smith then said more or less what Evie had just said, although in different words, and, after a while, Mrs Bowes gathered herself and sat up straight in a manner that was much more familiar to Evie.

Evie stayed for about an hour before she left (there was a hug between her and Mrs Bowes as she said goodbye at the front door), although Evie thought that it would be best if she waited until the next day before she broke the news to Mrs Bowes about the liquorice bootlaces.

On returning to Pemberley Evie crept past the parlour where she could hear the other PGs still chatting about Mrs SEW-and-SEW, and as quietly as a mouse she made her way up to bed. She knew she should eat or drink something, but her stomach clenched uncharitably at the mere thought.

All she wanted was a few hours of oblivion, and to her great relief, she felt herself falling asleep almost the instant her head, shockingly unscarved and with her brunette hair lying in a wild tangle about her face, touched the soft white pillow. It was the first time in almost a week that she had allowed herself to relax properly. It felt wonderful.

Chapter Twenty

The next day, Sukie persuaded Evie to go on a long walk with her. It was a lovely Saturday afternoon, and it was just the two of them, and they took sandwiches and a flask of Camp coffee.

Sukie had had to use all her wiles to get Evie to go, Evie pleading first a headache and then saying she wanted to lie in the orchard at Bluebells (to be out of the way of Peter) where she planned on having a snooze in the fresh air as she still felt very washed out, after which she would start a new book.

Evie had been to see Mrs Bowes first thing that morning, when she had mentioned the bootlaces and the possibility that the thieves were Frank and Joseph. Mrs Bowes had deep shadows under her eyes and looked very drained, and her response to the news was quite subdued, as she merely said, 'I'm surprised, Evie – it seems most out of character for those two.'

Susan backed up Sukie's plan for Evie joining her pal on a moorland walk, saying that Evie looked pale and in need of a good stretch-out that would blow the cobwebs away; then Susan quickly made the sandwiches and the flask of Camp coffee, and so reluctantly Evie heard herself agreeing to go, feeling it was something of a done deal.

As it turned out, the walk was exactly what Evie needed.

She and Sukie chose a relatively easy route across the moors, which would take them quite close to The Grange, the soon-to-be hospital where Sukie was now working; it would be a hilly climb towards the end, but for Dartmoor this qualified as a gentle perambulation. The weather was perfect walking weather as it was sunny but a gentle breeze prevented it feeling too hot. The heather hadn't yet come into flower (on a good year, the moorland undulations coming into autumn could look from a distance as if someone had draped a series of glorious purple blankets across them), but there was plenty of yellow gorse in bloom even though it was still too early for the gorse to have massed abundantly in its full golden-coloured flower.

There seemed to be a lot of Dartmoor ponies around, grazing in small herds of mares that were each carefully watched by an imperious, long-maned stallion as he stood a proud guard against marauding stallions stealing any stray mares to make up their own herds.

A relatively mild winter had led to a profusion of foals this year, although Sukie said that as a small airfield was being prepared close to the hospital she thought it might be that the ponies would soon choose quieter areas of the moorlands to congregate on.

The mares and stallions had shiny hides, having shed their woolly cold-weather coats, and the mares now looked to be quite stout as they had clearly put on the weight they had lost when the poorer winter grass didn't offer up the same amount of nutrition. The long-legged foals looked much more scruffily coated than their parents, and had bushy short tails as well as manes that stuck up in all directions.

'They're so adorable, those foals,' said Evie as she looked at the gangly-legged creatures gambolling around.

They could see the odd scraggy moorland sheep too, and on one sunny strip of sandy pathway, Evie and Sukie, who'd both taken the precaution of wearing their stout walking shoes, saw the distinctive v-shaped pattern on the rear end of an adder snake as it slithered from the patch of dry-earthed path on which it had been sunbathing into the bracken and heather beside the path at the sound of their approaching footsteps.

As they ambled along (Sukie had had to promise to Evie that

their pace would be sedate), Sukie said the hospital opening was being slightly delayed as there had been a bit of a set-to between the authorities and the church in the small village of Plumpton that The Grange and the airfield were close to.

The church in Plumpton had been requested by the military to remove its spire for the duration of the war (saving all the tiles, and the lead and timbers, of course). The spire, which was a tall one for a country church, was deemed by the military to be too close to the airfield and thus a danger to aeroplanes taking off. The church authorities were digging their toes in though, saying the spire wasn't a danger, especially if the aeroplanes took off in the opposite direction, although Evie pointed out that if the direction were switched then surely it just meant that the spire would be a danger for aeroplanes coming in to land.

'Yes, you may well be right on that – I hadn't thought of it, but it does make sense, unless they use the same direction for landing and taking off. Goodness knows how this is all going to turn out. There's a right royal hullaballoo as the villagers are furious, especially as their noses had already been put out of joint by the military lorries going through the village at all hours on the way to take things up to the hospital,' said Sukie.

As they walked, they linked arms, and gradually Evie started to relax. The pleasant companionship, the smell of the gorse and the heather, the heart-warming sun and the breathtaking scenery were a wonderful fillip to the soul, she realised, even a soul as bruised as hers. It wasn't long before she felt able to open up to Sukie about her feelings regarding both Timmy and Peter.

'I see now that I was far too inexperienced when I began seeing Timmy, and I was stupidly idealistic too. I was so flattered he'd noticed a girl like me—'

'That'll be the very charming and extremely lovely Evie Yeo,' interrupted Sukie. Without breaking stride, Evie nudged Sukie in the ribs playfully with her elbow.

'Well, the truth of it was that I felt Timmy to be way out my league. And so when he noticed me I was so taken aback that I think I failed to notice that really we don't have that much in common. Or, even back then, that I perhaps didn't like him very much. I liked the *idea* of him much more than actually him, I fear. You are the only person I could ever say this to, Sukes, and so I'm trusting you to keep my confidence.

'And while Timmy was always just the same, laughing and joking and trying to sneak his fingers inside my blouse, like a silly fool I kept waiting for him to settle down and be a bit *better*, if you know what I mean. And I thought I was doing the right thing by both of us by agreeing when he suggested that we should get engaged. I couldn't imagine that I could ever find anyone better than Timmy, and I suppose that I wanted to be able to boast (even if I was going to boast about it only to myself) that he could have had anyone as his wife, but he had chosen *me*.

'It was only after that terrible evening with Dave Symons – and honestly, what an ugly lump *he* is – and I found out about Tricia and all the others, that I realised what a hole I'd dug myself,' said Evie unhappily.

Sukie quickly mentioned that she'd heard a day or two ago that Dave Symons was apparently now making hay with the friend of Tricia's who had been so rude to Sukie that night in The Wheatsheaf.

There was a pause, and then the friends paused and looked at each other as they shared a grimace and shudder.

Then Sukie asked her friend why she thought Timmy had wanted to get engaged when he clearly adored being a lad about town.

'I think you mean "lad about the village", although poor Timmy would hate to hear me point out the smallness of his ambition. To be honest, I think he wanted to please his mother. Whatever one might think about Mrs Bowes – and I have had a lot to think about in *that* respect – she's not a fool, and therefore she can't have been happy with the way he was carrying on. And so I think to offer her an engagement before he left to fight was, Timmy must have felt, something his mother could take as a sign of him growing up. And I think he liked me enough that he wanted to write to me; or more probably, that he wanted me to write to *him* while he was away fighting,' said Evie.

'Actually I doubt he thought about it all very much at all. Timmy has always been impulsive, I would think, and he has often acted before thinking. And of course there were a lot of people getting engaged suddenly, and so it seemed to Timmy that perhaps I'd pass muster as someone for him. And if I'm honest, I probably got caught up in that tide of feeling of those months when everyone was signing up too, and suddenly getting engaged or even married before they left, and so I must have thought, in a moment of madness, that he'd do for me. It all seems like such a terribly long time ago, although really it's not, and so it's hard for me to remember quite why I was so keen. I just remembered that it seemed at the time absolutely what should happen.'

Evie went on to say how peculiar she felt now when it came to Timmy. She didn't love him any longer, but she was desperately worried about him, and also about what would happen over the next few months.

'I can't distinguish between these feelings of worry, but it just feels like a horrible sinking pit in my tummy all the time. Mrs Bowes doesn't yet seem to know anything about Timmy's behaviour, and she's got no idea about what Tricia's going through. My heart sinks every time Mrs Bowes talks to me about me and Timmy getting married, which she assumes will be sooner rather than later. When Timmy is home and well enough, of course,' said Evie. 'But Timmy's poor baby isn't going to go away, that's for certain. And I've not been a model of good behaviour myself. Aside from the rights and wrongs of me getting engaged to Timmy, I've treated poor Peter extremely badly, and that makes me feel beastly. I should have made Peter aware that I was spoken for, and even if I didn't have the courage to do that, I should never have let him kiss me or, a minute later, allowed him to touch my face or kiss me again when we were on our own in the damn Nissen hut with the piglet in the dratted box beside us.'

Evie still hadn't seen Peter in the days since they had had their difficult conversation about Timmy and her engagement in the kitchen as she was making her bedtime drink, and so she could only guess what Peter might be feeling.

'The worst thing about all of this – other than Timmy being wounded, of course – is that now I have met Peter, I have an inkling of what a true love might be like. I know we only had those two kisses, and they lasted just a second or two, but in those moments I knew that I would cheerfully lay down my life for his. Every time I think of what we did, I feel it all over my body.'

'Just think what you'd feel like if he'd kissed you thrice!' teased Sukie, this time poking her own elbow into Evie's ribs.

'Don't!' sighed Evie wistfully. 'The thought that I might already have had the very best experience of my life hardly bears thinking about.'

The friends continued to talk through what Timmy and Peter might each be feeling, with Sukie reasoning that perhaps Timmy's injuries would be such that he would offer Evie the honourable way out of their engagement, and that perhaps Peter felt it had been he who had taken advantage of Evie in a moment when she was excited and her normal barriers of good behaviour were down.

'I think you are just being kind to me, and I can't see any of that. I feel the onus was on me to mention the engagement. I don't know why I didn't from the moment I met Peter. And then after a while I couldn't bring myself to,' confessed Evie quietly. 'The odd thing about Peter is that I hardly noticed him when he first became a PG at Pemberley, and in fact I thought him downright awkward and ungainly, with his stammer and his blushing, and so perhaps to me then he didn't seem to be someone I should take care over. I never noticed him changing before me, until it was too late. I feel so dense and stupid, and he must think me an idiot, and a cruel one to boot.

'And what's just as bad is that if Timmy were to do the honourable thing and offer me a way out, I suspect I might feel then that I'd *have* to marry him come what may, because for once he'll have done the right thing, and I'll feel too ashamed by me not doing the right thing beforehand not to insist that we do go ahead and marry, especially as I have to go on living in Lymbridge. You can imagine the tittle-tattle if I break my engagement with a wounded serviceman, and especially so in the case of someone known to everybody, as Timmy is. And if someone as morally weak as Timmy were to find it in himself to do the right thing, what would it say about me if I didn't respond in kind too?'

Evie gave a sigh of frustration, and then added, 'Obviously Mrs Bowes might think otherwise, when it's public knowledge about Tricia, and so I daresay she'll have an oar to throw in. But even though the poor lass is carrying Mrs Bowes' first grandchild (that we know of), I can't envisage her allowing Dear Timmy to marry a dairy parlour maid. Ugh. It's all such a dreary mess.'

Sukie agreed, and then added that when Timmy was back in Lymbridge he might find it very prudent, if Mrs Bowes were on the warpath over The Tricia Trouble, to fake a relapse of his coma until everything calmed down. Evie and Sukie couldn't help but snigger briefly at the thought of this.

Then Evie felt they'd talked for quite long enough about the disastrous state of affairs concerning her love life, and so she began to ask Sukie about The Grange and the new airfield.

They were now standing midway up a tor and had a bird's eye view of what would soon become the runway. The sight revealed it to be the only reasonably level piece of ground for what looked like miles around.

They could see the local villages and the outlying farms and fields lacing the edge of the moorland, and the roads crisscrossing both the hilly arable land and the moorland. Even though it was a Saturday, there were lorries and workmen hard at work marking out and preparing the site, and constructing a road between the airfield and the hospital, and between the local road and the airfield site.

Sukie said she had heard that there would be some temporary

hangars erected within the next couple of weeks, as well as some sort of mess hall for the servicemen who'd be using the airfield.

'I heard a rumour circulating at The Grange during the week that this area is going to become an area where the Army, the RAF and the Navy will all have various billets and training. It might not happen for months, but I've heard tell that in time it could be that there will be thousands of troops hereabouts,' added Sukie.

'Goodness,' said Evie. 'If that happens then Pattie will be beside herself with delight, unless she's still going steady with John, not that I can quite see what she finds attractive in him – he looks a bit of an amiable lummox to me. And if we do get an influx of troops then I can see that Tina and Sarah could well feel they made a wise choice in moving to Pemberley when Lymbridge turns out to be awash with muscular men on training.

'And if you're still doctorless, it will give you a spring in your step too,' said Evie, turning to look Sukie in the eye, who merely replied with a toss of her blonde curls.

Evie added, 'When I look around me now, it makes me think we're in for a longer haul with this damn war than we hoped for. I can't tell you how much I hope that it's all over before James has to go off to fight too – I don't think mother and father could bear it if he were lost on some godforsaken battlefield.'

For a minute or two Evie and Sukie held hands in the bright sunshine as they stood on the springy moorland each lost in her own thoughts, staring down at the ant-like men and the tiny lorries beavering away far below them in the sunshine.

Chapter Twenty-One

The next day, Mrs Worth, with help from Mrs Whitstable from the village who didn't usually work on a Sunday but who had been persuaded to come up to Pemberley especially to help out, was able to dish up a roast Sunday lunch that harked back to the pre-war times of plenty. It was a lunch purely to cement friendships and to give thanks that they had all survived so far.

It was intended as a real treat and Mrs Worth had pooled all the Pemberley residents' meat rations to provide a gigantic rib of beef which, against all odds, the butcher had managed to secure for her.

Mr and Mrs Worth, after their initial irritation at having to make Pemberley over as a guest house, were now obviously rather enjoying their new role. And a knock-on effect had been that they now had a much wider acquaintance in Lymbridge than previously, and so Mrs Worth was revelling in being asked to the occasional coffee morning at the church hall or to a village woman's house for tea, while Mr Worth now went each Friday evening to The Haywain for a couple of beers, where he would enjoy a chat with Barkeep Joss as they put the world to rights.

Julia pointed out to Evie that it was another example of a silver lining in any grey cloud.

The whole Yeo clan had also been asked by Mr and Mrs Worth to Sunday lunch at Pemberley, along with Sukie and

Linda, and of course all the PGs would be there, and Mrs Bowes had been invited too.

Frank and Joseph carried two garden trugs groaning with potatoes and greens up to the house, the heavy trugs knocking against their bare knees poking beneath their short trousers as they each manhandled their trug from hand to hand. Susan provided the Yorkshire pudding, carrying the mixed ingredients in a large bowl (this was because the Yorkshire pud mixture needed to stand for at least an hour, she said, before going into a hot oven), and Marie and Catherine, looking sweet in their Sunday best (which were ancient hand-me-downs that Evie, Julia and Pattie had all worn as small girls) took it in turns to carry a little jar of last year's honey from the hives at the bottom of the orchard at Bluebells. Robert had picked some of the wild flowers from Bluebells' garden, and somehow had persuaded a shiny-faced James (Susan had obviously been at him with a damp flannel immediately before they left) to carry the flowers as a thank-you gift for Mrs Worth for the lunch. The rest of the family only noticed Robert had avoided carrying anything himself as they got to the steps to Pemberley's front door.

Mr Smith had walked down to collect Mrs Bowes, who contributed a large bowl of soft fruit from her netted-in fruit cage in her back garden, although Mr Smith had been sent out to pick the fruit on her behalf as she said she didn't really have the outfit on that would enable her to go tromping around in her fruit cage. And then he had to carry the ungainly earthenware bowl to Pemberley, rather wishing that he'd driven down to collect Mrs Bowes as that would have saved a lot of effort on his part as she lived at the far end of the village.

Mrs Worth had said to Evie the morning previously that she was going to get a large joint of pork for the lunch 'as everybody loves crispy crackling, don't they?'

But Evie, dreading the thought that she and Peter might catch each other's eyes over the pork joint when of course that dear little piglet had been so significant in bringing them together, had said quickly that her father much preferred beef, at which comment Julia shot her head up and cast Evie a penetrating look of bemused puzzlement as it was well known in the Yeo household that Robert was extremely partial to a bit of heavily salted crackling.

Evie widened her eyes and pursed her lips in her sister's direction, at which Julia frowned in a significant manner that she knew Evie would notice, before meekly turning her head once again to reading the *Western Morning News*.

The lunch was delicious, in part as nobody had had anything like that to eat since Christmas, when of course there hadn't been the current abundance of fresh summer fruit and vegetables. Evie and Peter were careful to place themselves at opposite ends of the gigantic, cloth-swathed table, although on the same side in order that they didn't have to look at each other unless very determined to do so.

And they'd kept at either side of the terrace during the pre-lunch drinks outside, Sukie making sure that Evie could talk with her at all times. When it was time to go inside, Evie and Peter walked to their places at the table with downcast eyes and without saying a word to each other. They appeared to have worked out an unspoken system of avoiding difficult interactions between themselves.

Evie felt thoroughly uncomfortable, and she was convinced she wouldn't be able to face eating a thing. But when Mrs Whitstable struggled in with hot serving dish after hot serving dish, and the tempting smells of the roast meat wafted around, even Evie's disloyal tummy began to rumble.

Shady was allowed special dispensation to be inside the house, as ordinarily Mrs Worth thought dogs to be dirty, smelly things who should remain outside, but she had noticed Marie and Catherine's pleading looks and so she had relented in good spirit, saying to the small girls that as long as Shady watched his Ps and Qs, he could come in.

Evie hoped that Shady hadn't had a particularly wind-inducing breakfast, as that would definitely put a huge dampener on the occasion. And when Shady began to drool copiously at the arrival of the roast beef, she had to distract Mrs Worth from looking in his direction.

It was a ploy that worked, and the meal was eaten in the generous and happy spirit in which it had been provided by the Worths.

Much of the conversation was to do with bottling, salting and pickling methods of the current surfeit of garden produce, before it moved on to various interesting (or not) recipes for reconstituted egg powder, and how shredded carrots could be added to a whole lot of savoury and sweet recipes. It was actually a much more interesting conversation than it might have at first sounded.

And once the roast had been consumed and the used dinner plates cleared, and just as Shady could be heard in the kitchen slurping his own lunch of some now cooled leftover roast potatoes that Evie flavoured with a little bit of watered-down beef gravy, Mr Worth stood up and then tapped on a water glass to get the table's attention.

'Mrs Worth and myself wanted to throw a little lunch party as it has been a difficult and busy few weeks for some of us, and so we – that's Mrs Worth and myself – wanted to treat everyone to some tasty fare as our way of saying to those of us who are at the table today that these might be difficult times, but our British Bulldog spirit will never be defeated by that B-word Adolf Hitler.'

Mr Worth sat down to a round of applause and a little table-thumping in approbation of his patriotic thoughts.

Robert then stood up to say thank you on behalf of the table, before adding that he wanted personally to thank Mr and Mrs Worth for providing Evie and Julia with such a pleasant home. Mr Wallis then stood up to say more of the same, although not to do with Evie and Julia, of course. Tina stood up quickly to say that she and Sarah were delighted to be living at Pemberley too, and they wanted to thank everybody for making them so welcome in Lymbridge.

Pattie, sitting opposite Evie, made a comical face at all this mutual appreciation, and quickly Evie had to reach down to give Shady a pat so that nobody could see her answering smile.

Mrs Whitstable was clearly itching to get the pudding course on the table as she was hovering just on the other side of the doorway with a tray loaded with dessert bowls, but with an apologetic smile in her direction Mr Smith delayed her, as with a raise of his hand that caused an infuriated tut from the doorway, he then stood up to speak too.

'There are two things I want to say. Firstly, I wonder if we can have a minute or two's silence while we remember those loved ones we know who are fighting, and especially Timmy, who is very much in the thoughts of his mother and fiancée.'

Heads bowed in silence around the table, and Evie felt hot and bothered as she stared at her lap. Mr Smith's unexpected words had caught her completely on the hop, and she was painfully aware of the stiffened posture of Peter just three people along the table from her, and that Timmy's mother was close by too.

Then Mr Smith said, 'On to happier matters, and I think now is the time to clear up the Mrs SEW-and-SEW mystery. It's all down to me, I confess.'

There was a moment of shocked silence. Julia and Pattie looked thunderstruck. Evie wished they could see their own dumbfounded faces.

Mr Smith went on to explain that he was employed by the British Board of Trade, in what he then made sound like quite a dull role to do with making sure that BoT instructions were running smoothly to the west of Bath, and that various regulations were being followed. He had an office in Plymouth, but he actually spent quite a lot of time checking on various BoT responsibilities in Truro or Barnstaple or Exeter or Bristol or wherever – so this was why he had his own car and what seemed like unlimited petrol, thought Evie – but often he had to go to London to present various reports to the Board of Trade HQ.

As Mrs Whitstable could be heard stomping back to the kitchen with her tray and gruffly plonking it down on the kitchen table with a peeved rattle of crockery, eventually Mr Smith arrived at the long and short of what he wanted to say. This was that, not long after he had moved to Pemberley, Mr Smith had been sitting in his favourite chair in the corner of the dining room doing a crossword in the newspaper when he had noticed and been amused by Julia and Pattie's creation of Mrs Sew-and-Sew whilst they and the other members of Lymbridge's sewing circle chatted about this and that as they worked up new wardrobes from scant beginnings.

At first he couldn't grasp what there was about this bossy and officious creation that made everyone laugh so much. But, Mr Smith continued, the more he heard from the officious Mrs Sew-and Sew, the more she got under his skin.

At this point Evie, Julia, Pattie, Linda and Sukie all shared a quick glance with each other of unreined horror, and there was a corresponding tightening of all their jaws.

For of course in large part the fun of Mrs Sew-and-Sew had been to do with poking mischief at Mrs Bowes. Who was now sitting beside them and, because of her distress concerning Timmy, simply could never be allowed to discover her role in the genesis of Mrs Sew-and-Sew.

Sarah and Tina were quick to pick up on the glance between the sisters and their friends, although their looks were more questioning.

And then to the further horror of the Yeo sisters, Susan flashed them all a look of warning – her mother's intuition rarely let her down, and she had clearly twigged precisely what had occurred, and was now signalling furiously that they must all take extreme care.

All of this happened in less than a second or two, causing Evie to think the very next moment that if the bush-telegraph powers of Devon women could be harnessed and put to good patriotic use, surely it wouldn't be long before the war would be over and won.

Fortunately Mrs Bowes seemed quite oblivious to the round-robin of significant looks between the younger generation of women sitting around the Worths' dining table, being perhaps too entranced as she gazed with an expression of utmost concentration and open admiration at the well-dressed gentleman who was standing before them.

'And the more I listened to Mrs Sew-and-Sew, the more I thought she deserved a wider audience. She is an amusing creation of the sort of busybody we all recognise, and yet she talks sound sense – and she knows a lot about sewing and making do and mending.

'I became convinced that she would strike a chord with all sorts of women, from young ladies right through to the older generation. So I made a note of some of Mrs Sew-and-Sew's sage advice, and then I roughed up a plan of how she might work as a sort of help-mate to pass on useful tips to the type of women who are inexperienced with needle and thread and who might now be trying to sew for the first time. After I'd done that I telephoned the propaganda department at the BoT, who put me through to another department who, once I'd gone through it all again several times, expressed a strong interest in Mrs Sew-and-Sew,' Mr Smith explained.

'I posted the relevant people at the BoT some more carefully thought through ideas, which were pretty much just me listening to you clever young ladies – and you've no idea how much useful information I got during that week of you all making up Miss Sukie's new wardrobe for her ready to start work at The Grange – and writing down what you said. The rest is history, as the BoT then got their illustrators on to making the proper diagrams to go with the text, and within just a few short weeks the first two leaflets were ready. It was the BoT's idea that the "sews" in Mrs Sew-and-Sew's name be capitalised, in order to drive home the point a little more that the leaflets were about sewing.

'Anyway, I drove to London early on Monday and proofread the copy. And we printed the leaflets that very evening, thousands and thousands of them. I took a couple from the first runs of each leaflet and posted them to Mrs Worth. I couldn't resist sending them anonymously, just for a little bit of fun. And I heard earlier today, that the leaflets have been deemed such a success that they are going to do a second printing, and distribute them nationwide, and not just in London as originally planned. And these two pamphlets are just the start, as Mrs SEW-and-SEW looks to have a whole lot more to say about patching and pockets and unpicking.'

Mr Smith added that there definitely was going to be some sort of cartoon strip in the national press, although quite how this would end up was still to be decided.

He went on to say that within the next few weeks the Board would be sending someone down to interview Julia and Pattie. The BoT wanted to wait until women right across the country were familiar with Mrs SEW-and-SEW, and then they would feed the story of how she came to be to the press.

At this Mr Smith sat down to a loud round of applause, and at long last a long-suffering Mrs Whitstable was able to bring in the fruit and whipped cream for pudding (Linda had brought the cream with her as her contribution to the lunch, knowing that everyone was getting bored of the much less appetising mock cream they would normally have), and of course there was the honey from the Bluebells' hives as an added treat.

Mr Smith nipped out to the scullery. He had had the foresight to leave standing in cool water four bottles of precious champagne, brought especially to Devon for the purpose from his own wine cellar at his Mayfair house in London, and these he now delivered to the table with a flourish.

Mr and Mrs Worth scrambled to find some clean glasses, and soon everyone, even Frank and Joseph (although not little Marie or Catherine, who – Mr Smith hadn't forgotten them either – were given some special rosehip and orange cordial he had obtained from an Italian foodstore close to Berwick Street Market in London), was raising a toast to the success of Mrs Sew-and-Sew, and then to the value of family and friends, and then to the British servicemen, and to Timmy, and then Winston

Churchill. After that there were toasts to just about anything those sitting around the merry table could think of.

It was the first time that any of the Yeos had had proper champagne. Robert gave Susan a slightly mystified look as if to ask what all the fuss concerning champagne was about, while Julia and Pattie both laughed at the way the bubbles were going up their noses, and meanwhile James swigged his glass down in one hasty gulp and then had to endure some embarrassing wheezing and watering eyes, as he wasn't used to the fizzy sensation.

As Evie felt the alcohol surge around her body, she was brave enough to look over vaguely in Peter's direction, daring to sneak a peek at him as she casually leant back to give Shady another pat. Peter was already staring at her. They looked away at the same instant, and then immediately glanced back at each other again. Evie felt tingly, although she couldn't say for certain that this wasn't the effects of the champagne.

When Mr Wallis said that as it had been such a lovely lunch, why didn't all the men present, including young James, join him for the last half hour of Sunday lunchtime opening at The Haywain (all drinks on him, of course), Evie ventured the smallest of smiles in Peter's direction, at which Peter gave a tight-lipped smile that was just as modest in return.

The sight of this tentative tiny smile was a start, Evie felt, although she knew that it was nowhere near the dazzling smile of Peter's of which she was so fond.

Chapter Twenty-Two

At school on the Monday morning, Mrs Bowes told Evie she had had a telephone call just as she got home after the lunch at Pemberley, to say that after morning playtime the local police constabulary at Bramstone would be sending over a police constable to talk to the children about the spate of thefts.

Mrs Bowes had that morning dropped in to the village shop on the way to school in order to have a word with Mrs Coyne. The shopkeeper had said to Mrs Bowes that she had, as she had indeed threatened, called the police on Saturday morning concerning the theft of the liquorice bootlaces. She hadn't wanted to, especially as Susan's evacuees were among the boys, but she felt it was crucial that an example was made of the thieves in order that this petty thievery be knocked on the head before it got out of hand.

The police had taken the theft quite seriously, sending the PC who would be coming into the primary school later in the morning to Mrs Coyne's house and then over to Bluebells during Sunday afternoon to talk with Susan and to take a statement from her about the loss of her purse. Evie and Julia hadn't known of this visit by the police to their mother, and so Evie presumed that her parents had decided that it had been such a wonderful lunchtime at Pemberley that it would be a pity to break the happy mood by letting the girls know of what had been going on at Bluebells just a short time later.

At the PC's arrival Robert had taken James, Frank and

Joseph to the well-tended back garden to do a little more Very Important Weeding, and in actual fact the PC had left Bluebells without wanting to speak to the boys from Peckham.

Finally the PC had called at Mrs Bowes' house, leaving his police bicycle propped against the front wall to her garden, in plain view of any Lymbridge resident who wanted to look. Once she had been calmed down by Mr Smith, who'd escorted Mrs Bowes home, as the sight of a uniformed policeman walking down the garden path had convinced her that Timmy's condition must have taken a turn for the worse (she didn't notice the bicycle leaning against the wall until later, which would have upset her even further in case any villager had thought she might be implicated in something unsavoury), the PC told Mrs Bowes that although on a superficial level the evidence of the thefts did rather point to the culpability of Frank and Joseph, he was rather inclined to take a wider view.

This was because in his experience, lads of Frank and Joseph's age would be wilier and more cunning if they were committing these crimes. The fact that the evidence seemed to point so obviously towards them might be, according to this reasoning, in fact a point in their favour. It all seemed too easy, and indeed a bit childish.

'So PC Tucker and myself decided last night that probably the best way of dealing with this problem is for him to come in and give the whole school a talking to,' Mrs Bowes said to Evie.

'He thinks it unlikely we'll ever find out who the thief or thieves are, but that if he is stern enough, then the problem should melt away of its own accord as the child or children responsible should be too scared to contemplate doing it again.'

'Let's hope that's true,' said Evie. 'Only I hope PC Tucker isn't too scary for my little ones, as I don't really want to have to wash out a lot of damp underpants and knickers tonight.'

When PC Tucker arrived, Evie was pleased to see that he was a comfortingly large and cheerful-looking middle-aged man, with a jolly smile and a strong Devonian accent.

Red of face and damp of forehead after cycling up the steep hill into Lymbridge on the Plymouth road, he got off his ancient push bike, removed his helmet and dabbed at his face with a huge white hankie.

Evie ran to get him a welcome drink of water, which he downed in one long swallow and Evie could hear the water glug down his throat, before declaring that if it were all right with Mrs Bowes and Evie, he'd take his uniform jacket off and then stand in the shade under the large sycamore tree at the edge of the playground (the same tree that donkey Susie had rested under between giving rides at the Revels) and talk to the children as they sat cross-legged in a semi-circle around him.

Evie and Mrs Bowes both thought that an excellent idea. It wouldn't be too threatening, but because it would be a serious talk and one that was taking place outside of their classrooms, hopefully it would be the more memorable for that, and the important message of PC Tucker's talk would thus sink in to the pupils' heads.

The children were all very excited to see a real policeman in their midst, and PC Tucker was very patient with them, allowing those that wanted to try on his helmet, and to blow his official police whistle. It was a very loud whistle, and so after its first ear-shattering blast, Mrs Bowes was quick to cut in with the instruction that there be three more whistles only from pupils at Lymbridge Primary School.

PC Tucker was obviously used to talking to children, speaking to them in a relaxed but gently authoritative manner. He asked them lots of questions, and then without them noticing it, he started to get them to play some games where somebody might be a pretend grown-up, and someone else a child who was telling a lie, with the audience of other children yelling out when the lie happened. He graduated to a game of shopkeepers and shoppers, and what might happen when a shopkeeper might be told a lie.

He then got all the children to sit down close to the adults, and in a quieter, graver voice he began to talk to them about their own mummies and daddies, and whether it would be fair if somebody was to take something that belonged to their mummy or daddy.

The children became very quiet as they thought about this. And then PC Tucker asked them what they thought about somebody who wasn't their mummy or daddy having something taken from them – was that fair? No, it wasn't! was the vehement response from his rapt audience.

There were several more questions like that, and then PC Tucker made the discussion slightly more abstract. Evie knew that much of this would pass over the heads of her infants, but she could see that the older children were thinking about the implications of small thefts of food really being a crime against the war effort and thus against Britain itself. And that theft of money, even when the money belonged to just one person, was really a crime against the whole community.

After that, PC Tucker dealt with police stations and courts, and the concept of fines and even prison. And he asked the children if they could imagine, just for a moment, what it would feel like to have to use all their pocket money to pay a fine if they had done wrong, or if they had to leave their mummy or daddy if they themselves were ever sent to prison.

'But of course good boys and maids'll will never 'ave to pay a fine or go to prison. If you never steal or get into trouble, then you'll never need to see the inside of a police station or a courtroom. Remember, nobody expects anything from any of you other than that you treat other people well and always respect other people's belongings, just as you all expect other people to treat you well and not to take aught what doesn't belong to you,' said the PC. The children were wide-eyed, and they were all sitting very still. Many of them nodded in agreement with what he said.

PC Tucker stopped speaking, and there was a silence. He asked if anyone had any questions about ownership or doing wrong by thieving. The children shook their heads. They all – even the youngest children of just five years – understood that thieving was wrong, and that to be a thief was very bad. PC Tucker stood still and looked at the children with a stern expression on his face, and they stared in awe back at him.

Mrs Bowes then broke the tension by stepping in front of PC Tucker, saying that Lymbridge Primary School was very lucky that such an important and busy man as PC Tucker had found time to spend with them that morning. To say thank you, would the children like to say three hip hip hurrahs to PC Tucker? Yes, of course they would, and Evie was amused to see the policeman look coy and a trifle abashed at the enthusiasm of the hip hip hurrahs yelled in his direction.

Evie's infants then ran to her with lots of questions about policemen, and the difference between right and wrong. Evie saw Mrs Bowes deep in conversation with PC Tucker as he wheeled his bicycle towards the school gate, Mrs Bowes listening to what he said with a serious face.

Evie walked home to Pemberley at the end of the school day with more gusto than she had for over a week. Only one more day of teaching to go, and then a day of administration, and at last she would be free.

Mrs Bowes had made no mention of Evie returning to teach in the autumn term, and so Evie presumed that other arrangements were being, or were going to be, made.

And bearing in mind The Tricia Trouble that was becoming an increasingly pressing presence in Evie's head, that was probably just as well, she thought. She couldn't see that Mrs Bowes was going to want her back in the autumn once it was out in the open that Timmy had impregnated another woman.

At Pemberley Evie had a drink of water and then took her book – it was *Pride and Prejudice*, and so Evie felt that Pemberley's name was having some influence on her choice of reading – to the same lichen-covered stone bench where Pattie had so tactfully broken the news to her about Tricia's rounded stomach. It was a hot afternoon, and the large tree behind the bench offered enticing sun-dappled shade.

Evie was so lost in the world of Regency England, and the travails of Elizabeth Bennet, that she failed to notice she was no longer alone until an unexpectedly large shadow flitted across her page.

It was Peter. He asked if he might sit at the opposite end of the stone bench, and Evie could only nod at him.

He sat down, and there was silence between them. Evie couldn't think of a single thing to say, and it seemed as if Peter couldn't either.

'Peter—'

'Evie—'

They had both spoken at the same time. And now they both stopped, each waiting for the other to go on.

'Peter—'

'Evie—'

Oh no. Exactly the same thing had happened for a second time. This was terrible.

And then they both saw the funny side, and as they laughed, the moment of tension passed and they each relaxed.

Peter indicated that Evie should go first.

'I am so pleased that you have come to talk to me. I wanted to speak with you but I wasn't brave enough to make the first move,' said Evie. 'I wanted to say that I owe you the biggest apology. I should have made it clear from the outset that I was engaged to be married to Timmy Bowes. I have behaved abominably and treated both you and Timmy very shabbily. I feel ashamed of my behaviour, and I am very sorry that I have put you in a difficult position, especially when you have done nothing to deserve this.'

Peter had gone a deep shade of crimson under Evie's unwavering stare.

'The fault is all mine, Evie. I should never have presumed that a young woman as beautiful as you would not already be spoken for, and I should have checked to make sure that you were under no romantic obligation,' Peter replied, staring back just as intently at Evie.

She felt her blood course around her body; every capillary seemed engorged with longing and emotion. Her mouth felt dry and she clung to the sight of the gold flecks in Peter's eyes that the sunlight was enhancing.

Peter wasn't finished yet. 'I should never have kissed you without asking, and nor should I have been inappropriate in the Nissen hut. It was ungentlemanly and the fact that I did so put you in a terribly difficult position.'

Once again Evie was struck dumb. She contented herself by drinking in the sight of Peter so close to her, and by imbibing the longed-for Peter smell, which was of clean clothes, a little soap and just the slightest whiff of manly sweat.

Peter leant forward for a moment. And then he thought better of it and abruptly pulled himself upright and stood up to leave her.

'I've said what I wanted to say to you,' said Peter. 'I very much hope that we can be pleasant with each other. It is very likely that I will be leaving Pemberley quite soon, and so you won't have to endure the sight of me for much longer.'

He turned to go, and before Evie could stop herself, she called after him, 'Peter, I wanted you to kiss me. I wanted it more than anything else in the world.'

He paused momentarily but didn't look around, although Evie noticed his buttocks clench. And then he walked smartly towards the house without glancing back at her. Evie wasn't sure whether he'd understood her or not, or what he might have thought about what she had called to him.

Indeed she wasn't quite sure herself precisely what message it was that she'd been trying to convey to Peter with such urgency.

After tea an hour or two later there was a telephone call, the ring ding-dinging from the telephone on the narrow wooden table in the hallway. Mr Worth answered it, and then he told Evie that it had been Mrs Bowes wondering if Evie could pop over.

Evie sprang up from the kitchen table where she had been

doing the crossword puzzle in that morning's *Western Morning News* with Mr Wallis, while on the wireless that Mrs Worth had moved into the kitchen there was Dr Hill, commonly known as The Radio Doctor, pontificating on the digestive system and the need for regular bowel movements.

As she hurried down the drive to Mrs Bowes', Evie didn't spare a thought for Timmy as she was too busy thinking about Peter. What was it about him that she found so compelling? She wished she knew.

Julia, Tina and Sarah all liked Peter well enough, from what she could tell at least, but in none of them had Evie been able to detect any sign of that same frisson that she felt radiated between herself and Peter.

He hadn't been at the tea table just now at Pemberley, and Evie couldn't decide if that were a good thing or a bad thing. She sighed as she thought that so much of what she felt about Peter seemed to be evenly weighted between the positive and the negative.

At Mrs Bowes' Evie expected an update on Timmy's health, but that proved not to be the reason for which she had been summoned.

Instead, Evie was surprised to see the ruddy face of PC Tucker, his immense frame dwarfing the chintz sofa and the ornament-strewn sitting room.

'Evie, PC Tucker has solved the mystery of the thefts,' said Mrs Bowes, and then took a breath, clearly intent on going on with the story herself.

PC Tucker shut his mouth as he had obviously been just about to say something. Then he changed his mind.

'Yes, yorn 'vacuees Frank and Joseph are in the clear, you'll be pleased to 'ear,' PC Tucker said quickly to Evie. Mrs Bowes shot the policeman a wounded glance in recognition that he had stolen her thunder.

Evie beamed at PC Tucker.

'As I was talkin' to the children today I was keeping a close eye out, and as your mother had mentioned that she and your pa were worried that the lads they had taken in 'ad done the thievin', I made special sure to watch their reactions to what I was sayin'. But I could see no sign of any guilt or suspicious behaviour, and this bore out my idea that they weren't who I was looking for.

'I then concentrated on lookin' at the other older children, in the end concentratin' on Vince Short, because of his sticky-fingered family and also because your ma had said he'd tried to convince you that Frank and Joseph were lookin' to steal on Saturday at the school shindig. I caught his eye and he looked rightly wrong to me.'

PC Tucker said that from then on Vince had refused to look at him properly, and he was the only child to behave in that way as the PC talked to the children. And that when he had gone to the Shorts' house after school, it hadn't been long before Vince had confessed all.

Apparently, near the start of term there'd been some talk at his house about Jews starting the war, and then somebody had said that Frank and Joseph had had their names changed as they were Jewish, and so Vince had decided they needed to be made to pay for getting Britain fighting against Hitler.

Evie thought it ironic that her parents had thought it best to change Franz and Josef's names to Frank and Joseph to draw attention away from their background. Now this pretence looked in large part the very reason that Vince had become interested in them.

PC Tucker said he had told Vince that the Jews hadn't started the war, but he was going to let Mrs Bowes deal with the wider issues at the final lesson of term tomorrow.

'I'm now off to see your ma 'n' pa, Evie, and then I'm over to Mrs Coyne's. I think I can persuade 'er not to press charges, now that Mrs Bowes has said she's not goin' to, and I know your ma doesn't want to either. I don't think anything is to be gained by taking things further with Vince, because 'e was cryin' and right contrite when I left him, and hopefully Mrs Coyne'll be willin' to see it in the same light. The bootlaces have all been eaten, but Vince 'adn't dared to do anything with the money or purse other than 'ide what 'e'd stolen, and so I will be able to return that to Mrs Yeo and Mrs Bowes. And I've agreed with Vince that he can pay Mrs Coyne his tuppence pocket money every week until the bootlaces are paid for,' PC Tucker said. 'I don't think Vince is a bad child as such, but it's not easy for him at home as those Shorts get up to some rum do's. I don't think 'e's got anything particular against Frank and Joseph, aside from them being evacuees, and so I doubt 'e'll steal for a long while, or try to pin the blame on anyone else for something bad that he has done.'

As Evie and Mrs Bowes waved off PC Tucker, they agreed it was a relief that the perpetrator of the thefts had now been exposed, and that Frank and Joseph had been exonerated.

Hopefully the two boys from Peckham would never know quite how close they had come to being accused of this spate of unsettling thefts.

'I'm not sure that Vince won't carry a chip on his shoulder about it though; I think PC Tucker might be taking a more kindly view about this than I would. While it probably started as something of a game that escalated out of hand, I think it's probably indicative of a less than charitable attitude prevalent among some people,' said Mrs Bowes. 'I'm glad Vince is off to secondary school next term, as I think I'd have difficulty in looking such a dishonest lad in the eye for long.'

'Yes, it's never nice to have one's trust broken,' agreed Evie, before she realised that she had been breaching the trust of Mrs Bowes for quite some weeks by keeping secret what had been going on behind the scenes. And then for an instant, she felt a sudden chill. It was as if someone was walking over her grave.

Chapter Twenty-Three

The infants were adorable the next morning, the last day of term, and Evie felt as if she wanted to cuddle them all. She realised that she was going to miss teaching them.

Nearly all of them had made cards at home from odd scraps of paper or card, to thank Evie for being their teacher. Bobby Ayres' effort stood out particularly as it was covered in what looked like some sort of hair; indeed it *was* fur, he explained proudly, as he'd brushed his pet rabbit until he had enough downy rabbit fur (the best bits coming from her TUMMY, he bellowed happily to Evie), which he had then gummed on to the front of his card as his very personalised form of decoration, Mr Cawes having supervised the gumming, apparently.

Evie thanked Bobby and said with a smile that she would always treasure his very special thank-you card.

Several of the infants had brought her presents of food. There were a couple of onions, a crumpled brown paper bag containing some runner beans and one of the jars of the 'most inventive' jam batch, this one being apple and parsnip, coloured by a couple of blackberries, bottled from the previous autumn as well, as what looked like a little grated carrot. Evie said with what she hoped sounded like gusto that she couldn't wait to try it and she was already very much looking forward to spreading it on toast for her breakfast tomorrow.

Evie and Mrs Bowes were only going to teach until lunchtime, and the children would be allowed to leave before lunch. And then school for the pupils would be over for the year.

Although it was still quite early, the infants were already in a noisy, restless mood, with most of them appearing excitable, whilst a couple were already heading towards the tearful and irritable stage.

Evie had sympathy for those of her charges who were looking to be at the end of their tether, as she had kept them very busy since she had taken over the class after Easter, and she was sure that some of her pupils were genuinely tired out. Just the routine of school was exhausting for the youngest children, she knew, and so the end of term was here not a day too soon for them. Or for herself either, Evie thought a trifle glumly, as once again she had the too familiar feeling of being drained of energy.

Right then. This enervating mood meant that it should be the last nature table of the year, Evie decided, as she asked the infants this time for as many different types of grasses as possible. She explained to them what grasses were, and then picked a couple of blades of one variety of grass as an example. Then she set her class off on The Great Grass Hunt, reminding her pupils that it was very important that they mustn't go on Mr Cawes' vegetable plots.

The winner would be the child who could find the highest number of grasses, the prize being called king or queen of the grass, and being allowed to wear Evie's old dressing-up crown for five minutes (the crown having done sterling work in this respect over the term, with all of the pupils wearing it at least once, even if on occasion Evie had had to wrangle a result so that a child who hadn't previously been crowned could have the honour). If there was a tie in the number of grasses collected, then each winner would get to wear the crown for one minute.

As her young pupils searched the grassy areas in the playground and school field before her in the morning sunshine, punctuated by the occasional buzz of gigantic bumble bees going about their business, Evie could hear Mrs Bowes dealing with the causes of the war, and the German aggression, and the oppression of Jews in Germany and Poland.

Mrs Bowes gave the juniors a simple but enviably thorough explanation of how Britain had come to be fighting against Germany, using the cloth map of the world rolled down from its wooden casing above the blackboard, to judge by the occasional rather odd slapping sound that Evie wasn't used to hearing. Evie was impressed with the headmistress's clarity and presumed the slapping sound was made by some sort of pointer hitting various territories of the shiny-sided canvas map as Mrs Bowes explained what had happened in various countries, and when.

There was then a question and answer session, during which Evie was content to relax while sitting on the steps into the school as she watched her infants with their heads bowed as they searched for different varieties of grasses. They were being helped by Mr Cawes who had been persuaded by Bobby Ayres to get involved. He had obviously decided that his vegetables would stand less chance of getting trampled if he stepped in to keep an eye on things, as it didn't look as if Evie would be budging from her sunny step.

Evie heard Mrs Bowes ask specific questions of Frank, Joseph and Vince. It sounded as if the lesson was timely, and as if it went well. Frank and Joseph weren't asked outright if they were Jewish, but they seemed happy to talk to their classmates about coming to Britain by train from Poland, and the other pupils, including Vince, were encouraged by Mrs Bowes to ask them about life in Poland and what they would have for breakfast there, and so forth. Evie hoped that the more Frank and Joseph were made to seem like ordinary boys, just like any lads who had been born and bred in Lymbridge, the more any threat of discrimination against them would retreat.

An hour later and all the children had gone home, each one of Evie's pupils having given her a hug, with her warmly embracing them back and giving them a biscuit she had baked the night before.

'Right, you scoot along home too now, Evie, and I'll lock up. We'll get an early start in tomorrow, and put a good day in ourselves, finishing off this year, and we'll also make sure everything is shipshape for next year in terms of paperwork and organising any bumph. I know that on Thursday Mr Cawes wants to make a start on repairs to the classrooms, and so I want you and I to have finished our wrapping-up mumbo-jumbo by then in order to give him a clear run,' said Mrs Bowes, adding as an afterthought, 'I'm going to bake him a thank-you cake tonight as he's worked hard too this term.'

'What a nice thing for you to do, and especially at this time when you've got so much to think about – I'm sure Mr Cawes will be very touched. And I'll see if I can get someone from Pemberley to go to The Haywain to check if they've got a couple of bottles of stout that Mr Cawes can have too,' said Evie.

'That's a good idea. And if it's Mr Smith who volunteers to go to The Haywain on your behalf, perhaps you could ask him then to come over to my house tonight to drop off the bottles, and then that will save you having to bring them in to school tomorrow,' said Mrs Bowes.

Evie said what a good idea. But she couldn't help chuckling to herself. Mrs Bowes was becoming quite shameless in her pursuit of Mr Smith. And he seemed just as keen on Mrs Bowes.

If this goes on as it is at present – and I see no reason as to why it wouldn't – I wonder what Timmy will make of this state of affairs when he returns, Evie mused as she headed towards Pemberley. And when I think of how furious Mrs Bowes was when I told her all those weeks ago about me having chatted to Mr Smith when we were breakfasting together, and how she intimated he might not be as morally upright as he claimed to be, it does make me smile.

The stout was duly delivered by Mr Smith to Mrs Bowes later that evening. Evie and Mrs Bowes completed their day of paperwork the next day, and that teatime news came through that Timmy's condition had improved, and that he was now on a hospital ship bound for Southampton, from where he would be transferred to a hospital with a spinal unit for specialist assessment.

Understandably Mrs Bowes was thrilled that Timmy was going to be on British soil soon. Evie was pleased too that he was improving, but she couldn't say, hand on heart, that she was delighted that it looked like she might be seeing Timmy face to face quite soon. She had got used to him being out of the country.

Later that evening Mr Smith had a quiet word with Evie, catching her in the sitting room at Pemberley when it appeared as if all the other PGs had gone to bed and she had just finished the final pages of *Pride and Prejudice* and was looking in the bookcase just in case there was a copy of *Northanger Abbey*, as this was the only Jane Austen she'd not read.

Mr Smith said he was sorry to interrupt Evie when she was probably tired, but he had just come from having a cup of tea after supper with Mrs Bowes and he wondered if Evie could do something very magnanimous.

He thought it very likely that once Timmy was back on British soil it was most probable that he would be taken to Stoke Mandeville Hospital in Buckinghamshire. It was a large hospital where many military casualties were being treated, and it was building a reputation for pioneering work with back injuries.

'I know you will be most anxious to see Timmy as soon as you can,' Mr Smith said, 'but if it is Stoke Mandeville he is sent to, I wonder if you can find it in your heart that in the first instance you could let me drive Mrs Bowes to see him on her own? I think she, and myself, would really value that; she is desperate to see Timmy and have the sort of time with him that only a mother can have with her son. I'd be very happy to take you then to see Timmy a day or two later, of course, and I would feel forever in your debt. It might not be Stoke Mandeville Hospital he is sent to, of course, but if I were a betting man I'd be putting money on him going there. It's probably about three or four hours' drive away.'

Evie felt a weight shifting off her shoulders slightly.

She knew that at some point she was going to have to be brave and see for herself what sort of condition Timmy was in. But in some ways she was reluctant to go. It would almost definitely be a very upsetting experience seeing him lie poorly and unable to fend for himself in bed, plus if she insisted on going to see Timmy at Stoke Mandeville along with Mr Smith and Mrs Bowes, just the fact that they were having to spend enforced time together on the journey might provoke uncomfortable conversations and assumptions as to her and Timmy's future together.

'No, of course, I completely understand. And I agree that Mrs Bowes deserves to see Timmy first,' said Evie in what she hoped was quite a firm and efficient manner (her weeks of teaching having given her a bit of backbone in this respect). 'You can speak to the doctors along with Mrs Bowes, and then she can have some time to get accustomed to whatever it is the doctors say to her, without her feeling any need to take me into account.

'She is a wonderful mother to Timmy, and I'm very aware that he is the whole world to her. If I am there, she might think that she must make me feel better, and that Timmy should be planning for his future when in fact, according to his condition, what in a perfect world he'd like to do, might not in fact end up as what is either appropriate or best for him.'

Mr Smith smiled at Evie, and thanked her for being so considerate. 'Mrs Bowes doesn't know that I have asked you to make this sacrifice, Evie, and so it might be better if you and I were to keep it that way...' They shared a conspiratorial look.

Mr Smith was a sensible and exceptionally kindly person. He always was a very nice man, Evie thought, and Mrs Bowes may be luckier than she knew if their relationship were to progress to something deeper and serious.

Suddenly Evie had an idea that pleased her.

Perhaps she should try to get Mr Smith to help her deal with Mrs Bowes, and Timmy too (assuming Timmy was up to anything as tricky as this promised to be), over The Tricia Trouble. Or if not to help, as such, at least if Mr Smith knew what had gone on back in Lymbridge, then he could provide a shoulder for Mrs Bowes to cry on when the news about Tricia became public knowledge.

Mr Smith seemed sage and wise, and not at all to be the type of person to go off the deep end over anything; and he had the huge advantage of genuinely seeming to care for Mrs Bowes, and also to have her ear. Mrs Bowes tended to be hectoring and too forceful with most of the Lymbridge residents, but with Mr Smith she was meek and much calmer. That might prove to be a very valuable state of affairs as far as Evie was concerned.

'Mr Smith, I wonder if I can speak to you in absolute confidence?' Evie ventured cautiously.

'My dear girl, you are looking very serious,' replied Mr Smith as he looked at her in a more penetrating manner. 'Whatever is on your mind won't go further than these four walls, I assure you.'

'It is imperative that that is true,' said Evie. 'Mrs Bowes especially cannot know just yet what I might be about to say to you, and indeed you might never be able to tell her. If that puts you in a difficult position, please stop me before I start. I don't mean to sound hysterical, but it's crucial that you, for now at least, keep my confidence.'

Mr Smith looked for a second bemused, and slightly as if he was expecting now to hear some girlish secret. But Evie continued to stare at him with a look of extreme gravity, and his expression correspondingly deepened.

'Evie, you are concerning me. I cannot imagine what it is that is burdening you so, but I repeat that anything you say to me stays in this room, and is between us alone.'

Evie said that she felt she needed the advice of an older and more experienced person. Her problem was becoming increasingly pressing, and it was a delicate matter.

Mr Smith's expression altered once more, and with a jolt Evie realised that he now thought her to be expecting a baby. 'No. No! It's not that,' she said quickly, 'although actually I think it is a trickier but related matter.'

Once more Mr Smith resumed his serious expression, although now tinged with a look of puzzlement.

Quickly Evie summarised her problem. She explained that she and Timmy had rushed into their engagement, and in some ways Evie felt this had then led to Mrs Bowes offering her the summer term as the teacher of the infants. She had assumed that she was in love, although Susan had had reservations that Evie had brushed aside. But when Dave Symons had told her about the lengthy list of women Timmy had, allegedly, had relations with, she had had to start her new job knowing that he had cuckolded her, and that his adoring mother had no idea.

Mr Smith's face changed from serious to sympathetic. He was clearly imaging what these months since Easter had been like for Evie in the face of Mrs Bowes' adoration of Timmy.

'Timmy has many good qualities, and in most ways he's a fine chap. It's more that he's just a lousy fiancé. And his shoddy behaviour has led me to scrutinise my own feelings for him, and I see now that I don't, and in fact never did, love him, at least not properly in the way a fiancée should love her intended,' confided Evie.

'But then the situation worsened. Pattie told me that one of these women, a dairy parlour maid called Tricia Dolby, looked to be carrying his child; and a month or so ago, Tricia confirmed to me that, sadly, this indeed is the case. Tricia doesn't have expectations of marriage as she thinks she's not good enough for Mrs Bowes or Timmy, but she is understandably very frightened as to her and her baby's future.'

Evie then told Mr Smith about asking Timmy about his relationships with other women by letter, and his rather evasive reply.

'And then he was sent abroad, and immediately he seemed to be having a horrible time. And the more I thought about it, the more I thought I should end our engagement after the end of term, once Mrs Bowes and I were no longer working together, especially as she's not given me any sign that she wants me to come back to school in the autumn term. I daresay I am going to get the blame for what Timmy got up to here in Lymbridge before he left, and now I have had time to get used to that idea. And in that case at least me and Mrs Bowes don't have to go on working together,' Evie said.

'Ah, I see your reasoning,' said Mr Smith. 'Mrs Bowes *is* going to be furious, there's no doubt about it. What a situation. Tricia doesn't sound like the sort of woman Mrs Bowes had imagined that Timmy would have to marry. And, at first at least, she will be livid with you for having the presumption to reject her Timmy as your suitor, no matter what he's done.'

'Yes, she will,' said Evie. 'I think she shall soften once she gets to thinking about her very first grandchild being born this autumn. But it is all going to be very difficult for a few weeks, that's for certain. And Timmy being so poorly is in itself an extra level of complication. And of course another layer of difficulty as far as I am concerned is that my parents are also unaware of what is happening around them, and they are going to be exceptionally angry with Timmy on my behalf. I've confided to Julia and Pattie about what has been going on, and we've decided that because of Timmy's condition, I need, although this goes against every fibre of my being, not to tell my parents until after I have dealt with the situation with Mrs Bowes and Timmy.

'What I do know beyond any doubt is that Timmy and I don't love each other as we should, and that it will be disastrous if we were to persist with this sham of an engagement.'

Evie's urgent flow of words dried up, and Mr Smith didn't say anything for what felt like a long while as he stared into the fireplace. Then he looked at her, and Evie felt reassured by his compassionate look.

'Evie, my dear, you have been put in a very difficult position, and you have behaved exceptionally gracefully in the face of extreme provocation. Timmy's behaviour has been poor at best and abominable at worst. And although Mrs Bowes might at first want to try and blame somebody else for the situation as it stands, I think even she will soon realise the failure of moral responsibility on the part of her son,' said Mr Smith. 'This needs careful thinking about. There are several people who need to be taken into consideration, including the unborn child, of course, and I can't pretend to have all the answers at my fingertips. Mrs Bowes, who is already under pressure with Timmy's injuries, is going to feel cross and very let down – I can't see any way around that.

'But I am glad you have told me, Evie, as I don't like to think of you trying to come to the best resolution more or less alone. I know your sisters and friends have been sympathetic, but there is little real help they can give other than to make you feel it's not all your fault. Anyway, whatever the rights and wrongs of the matter, I don't feel anyone should rush to do anything for the next week or two. We need to see how Timmy is and, if he's well enough, what *he* thinks should happen. But rest assured, my dear, that I will be thinking about this, and be doing all that I can behind the scenes to help you all.'

As Evie thanked the older man with heartfelt gratitude, she was glad she had enlisted his help.

The closer it had got to her having to end the engagement, the more frightened she had been feeling (and especially if she awoke in the pre-dawn hours, when it all seemed even more terrible), and she often felt very alone in spite of the loving backing of her sisters and her friends.

But with Mr Smith as an ally, even if he never did anything concrete to help her, at least now she no longer felt quite so exposed or isolated. In him Evie now felt she had a steadying and influential friend on her side.

Chapter Twenty-Four

The next morning it was Julia who was up and about before her sister, leaving Evie to luxuriate in her comfy bed as she allowed herself an extra hour to lie in. It felt very naughty not to be springing out of bed on what was usually a work day.

Susan wanted to go to Oldwell Abbott that morning as she had a couple of errands to run, and so Evie was going to fill in for her mother at the shop. But she didn't need to be there until nine-thirty, after which she was going to keep an eye on the four evacuees for her mother, taking over from James, who although generally happy enough to keep order for an hour or two, wasn't particularly reliable for a whole day.

She heard the scrunch of Julia's bicycle tyres on the gravel drive as she pedalled off to deliver the mail, and as Evie stretched out, a patch of early morning sunlight illuminated her bedcovers, and she realised that there'd been no night-time flying for a week or two, and nor had there seemed to be any bombing activity in Plymouth or Exeter, at least that she had been aware of. Certainly there had been nothing like the same activity of a while back when Evie had been able to see the glow caused by fires in Plymouth. Whether this meant that the Germans were changing tactics for something even more dreadful, or that they'd been disheartened, she couldn't say, but she felt distinctly better for having had a good night's sleep, helped in this in large part by the calming influence of her and Mr Smith's pragmatic discussion before bedtime. And it was always hard not to feel cheerful at the sight of such a lovely sunny day.

She dozed for a while, and when she next woke she could hear that Peter seemed also to be sharing Evie's lighter mood. For the first time in ages, she could hear him whistle a jaunty tune. He seemed to be in the garden, and so Evie sat up and inched across her bed to peek out of the window under Pemberley's eaves while, hopefully, keeping herself hidden from view.

Peering down to the stone-flagged back yard, Evie could see Peter kneeling down on a square of old newspaper as he oiled and fiddled with the chain on his bicycle. He was wearing the suit he wore to work, although he had removed the jacket and rolled up the sleeves of his white cotton shirt, and so presumably there had been a problem with the chain when he went to cycle off from Pemberley that morning. As Evie watched she could see that he worked in a methodical manner, taking care to wipe his hands frequently on a piece of old towelling in order not to get oil or dirt on his clothes.

Evie smiled to herself as she watched him – he was concentrating on what he was doing, and Evie felt she could be greedy in her observation of him. She'd seen so little of Peter since the Revels, and even when they had been in the same room, they'd taken pains hardly to look at each other. They had had that bad moment in the kitchen, and they had spoken more reasonably when Evie had been reading *Pride and Prejudice* sitting on the stone bench, but this had merely made her long for their former days of being able to plan the Revels together and chat about this and that.

Now, it was wonderful to be able to drink her fill of this man whom she thought about constantly.

And then suddenly – goodness! for a moment she was really shocked by this unfamiliar impulse – Evie had an almost uncontrollable desire to take off all her nightclothes (and her seen-better-days sleeping scarf), and then kneel there upright on the bed in her nakedness as she tapped on her small-paned

232

bedroom window to get Peter's attention so that he could see her too.

She didn't for a moment think she would actually do it, but it was a powerful thought all the same.

And as she continued to watch Peter work on his bicycle, Evie noticed Mr Worth wander across the yard to speak to him, waving a cigarette about as he did so (Mrs Worth being adamant that ciggies and pipes were without fail to be enjoyed *outside*), and so Evie lay back down on the bed again, smiling to herself at the idea of Peter and Mr Worth's astounded faces if she had dared to wrest her clothes off and bang on the window to attract their attention. What a turn-up for the books that would have been, if she had been so bold, she thought.

Pre-Timmy, the old Evie would never even had had such thoughts, she was sure, and she felt it was through her association with him and her seeing how Timmy's daring and his love of life could signal a depth of exciting experience she had never previously dreamed possible. This had led now to her no longer wanting to tamp down this unfamiliar and more intoxicating side of herself – she couldn't, and she didn't want to, return to being the staid and dependable Evie of yesteryear.

And while they might not be the type of thoughts that nice girls should think, there was something undeniably enticing about them all the same. In fact, Evie could see now, being a 'nice girl' might not be everything it was cracked up to be. Indeed she liked the slightly bolder Evie of the past month or two – and so perhaps she did have something to thank poor Timmy for, after all.

Evie did her stint at the village shop, and then headed to Bluebells to keep an eye on Frank and Joseph, and Marie and Catherine. She got them all to help make bread, and she laughed to see the four of them standing around the kitchen table, the girls on the wooden crates Susan used to place Evie and her sisters on when they were too small to be able to work at the kitchen table if they stood on the floor when Susan was trying to teach them simple recipes. Now the evacuees were all kneading and pummelling the soft dough, and then within a minute or two, they were all complaining that it was Hard Work and they were Tired Already.

Susan arrived home just as Evie was suggesting that when the dough had had chance to rise a second time that perhaps each child could make a bread roll in the shape of an animal. Marie and Catherine, who always seemed to want to do the same thing at the same time, said they would make their rolls in the shape of Keith, the school cat. They went off to get a pencil and some paper so that they could practise drawing Keith first. Having done many a painting session with them, Evie didn't hold high hopes for Keith being very recognisable in her bready incarnation.

And Frank and Joseph decided on dinosaurs as these were more fierce than a fluffy old puss, and off they went to find pictures in James's old boys' encyclopaedia, with Evie's words of 'maybe more stegosaurus than brachiosaurus?' chasing them up the stairs, as she was concerned that long necks and tails would very probably burn to a crisp in the bread oven in the cast-iron range.

'Mother, dear,' Evie then began, at which point Susan gave her that look well known to parents the country over when faced with a wheedling voice from one of their offspring.

Evie smiled, and went on, 'I'm a bit worried about Keith over the summer. I think she'll miss all the children and being centre of attention, and although Mr Cawes will feed her I'm sure she'll miss the fussing she's been getting from my infants. I don't think she goes back to Switherns at all any more as she always seems to be at the school. And Marie and Catherine are so *very* fond of her, and therefore I was wondering that if I went to get her, and if Shady didn't take umbrage about the whole thing, or Keith either, for that matter, whether you'd mind having her here at Bluebells for the school holidays? I'm sure it would make Marie and Catherine very happy. And I'm sure father would enjoy sitting by the range with Keith purring on his lap.' Evie thought it prudent not to mention how loud Keith's purr was.

'Yes, I was wondering how I was going to fill my time – four eleven-and-unders, as well as James and Pattie, and your father too, of course, who's the biggest baby of the lot. My job at the village shop. And Shady. And Shady's windy behind. Yes, I've plenty of time to spare, and I definitely need another hungry mouth and somebody else to clean up after,' replied Susan.

Evie could see the sparkle in her mother's eye, which was quite at odds with what she had just said, and so Evie just raised her eyebrows as she mimicked Shady's squeaky whine that he always made when he was begging for something.

Susan turned so that she was directly facing her daughter, put her hands on her hips, and tried to give Evie a forbidding look.

But Evie's comical expression, her unabated squeaky whines and her two hands now flopped forward from her chest in Shady's begging position (after many hours of drilling by James, Shady was now very good at sit-up-and-beg) couldn't help but make Susan laugh.

'Darn it! I'm going to regret this, I know it, but if you help provide food for Keith, I suppose she can come, Evie,' said Susan.

Not long afterwards Evie went to see Mrs Bowes, and Mr Smith had been correct in his assumption that Timmy would be sent to Stoke Mandeville Hospital. Mrs Bowes had just been telephoned with this confirmation, and she and Mr Smith were leaving for Buckinghamshire later that afternoon.

'I can't wait to see my dear Timmy, Evie sweet. Is there anything you want me to give him from you?' said Mrs Bowes, whose sentimental words and dropped guard revealed she was clearly distracted and very pleased that she was able to do something useful at last.

Evie could see on the kitchen table some things for Mrs Bowes to take to Timmy, including a towel, some shaving gear and a small bar of soap.

'Why don't you see how he is, and then when I've spoken to

you again, I can have a think of something that I can give him?'
Evie said. 'I'll pop back later with a card for him, of course. And
I'd like to send some books, or maybe bake him some biscuits,
but he might not be up to either of these things, in which case
I'd rather save them for when he is feeling a bit better.'

When Evie came to go, she found that this time it was she
who initiated the goodbye hug. She was much fonder of Mrs
Bowes, she realised, than she had been when they first started
working together.

And while she stopped short of saying to the older woman
that she was sending Timmy her love, Evie did feel able in all
honesty to say, even if the actual meaning wasn't quite what Mrs
Bowes would assume, 'Please tell Timmy that I think about him
all the time and that I'll see him very soon.'

When it came to taking Keith over to Bluebells just before supper-
time, Evie was delighted to discover that Mrs Worth had an
ancient wicker cat basket she could borrow. Carrying the basket,
she went to the school playground, and Keith trotted up happily
when Evie called her.

Once incarcerated in the basket, however, Keith was much less
delighted about the whole deal, sending out heart-rending yowls
as Evie turned to head back into the village. She'd only carried
her a little way when she realised that a cat basket was a very
unwieldy thing to carry with a cat inside it, and especially so if it
was imperative that if the wickerwork wasn't to snag her stockings it meant that the basket then had to be held uncomfortably
at arm's length with her arm almost at right-angles to her body,
whilst even a cat as small as Keith proved to be a surprisingly
heavy burden.

She was barely out of the school gates and already Evie was
beginning to regret her idea about Keith's summer holiday. And
to think I was mean to those poor children earlier at Bluebells
when they found kneading the bread to be such hard work –
here am I, on the verge of giving up just as easily on carrying
what is after all a very small cat, thought Evie.

There was a slight squeak of bicycle brakes beside her, and Evie looked up to see that Peter had halted in front of her. He must have been cycling back to Pemberley, when he had seen Evie struggling with the cat basket. 'Is there a problem? May I help?' he enquired. There was virtually no stammer today, Evie was heartened to notice.

'I'm taking Keith to Bluebells for the summer. Marie and Catherine love her, and so I thought they might like to look after her. That was before I realised how heavy she is, of course. And how noisy. She's obviously very thrilled about the whole thing,' Evie replied ironically.

'Yes, she's got a good pair of lungs and a very fine set of vocal chords, that's for certain,' said Peter as he hoisted the cat basket with Keith inside on to the seat of his bicycle. Together they walked a still-yowling Keith over to Bluebells.

As Evie watched Peter lift the cat basket into the kitchen, she realised that it was the first time she had ever asked a man into Bluebells. She had tended to meet Timmy at The Haywain, and Peter had never been with her to her much-loved childhood home.

Peter fits in rather well, Evie couldn't help but think as she watched him make sure the kitchen doors were shut, and the windows too, before he bent down to unbuckle the leather straps to release a furious Keith from her wicker prison.

Shady backed away in horror when he saw there was a C.A.T. in *his* kitchen, and went to sit by the door with a wounded look on his droopy face as he looked at Evie. How *could* you? he seemed to be saying to her.

Keith, purring her rambunctious racket of a purr now she was out of the dreaded cat basket, immediately hopped on to Robert's chair by the range, turned around a couple of times and settled down as if for a nap. She didn't give Shady a second glance, and seemed quite happy to have a dog in what was after all destined to be *her* kitchen.

Peter and Evie looked at each other and burst out laughing.

The rest of the Yeos came in for supper, and Keith didn't bat an eyelid; in fact she didn't even open her eyes.

Marie and Catherine were delighted at the surprise of seeing their beloved companion, and Evie felt heartened by their enthusiasm. It hadn't been that long ago that they'd been too traumatised to utter a word.

Later, as Peter and Evie headed back to Pemberley together (although Evie couldn't help but note that Peter had placed the bicycle between them as he pushed it along), Evie grasped the Timmy nettle and told Peter that Timmy was probably, even as she spoke, being settled in to a bed at Stoke Mandeville Hospital, and that she would be going to see him soon.

Peter wheeled his bicycle along in silence for a second or two, apparently staring very intently at his front wheel. 'I am sure that when Timmy sees you, that will be the best medicine he could have. I know it would be for me, if I were in his position,' he said.

At this Evie managed to feel both happy (at Peter implying the sight of her would make him feel better) and a trifle deflated (as she didn't really want this to be the case for Timmy).

They were just passing Mrs Bowes' house, and Evie sped up the path to drop off her get-well-soon card for Timmy.

Peter stood with his bicycle leaning against him, watching as Mrs Bowes and Evie had a word on the doorstep, Mrs Bowes' travelling case visible just inside the doorway. He waited for Evie, and they walked back to Pemberley together as they talked about the likely weather for the coming week and other safe subjects.

Back at Pemberley, Julia was having a cup of tea with Linda and Sukie, and Tina and Sarah. 'Mrs Worth was looking for you about twenty minutes ago,' Julia said to Evie. Peter seemed to have vanished into thin air as they walked down the hall to the kitchen where the friends' voices could be heard.

Evie found Mrs Worth upstairs. News of Timmy arriving at Stoke Mandeville had spread through the village like wildfire.

And Mr Smith had told the landlady that he was taking Mrs Bowes to the hospital to see her son.

'Mr Smith is going straight from Plymouth this evening to pick up Mrs Bowes, he tells me. I think it very nice of you to let Timmy's mother have the first visit, as that will mean a lot to her, I'm sure,' said Mrs Worth to her young PG. 'Evie, I don't know if you will be interested, but I've got several striped flannel sheets that have already been turned edge to middle, and that have definitely now seen better days as sheets. I was wondering if you would like them so that you could run Timmy up a pair of pyjamas.'

Evie was very touched at Mrs Worth's thoughtfulness; she was sure in part it was prompted by her landlady's loss of her fiancé during the Great War.

And yes, cross and awkward as she felt about Timmy and The Tricia Trouble, Evie realised that in spite of this she would like to make him the pyjamas: they would be useful, and although her feelings for Timmy had changed, she wanted him to be as comfortable as he could be while he recovered.

Clutching the candy-striped flannelette sheets, and a pair of Mr Worth's clean and pressed pyjamas to use as a pattern, Evie headed back to the kitchen.

'Right, girls, all hands to the pump please – I'd really appreciate it. If we make a start now, and all chip in, I think we – and Mrs Sew-and-Sew, of course – might even be able to finish these pyjamas for Timmy tonight,' said Evie, with what she hoped was a persuasive smile.

And making sure that they kept the pyjamas as simple as possible, and despite Mrs Wallis and Mrs Worth having promised to go out to a whist drive in Bramstone and being therefore unavailable to help, that is exactly what they did, the last button (donated from an old blouse that Tina dug out of the perennial sack of jumble when she nipped over to the church hall on her Project Button mission) being sewn on and the final stray thread snipped at nine-thirty. Mrs Sew-and-Sew pronounced herself very pleased with their efforts, adding that multi-coloured candy-striped pyjamas were surely destined to become all the rage in the best-dressed hospital wings.

The only thing that was missing was something to thread through the waistband of the trousers that could be tied to hold them up. Linda had a brainwave, and popped over in the last rays of daylight to the milking parlour at Switherns; when she had been trimming the cows' hooves there a week or so ago, she'd noticed a pile of feed sacks that had a thick hemming. Cut and stitched to length, and with the loose side turned over to stop fraying, and after a much-needed hot wash in some bicarbonate of soda to remove the dairy-parlour smell, here was a functional make-do-and-mend tie belt that would preserve Timmy's modesty once (pray to God) he was up and about on the hospital ward. A final rinse and the belt was hung up on the towel rail above the range to dry overnight.

During the evening, nobody mentioned Timmy's unfaithful behaviour, or Tricia. When a young man was lying badly injured in a hospital bed there were more important things to worry about, the young women sitting around the grand dining-room table tacitly agreed.

Even Peter returned to his old role as teaboy, bringing in a welcome tray at about nine o'clock. Evie knew this would have been hard for him to do, and she was immensely touched by his efforts at doing the right thing.

The next morning, Evie got up early to thread the now dry tie belt through the waistband of the pyjama bottoms, and then she gave Julia the pyjamas wrapped in brown paper and tied up with string. The parcel was neatly addressed to Timmy Bowes, c/o Stoke Mandeville Hospital, with Evie's name and address clearly marked as sender, and Julia had promised to post the parcel off for her sister.

Evie handed it to her sister, and then she snatched it back so that she could give it a kiss for luck, and then she passed it to Julia once more, along with some coins to cover the postage.

Chapter Twenty-Five

It was a week later that Evie got to see Timmy for herself. Mr Smith had pulled a few strings to arrange a lift for her with a vehicle that was going from his office in Plymouth to London, and then another one that was going from a depot of medical supplies out to Stoke Mandeville with various deliveries for the hospital. Something urgent had come up for him at work that had meant he was unable to drive her and it was a roundabout way of getting there, and it meant a very early start for Evie, who was driven to Plymouth just after daybreak by Mr Smith. But it meant too that she didn't have to pay for her travel and, crucially in these days of rationed petrol, that nobody was going to be put out as these journeys were being made anyway. Mr Smith had also found short-terms lodgings for Evie at the guesthouse within walking distance to the hospital, the same guesthouse that Mrs Bowes was staying in.

During their drive to Plymouth Mr Smith said that he had explained to Mrs Bowes that serious injuries did tend to change relationships romantically, and he'd tried unobtrusively to prepare Mrs Bowes for the fact that it could be the case that either Timmy or Evie might not want to hold each other to their engagement. 'I was very subtle, and didn't go into any detail. But she did agree that often that was the case,' said Mr Smith, at which Evie shot him a warm glance of appreciation.

He went on to add that he had several conversations with

Timmy, and he was hopeful that Timmy was going to act in as honourable a fashion as he could to retrieve the situation. Timmy had told him, said Mr Smith, that once he had seen Evie, he would break the news to his mother about Tricia.

Without bothering to drop off her overnight bag when she arrived at her destination, Evie went straight to the hospital.

Mrs Bowes was sitting by Timmy's bed, but when she saw Evie she stood up and said that she would go and stretch her legs outside, so that Timmy and Evie could say hello to each other in private, and off she bustled with a slightly teasing smile.

Evie peered appraisingly at Timmy, who was wearing the pyjamas she'd posted; they were a bit baggy but they looked comfy. In fact he appeared very much at home in them.

Timmy himself didn't look too ill, or at least not as much in pain as she had feared he might, although he had dark shadows under his eyes, one of which had an eyelid that was drooping badly. He had lost an alarming amount of weight so that he looked positively bony, or at least the bits of him she could see did. She couldn't see any other outward sign of his injuries.

Then Timmy grinned at Evie with a hint of his old vivacity, and for a moment Evie could remember what had first attracted her to him.

'Evie, dear, you *are* a sight for sore eyes,' he said in a slightly drunken-sounding voice. 'Actually my eyes are the only parts of me that aren't sore, I think, but you know what I mean. Mother has tried to be by my side morning, noon and night since I got here, and the doctors have to be very strict with her at times, otherwise I'd never get any peace.' He sighed with feeling. 'Evie, I've been simply longing to see you. You look so beautiful, and exactly as I remembered you.'

'How are you feeling?' asked Evie, as she sat down on the bedside chair that Mrs Bowes had just vacated.

Mr Smith had warned Evie before she left Lymbridge that it still wasn't clear how severe Timmy's head injury would prove to be ultimately, or his back injury either, for that matter. The doctors were cautiously optimistic he might regain some, or even all movement in his lower body, but his spinal cord was still swollen and so the eventual outcome couldn't yet be predicted. He had obvious memory loss, and he got muddled and confused when tired, plus his speech sometimes slurred and he was clumsy with his hands. But again, it was too early to tell if these symptoms would continue.

'I feel a bit rum, to be honest. I've constant headaches and I always feel as if I'm seasick, and half the time I'm not quite sure what's going on. It's all a bit of a dream, and not a very nice one. And I don't like being stuck in bed. But each day I feel a bit more chipper and a little more like the old me,' Timmy explained.

There was a pause while Evie wondered how to broach the difficult things she wanted to say.

Timmy grinned at her again, and went on, 'But I'm bored with me, and so can you tell me about you, Evie my dear, and what all of you in Lymbridge have been up to?'

Evie felt it wasn't quite the time to head for choppy waters. And so for a little while Evie and Timmy chatted companionably about this and that, mainly about her time teaching at Lymbridge Primary School, and life at Pemberley (no mention being made of Peter, of course).

After a while Evie concluded that Timmy very probably didn't remember that she was, theoretically, cross with him or that he might have behaved badly by her and Tricia before he left. His speech seemed good, however; certainly better than she had been prepared for. And she found their mundane conversation surprisingly genial and relaxing.

Then Timmy surprised her by saying in a much more reflective tone, 'Evie, I have something very grave to discuss with you, so let's be quick before Ma hoves into view again.

'While Ma was distracted by speaking to the doctor, Mr Smith told me last week about Tricia Dolby's impending motherhood being definite, and that you and her have spoken, and yesterday Dave Symons sent me a note with a cryptic message that I think might suggest that he is toying with the idea of asking Tricia to marry him. My mother doesn't know yet about Tricia, but I must tell her before she returns to Lymbridge as otherwise she is going to hear gossip from somebody else, and that won't do.

'This means I release you from our engagement, of course. Mr Smith has made it most clear to me that this is what I must do, and in quite a firm way too. And so I will tell my mother that this is the position, and there's nothing she can do about it, and that there's absolutely no slur on you in any way. I will make it clear that it is all completely down to me, and that it is me who is ending our engagement – you know how she is! I am so very sorry, and it quite breaks my heart to let you go in this manner as you are a wonderful, wonderful girl whom I never really deserved. I see, however, that I cannot make you go through with marriage to me now as it would be vindictive and cruel. You have behaved very well, and I do appreciate it. But there is nothing for it – I don't know what I was thinking. I wouldn't have hurt you intentionally for the world.'

Evie gave a small snort. Timmy was thinking too well of her. She didn't think she had behaved very well at all. She had lied, and if she were honest, some of the reason she hadn't gone around railing at Timmy to all and sundry is that she was ashamed of the ease with which he had been able to dupe her and so she hadn't wanted her obvious foolishness to add grist to the rumour mill. And she was embarrassed by her own inconstant heart; it hadn't taken her long at all to fall for Peter.

Now, looking at Timmy, in some ways she felt they were both spiritually reduced, and that she couldn't take the moral high ground. And especially so, considering the situation with Peter.

She held Timmy's hand and stared into his eyes; they looked pensive and grave. This was indeed a subdued and very different Timmy from the perennially happy-go-lucky chap she'd got so fond of at the start of the year. Although some might say that if he hadn't wanted to hurt her then he shouldn't have messed around with other Devon lasses, Evie decided to bite these words back and that she should treat him with an equal seriousness and a certain kindness.

'Timmy, it's all been horrible, and a very difficult time. I'd be telling yet another untruth to intimate otherwise. For a long while I wanted to strangle you, although it's fair to say that I don't feel like that any more. Most of all, I feel bad that I've been lying to your mother for months now. I've grown to like her and care for her very much, and I'm sorry that I, and you, have let her down so. It's also meant that I have lied to my parents by omission, and I have never been dishonest with them before—'

'What, never?' Timmy interrupted incredulously. So, the old chancer side of Timmy hadn't been completely eroded then, Evie thought with a certain cheerfulness.

'I also feel dreadfully sorry for Tricia too, who must be simply terrified when she thinks of her future and her loss of reputation. Surely Dave Symons can't be serious in marrying her? He couldn't make anybody happy, the great lump of him, I shouldn't think,' said Evie.

'Well, no, I suppose he can't. But he can probably make Tricia feel better than I can right now. And I think Dave has always tried to make use of my seconds,' pointed out Timmy. 'I suppose though I'll have to ask Tricia to marry me. Meanwhile Ma will want me to get better just so that she can then flay me alive for making her become part of the gossip herself.'

'Look, you mustn't rush into anything,' Evie cautioned. 'It's probably a good thing that you are considering making an honest woman of Tricia, but it will be a mistake if you can't honestly imagine loving both her and the baby. I think you need time to get used to the idea. You've been through a terrible time since you left Britain, and I feel sad for that, but you are right in that you can't now delay in telling your mother. She might have something to say about Tricia as a prospective daughter-in-law, and how she thinks you should behave from this point on.'

There was a significant pause as they each thought about this, and then they couldn't help smiling as they caught each other's eye. If Mrs Bowes had baulked at the thought of Evie as the next Mrs Bowes, then it would be chocks away on her disapproval when it came to thinking of a very pregnant Tricia in this respect.

Evie realised she could spy the hand of Mr Smith at work behind the scenes.

Boldly, she asked Timmy outright if his release of her from their engagement was his own or Mr Smith's idea. Timmy replied that while he would love to take the credit for 'this one time, doing the right thing off my own bat', of course the forthright ending of their engagement had indeed been Mr Smith's suggestion of 'the right thing for a gentleman to do in this circumstance'.

'I'm not pretending to be a gentleman, Evie my dear,' said Timmy, with a slight croak in his voice. 'But Mr Smith explained the repercussions of what has been going on in Devon, and although I didn't want to for a while as I dearly wanted you to become the next Mrs Bowes, eventually I realised that I owed it to you to let you go without any stain on your character. I don't particularly want to marry Tricia, but I do want to acknowledge my child – it's been made clear to me that I might never be able to have another – and so I feel my life has suddenly gone in a direction I could never have expected. Mr Smith has said that he will help me handle Ma; I think I'm going to need all the help I can get there. And he's told me too that I need to watch myself when it comes to how I behave from now on. Between you and me, what a total bore!'

Evie had to smile once again. She thought that Mr Smith might have expected Timmy to be more amenable to doing the right thing than he would in actual fact turn out to be.

They talked for a while longer – really, Mrs Bowes was being very considerate by leaving them on their own for quite such a long time, they agreed – and they decided that Evie should visit Timmy again during the next day's visiting hour, for form's sake. Then she would leave, saying she had an interview for a school-teacher's post in Exeter if Mrs Bowes were to ask, although she almost definitely wouldn't ask as she didn't seem able to think about anything else other than Timmy right now.

And then Timmy would somehow have to find the courage to confess all to his mother, and tell her that his and Evie's engagement was now broken for ever, and that Mrs Bowes would be a grandmother in just a few short months. Evie didn't envy him this conversation at all; it would certainly be a very sticky hour or two as far as Timmy was concerned.

'To be honest, Evie dear, when I got your letter about the rumours of me and Tricia, and the other maids too, I thought if I ignored it, somehow it would all just go away. I was such a long way from home, and what had happened before I left seemed so trivial somehow, and I couldn't believe that the grope with Tricia that evening, which meant nothing to me by the way, was going to lead to an actual baby, and so I more or less refused to accept what you were suggesting,' said Timmy. 'But talking to Mr Smith brought it home to me what a devil I'd been. And you deserve better, Evie – not some man that might never walk and who's the father of somebody else's child.'

This was the truth of it, but hearing it put so bluntly was still shocking.

Evie's eyes filled with tears. Perhaps it was the sight of the previously vigorous Timmy lying so still and pale and thin in bed, or perhaps it was Timmy openly talking about the things that had caused her such immense hurt since Easter. She remembered the evening in the snug with Dave Symons, and the hot rush of shame and jealousy; and she thought of Timmy's cheerful letters that never acknowledged his poor behaviour, and the weeks of being trapped into lying implicitly to Mrs Bowes by not telling her about Tricia. Suddenly Evie found herself cresting on a tide of emotion. She looked at Timmy, and saw that his eyes were welling up too. Immediately her anguished feelings switched to something more sympathetic, as she considered Timmy's emaciated body and his droopy eye.

'What a pair we are,' she whispered sadly.

And then she noticed Mrs Bowes talking to Sister at the end

of the ward, and bucking up, she quickly dabbed at her eyes with her hanky and then leant over to give Timmy a quick mop-up too, with the result that the pair were sharing only slightly damp looks but coyly warm smiles by the time Mrs Bowes rejoined them.

Evie left early the next afternoon as planned, exchanging a surprisingly sincere hug with Timmy. She realised that for the first time she could honestly say that she now liked him as the person he was. She didn't, of course, approve of how he had behaved, but the fact that there was a resigned humbleness about him as he lay in the pyjamas that Mrs Sew-and-Sew had overseen the making of had rather endeared him to her.

While Evie didn't necessarily think this contrite mood of Timmy's would last, especially if he were to make anything like a full recovery, for now at least the fact that he didn't seem to want to be evasive or the old devil-may-care Timmy any longer, and that he realised that his behaviour had put her and Tricia each in a very difficult position, had gone a long way in improving things between the two of them.

When later she waited on the platform at Paddington train station for a train to the West Country, Evie found herself considering that the remorseful Timmy who lay in the hospital bed might almost end up as a good fiancé after all.

Then she thought back to those weeks when she had just started working with Mrs Bowes at the school, and how very much Timmy had hurt her, and she chided herself. Whatever was she thinking? She shouldn't be sentimental about him just because he was lying in a hospital bed. There was a baby coming and a scared young mother-to-be without a wedding ring on her finger, and Timmy needed to get his priorities in order.

And, she knew, although her visit to Stoke Mandeville hospital had gone much better than she could ever have hoped in terms of how she and Timmy had resolved their differences (the terrifying glimpses of servicemen more severely injured than Timmy bringing home to her most assuredly that it could well have been a very different story in this respect), the reality was that she didn't love Timmy, and that she had fallen in love – she could now say this to herself for the very first time – with somebody else.

She couldn't wait to see Peter to tell him of her release from her betrothal.

The public news of the broken engagement might have to remain a secret for a while, of course – well, after Peter, there would be Julia and Pattie, and Linda and Sukie to be brought into the know – but once it was definite that Mrs Bowes had been told of the breakdown in their relationship, then it could become open knowledge and Evie would be able to break the news to her parents.

She thought Robert and Susan would feel that Timmy had behaved very badly by Evie, but that generally it would be a good thing Evie had been released from the engagement with no stain on her reputation.

Evie felt that the burgeoning romance between herself and Peter would have to be kept under wraps for a while (well, besides for Sukie, who knew already), as it just wouldn't do for her to be seen rushing straight from one romantic entanglement to another.

To her horror, Evie arrived back in Lymbridge very late at night to discover that the previous evening – and she had only been gone the one night, after all – Peter had been seconded suddenly to somewhere in the north of England.

He'd mentioned to Mr Wallis that his posting with the Signal Corps had suddenly been altered, and that he'd had no choice in the matter. And that very morning an official looking car had been sent for him before the other PGs were up, and off Peter had gone.

'You mark my words, young lady, that young Pipe has gone to do something with our spies or with our codes, or with breaking Jerry's codes. It's obviously important to judge by the car that came for him, and so I doubt he'll be back in the West Country,' said Mr Worth to Evie at breakfast the next morning, who was determined to have his tuppence-worth. He didn't know that he was inadvertently striking a dagger deep into Evie's churning heart.

Peter had paid for his next month's rent, apparently, and had left most of his possessions behind. But there was no forwarding address and no one really seemed to know where he was or what official body he'd been seconded to, and so Evie was unable to think of any way that she could let him know that she was now a woman free of any romantic obligations.

Evie could only, quite literally, grind her teeth in exasperation.

Just as bad was the next evening. After supper there was a ring of the telephone in the hall, and it felt that almost immediately Mr Smith came in with worrying news following a conversation with Mrs Bowes.

He asked Evie to join him on the terrace so they could have a word in private.

Apparently, not long after Evie had left, Timmy had told Mrs Bowes of Tricia Dolby's condition and the end of his engagement with Evie, and Mrs Bowes had been so furious that she had had to vacate his bedside, leaving Timmy in no doubt that she was livid.

Within an hour or two Timmy had developed a fever, and now he had what the doctors thought was pneumonia, his condition deteriorating rapidly as he no longer seemed to be responding to any of the medication the hospital could provide. He'd had seizures, and his condition had worsened to the point that it now looked as if he might not make it after all.

Instantly Evie felt drained and devastated. Timmy had looked weak and a little poorly when she had seen him so recently, but nowhere near how she imagined someone facing death might look. To hear of his rapid decline was truly terrible.

Without quite understanding why she felt so compelled to be there, early the following morning she dipped into her meagre savings to catch the next train to London from Plymouth, and from there another train from Marylebone station to Aylesbury.

When she arrived back at Stoke Mandeville Hospital, Evie could hardly recognise Mrs Bowes. In the short time since they had said goodbye, Mrs Bowes had aged what looked to be a decade, and her sensible tweed skirt now very obviously bagged at her rear and gaped at her waist.

Timmy's condition remained ominous. He was too ill to have anyone sitting by his bed, and so Mrs Bowes was seated very upright on the edge of a hard chair in a depressingly grim visitors' room.

She clasped Evie to her, and broke down with wracking sobs. Evie heard her own voice cracking as she suggested a walk outside, although within calling distance should anything change in Timmy's condition – the hospital and Timmy's fight for life felt unbearably oppressive.

Once in the fresh air, Mrs Bowes was persuaded to take Evie's arm, and the two walked slowly in the summer afternoon.

'I didn't expect you to come, Evie, that's the truth of it. It is an extraordinarily selfless act on your part, and I cannot tell you the high regard it makes me hold you in. Once you left here the other day, Timmy told me all that has happened, and about him releasing you from your engagement. He has behaved very poorly, I'm afraid, and I am very shocked at how badly he has acted. I'm still getting used to the idea that I am to be a grandmother,' said Mrs Bowes. 'I was so angry with him that I'm afraid I shouted at him – I didn't even care that people could hear us, can you believe? I had to march up and down outside in a temper! Then Timmy became so ill within what felt to be an instant, and I thought he would die. Mr Smith rang me back after he'd told you the news, and we had a long conversation and he calmed me down. He's helped me see that it might be a good thing that Tricia Dolby is having Timmy's baby – I admit that at the moment I don't agree wholeheartedly, but I do take comfort that something of Timmy will pass to the next generation. But I feel very, very badly about the way Timmy has treated you, Evie.'

Evie patted Mrs Bowes' hand in acknowledgement and said in reply, 'I'm so sorry that I had to be less than honest with you for all those weeks, but I didn't feel it was my place to tell you about Timmy and what he had been up to. Tricia seems nice enough – I have talked to her, and it's all been very frightening for her too, of course. And I am sure you will have a lovely grandson or granddaughter.

'Although Timmy and I are no longer promised to one another, I felt I had to be here with you – I can't quite find the words to say what I mean, or why I wanted to come back to see Timmy and you. But I suppose that I believe now that I am the person I am today because of the time I spent as Timmy's fiancée. And I want him very much to know that people in Lymbridge care about him, and that we are all rooting for him to get better. I do so wish him better.'

'Evie, I don't know where I went wrong with him – he was brought up to behave properly, as I'm sure you know. I admit I thought at first he had made a rash choice when he told me of your engagement, but I have seen you since in a different light, and now I believe that you would have made him a fine wife,' said Mrs Bowes.

To quell this line of conversation, gently Evie took Mrs Bowes' hand and in it placed the family heirloom. It was Timmy's grandmother's ring which he had given her as their engagement ring. Evie had been keeping it safe since she removed it from the delicate gold chain around her neck when she had arrived back at Pemberley after her visit to Timmy in the hospital; she hadn't been able to take it off until then.

Evie's smiled at Mrs Bowes to show there were no hard feelings on her side at least. Mrs Bowes looked at the ring, gave a deep sigh that seemed to reach every part of her body, and then she put it in her pocket after wrapping it in a neatly pressed and folded, lace-edged linen handkerchief.

'Shall we go back inside to see if there is any further news of Timmy?' said Evie, and together they turned around and slowly headed back inside the hospital.

The next few days were relentlessly depressing. Although the sun shone brightly, with just an occasional small, fluffy white cloud scooting across the sky, Timmy's life remained hanging in the balance. Fevers and pneumonia were quite common in hospital, but Timmy had already been very weak and with his brain and spine compromised, he had been hit hard and was once again in a deep coma, unresponsive and with a fluttering heartbeat and eyelids. It seemed as if every hour brought news of some further deterioration in his health.

Evie hoped that he would live, although when she saw how ill he was, there was a tiny bit of her that wished, should he recover only to be very incapacitated afterwards, that instead he would die, just slipping quietly away in his sleep this night or the next.

She even said as much to Julia, when she made a horrifically expensive reversed-charge call one night to Pemberley (Mr Smith assuring Mrs Worth that he would pick up the bill). Julia went very quiet for a few seconds, and then she just said, 'You sad thing, you,' after which Evie couldn't talk for the lump in her throat. Mrs Bowes, Timmy and herself were all sad things, Evie felt. She ended the call without thinking to ask if anyone had heard from Peter.

Mr Smith was still having to deal with the crisis at his office, and was thus unable to leave work to be with Mrs Bowes, and when Evie realised that Mrs Bowes had no close friends nor any family to be with her, she was very glad that she had made the effort to return to the hospital. It wasn't always easy being with the older woman, but actually they didn't talk much, and both of them seemed to find the other's company comforting and reassuring.

Then, almost without them noticing, they realised Timmy seemed to be holding his own. Or at least he wasn't getting any worse. And in a day or two more he started imperceptibly to improve.

Evie had been in Aylesbury for two whole weeks before Timmy was well enough to have a conversation.

'Ma was so livid with me when I told her about ending our engagement and about Tricia that I had to stage an evasive rear-flank action and retreat into fever...' he gasped out in such a quiet voice that Evie had to put her ear close to his mouth to catch every word.

It wasn't much of a joke, but Evie found herself smiling down at him as relief flooded through her body, and then she kissed him on the cheek. She laughed to see him looking bashful at her impulsive action. She remembered Sukie saying something similar the day the two of them had walked on the moors, and now Evie thought about how prescient people could be at times. It was enough to make one think there was some larger plan for everybody, although Evie couldn't begin to guess what this plan actually might be.

Several days later Evie returned to Devon, charged this time with having a word with Tricia on Timmy's behalf. This was to say that if Tricia wanted to, Timmy would be prepared to marry her, and that Mrs Bowes would welcome her and the baby into the family. Evie carried with her a note Mrs Bowes had written to Tricia to that effect.

How ironic, thought Evie. My parents are going to think I've lost my mind to have agreed to do this; on second thoughts, it's probably best that they never know. One minute I'm all set to marry the man, and the next I'm trying to help someone else marry him. I'd feel very differently if there wasn't a baby involved. And if I still loved Timmy. Or if I hadn't seen with my own eyes how very close to death he had got.

She didn't dare think about Peter. It was weeks now since they had spoken.

Chapter Twenty-Six

Sukie was the person Evie chose to confide in. Sukie was reasonably unshockable, and she was very much a 'take people as she found them' sort of gal. She also knew about Peter, of course.

'Sukes, if anybody had told me three months ago I'd be planning on seeing Tricia like this, I'd have thought them quite mad,' confessed Evie. 'But somehow me seeing her to say that Timmy will marry her, if she wants, and that Mrs Bowes has written her a letter "welcoming" her to the Bowes family, seems the right thing to do. I'm not certain that Timmy will ever make a wonderful husband, or that Mrs Bowes will be able to resist putting her oar in now and again if they do go ahead and do the deed, but from Tricia's point of view this might be a better alternative than tying herself to Dave Symons.'

Sukie gave a dramatic wince at the thought of Dave Symons as a husband, and then she and Evie roared with laughter, Evie gasping to her friend, 'You're a caution!' It wasn't that what had been said was funny as such, but that it was a welcome release of tension.

Sukie said that as The Grange was only a mile or so from the milking parlour where Tricia was working she would cycle over in her next lunch hour with a note from Evie suggesting that Evie and Tricia meet at The Wheatsheaf for a talk.

Evie thought this a good plan, and so the note she wrote was simple: 'Dear Tricia, I wonder if you and I could have a word? I have news that you might like to hear. I've nothing cross to say, I promise, and so perhaps you could meet me at The Wheatsheaf either tonight or tomorrow at six p.m.? Evie Yeo.'

The 'tonight' was actually tomorrow, and the tomorrow the day after, as Sukie would give the note to Tricia in the morning and then let Evie know what the answer was re: meeting up.

Once the writing of the note to Tricia was out of the way, Sukie looked at her friend – they were sitting on the grass in the shade of a tree at Pemberley, with (scandalously) their bare legs stuck out in the sunshine to get a bit of a suntan, their stockings carefully rolled beside them – and said, 'What about Peter?'

'I'm at my wit's end,' said Evie. 'We'd got to the stage where we weren't avoiding each other any more. And the moment Timmy had released me from the engagement, all I could think of was telling Peter that, if by any remote chance he were still interested, I was now a free agent. I raced back to Pemberley from Aylesbury itching to see him, only to find he'd gone and there's no obvious way of me contacting him.'

'There must be! I can't believe not,' said Sukie.

'Well, I can't think of one,' replied Evie. 'I think it's written in the stars that I'm to be unlucky when it comes to Peter.'

Despite it only being mid-August, it was a chill and blowy evening when Evie sat in the ladies bar in The Wheatsheaf the following evening waiting for Tricia, who was late. She hoped Tricia would arrive soon as she wanted to get their meeting over and done with as soon as possible.

At last the door creaked open and Tricia came in. She looked healthy but quite large of stomach now, and Evie could see that her ankles looked to be on the swollen side.

Evie tried to give Tricia a reassuring smile, and Tricia attempted to smile back. Neither smile quite worked – they obviously both felt tense and uncomfortable.

'May I get you a drink, Tricia? Or would you prefer to have a walk outside?' said Evie.

Tricia decided she needed a lemonade as she found the

pregnancy was making her thirsty all the time, but that then she would like to go for a walk. Evie pushed her own lemonade towards Tricia, saying she'd only just got it and she hadn't taken a sip. Tricia drank it quickly without bothering to sit down, and Evie then stood up and held the door to the ladies bar open for Tricia, and they stepped outside into the coolness of the blustery evening.

'Tricia, I'm sure you've heard that Timmy is now in hospital. He's got head and spinal injuries, and it's still too early to say how well he will recover or if he will ever walk again,' began Evie. 'I have seen him, and we have broken our engagement. He has now told his mother about you. And the long and short of it is that he will, if you want to, marry you to give your baby a father and to give you a wedding ring. Mrs Bowes says that you can live with her, and she can help you with the baby, and then when Timmy comes out of hospital you can all decide where you can live – if Timmy needs constant care, as could be the case, it might be best if he moves back to live at his mother's house. I have here a letter to you from Mrs Bowes.'

Evie had been watching Tricia's face as she had been breaking this news. Tricia's expression had remained oddly blank throughout, and Evie couldn't tell if she was pleased at what Evie had to say to her, or not. Evie decided to wait and let Tricia be the next to speak. She did, however, push the envelope containing Mrs Bowes' note in Tricia's direction, and as if she weren't really aware of what she was doing, Tricia took it without a glance and didn't open it.

'I don't understand,' was what Tricia said as she gave a confused glance in Evie's direction.

Evie tried again.

'I think Timmy has realised that he will have a son or a daughter in three or four months. And he has been extremely poorly and very nearly died, and of course he still is very ill. And so I think that because Mrs Bowes nearly lost him, this has made her think perhaps more kindly than she would have done otherwise towards both you and the baby you are carrying – it is Timmy's child, after all, and so she sees that she is to be a grandmother, while Timmy sees that come what may there is a part of him that is going to be living in the world that he's been fighting for. It could be that you are carrying the only child that Timmy can ever have, and he and Mrs Bowes are very aware of that. While it wouldn't necessarily be as anyone has planned, I think the past month has taught Timmy and his mother how precious life is, and so your baby is someone they want to celebrate and look forward to, especially as it might be the case that this baby will be the only Bowes of the next generation.'

There was another silence.

'Dave Symons 'as dumped my friend Kate an' said 'e'll make an honest woman of me,' said Tricia rather flatly.

'Do you love him?'

At this Tricia gave a derisive snort. And then she added, 'To be fair, I don't love Timmy either. But I think I 'ave to marry one of them as my parents have made it very clear I can't live with them when the babby is born, as they can't afford it and they don't 'ave the room. They say I've made my bed and now I've got to lie in it. I won't be able to support me and the baby on my milkin' wages, and that's even if I could find someone to sit for the baby if I were at the parlour. I've nowhere to go, and no savings of me own. If I marry Dave, I won't have Mrs Bowes tellin' me what to do. But if I marry Timmy, then the babby will be part of 'is or 'er proper family. Mrs Bowes was always wicked to me when I were a nipper though, and that's 'ard to forget.'

Evie sympathised, and said Tricia needed to think carefully about all of this, and that she needed to read the letter that Mrs Bowes had written to her. Evie added that it did seem as if Mrs Bowes was quite a changed woman over the last month or two. Finally Evie pointed out to Tricia that if she decided to go ahead, it would mean her going to Stoke Mandeville Hospital for the ceremony, which would be performed at Timmy's bedside, but she was sure that Mrs Bowes would pay for Tricia's travel and accommodation.

They talked some more, with Evie telling Tricia what she knew about Timmy's medical prognosis, from the worst to the best scenarios, Evie saying that she wanted Tricia to have all the information before making up her mind about what she should do.

Evie suggested it might be an idea for Tricia to write to Mrs Bowes to set her mind at rest that the offer was genuine. When she saw Tricia's horrified expression at the thought of this, Evie realised that Tricia felt (and she was probably right in this assumption) that Mrs Bowes would be very critical of any misspellings, or unclear or sloppy sentences, and as Evie knew that Tricia had struggled at school and had left when she was only fourteen, she added she could help Tricia write the reply if that made her feel better.

When they came to part Evie was rather taken aback when Tricia clasped her hand and shook it rather formally. 'I do appreciate you seein' me, Evie. There's not many a maid who'd do what you 'ave just done with me, when I've gone behind your back and rolled in the 'ay with yorn intended,' Tricia said with the slightest of trembles to her chin.

'There would have been a time when I wouldn't have done what I've just done either, Tricia,' Evie replied honestly. 'But when I saw poor Timmy lying so ill in his hospital bed, and when I thought of you carrying his baby, and what you must be feeling, it seemed to me to be exactly what I should do. Even if you decide not to marry him, Timmy's and my engagement is over, and I definitely won't be marrying him. And if you do marry him, I do wish him and yourself well, and the baby too, of course. It may be one of those situations where it all works out for the best in the long run. I truly believe that.'

As Evie started to walk back to Lymbridge a few minutes later, she thought the conversation between herself and Tricia had gone probably as well as it could have done. Once the letter from Tricia to Mrs Bowes was written it would be up to Timmy,

Mrs Bowes and Tricia to sort things out between them, and Evie could stop worrying about them all.

Now, Evie knew she had a trickier conversation to have – breaking the news to Robert and Susan that she was no longer engaged.

Evie headed straight to Bluebells as she wanted to get the next bit of unpleasantness out of the way as soon as possible. The minute she arrived she said she needed to speak to Robert and Susan alone.

Pattie twigged immediately what Evie was planning to say, and so she offered to put the younger children to bed. James was having a night in, and his head popped up in curiosity from the boots to which he was threading new laces – Evie looked at him and then with a shrug of her shoulders she said he could stay. She felt she might as well face all the likely unpleasantness at the same time, and as James was practically an adult now it was time she treated him like one.

So she and James, and Robert and Susan sat around the kitchen table, while vague noises of mischievous children laughing and having fun drifted down to them from upstairs.

Evie took a deep breath, and began.

'My engagement with Timmy is officially over. He has made Tricia Dolby pregnant, and she will have their baby in late November, I think it is. Our engagement ended on my first visit to Stoke Mandeville, and Timmy has now told Mrs Bowes about the pregnancy, and he has offered to marry Tricia. I have known about this since just before I started at the school, but I couldn't say anything, except to Julia and Pattie. Mother and Father, I'm sorry I've been keeping you all in the dark,' she said, increasingly rushing through saying what she wanted to.

Predictably Robert and Susan were outraged on Evie's behalf, while James became a typically protective brother, saying that when Timmy came back to Lymbridge he would 'sort him out'. Robert replied grimly that 'you'll have to get in line, son'.

'Stop it, both of you,' said Evie, a trifle wearily. 'I've had a while to get used to the idea and actually I think it a very good thing that Timmy and I are no longer engaged. We weren't right for each other, and we never were, as you guessed, Mother. We would have made each other unhappy if we had married. Timmy and I *both* feel this, and so when Timmy comes home, I want every single Yeo to treat him nicely – and that means all of you around this table – I simply will not allow this to degenerate into any sort of long-running family feud, do you all understand me? And I want Tricia Dolby, or Tricia Bowes as she may well be soon, and the baby too, of course, to be treated well by us all too. This is the time for the Yeos to put on a united front of magnanimity, and for us to lead by example. The gossip mill in Lymbridge will be busy, but we will rise above it. Is everybody clear on this?'

Susan put a hand on both Robert and James's arms, and told them to listen to Evie. If Evie were content with the situation, then neither of them had any right to put their two-penneth in.

The male side of the Yeo family was not to be so easily placated, however, and the more they continued to say what a scoundrel Timmy was, the more Susan began to see their point of view and to become cross on Evie's behalf.

Evie tried to calm things down, but it was clear her family were simply furious with Timmy and his callous treatment of her.

In the end, Evie stood up abruptly, saying, 'This is ridiculous. You're all behaving as if I should marry a man who has been unfaithful to me, and as if I should be mourning the loss of the promise of this already doomed marriage. I like Timmy but I don't any longer want to be married to him, please understand that. There is no harm done as far as I am concerned; he and I never had relations –' at this confession Robert and Susan both looked relieved, while James looked a little puzzled as to quite what Evie was driving at '– and I would prefer to wait for a man who will treat me better. And let us all remember Timmy is still very ill, and that we should all be praying for his recovery rather than thinking of ways to give him a bloody nose. I thought better of you all, really I did.'

And with that rebuke, Evie stomped angrily out of the kitchen and back to Pemberley, where the absence of Peter seemed to be weighing even more heavily in the air than usual.

Evie felt she couldn't face going through all of this again, and so she decided to have a word with Mr Smith and beg him to break the news of the broken engagement, and Tricia's impending motherhood, to the Pemberley household.

She felt exhausted – trying to do the right thing was much more exacting than one might imagine.

Chapter Twenty-Seven

Mr Smith stepped into the breach as she had hoped, and by the following evening it was obvious to Evie that he had spread the word, with the welcome result that everyone at Pemberley now obviously knew that Evie's engagement with Timmy was broken.

Sympathetic looks were cast in her direction, and the sort of smiles that weren't happy exactly but were more the sort of smile that pressed the giver's lips together to result in a look of what was intended to be kindly commiseration.

Mrs Worth said to Evie when she came across her in the hall how extremely sorry she was to hear the news, and that if there was anything she could do, Evie only had to say the word. Mr Worth managed more than Evie would have expected, with his 'chin up, old girl, chin up' as she passed him on the way to wash her hands. And Mrs Wallis confessed in a quiet voice when Mr Wallis had gone to refresh their pre-dinner drinks (sadly non-alcoholic as the gin had long been finished), and had his back to her and Evie, that she had had three broken engagements before Mr Wallis had been the one to walk her down the aisle. 'Always hurts like hell, Evie, but time heals, it really does. You remember that, my dear. You will get over it, I promise. Mr Wallis is older and not at all what I expected I'd settle for, but I've surprised myself how happy we've been, and so now I think affairs of the heart are sometimes rocky but always mysterious waters,' the older woman said in a wise tone.

Tina and Sarah tried to be positive about the latest turn of events by insisting that if Lymbridge really was poised to get all the thousands of servicemen and ancillary support staff as was being rumoured, then Evie wouldn't be left on the shelf for long and so she mustn't allow herself to be downhearted for too long.

Evie wanted to say to all and sundry that she felt it was a good thing she and Timmy were no longer getting married, and that even a stickler for etiquette such as Mrs Bowes now agreed that a broken engagement and a different wife for her son were positives to be embraced.

But Evie decided to keep these thoughts to herself, feeling a dignified silence was the most sensible option. She was sick and tired of being the centre of attention, and so she thought that if she adopted the policy of remaining as quiet as possible about the whole thing then it was likely to become yesterday's news just that bit sooner. And so she tried to smile graciously when the Pemberley PGs commiserated, and to not really get drawn in to commenting one way or another on what had gone on between herself and Timmy.

Evie had had a good heart-to-heart, however, with Julia as they lay in their bedroom, although without any mention of Peter on Evie's side. Evie noticed that Julia mentioned him a couple of times, but whenever that happened she would deftly change the subject to draw her sister off the scent. Evie didn't want to muddy the water by talking about herself and Peter – and certainly not anything to do with piglets or the blessed Nissen hut – and Evie gambled that although Julia probably had the sneaking suspicion that Peter had piqued Evie's interest, she wouldn't be aware that anything had actually happened between them.

The next teatime Evie and Julia went to Bluebells for tea, and Evie apologised unreservedly to her parents for being uncharacteristically short-tempered with them the previous evening.

Susan told her not to give it another thought and that she and Robert quite understood Evie's point of view; Robert harrumphed and headed out to the back garden for a little remedial weeding in the vegetable plots.

'Robert's still beside himself with Timmy, naturally, but he'll come around, lovey, as will James. And Pattie and Julia and me will make sure that Robert and James are nice to Tricia if they run into her,' Susan reassured her daughter.

Evie smiled at her mother and then sank into Robert's chair by the range. She felt tired suddenly, and content to let Julia and Pattie take care of supervising Marie and Catherine setting the table for tea. They were just at the age where they loved to feel grown-up by helping out with simple household chores.

As Evie allowed herself to relax for a couple of minutes, Keith jumped on to her lap and purred happily as she turned around a couple of times before settling down, while Shady, determined he shouldn't be outdone, went to lie at Evie's feet. It was as if the pets knew that Evie had had a trying time recently, and she felt very comforted by their furry presence.

The next week or two dragged by at a snail's pace for Evie. The heather and the gorse flooded the moorland hills with hues of lavender and gold, and the wild Dartmoor pony foals lost their babyish looks and started to look coltish. It was the time of year that Lymbridge looked at its most idyllic, and normally it was Evie's favourite season. The weather was fine generally and there was no rain, but Evie hardly noticed as she felt distinctly out of sorts and unable to concentrate on anything much.

Sukie and Linda tried to cheer her up but they only had middling success. Evie didn't much feel like going to either The Haywain or The Wheatsheaf as they suggested, and although she allowed herself to be persuaded to go to Oldwell Abbott a couple of times to accompany her chums to the cinema, it was very obvious to them all that her heart wasn't really in it. Her friends stopped pressing her to go out when they realised that Evie was struggling to follow any dramatic storyline over the length of a movie, and they'd noticed too that when she chatted with them, she would often ask a question that one or other of them had just given the answer to with their previous comments, something Evie would have realised easily if she had been paying attention.

Julia put all efforts into interesting Evie in her growing hair-dressing work with the women of Lymbridge, while Pattie tried to involve Evie once again with the sewing circle, as now that Linda was officially walking out with Sam Torrence, they were all making do and mending to ensure that Linda had a couple of presentable summer dresses, and a nice jacket to wear on their nights out together, Linda having been able (miraculously) to persuade Sam that it was nice for her to do something occasion-ally in her free time that meant she didn't need to wear her breeches and that would necessitate him having a bit of a wash and brush-up too. But neither of the sisters' efforts really bore fruit, as although Evie appeared happy enough to sit at the dining table at Pemberley along with the other members of the sewing circle, she didn't say much and nor was she especially productive when it came to the actual sewing, no matter how much Mrs Sew-and-Sew tried to cajole her otherwise.

Meanwhile, Evie had met with Tricia, as she had offered, and together they had written Tricia's reply to Mrs Bowes' note. Or, to be more precise, Evie had drafted a reply, and then Tricia had copied it out in her loopy writing, which slanted this way and that as if it had had one too many slurps of scrumpy.

'Dear Mrs Bowes,' said the letter, 'Thank you very much for your note to me. It was a kind and unexpected gesture and I am very grateful for your thoughtful words. I was wondering if I should come to see you and Timmy at the hospital, and then we can discuss things further? I look forward to hearing from you. Yours sincerely, Tricia Dolby.'

Tricia's note had the desired effect, and several days later Mr Smith drove Tricia to the station, bought her a return ticket and waited until he saw her safely on the train towards Timmy and Mrs Bowes.

That evening Mr Smith and Evie agreed honour had been served all the way around regarding Timmy and Tricia and the forthcoming baby, and that it was a good thing Tricia was going to see Timmy and Mrs Bowes in an open frame of mind.

Evie didn't feel particularly relieved, or unhappy – she was just glad that her responsibilities had now ended and that she didn't have to do anything else in respect of aiding and abetting Timmy's love life.

There was one day when Evie's mood lightened, and even then it was only for an hour or so. This was after Mrs Worth opened a package posted to her from the London offices of the British Board of Trade – it contained a selection of newspapers with the first cartoon strips of the antics of Mrs SEW-and-SEW. Even Evie found it quite exciting to see the cartoon strip; it was almost as if Mrs SEW-and-SEW was a flesh and blood member of the Lymbridge community who'd unexpectedly found national fame.

A few days later, a man from the public relations department of the BoT interviewed Julia and Pattie over the telephone, and the same *Western Morning News* photographer that had been to the Revels was sent out to Pemberley by the BoT to take their picture.

Sukie joked to Evie that as Linda had been written about by the *Western Morning News* after that horrible day when poor Mabel was killed by the strafing from the German light aeroplane, from the group of the five of them, it was now only she and Evie who had not had a story about them appear in the press. Evie smiled tolerantly in Sukie's direction, but she didn't come back with a rejoinder as the Evie of a month earlier would have done.

The resulting Mrs SEW-and-SEW good-news story was press-released across the national papers, and for a short while Julia and Pattie were Lymbridge's most famous inhabitants, although Pattie had to laugh a few days later when she went out one evening in Oldwell Abbott to find that her treat of fish and chips that she was scoffing merrily had been wrapped in newspaper containing the story of herself and her sister, and the creation of their bossy sewing helpmate, and that there was a greasy spludge across her and Julia's photograph.

'Back to earth with a bump, that's me now that I've had a piece of battered rock salmon rubbing against my cheeks,' Pattie announced to the world at large. 'Here today, and gone tomorrow.'

'At least you know your plaice,' replied Sukie. 'Whoops – only codding.' And then, after Pattie had swung a cushion in her direction, 'It doesn't become you to carp!'

Meanwhile there was no news at Pemberley about Peter or his whereabouts, or any plans he might have to return to Dartmoor.

One evening Evie heard Mr and Mrs Worth discussing whether they should move his things into the tiny box room that could just about squeeze in the narrowest of single beds, as this would mean they could let his nice airy bedroom to another PG.

Although Evie had suspected for a while that it didn't look as if Peter were coming back, her crushing disappointment with the casual and rather mercenary way Mr and Mrs Worth were discussing Peter's absence made her realise that secretly she had been hoping that one day he would simply turn up as if he'd never been away.

In a half-hearted manner Evie supposed she should think about applying for another teaching position, but every day she kept putting off any serious attempt at looking for anything that might suit her. She knew that if she didn't get herself sorted soon, she wouldn't be able to continue living at Pemberley for very much longer, but somehow even this thought didn't seem enough to galvanise her into taking proper action.

Luckily Mrs Bowes gave Evie a little temporary work, and this helped eke out her slender funds for another couple of weeks.

As it was clear Timmy was going to be at Stoke Mandeville Hospital for a while longer, Mrs Bowes had telephoned Pemberley to ask if Evie could spend a day or two sorting a few things out at Mrs Bowes' house. Mr Cawes was keeping the garden going, and as Mrs Bowes had a lady 'who does', the house was kept ticking over.

But Mrs Bowes wanted some clothes and other odds and ends

for herself and for Timmy, and a few important papers, and so Evie took careful note of everything required, and promised that she would find everything, pack it and have it ready for Mr Smith to take to Mrs Bowes when he next visited her and Timmy. Mrs Bowes also gave her some further administrative tasks for the school, and Evie carried them out with no trouble, although still feeling slightly as if she'd not surfaced from her old feelings of being underwater.

One evening Mr Smith asked if he could have a word with Evie, and she made her way after him on their familiar route out to the terrace. This sort of request usually meant unwelcome news in her experience

He made sure that Evie was sitting down, and then he said he had several things to tell her.

Firstly, Timmy and Tricia were indeed to marry; it had all been agreed, and Tricia was now the proud owner of the heirloom engagement ring. The ceremony would take place the following week at the hospital.

Secondly, Mr Smith and Mrs Bowes were to get married too. They were going to marry at the same time as Timmy and Tricia, and the hospital chaplain would officiate over a dual wedding. The bans for both weddings were in the process of being read.

Thirdly, because of Timmy's condition, Mrs Bowes had decided to rent a small house near the hospital for herself and Mr Smith. This meant Mr Smith was transferring temporarily to a British Board of Trade office nearer Stoke Mandeville Hospital for his work, and of course this also meant that he would be moving out of Pemberley at the weekend, although later he would be moving back to Lymbridge to share Mrs Bowes' cottage, once Timmy was out of Stoke Mandeville. However, Timmy still being in hospital meant that Mrs Bowes planned on taking at least a term (and very possibly longer) away from teaching at Lymbridge Primary School.

Evie realised she'd become fond of Mr Smith, and that she would miss his smartly dressed presence at Pemberley. She was also sorry that Mrs Bowes and her beloved tweed skirt wouldn't be back in Lymbridge for a while at least.

And fourthly, said Mr Smith, Evie and a guest (he assumed Evie would choose either Julia or Sukie, if either of them could get time off work), would be very welcome at the wedding ceremony, all their expenses to be paid by Mr Smith, of course.

'We would understand, my dear, if you felt unable to come, seeing as you would be watching Timmy and Tricia marry, as well as Mrs Bowes and myself. But you have been very much part of everyone's lives these past months, and so we would all very much like to have you there as we are each so very fond of you. It will be a quiet wedding as Timmy tires so easily, but we hope all the same that it will be a happy day for everyone,' said Mr Smith in his earnest voice.

Evie felt very calm about everything that Mr Smith had just said to her. And yes, she thought, she would try to make it to Timmy's wedding, as a guest. It wasn't exactly conventional – but what the goodness?!

Chapter Twenty-Eight

Forty-eight hours later and Mr Smith had moved all his possessions out of Pemberley. He had loaded his large and well-travelled suitcase and a couple of boxes, and also the things that Mrs Bowes had asked Evie to get packed for her, into the spacious boot of his car.

Mr and Mrs Worth, and the remaining PGs, waved Mr Smith on his way, a wedding present from all of them for him and Mrs Bowes sitting proudly on the back seat (it was a terracotta window-box that Mrs Worth had bought but never used, and that they all had decided would make an excellent, and pleasantly economical, wedding gift).

Evie noticed too that Mr Worth had packed up Peter's things and removed them to the small box room on the first floor. Mrs Worth now had the two best rooms waiting for new PGs.

It was almost as if Mr Smith and Peter had never been at Pemberley, Evie thought. What a strange feeling that was.

Julia wasn't able to get any time off work to go with Evie to the wedding as the local Post Office were already running on a shoestring staff. And, she added, there was now a string of ladies whose hair she would style of an evening; she didn't want to risk custom by letting anyone down and not meeting appointments already made. Evie quite understood.

Luckily Sukie was able to go with Evie instead – there had been yet another delay to the opening of The Grange as the recuperation hospital, and so Sukie's hours had been cut to two mornings a week while this was all sorted out.

Evie and Sukie caught the early train, changed in London, and went to the wedding (which went very well, all things considered). Evie didn't even feel a pang as she watched another woman say 'I do' to the man who had made her summer term at Lymbridge Primary School so filled with heartache.

And then, at Mr Smith's expense, Evie and Sukie headed for a luxurious night in London at The Ritz. Obviously Timmy and Tricia wouldn't be having a honeymoon, but Mr Smith said to Evie that he wanted to thank her for being such a brick over the past few months, and he thought a night at The Ritz might be just the ticket.

When she saw how grand the communal rooms at The Ritz were, with their gold-framed mirrors, Evie felt her home-sewn checked suit only just about passed muster. Sukie looked to be in her element, however, and the result was that several cocktails arrived at their supper table.

With each new cocktail Sukie would raise her glass in the direction of the person the waiter told her had sent it over, take a sip, and then, very coolly, continue talking to Evie as if nothing particular had happened.

Evie thought the expensive decor of The Ritz to be somewhat stifling, and she didn't find the experience to be quite the treat that Mr Smith had intended.

She admired, however, the aplomb with which Sukie handled herself, but it was all verging on the overwhelming as far as Evie was concerned.

A kindly waiter noticed she wasn't relaxed, and he suggested that perhaps they'd like to take their coffee and cocktails in a small sitting room rather than at their dinner table, and Evie smiled at him gratefully as by now she felt she had been on public view for quite long enough.

Soon she and Sukie were sitting on a comfortable sofa, with a tray holding their tiny, gold-rimmed coffee cups on a little table in front of them. They were the only guests in the sitting room, which was small and very comfortable.

They enjoyed a chat about the wedding earlier in the day – Mr and Mrs Smith looked very content and well-matched, while Mr and Mrs Bowes looked a bit shell-shocked and jumpy with each other, they decided. Still, Evie and Sukie hoped, everyone would be happy.

The good news was that Timmy's memory problems seemed to be receding, and he now had a little feeling in his legs, although he didn't have any discernible movement yet.

As she leant back on the plush sofa Evie realised she felt pleasantly merry. Although she had only had a sip or two of each cocktail, she wasn't used to alcohol and it had gone straight to her head. She was relieved she hadn't been so foolhardy as to drain her glasses.

She was laughing at one of Sukie's jokes, when from the corner of her eye she noticed a figure at the doorway to the sitting room.

As Sukie caught sight of what Evie was turning to look at, she seamlessly said, 'I'm away upstairs, Evie,' and rose and walked swiftly out of the room via another doorway.

Evie barely noticed.

Peter was standing at the door wearing black tie and evening dress, looking very smart and staring at Evie, as transfixed as she was.

'Peter!'

'Evie!'

Their greeting came out at the same time. They tried again; the same thing happened.

They laughed as each remembered this very thing happening to them before, when they were sitting on the lichen-covered stone seat at the bottom of the garden at Pemberley.

Peter came into the room, followed by a waiter, who took Peter's order for a large whiskey. Evie shook her head, curls bouncing, at the offer of another drink.

Gingerly Peter sat down on the sofa beside Evie. She hadn't been able to take her eyes off him.

'What are you doing at The Ritz?' Evie asked.

Peter answered glumly that he had been seconded to a more senior position, and after his brief sojourn in the North, it looked now as if he would be based in London for several months. He couldn't say what he was doing, but it was for the war effort. He was at The Ritz because he was having a business supper.

Evie made an effort to tear her eyes away from Peter's face. Now that she could see all of him up close to her, she noticed that he looked surprisingly confident and debonair, and that his clothes appeared to be expensive, and so Evie surmised this probably meant he was doing something important at the War Office.

At any rate, Peter looked like a young man used to being in a lavish setting such as The Ritz, and Evie saw that he was, in just a few short months, a far cry from the chronically shy person she had first encountered at Pemberley. Had she perhaps had something to do with this? She would like to think so, but the more sensible part of her felt it was unlikely to be true.

Peter's whiskey arrived in a chunky cut glass, and when the waiter had stopped fussing with the tray on the small table and had left them alone, Peter asked Evie what on earth she was doing at The Ritz. 'I don't mean to be rude,' Peter said, with only the slightest of stammers, 'but this is pretty much the last place I expected to see you, although, of course, it is very good to see you sitting there looking so well and representative of the good things in Devon.'

Evie saw him glancing surreptitiously at her wedding-ring finger, which of course was absent of either engagement or wedding rings.

'Peter, the very day you left Pemberley, I returned from seeing Timmy, ready to tell you that he had released me from my engagement, and that I was a free agent. Timmy had made another woman pregnant and so our engagement couldn't continue. I had known this since Easter but for a whole variety of reasons I was unable to say anything about what had gone on. I felt confused and awkward,' explained Evie.

'And today Sukie and I have been to Timmy's wedding to this woman, who is called Tricia. It was a double wedding that took place at Stoke Mandeville and that was also shared by his mother, Mrs Bowes, and Pemberley's Mr Smith, who tied the knot too as they didn't see the point of waiting once they realised they loved each other. The wedding took place at Stoke Mandeville Hospital in a small ward, and the hospital is where Timmy will remain for the foreseeable future.'

Peter took a large gulp of whiskey. He didn't look at all happy.

'That day I raced back to Pemberley all eagerness and trepidation in the hope you might not hate me too much,' Evie said, slightly less confidently.

'And I was gone. And I hadn't, on purpose, left a forwarding address,' said Peter, looking deep into his whiskey glass.

'No, you hadn't. It's driven me mad,' said Evie.

'Me too,' agreed Peter dolefully.

'I could think of no way of reaching you, although it was what I wanted to do more than anything else in the world,' Evie told him. 'Nobody knew quite where you worked even, let alone where you had gone to. Although, of course, once you'd left, the rumours within Pemberley started, until you were pretty much head of military operations for the whole West County. Us Pemberley girls laughed to think that we'd taken Mr Smith as the important one, when really it might have been you all the while.'

They smiled at each other.

But then Peter looked at Evie with a rather hard-to-read expression, and then he said it was 'all very difficult'.

It was likely to be a long while before he'd be sent back to the West Country, if at all. He did have an important job but, he was sorry, he couldn't talk about it.

And, worse, he was now involved with somebody himself.

Evie could hardly believe her ears. This was dreadful in any event, and also she couldn't fathom how Peter could have romantic inclinations towards another woman with such alacrity. Had she really been so easy to forget?

Peter explained that the person he was involved with was someone he had known for a long time, since they were children, and their families had long held hopes for them as husband and wife, although there had almost been a family rift a year or two back when this young woman had been swept off her feet by another man and she and this new man had announced their engagement. But then, unbeknownst to Peter, her fiancé had been killed in a car accident.

And although now she – her name was Fiona apparently, and immediately Evie decided that Fiona was her least favourite name – and Peter had been seeing each other for only a couple of weeks, after they had unexpectedly bumped into each other when Peter arrived back in London, both families approved of the match and pressure was being applied for them to move things along even more swiftly. It was taken by all concerned that there would be a marriage within weeks rather than months.

Peter explained that he would never have allowed this situation to occur if he had thought for a moment that there was any chance between himself and Evie. In fact he had only agreed to meet Fiona for a drink originally as he thought it might help stop him thinking about Evie constantly. Peter admitted he was fond of Fiona and he had been trying to convince himself he might be able to love her in the course of time as he once had.

At this, Evie felt as if she were crashing head-first down a cliff. It was as if she were falling to certain death.

After the good luck that had led to her and Peter's paths crossing once more, and the jump in her heart at seeing him, it was to be for nothing after all.

Peter was not the sort to break a relationship that had progressed to 'an understanding'. And there was clearly some sort of understanding between him and this woman, even if it might not yet be official.

Evie couldn't bear it.

'Ah. I see. I understand. Really. Really I do,' Evie cut in sadly, as her eyes pricked with tears. Then she rallied herself, saying very firmly and in what she hoped was a more positive, cheerful, professional-sounding voice, 'Goodness, is that the time? Sukie will be wondering where I've got to ...'

The jolliness sounded fake, Evie knew, but it was the best she could do. And Peter wasn't helping any, as he was just staring at her.

She stood up and brusquely offered her hand to Peter. Just a couple more seconds and she would be at liberty to howl her heart out in private.

'I hope you and your young lady will be very happy together. Fiona is very lucky, very lucky indeed, but I am sure she will be aware of that,' she managed to force out.

Peter rose to face her. He clasped her hand, and with a mutual jolt, together they realised they could feel each other's racing pulses. They looked into each other's eyes, unblinking, and it felt as if they could see down to the very essence of each other.

Suddenly and impetuously Peter pulled Evie towards him as, almost roughly, he backed her behind the open door to the sitting room. He swung her against the wall, and then he kissed her passionately.

These weren't the feather-light brushes of her lips she had relived in her mind so often from the day of the piglet and the Nissen hut.

These were probing, hungry kisses, with the whole length of their bodies pressed provocatively closely, with Peter's hands touching her neck, her back, her waist. Evie heard the faintest of moans escape her mouth.

The waiter had returned to the sitting room, thinking it now empty, but when he caught a glimpse of what was occurring behind the door, he backed silently away. He was an old softie at heart, and the young lady had looked sad and sorry for herself, and very much in need of the romantic attentions of someone to take her out of herself for a minute or two.

Suddenly Peter and Evie pushed each other away, and stared

aghast at one another as they tried to catch their breaths. Their eyes were bright and their skin flushed.

Evie dropped her eyes towards the ground, and dashed past Peter, her hand touching her temple as she hurried away. Her lips felt swollen and bruised, and her head as if she had drunk every last cocktail sent to their supper table. She wasn't sure but maybe Peter had called an anguished 'Evie!' after her.

On the train back to the West Country the next day, Evie and Sukie sat in almost total silence.

Evie was monosyllabic.

Sukie had tried all the wheedling tricks in her arsenal to get Evie to say what had gone on in the sitting room, but each time she'd mentioned Peter, Evie could only look at her friend with brimming eyes and a determined shake of her head. Sukie could tell that something *had* happened, but that the consequences weren't something making Evie dance with joy. Precisely what remained a mystery.

Fortuitously Mr Smith had arranged for a former colleague from the Plymouth office to be waiting to pick them up; he had to go to Oldwell Abbott on work business, and so he could drop them off in Lymbridge on his way there as he could drive to Oldwell Abbott using the scenic route.

As the car turned into Pemberley's impressive drive, Sukie noticed a dashing man who looked to be in his thirties, and a slightly younger man beside him, talking with Mrs Worth as they stood grouped on the imposing doorstep. There were suitcases beside the men, and several small boxes.

Maybe Pemberley was about to welcome its two new PGs, Sukie thought to herself.

Evie didn't notice either man.

All she could think of was Peter's anguished gasp or call of 'Evie!' as she had hurried away from him down the hall at The Ritz. Those few minutes were shameful, but she couldn't stop thinking of them. And now her heart was shattered into a million minute fragments.

With a pounding head, Evie leapt from the car, and ran straight past everyone and upstairs to her room where she flung herself face down on her bed, leaving Sukie to thank the man who had driven them from the station to Pemberley, and to apologise for Evie's rude behaviour to Mrs Worth and the two men on the doorstep, who were indeed introduced as the two new PGs.

Sukie made excuses on Evie's behalf, pleading that Evie was suffering a terrible headache, and then she set off towards her own home.

As she walked down the drive attempting to swing her overnight bag in an appealingly casual manner, Sukie was very aware of the appreciative looks from behind she was getting from the new arrivals.

'Evie, my dear, you think right at this moment that your heart is broken,' Sukie thought. 'But I think you need to look up and see what's before your very eyes – indeed Peter Pipe had better come soon to claim you, or else he's going to be in for a rude awakening. I'm not sure I've ever seen two such interesting men.'

What neither Sukie nor Evie had noticed was that one of the men was clutching an official-looking white envelope addressed to Miss Evie Yeo. Or that in one of the boxes a lesson plan, some chalk and a new blackboard cleaner, and a cricket ball, could clearly be spied.

To be continued...

Acknowledgements

I would very much like to thank Cathryn Summerhayes, Kate Mills and Laura Gerrard for their valuable editorial support and encouragement. And my mother, June, for being, well, June. Also my husband's children, Josie and Louis, for providing inspiration for Evie's pupils. There is, of course, a real-life Keith, although plumper and lazier than the Keith who cheers up the children. I couldn't have done it without any one of you.

Author's note

I grew up in Devon, and my mother June is the inspiration for Evie as, during World War II, she lived in a house that shares many similarities with Pemberley, while some of the events described are as she remembers.

However, *Evie's War* and its two sequels are very much novels, and so, although I hope to have recreated something of the mood of how ordinary people lived during those difficult times, and their corresponding hopes and fears, joys and disasters, I have set the story in an imagined place within the beautiful expanses of Dartmoor, with loose reference to historical events.

For readers wishing to know what it was really like, there are two writers I would recommend.

One is the redoubtable Julie Summers, who has written several bestselling books, including *Jambusters* (Simon & Schuster), which is based on interviews with people who were children during World War II. In fact, Julie often does personal appearances, and I would urge you to go if she is appearing at an event near you, as she is an absolutely riveting orator who is full of fun while at the same time incredibly knowledgeable.

The other is May Smith, whose *These Wonderful Rumours: A Young Schoolteacher's Wartime Diaries* (Virago) contrives to be both charming and fascinating. These diaries, which were not written with publication in mind, portray a time both more innocent and yet arguably more exacting than those we know today. When I came to write about Evie, I asked myself whether she'd be the sort of person the indefatigable May would have wanted to spend time with – I do hope she is.

Kitty Danton

Evie's story will continue in

Evie's Allies

Coming soon.

Turn the page to read the first chapter

The smell of the verdant gorse and heather cloaking the Dartmoor hills, crags and gullies that Evie loved so much in breathtaking shades of gold and purple, wafted through the open bedroom window tucked high beneath the eaves.

Evie was getting ready for the first day of the autumn term at Lymbridge Primary School.

It was early still, very early, but once again Evie had barely slept.

As she fumbled for her skirt and cotton blouse she had laid out the night before, while doing her utmost not to wake her slumbering sister Julia who didn't have to get up for another fifteen minutes or so, Evie remembered the start of the summer term, her very first day as an infant teacher.

Although barely five months past, what a long time ago that seemed now, as if a lifetime had passed. Now, if she cared to think about it, her old self seemed shockingly naive and childish, a completely different Evie, in fact.

But like today, back on that spring morning Evie had been suffering from a broken heart.

Or, she thought ruefully, what I considered a broken heart might feel like, the silly and babyish chump that I was. How innocent, and how foolish.

Evie knew differently now.

Her hasty engagement to Timmy Bowes, and the painful

discovery that as Timmy left to fight for king and country he'd been nursing a secret in the shape of Tricia Dolby and her unborn baby, had felt dreadful at the time.

Faint rays of September sunlight dappled her bed through the high-up window as Evie tried to pull her pin-curled hair into some sort of order, Julia having insisted the previous evening there should be at least one day this coming autumn term that Evie stood in front of her class of five- and six-year-olds with properly styled hair. Evie avoided her reflection. She knew there were shadows under her eyes and her eyelids looked puffy. She had lost weight and, Evie fancied, her face looked as if the bones underneath were just a bit too close to the smooth surface of her skin.

Timmy wasn't to blame for this, she knew.

It was her own fault.

No, it wasn't, she immediately chided herself with a shake of her head that sent the bouncy curls dancing into disorder.

It was Peter's fault!

Peter and his inconstant heart.

Her fault had been to fall for Peter.

Was no man she cared for able to hold back where other women were concerned? Or was it herself that was the problem? Perhaps she made other women seem more attractive by comparison. At these grim thoughts Evie felt defeated. As she stared down at her unstockinged feet, she fancied they looked sad too.

Evie sighed and dropped her head further as she leant her weight on to her hands holding the edge of hers and Julia's dressing table. A tear fell, its edges breaking into a minute splash as it struck the wood. Weary beyond measure, Evie felt her shoulders quiver as she gave in to her desolation.

Twenty minutes later, Evie was at the breakfast table at Pemberley, the guesthouse where she lodged as a PG, or, more properly, a paying guest, staring at the mark her deep red lipstick had left on the rim of her tea cup. Normally she wouldn't wear make-up to school, but today called for special measures to bolster her spirits as she felt so low. The lipstick, a present to

286

Evie from Timmy's mother to say thank you for Evie's gracious behaviour when Evie had stepped aside and Timmy had finally made an honest woman of Tricia Dolby, was the best booster to her frazzled spirits that Evie had been able to think of.

As she heard the first sounds of her fellow guests beginning to stir upstairs, Evie took her tea cup and saucer through to the kitchen, and quickly rinsed and placed them on the tiered draining rack. She picked up her newly knitted cardigan and her handbag, and then the sandwiches wrapped in paper she had made while she was waiting for the kettle to boil for her morning tea, and finally she grasped a large jug with just a little milk in it to avoid any danger of splashing her clean clothes. She hurried out of the door, hardly pausing to notice the splendid morning that promised an Indian summer over the next month or two. Evie wanted to delay having to face anybody for as long as she could.

It was a short walk to the school, down Pemberley's graceful arc of a sun-bleached gravel drive, and then in at the school gate, a mere stone's throw away along the single road that wended through the village.

Evie went to find the key to the schoolblock in its accustomed hideyhole in the wall, but no matter how she felt and fumbled around and then peered into the dim recess, the key was resolutely not there.

'Miss Yeo. Young lady, as you might be able to surmise, the classrooms are unlocked already.' The imperious male voice sounded as if its owner had called to her from within the vestibule outside the classrooms. Evie couldn't help but note that the owner of the voice couldn't be bothered to put his head out of the door to speak to her directly.

Evie pursed her lips and blinked as she let out a slow breath. These were, she knew, the unwelcome tones of Mr Leonard Bassett, the new temporary headmaster at Lymbridge Primary School.

And, unfortunately, also one of the recently arrived guests at

Pemberley, following the vacating of two spacious bedrooms now that Peter was working in London, and kindly Mr Smith was moving out to go to Berkshire to be with his new wife, Mrs Bowes, who was Timmy's mother – or, more precisely, Mrs Smith, as she now was. Evie would have to get used to calling her former headmistress Mrs Smith, but it felt very odd still to think of her as anything other than Mrs Bowes.

For the time being, Mr and Mrs Smith had rented a small house close to Stoke Mandeville Hospital, until Timmy would be well enough after his searing back and head injuries of several months earlier to be sent to the new recuperation hospital that was in a grand house close to Lymbridge and that would soon begin to take its first patients.

There was a Mrs Bowes still – but this was Tricia Dolby. Although heavily pregnant, she had returned to her job at the dairy parlour, hoping to get in another month or six weeks of work before Timmy's baby arrived. Evie believed the plan was that once Timmy was installed at the recuperation hospital and Mr and Mrs Smith has taken up residence in Mrs Bowes' old pretty cottage, then Tricia would move in with them.

Evie didn't mind at all having a new superior she must report to at Lymbridge Primary School. It hadn't always been easy working for Mrs Bowes (actually, that was quite an understatement), and at least she was no longer Timmy's fiancée and so she wouldn't have to begin the new term while going through the same charade as she had had to do the previous term, trying to keep secret the philandering behaviour of her headmistress's beloved son.

And Evie was all too aware she still had a lot to learn before she could claim to be a fully rounded infant teacher, as so far she'd only had just the one term of hands-on teaching experience following her qualification at teacher's training college. In fact, she was very relieved to have been offered the autumn term teaching too, as money had become tight for her over the summer. This was because the previous term had been a temporary posting. And so too was this autumn term, as it had been made clear to her by Mr Bassett.

Presumably after that the Board of Education would 'take a view', as by then Mrs Smith would be clearer as to her own plans of whether her sabbatical needed to be extended or not. It was still unusual for a woman teacher to be married, Evie knew, but if Mrs Smith wanted to teach, then Evie felt sure the feisty headmistress would make sure that was exactly what would happen. Evie knew there had been a bit of a set-to with the education authority many years earlier when Mr Bowes had left the family home unexpectedly following an unfortunate liaison and Mrs Bowes, as of course she was then, had demanded her old job back at the local primary school.

If Mrs Smith were to make her leave of absence permanent, then Evie assumed that the new headmistress or headmaster would want to appoint their own infant teacher, and it was by no means certain that either Mr Bassett or Evie would keep their posts under a new regime. Evie had told herself already that the best thing meanwhile would be for her to throw herself into this autumn term of work. All experience was valuable, and it could be that afterwards she could get a job at one of the other local schools if she had a good autumn term teaching at the primary school she herself had attended as a child.

However, Evie did very much mind having to report to Mr Bassett for the next few months, until Christmas.

Hard to age but very probably barely thirty, as far as Evie was concerned Mr Bassett's crime was that he treated her as if he were a grand old man and she a mere flippertygibbert. He was bumptious and conceited, and he never appeared to be the slightest bit interested in anything she had to say. And those were his better points, Evie felt.

Her best friend Sukie had tried to point out to Evie that Mr Bassett seemed suave and he certainly was good-looking, but to no avail.

Evie acknowledged that it wasn't Mr Bassett's fault that an eye problem had meant he was unable to join up – within minutes of their first conversation Sukie had got out of him that he couldn't see with the lower part of his vision, and that doctors were divided as to whether this was an optical or a neurological issue. But, Evie felt, he was a man inordinately fond of himself and as far as she could see he didn't really have anything much to talk about other than cricket.

Indeed, she had taken a firm dislike to him on sight, not helped by the fact that the day he'd moved into Pemberley, at the same time as a young journalist called Paul Rogers (whom had rarely been at the guesthouse since), was one of the unhappiest of Evie's short life.

And nothing Leonard Bassett had said or done in the ten days since arriving in Lymbridge had persuaded Evie that it would be pleasurable or informative for them to work together. It was irritating that Mr Worth, who ran Pemberley as a guesthouse with his wife (well, it was Mrs Worth who did most of the running, although Mr Worth tended to overlook this), and Evie's fellow PG Mr Wallace both appeared to think Mr Bassett a fine fellow.

And the fact that Mr Bassett had just proved himself to be an earlier bird in the morning than Evie was nothing short of plain irksome, as she prided herself on being up with the lark nearly every day.

'Good morning, Mr Bassett,' Evie said primly as she marched up the three stone steps and straight past him into her infants classroom, making sure she avoided directly looking at him. And how frustrating it was that the corner of her eye told her that he'd already lost interest in her, and instead appeared to be deep in concentration as he gazed at something written on an officious-looking clipboard, replying to her clipped good morning with something sounding suspiciously like a mere grunt.

Evie swept into the infants classroom, and then realised she'd forgotten to put her sandwiches and jug of milk for her tea into the old-fashioned cool-box in the staff kitchenette. She went back into the entry vestibule, and was relieved to note that Mr Bassett was now in his own classroom, meaning she didn't have to talk to him just at the moment and that she could stow away the sandwiches and milk in peace.

Evie's classroom was spick and span, and ready for the new term. She and the school caretaker, Mr Cawes, had spent a good hour the previous day arranging the tiny wooden desks and chairs in various new configurations, Evie ignoring, as they pulled the desks and chairs this way and that, the increasingly testy exclamations of 'newfangled nonsense' and 'I'll be damned' (alternating with 'I'll be jiggered', 'whatever next' and 'the maid's done it now', all of which Mr Cawes muttered only half to himself in his broad Devonian accent).

It was a daring new arrangement she'd decided on eventually, and Mrs Smith would be quite shocked if she could see the new placement of furniture, Evie conceded privately as Mr Cawes peered around in obvious disapproval with many a shake of his head. And after she had insisted on her way and returned to Pemberley, she thought suddenly that Mr Bassett might not approve either, although he hadn't commented one way or another to her after he'd been to check the school the previous evening.

What had provoked this upheaval in the infants classroom was that towards the end of the previous term Evie had found herself wondering if desks in a line were really helping her pupils, many of whom were still only five years of age. While she could see that such a way of seating could be better for the junior pupils, who were seven and up, as sitting in a more regimented manner might quell a little distracting chatter, it seemed asking a lot that her small pupils couldn't see each other's faces. And so Evie had broken up the rigid rows of desks into what she hoped would be less intimidating clusters so that four children could sit facing each other, with the desks in four little groups in a semi-circle around her teacher's desk.

Also new to Evie's classroom was a big chart on a large piece of hardboard Mr Cawes had found for her and painted white. The two WRVS (Women's Royal Voluntary Service) PGs at Pemberley, Tina and Sarah, had been instrumental the previous week in carefully transposing Evie's unruly pencil sketch of what she wanted into a simple but nonetheless professional-looking grid, along with the various names of the pupils and categories of lessons. Tina and Sarah had made such a wonderful scoreboard to lodge the competition scores at the village's Revels that Evie had organised in high summer, that she had co-opted them in this latest endeavour.

Once she had their agreement as to the grid-making, Evie had persuaded her younger brother James to cart the board from the school to Pemberley for Tina and Sarah to work on, and then lug it back again to the school a few days later. She was rather proud that she'd not had to bribe James to help her, but she thought he probably hoped he might run into her glamorous best pal Sukie if he ran these errands for his sister.

Down the side of the board in alphabetical order were the Christian names of each of Evie's sixteen pupils for this coming term, five of her previous class having moved up to the juniors now they'd been in the infants class for two years, but another nine children from the village of Lymbridge or the surrounding farms now being old enough to join the school.

Along the top of the grid were categories such as handwriting, spelling, sums, gym, history, painting and nature. Evie had begged Mr Smith to see if he could wrangle her some card in a range of colours and some blunt scissors from an art sup-plies shop when he was next reporting to the Board of Trade in London, and she'd been delighted the previous week when he'd sent a package down for her, especially as it contained twenty such pairs of kiddies scissors and quite an array of thicknesses of card in a rainbow assortment of colours.

Evie had made a template in a star shape and cut out some sample stars, sticking a single star of a different colour at the top of each column, making sure the green star was above the title 'nature', on the basis that lots of leaves and grasses were green. As nearly all of her children wouldn't be reading big words yet she had also hunted around in some old picture books she and her siblings had enjoyed as children, and had cannibalised a few suitable illustrations to go underneath the headings. She had also got Tina and Sarah to put in '1 + 1 = ?', 'My name is ?', 'C.A.T. spells?' etc., in the boxes immediately underneath the headings. If that didn't make it clear what each column referred to, then Evie wasn't sure what would.

The plan was that stars would be earned by the pupils for good behaviour or excellent work, with the aim that everyone should get at least one star per subject over the term. At the end of the term Evie would award a prize to whoever managed to get the most stars. The stars would be stuck up with a little flour-and-water paste, already prepared in a washed-out glass jam jar with the metal lid firmly screwed on. Evie was hoping such a mild glue would make the stars easy to remove at the end of term, meaning that the board could be re-used for the spring term, if necessary. This theory was yet to be tested, however.

The remaining coloured card Evie had divided into smallish sections, and had outlined in pencil smaller stars. It would be chaos, she knew, but she thought the children would enjoy cutting out the stars with the small round-ended scissors as a way of easing them in to the new school year, after which she would award everyone a star for their morning's work, and then put the rest of the homemade stars into another jar so they were ready to be stuck to the grid as harder-earned rewards over the coming weeks.

Evie had asked Mr Bassett the previous Friday if he played the piano, and he'd had to admit that it was something he couldn't do. Evie wasn't very good – and certainly nowhere near the dab hand as a pianist that Peter had been – but over the summer she had been practising hard on the piano at Pemberley under the tutelage of ancient church organist Mr Finn, and her reward had been that she made vast improvements to her still slim repertoire. While she practised and her fingers fumbled around on the black and ivory keys, Evie had had to force herself not to remember the happy times Peter had played Pemberley's piano. This was a plan that hadn't gone too well, as it turned out.

Anyway, yesterday she and Mr Cawes, with rather too much

huffing and puffing and the odd muffled swearword, had man-handled the ungainly school piano from the juniors classroom into the infants classroom. 'Well, I'm blowed, Evie. Mrs Bowes was an 'ard taskmaster, but she's a little'un to yer. Me knees and me back are rightly sore,' Mr Cawes said pointedly, and then Evie had promised him a stout the next time she ran into him in The Haywain, at which he looked somewhat mollified.

Mr Cawes had attached hooks for string on the back of the hardboard grid and hung it on the wall. Evie hadn't had the heart to point out that he'd nailed in the hook on which the grid hung so high up that every time she wanted to reward one of the pupils named towards the top of the grid, she would have to stand on a chair to do so. In fact, she was now having to discourage further conversation with the elderly caretaker, as she'd had to dodge his nosy questioning comments about her and Timmy, and 'that daft Dolby maid, mad's a brush an' wi' a belly t' size o' Christmus'; it had been rash of her to mention the stout if this was the result. A bit of a stretch to stick a star on the grid was a much more welcome outcome than having to fuel the old man's demand for scurrilous gossip that he'd likely be sharing down at the village pub before the day was out.

But alone this early morning in the quiet time before the new term got under way, Evie tried to compose herself as she took the seat at her teacher's desk, and then neatly wrote the name of each of her pupils in alphabetical order down the side of the first page of the register for the forthcoming year.

The church clock struck eight, and Evie realised she had nothing else she needed to do before the first pupils arrived, which wouldn't happen for another half hour or so. She sighed and tried to sit in quiet contemplation. It can't have been more than thirty seconds before she sprang to her feet and heading briskly to the classroom next door.

'Mr Bassett, I'm shipshape and ready for my pupils now, and I have some spare time. Is there anything you'd like me to do?' she said.

Her temporary headmaster was standing with his back to her

as he stared morosely out of the window in the direction of the moorland tors. There was a silence.

Still waiting for a reply, Evie crept forward. Mr Bassett looked rapt in the deepest of thoughts and Evie felt she'd never seen anyone look so far away. She didn't think he had heard her. Then she was taken aback and slightly shaken to see what looked as if it could be a tear glistening on his cheek. She halted, and then tried to back soundlessly out of the room, unfortunately bumping into a desk that was slightly out of alignment.

Mr Bassett jumped at the unexpected sound of the desk's legs scraping on the parquet wooden floor. He turned quickly to look at Evie, who said hastily, 'I do apologise for barging in, Mr Bassett, but I have a spare few minutes and so I was wondering if you would like a cup of tea?'

'No, Miss Yeo, I don't think so,' he said flatly. And without ado Mr Bassett turned once more to gaze on the majestic view of the moors, his back square-on to Evie.

It was impossible not to take this as some sort of rebuke, and Evie returned to her classroom feeling distinctly unsettled. It wasn't so much that anything particularly threatening had happened, but more that she sensed that whatever was affecting Mr Bassett was so very much outside Evie's experience that she didn't know what she should do. Whatever it was, though, it was deeply troubling to Mr Bassett.

Still, Evie didn't have the inclination to brood for long on her headmaster. Mr Basset might not be looking forward to the day ahead, but the parlous state of her own see-sawing emotions felt too all-consuming for Evie not to give in to her own thoughts for a moment. And with that, she dwelt on the happier times of preparing for the village Revels, and as she turned to gaze out of her own classroom window she caught her breath and her heart bumped uncomfortably against her ribs at the sight of the Nissen hut at the bottom of the school field.

For, hidden from prying eyes, that was where she had enjoyed two stolen kisses with Peter while the Lymbridge villagers enjoyed themselves at the Revels just a matter of yards away.

Only lasting a matter of seconds, nevertheless those secret moments were the highpoint of Evie's life. To think about them sent a whirl of emotions and sensations scudding through her mind and body.

It wasn't long before the children started to arrive, full of energy and chatter. Evie realised she was very pleased to greet her pupils from the previous year. Even though really it was only a matter of weeks since she had last seen them all together, it was notice-able how much some of them had grown. Almost everybody looked suntanned and healthy. It was obvious that lots of time had been spent running around outdoors during the summer holidays. Evie could remember that back when she was a child during the warm weather she and her sisters and brother had only come inside to eat or to sleep. Evie saw that there also appeared to have been a mass loss of milk teeth amongst her pupils, as nearly everyone seemed to be sporting gappy smiles.

As had happened last term, it looked like little Bobby Ayres was set to be the leader of the class. He arrived carrying, very gingerly, a small cardboard box. He opened it carefully to show Evie a dormouse he'd found the previous day. Evie thought it very lucky that the poor dormouse had survived so long (it actually looked surprisingly happy, sitting on an old flannel), but she didn't want to tempt fate. She promised Bobby that the minute everyone had arrived and she had got everyone seated and taken the register she would show them all the dormouse, after which Mr Cawes could release it behind the Nissen hut as it was 'much kinder to let wild animals live outside'.

Bobby's face clouded for an instant and then threatened to crumple, but he cheered up when Evie promised that he could go with Mr Cawes to set the small rodent free. And with that Evie put the box on the rather high window ledge as she thought the dormouse might appreciate a little privacy to do whatever dormice do when unexpectedly plucked from their habitat.

Evie said to her infants from the previous term that they could play for five minutes at the far end of the playground and that

Mr Cawes would be with them. She would be calling them in soon, she explained, but first she wanted to show the new pupils their classroom and where they could find the toilets. Indeed, it was probably a good idea if she made all the newcomers use the tiny porcelain toilets and then wash their hands. She knew that some of them would be feeling frightened, and too scared to ask to go if they needed.

As she led her little troupe of new arrivals into the schoolhouse, Evie noticed that Mr Bassett had cheered up remarkably from earlier. He seemed to have a nice way with the children, and was promising the juniors a cricket innings later in the morning. Evie also noted that nearly all the girls looked less than enthusiastic at the prospect, although it was hard to tell if this was because they'd been told they had to play, like it or not, or because Mr Bassett had said the girls could field while the boys bowled and batted.

It took Evie what felt like a surprisingly long time to get her new pupils settled. After everyone had used the toilets, she put two of her new children at each of the groups of desks, and one at the final group. And then she called in her older pupils and allocated them seats, attempting to make sure that in each set of four she had a balance of the shy and the forward youngsters, and the new and the old, in the hope that each set of four would balance out and that no one group would seem too raucous or withdrawn.

Evie went to each group to allow them a peek at the dormouse, putting a finger to her lips as she did so to encourage the children to be quiet, but she asked them to take a good look as they were each going to try to draw the dormouse later. Fortunately Evie had an illustrated book on wildlife on the bookshelf behind her desk that would help out too in this respect as it would remind the little ones what they had seen, and with a bit of luck it would detail habitat and food, and so she could turn a chance event into a nature and painting lesson.

She then gave the box to Mr Cawes, who'd been hovering

just inside the classroom door, and he and Bobby Ayres set off to release the tiny quarry.

Evie was just about to shut the classroom door behind them and start explaining to the rest of the class exactly how they would go about the cutting out of the card stars, which would then be collected to be used as rewards, when a lithe, slim, furry body squeezed through the closing gap between the door and jamb.

It was Keith, the school cat.

Evie laughed out loud, and so did the pupils who knew the puss.

Keith had spent the summer living over at Bluebells, Evie's parents' house at the far end of the village. She – and indeed it was a she, and not a he, despite her name – had clearly been spoilt and had had a good summer, as Evie could see a hint of rounded belly as she cavorted by. How had Keith been able to sense it was time to return to school? Evie had planned to collect her at lunchtime, if she could persuade Mr Bassett to watch her pupils as they ate their packed lunches. But now Keith had obliged by saving her a job – perhaps cats really did have something of the 'other world' about them as some of the elderly folklore-loving village women had tried to persuade Evie when she herself had been young.

The infants were delighted to see Keith too, and it wasn't long before the tabby and white cat was introducing herself to the new pupils.

As Keith's famously booming purr rang out, Evie thought that the school term had got off to a reasonable start that morning, all things considered. But it probably was a good thing the dormouse had made such an early exit. Keith was a dear, but cats were cats and a captive dormouse would have been nothing short of a delicious temptation.